*Bridget, Thank [you for coming] on this journey with me ♡
R.H.*

The Midwinter Queen

Book One of The Ulvvori Chronicles

R. H. Linehan

Copyright © R. H. Linehan

All rights reserved.

ISBN: 979-8-3204-8326-9

Cover art created using Canva Pro

Map created using Inkarnate

Chapter header artwork by Chelsea Best
(follow her on IG @chelsea.face)

For my daughters, my own little lights in the darkness.

For my younger self, the girl who poured her soul into thousands of pages that never saw daylight. You got me here.

And for all Indigenous people who are still waiting to go home.
#LandBack #EverythingBack

Land Back

First Nations Development Institute

CONTENT WARNINGS:

- Violence/Gore/Death
- Themes/Mentions of Genocide
- Strong/Suggestive Language
- Suicide/Suicidal Ideation
- Emotional/Physical Abuse
- Sexuality & Romance
- Animal Death
- Alcohol Use
- Children/Childbirth/Breastfeeding

Dear Smut Sluts,

This book is **one** chili pepper emoji, *maybe* two, depending on how desensitized you are. I tried to give you the smut you deserve, I really did, but it was seriously some 2007-fanfic-level cringe. I hope some of you can still get off on banter and emotional intimacy.

Enjoy

CONTENTS

	Map	i
	Prologue	1
1	The Heir	19
2	Commander	31
3	The Twins	43
4	Hunter	58
5	The Forest	72
6	Deserter	84
7	The Lullaby	97
8	Defender	110
9	The Pact	125
10	*Vikmiri*	138
11	The Resistance	159
12	Ulvvori	177
13	The Invasion	197
14	"Traitor"	219
15	The Rescue	241
	Carro's Epilogue	257
16	The Midwinter Crown	260
	Asenna's Epilogue	270
	Ulvvori Language Guide	273

The Midwinter Mountains
The Den
The Valley
Southrun River
Ossesh
Kashait
Anburgh
Bridge
The Forever Forest
Ruins
Oragos River
Sciala
Farm
Sinsaya
Ulvvori Village
Villa
Esmadia

PROLOGUE

A wailing gust of sea air hit Asenna in the face as she stepped out of the carriage. At least, she assumed it was sea air, but she had never seen the sea so she couldn't really be sure. Whatever it was, she disliked the feeling of the salt chapping her lips and stinging her eyes. Turning her back to the wind, Asenna shaded her face to take in the sight of the sprawling villa before her. She had never seen such a structure. It was made of smooth red stone with white marble accenting the dozens of windows and balconies, and a massive portico wrapped around the entire first floor. It seemed so unyielding and permanent, even though she knew that her time here would only be temporary. A cadre of servants stood outside, backs straight and eyes averted. Asenna noted their mismatched uniforms and she realized that the effects of the war had reached even here, to the southern shores of Esmadia and the luxurious seaside retreats where the wealthiest families spent their summers.

Standing at the top of the wide staircase that led up to the portico was a severe-looking older woman in a plum-colored gown and high lace collar who Asenna could only guess was Lady Ilmira Sinsayed, her future mother-in-law. The woman beckoned for Asenna and she lifted her skirt to climb the stairs. Had she not spent her entire childhood scaling the cliff faces and scree fields of her mountain home, she might have been winded when she reached the top, so heavy was the gown they had insisted she wear. When Asenna reached the portico, Lady Ilmira looked her up and down with a sour expression.

"So," she croaked, narrowing her steely gray eyes, "*this* is my son's future bride? The future queen of Esmadia? The....wolf girl?"

Asenna lifted her chin. "I'm twenty-two," she said, "not a girl."

"Indeed," Ilmira pursed her lips, "can you at least read and write?"

"Not as well as you, I'm sure," Asenna answered, doing her best to match Ilmira's icy tone and make it clear that she would not be bullied simply for who her family was.

"Aside from a bath and a hairbrush, it seems you are sorely in need of a lesson in manners, girl. You will address me as Lady Ilmira or Madame, and you will watch your tone." She turned on her heel and swept through the massive double doors, which were carved from rich redwood and fixed with wrought iron spirals and leaves. Asenna followed her into an atrium with real vines curling around the columns and lily pads floating in the rectangular pool. The roof was open for rainwater to fall directly into the pool, so Asenna first imagined it must be for bathing or to water animals, but she realized as they passed that it was merely decorative and wondered what she had gotten into, being married off to the type of people who used water as an ornament.

"So the war is going well then?" Asenna asked as she almost skipped to catch Ilmira, "Azimar will be King?"

"Do *you* not believe so?" Ilmira snapped, leading her into a vast, echoing entrance hall. Asenna spun around as they walked, trying to take in the entire marble-tiled room with its high ceilings and richly painted walls.

"I'm afraid I don't know much about wars or kings," she admitted as they climbed yet another grand staircase. It was true that Asenna's own people, the Ulvvori, kept to themselves in the Midwinter Mountains, so she had known little of what was happening in the rest of Esmadia. But when Azimar Sinsayed, the young General-turned-would-be-usurper, had come to the Ulvvori seeking an ally for his rebellion, they had leapt at the chance to be rid of King Rogerin Godmere. Azimar had promised them self-determination and freedom from Rogerin's oppressive regime, and had asked in return for the Ulvvori to commit their fearsome Wolf Riders to his cause. He had also asked for a bride, to seal the alliance and provide him with an heir that might possess the Ulvvori's unique ability to communicate with the giant dire wolves who roamed the mountains. When they had met and then Azimar had asked for her specifically, Asenna had agreed to the arrangement knowing that another opportunity to help her people might never present itself. Now, however, chasing the stiff and pompous Lady Ilmira up yet another staircase, Asenna was beginning to second-guess her decision.

"Well, you will learn all of it soon enough," Ilmira said, stopping in front of an ornate carved door, "this will be your room until you and my son are married." Asenna stepped inside and let out a loud gasp. It was like nothing she could have imagined, having only lived in tents and caves with little to no furniture or privacy. The far wall was made of archways which led onto a wide balcony and shifting patterns of sandstone and marble tiled the floors, while the furniture was carved of the same sumptuous redwood as the front doors. A massive four-poster bed sat against one wall, beside a vanity with a real mirror, which Asenna had never seen before. There were also two enormous wardrobes, and finally, lounging in a chair on the balcony, was Azimar, her future husband. He stood up as they entered the room and Asenna noted that he looked much cleaner and happier than when she had first met him several months before, having exchanged his blood-stained chain mail for a loose black shirt, and his strained frown for a broad smile.

"Mother!" he crowed, and Asenna could tell that Ilmira was surprised.

"Darling! What on earth are you doing here?" Ilmira embraced her son and kissed his cheek, "they told me you were riding to Anburgh to meet Rogerin's latest reinforcements."

"The coward never showed up, so I left Roeld in charge, rode down, and snuck in through the kitchens," Azimar said casually, taking Asenna's hand and kissing it, "I had to make sure that my bride-to-be is pleased with her new home. What do you think, Asenna?" He stepped aside and Asenna walked out onto the balcony. Her breath caught in her throat when she saw the endless stretch of writhing, churning blue that touched the horizon beyond the cliffs. It made her feel incredibly small.

"It's...overwhelming," she said softly.

"It's all yours," Azimar said, "the villa, the servants, the carriage and horses. There's a beach down below the cliffs as well, but you shouldn't go too far. Rogerin hasn't tried to attack my home yet, but I wouldn't put it past the old bastard."

"Language, my dear," Ilmira chided.

"Of course, forgive me. I've been living in the camp too long. Asenna, I know you've had a long journey, but I hoped that you would join us for dinner tonight. Is that alright?" Asenna was exhausted, but she felt the intense need to ingratiate herself with both of them, so she gave a dutiful nod.

"That sounds wonderful."

"Mother, could I speak to Asenna alone for a moment?" Azimar asked, giving a rather mischievous smile.

"Alone..." Ilmira's eyes narrowed again, "I shall wait by the door." She swept over to stand in the open doorway, watching them from afar. Azimar motioned for Asenna to sit and he sat across from her, running a hand through his wind-tangled curls. Asenna noticed that his hair was not black, as she had thought, but rather a deep mahogany that shone like polished wood in the sunlight. They had never been this close before and she was absolutely certain he was the most beautiful man she had ever seen. Something about the way he looked at her made her smile involuntarily and she could feel her face burning red.

"I'm sorry about my mother," Azimar said softly, "she is harmless, just very attached to all her traditions. I wanted to talk to you for a moment because I know this can't be easy. I was raised with the idea of an arranged marriage, like my parents had, but I know that isn't how the Ulvvori do things. I need to know you are at least comfortable with it, and with me, before we go through with this." His eyes, the same translucent blue as the sea beyond the balcony, cut straight through Asenna and she shivered.

"I made my choice," Asenna told him, "my people have suffered enough under Rogerin and if they're willing to fight to be rid of him, then I should be brave enough to do this. I think it's hardly a sacrifice compared to what they've already endured…and what they will endure in this war."

"Well," Azimar moved closer and Asenna's entire body started humming like the string of a fiddle, "I promise I will do everything in my power to make sure you never regret your decision." Before she could respond, he leaned in and briefly pressed his lips to hers, pulling away before Ilmira noticed anything. Asenna's head spun as he stood up and winked.

Asenna watched him leave the room with Ilmira on his heels and then touched her lips. *I certainly don't regret that,* she thought, getting up and walking over to the mirror perched on top of the vanity table. It was startling to see how detailed her reflection was in the glass. The Ulvvori didn't use mirrors, so Asenna had only ever seen herself in the blade of a freshly polished ax or a still pool of mountain water. A smattering of light freckles covered her skin, and long, obsidian-black hair fell in messy waves around her thin shoulders. Slowly, she ran her fingers over the pointed face and deep brown eyes that were, apparently, her own. As she examined the bump on the ridge of her nose that her father had always said made her look like an eagle, she smiled, seeing the resemblance for the first time.

On the vanity was a set of combs that looked like they had been carved from the antlers of a giant deer like the ones the Ulvvori hunted in the winter. The feeling of the rough, unpolished antler against her skin was strangely comforting and Asenna tried to pull it through her hair, but there were too many knots and she put it back down quickly. Wandering around the room, Asenna drank in every luxurious texture and color that she had never seen or felt before. The bedposts had been carved to look like trees, even branching out at the top and intertwining with one another to form a sort of canopy, and a length of pure white cloth had been woven through the branches all the way around the top. When Asenna touched it, she realized it must be silk, which she had heard of, but never seen or felt. Her brother, Ivarr, had told her it came from one of the island nations to the east, and it was woven from webs made by tiny white worms. As disgusting and unlikely as that sounded, Asenna marveled at how smooth the fabric felt between her hands. Without thinking, she began to pull it out from between the carved branches, wrapping it around her body until she was fully encased. She fell back on the bed, giggling like a child at the absurdity of it all. There was a sudden knock at the door and Asenna got tangled in the silk as she panicked and tried to extricate herself. A squat, elderly woman with a large gray chignon bun atop her head opened the door and her eyes grew wide when she saw Asenna's predicament.

"What are you doing, my lady?!" she asked, hurrying over.

Asenna felt her face burn. "I was just…I wanted to…It's just I've never seen silk before…" she tried to explain. The woman's demeanor softened.

"I see. Well, my name is Ephie and I'm to be your lady's maid. That means I do whatever you need me to do so you can be comfortable here. First, Lady Ilmira wants me to get you a proper bath and fix that hair before supper."

"Pleased to meet you, Ephie," said Asenna, following her into an antechamber where a massive copper tub was sitting on tiny legs made to look like clawed feet at the ends. Asenna stifled another laugh as she pictured the tub coming to life and hopping down the corridor. On the list of new experiences that day, the hot bath was by far the best. It reminded her of the hot springs pools that dotted the foothill valleys around the Ulvvori's winter settlement. After a long, cold day of work, everyone gathered in the pools to bathe and talk while the children swam. The copper tub was not quite as comfortable as the moss-covered stones in the springs, but the way the hot water enveloped her body made her feel suddenly and desperately homesick.

"Ephie, how long have you worked for the Sinsayeds?" asked Asenna.

"Only six months or so, my lady," Ephie replied, "since just before the war started."

"Can you tell me what I've really gotten myself into? I mean…Azimar seems kind enough, but Ilmira…"

"Oh," Ephie's voice sounded a little strained, "I admit, I haven't spent much time around him, my lady. I was hired to work for Lady Ilmira and she is…tight-fisted, to say the least. I don't want to frighten you, but I hope we can be honest with one another."

Asenna slipped down a little farther into the tub. "No, thank you for the honesty. I'll admit to maybe being a little afraid. I've never been away from my family for a single day, and now…" Asenna felt a lump in the back of her throat as she pictured the faces of her mother, brothers, and uncle.

"I know it's not my place," Ephie said softly as she combed the knots out of Asenna's hair, "but I want to thank you for what you're doing. Our people will remember your courage." Asenna turned around in the tub and realized that there was something familiar about the way Ephie's face was shaped and the shade of her brown eyes.

"You're Ulvvori?"

"Yes, but I left a long time ago."

"Why?"

"I had three sons," Ephie said, her eyes shining with emotion, "they were all taken by Rogerin, by his conscriptions. I came south to try and find them. Oh, I don't mean to burden you with this, my lady, but I wanted you to know how grateful I am. This alliance will win Azimar the war and then no Ulvvori mother will have her sons taken from her again."

"It's not a burden to hear your story, Ephie," Asenna murmured, reaching out to take the older woman's hand, "thank you for telling me. It's good to remember why I'm here." Asenna didn't know what else to say, but her words seemed to help and Ephie continued combing and humming softly. Rogerin's decades-old policy of forcibly conscripting young Ulvvori boys into his army was the primary reason the tribe had allied itself with Azimar, who had sworn to end the barbaric practice if he took the throne. Every Ulvvori family had lost at least one boy to the conscriptions, and when Asenna had agreed to marry Azimar, her first thought had been finally ending the brutality and heartbreak that had touched three generations of her own family, along with countless others.

Once she was clean and her hair free of knots, Ephie helped Asenna out of the tub and dried her off, then opened the wardrobes, revealing at least two dozen beautiful gowns in all different fabrics and colors and patterns. Asenna ran her hands over them and pressed them to her face, feeling how each one moved and watching how they glimmered in the evening light.

"All of these are mine?" she asked Ephie, who nodded. Asenna chose a gown made of green silk with gold embroidery around the collar and sleeves, but the sight of all the elegant clothes made her feel that she was woefully unprepared to face the situation she had found herself in. "Can you tell me about Azimar's rebellion, Ephie? I'm afraid…I don't actually know much of what's been happening and I don't want to look like a fool at dinner."

"Hmm," Ephie mused, pulling Asenna's sleeves down and straightening her skirt, "it started about six months ago. Everyone knows Rogerin is on death's doorstep, and he has no heir, not even a daughter. He's run through so many wives I've lost count, but none could produce a child. The rest is rumors, but they say Rogerin had sworn to name Azimar his heir but he reneged on the deal. Apparently, a soothsayer told him that Azimar would be his downfall. Well, Azimar didn't take kindly to that, and as a popular soldier, it wasn't hard for him to find support inside the army, so I suppose the soothsayer was right. Or at least…they will be right if Azimar wins his throne." Ephie began to pull the laces at the back of the gown and

Asenna tried not to breathe while she worked. Her mind was tumbling over itself trying to make sense of all the intrigue. Life in the mountains had been so straightforward that this new world felt like walking into a saber-tooth lion's den unarmed and naked.

"This all seems like it's too far beyond me," Asenna confessed as she turned to look at herself in the mirror. The effect of the green fabric against her tawny skin was attractive, but Asenna could not help feeling like a child trying to play dress-up with her mother's clothes.

"The best advice I can give you is to keep your mouth shut and smile," Ephie told her, "at least when Ilmira is around. Anyway, you're not meeting any Lords tonight. It's just Ilmira and Azimar and his little pack of hunting hounds. Those boys won't expect anything resembling manners from you, since they have none themselves."

"You don't like his men?" Asenna laughed, twisting her damp hair around her fingers so that it would dry into waves.

"They're just men," Ephie snorted, "and if I've learned anything in all my years, it's that men are only good for two things, neither of which I will repeat here." She bustled away to drain the water from the bathtub while Asenna spun in her gown, watching the way that the candlelight flickered on the pleated skirt. There was a knock at the door and Asenna opened it to find Ilmira.

"Never answer your own door," she scolded, stepping into the room, "that is a job for your lady's maid. Are you ready? Dinner is waiting." Asenna nodded and followed Ilmira out into the corridor, where a pair of guards in red and gray livery were waiting to escort them. Asenna could hear raucous voices coming from somewhere downstairs and she felt like her whole body was on fire with nerves. When they reached a large pair of double doors on the first floor, Ilmira stopped and turned.

"I am not sure what you are used to…*at home*, but here you do not speak unless you are spoken to, do not drink more than two cups of wine, and do not eat with your fingers. Understood?"

"Yes, Madame," Asenna felt the edge return to her voice and tried to shake it off before the guards pulled the doors open. The dining room was illuminated by an enormous, roaring fire set back in a hearth taking half the wall up. At least three dozen young soldiers were gathered around long tables covered in platters of food. Looking around curiously, Asenna spotted Azimar sitting at one of the tables, holding a hand of cards and engaging in a good-natured shouting match with the young man beside him. When he saw her, he sprang to his feet and pounded the table with his fist, causing all the men to fall silent and look over at her. Asenna's face burned even hotter and she was suddenly glad for the dim lighting. Azimar climbed on his chair and held a cup out.

"My friends!" he called, "you have stayed loyally by my side these past months, and now I wish you to be the first to greet Lady Asenna of the Ulvvori, my future queen!" A deafening cheer erupted in the dining hall and Asenna put on what she hoped was a gracious smile. Azimar jumped down and escorted her to a table on a dais at the head of the room, also set with food and plates.

"Do you drink wine?" he asked, sliding into the chair beside her and motioning for a boy standing nearby with a pitcher to fill their cups.

"I've only tried it a few times," Asenna admitted, "am I *supposed* to drink it?"

"You are *supposed* to do whatever you like," Azimar shot an amused look at his mother, "and don't let anyone tell you otherwise. Try it." Asenna took a sip of the wine. It was sour and strong, but she also knew that it might help her nerves, so she drank more.

"It's lovely," she told Azimar, "thank you." He gave her a winning smile and then began filling his plate. Asenna looked down the table and felt overwhelmed by all the choices. There was a large roasted bird of some kind, stuffed with vegetables and herbs, a plate full of small bread rolls in various shades of brown, and tureens filled with soup sitting alongside dishes of fresh fruit, hand pies, and other foods Asenna could not name.

"What do you normally eat at home?" Azimar asked, leaning over.

"*A lot* of venison and mammoth," Asenna laughed, "boiled eggs and dried salmon or rabbit. Apples and wild honey in the autumn. Flatbread in the summer, when we can get flour from the traders, or black moss bread filled with mushrooms, or made into porridge with berries."

"Moss bread?" Azimar looked up at her and raised an eyebrow.

Asenna laughed at his expression. "It's actually quite good."

"I'd like to try that sometime," Azimar's eyes twinkled. "We'll go slow then, since this is…much different." He leaned forward and pulled a whole leg off the cooked bird, then set it on her plate. Asenna gave Ilmira a sideways glance and saw that she was cutting her meat daintily off the bone with a fork and knife.

"Can I just…pick it up?" she asked, and Azimar nodded.

"No need to stand on ceremony around these heathens," he waved his hand around the room at his men. Asenna could feel the strings on the back of her gown becoming taught as she sampled something from each plate on the table. Azimar was patient and stifled many of Ilmira's expressions of disapproval, so Asenna let herself drink far more than two cups of the sour wine. With each sip, everything in the room began to feel softer and less threatening, and she found Azimar much easier to talk to and far more attentive than she had imagined he would be. By the time the plates were cleared away, her cheeks hurt from smiling and laughing.

When the fire started to burn low, Azimar drained another cup of wine and then beckoned to one of the men sitting nearby, who approached the table. Asenna guessed that he was younger than Azimar by a few years, but a little older than she was, with a nervous, crooked smile framed by deep dimples and cropped reddish-brown hair. His dark eyes struck her as being older than the rest of his features, and she could feel them searching her with an intense curiosity that she had seen on many faces during her journey south, usually when people realized she was Ulvvori.

"Asenna, this is Captain Carro Morelake," Azimar said, slurring his words slightly, "my oldest friend and probably the most loyal soldier you'll ever meet. You will never see me without him, nor him without me!"

"My lady," the young man bowed.

"It was the Captain's idea to ask the Ulvvori for an alliance," Azimar explained, "so whatever successes we see with it, they are thanks to Carro." He leaned over and kissed Asenna's hand, making her stomach flip.

"Then my people and I are in your debt, Captain," Asenna said.

Carro dipped his head and then turned his attention back to Azimar. "Sir, we still need to discuss how we're going to--"

"Tomorrow!" Azimar laughed, "when I've sobered up."

"Yessir," Carro grinned.

Azimar stood up and took Asenna's hand. "Come on. I want to show you something."

"Where are you going at this hour?" Ilmira barked, "you shouldn't be alone with her. What will people say?"

"There's no *people* here, Mother. Just you and my men and the servants. No one will gossip about us walking down to the damn cliffs and looking at the ocean," Azimar chuckled and Ilmira's face turned bright red, "you are welcome to chaperone. If you're too tired, I'm sure the Captain wouldn't mind accompanying us." Ilmira's eyes shifted over to Carro and narrowed even further until they were tiny slits in her face.

"Come on, Ilmira," said Carro gently, "have I ever let him get into trouble?"

"It's not *you* I'm worried about, Captain," Ilmira said, looking at Asenna, who felt a tiny flare of anger in her chest, but said nothing, "very well, Azimar. If you must." She left the dining room in a huff. Azimar smiled and led Asenna out of the manor with Carro several paces behind. There was a narrow path that led down to the cliffs and Asenna gasped softly when she looked out over the sea. A full moon was hanging low over the dark water, which reflected its light back in shining strips between the waves. Asenna thought it looked like line upon line of polished swords moving toward them. Farther along the coastline, parts of the cliff face had eroded away, leaving a magnificent stone archway standing in the surf, like a gateway into another world. Asenna closed her eyes and tried to soak up the moonlight.

"The old family legend says that a Sinsayed can't really die," Azimar told her, "when we're ready to go, we're supposed to come to this cliff and make a leap of faith, then the wind will catch us and turn us into a gull so we can live at sea forever."

"Is that true?" Asenna asked.

Azimar let out a loud, barking laugh. "Of course not! Just some silly nonsense my ancestors made up to try and make our family seem more interesting," he paused for a moment, "your people's legend is true though, isn't it…the Wolfsight…"

"It's true," Asenna said, as they moved along the top of the cliff with Carro straggling behind them, trying to keep his distance.

"You know, I was always skeptical," Azimar said, "I never believed in all the legends and fairy stories and magic. Rogerin and those like him, including my own father, put too much faith in soothsayers and their omens. I've seen the damage it's done to this country. It makes people weak and malleable, and that's not what I want to be. But then I met your people, with their golden eyes, and their dire wolves…and I still don't understand it, but how could I not believe?"

"I'm not sure the Ulvvori even really understand the Wolfsight," Asenna said quietly, "some of us are just…born with it, with the golden eyes, then the baby is bonded with a dire wolf pup as a companion when they're newborns. There's a connection between them that's stronger than anything. It lets them share their thoughts and feelings, and they train as Wolf Riders so they can hunt and fight for us. My mother, my brothers, and my uncle all have it, and my father too, before he died. I'm the only one in my family without."

Azimar nodded slowly. "Well, I'm certainly glad they're my allies now. I understand why Rogerin could never control them the way he wanted to."

Asenna stopped in her tracks. "He couldn't control them because they were kidnapped children," she said with an edge in her voice.

"I'm sorry," Azimar said, putting a hand on her arm, "I'll admit, I don't know everything that happened between Rogerin and the Ulvvori. It's a bit taboo…for soldiers to talk about it."

"Well, if you're going to be allies, then you should know," Asenna took a deep breath, "soon after Rogerin came to the throne, he asked the Wolf Riders to join his army and they refused, so he started kidnapping children with the Wolfsight, and their wolves. He wanted to raise them to fight for him, but he quickly learned that the young dire wolves were too hard to control. You can't just take a wolf pup away from its pack and expect it to do as you say. That was when he started to send raiding parties, trying to kill the wolves off. We lost so many wolves and Riders that Rogerin was able to force a treaty. The conscriptions were one of the conditions that allowed us to stay on our land, but now any Ulvvori boy without the Wolfsight is fair game for the army as soon as he turns five." Her voice broke and she had to stop walking for a moment.

Azimar ran a hand over his face. "It's awful...unconscionable."

"You're going to stop the conscriptions, right?" Asenna asked.

"I've already done what I can to stop them, yes, but the war still needs to be won to keep it that way," Azimar paused for a moment, "who did they take...from your family?"

Asenna drew in another deep breath. "All four of my grandparents lost a brother *and* at least one son. My father had two brothers taken. And then...well, you met my uncle, Tolian. His son Kirann was taken and his wife was killed trying to stop it. Tolian probably would have died too if my parents hadn't held him back. I was five and...my brothers and I watched the whole thing." Azimar put his hand on her waist and moved a little closer to her. Asenna felt dizzy as she breathed in his scent and his blue eyes cut right through her.

"I'm so sorry, Asenna," he murmured, running his fingers along her cheek, "I swear to you, it will never happen to *any* family ever again."

"Thank you," she whispered. Azimar leaned in to kiss her and Asenna felt like she had fallen off the cliff and was plummeting toward the beach, her heart racing and skipping beats so wildly that she was certain it would simply stop as she put her hands on his back.

"Hey!" yelled Carro from farther down the cliff, "are you trying to get me in trouble?" Azimar pulled away and grinned.

"I would never!" he called back, taking Asenna's hand and walking toward the house. By the time they stepped inside, Asenna found herself fighting back a sudden wave of exhaustion.

"I'll see you in the morning," Azimar said softly, kissing her cheek and sending a lightning bolt tearing through her stomach. When she reached her bedroom, Asenna collapsed on the mattress facedown while Ephie undid the laces on the back of the gown and gave her a gentle lecture about drinking too much wine. Asenna's dreams were fitful that night. She saw the golden eyes of her family surrounding her but could not see their faces. The dire wolves howled and keened all around her, but she could not find them as she wandered down the mountain paths of her home. A huge, black dire wolf with Azimar's sparkling blue eyes began to follow her as she stumbled over rocks and roots. She could feel its hot breath on the back of her neck, but it never caught up.

The next morning, Asenna woke to the sound of waves crashing and gulls screeching in the distance. Ephie was nowhere to be found, but she had laid out a simple, light blue linen dress at the end of the bed. Asenna slipped it on and fumbled with the laces for a few minutes before she figured out the trick to tying them, then she peered out into the hall, which was empty.

"Azimar did tell me to make myself at home," she said to no one, stepping out and wandering down the stairs into the deserted entrance hall. Asenna heard voices drifting in from outside and she slipped between the front doors onto the portico. The sound of scraping and clanging metal punctuated the conversations and Asenna realized that Azimar and a few of his men were sparring on the side of the house. As she approached, she heard her own name and stopped, then hid behind a column to watch and eavesdrop, being nothing if not nosy.

"She's a liability!" Carro was saying as he and Azimar faced off beneath her. Azimar was armed with a single broadsword, while Carro wielded a pair of long, curved sabers. Asenna watched in fascination as they danced around each other, blades flashing in the morning sun.

"What would you have me do?" Azimar hissed, striking out and forcing Carro to jump backwards. "We need the Wolf Riders."

"You *should* have left her in the damn mountains," Carro retorted. He lunged at Azimar, who leaned back and easily knocked the swords aside.

"Why do you care so much?" Azimar asked, circling around Carro and pointing the broadsword at him, "are you jealous, my friend? I'm sure I could get a wife for you too." Carro turned slowly on the spot, his eyes never leaving Azimar, and Asenna found herself holding her breath as if it were a real battle.

"I care that you're distracted!" Carro suddenly dropped to the ground and used his foot to sweep Azimar's legs out from under him, then swung his blades up in an arc, bringing them down above Azimar's face and stopping just short of an actual blow. "See? Distracted. You'd never let me do that normally." Azimar rolled to the side and stood up, his teeth bared in frustration as Carro casually spun one of his swords and laughed.

"And *you* would never question my judgment normally." Azimar lunged again, but Carro caught the broadsword between his sabers, holding it as Azimar tried to pull back.

"How can I not? You're so fucking spun up over this girl that you're ignoring the strategy we agreed on and to run back here and play husband," Carro growled in his face. Asenna watched Azimar closely and could see his irritation building. Carro released his sword and Azimar stumbled backwards, then pushed his dark curls out of his eyes and smirked.

"If I was playing husband, I wouldn't have spent all night shuffling cards around with you," he said with a cut in his voice. Carro attacked again, but Azimar knocked him back harder this time, "we've been living in a damn war camp for six months. Why shouldn't I enjoy myself for a few days?"

"How much enjoyment are you really getting from her? I know you wouldn't trade everything we've worked towards for a few stolen kisses," Carro shot back. Asenna realized that Azimar was slowly backing Carro up against the side of the staircase as they continued to spar. Some of the other men had stopped their own practice to watch and Asenna leaned out from her hiding spot to see better. Carro was becoming more and more agitated as Azimar continued to smirk while thwarting his attacks.

"I'll get plenty out of her soon enough. Besides, nothing Rogerin does will matter once we have the Wolf Riders," Azimar said.

"The Ulvvori cannot end this war on their own!" Carro shouted as their blades met again with a loud scrape, "don't you think they'd have done it already? You're the one who started this rebellion, Azimar, and I've been with you every minute, but it *will* fail if you don't go out and stand with your men!" Azimar swung down hard, knocking the sabers from Carro's hands, then grabbed him by the front of his shirt and hit him hard across the face with the pommel of his broadsword. Carro cried out in pain and doubled over, but Azimar shoved him back against the wall, pressing his arm into Carro's throat. The other men exchanged nervous glances and Asenna felt her stomach twist.

"How dare you?" Azimar's smirk was gone and his voice was full of venom, "I didn't pull you out of the fucking gutter to have you order me around! My decisions are not up for debate, especially not by you. Is that clear?"

"Y-yes, sir," Carro groaned, turning his face away as a trickle of blood ran down from the cut on his cheek. Azimar released him and took a few steps back.

"We're done," he said to the rest of the men, who scurried away up the stairs. Azimar followed them, leaving Carro hunched over alone by the staircase. Asenna emerged from her hiding place to make it look like she had just come out of the house and tried to put a smile on.

"Asenna, there you are!" said Azimar, his voice suddenly calm again.

"Is everything alright?" she asked, "I thought I heard arguing."

"Everything is perfect," Azimar smiled, "you have brothers, you understand how it can be. Carro is the closest thing I have to a brother. Sometimes we just…disagree. Now, let's find some food and then I'll show you the beach!" He wrapped an arm around her waist and Asenna felt her heart start to skip again. She couldn't deny that her own brothers had nearly come to blows with each other before, but Asenna still couldn't shake the feeling of disquiet. Azimar took her into the dining room, where breakfast was already being laid out, and they had a few minutes alone before Ilmira appeared and began to demand that Asenna begin her training. Azimar shut his mother down quickly, however, and she stalked out of the dining room looking and sounding like an irritated buzzard.

When they had finished eating, Azimar led Asenna back down to the cliffs alone and showed her a spot where it jutted out toward the sea. In the corner, someone had carved stairs directly onto the face of the cliff that wound all the way down to a wide, white sand beach. There was no handrail to speak of, so Asenna kept one hand on the cliff face as they descended carefully. She was no stranger to heights, but the wind whipping her skirt and hair into a frenzy made her feel more unsteady than normal and she grabbed onto Azimar's shoulders a few times. Once they were on the beach, the wind seemed to die down and Asenna slipped off her shoes. She had been on muddy lakeshores and riverbanks thick with clay, but nothing like this before, and the feeling of the sand between her toes delighted her. Azimar showed her how to search for seashells in the surf and they spent some time chasing the tiny minnows that lived in the shallows. Asenna felt like she could finally see Azimar for how young he actually was, when he wasn't trying so hard to be a general or a future king. In the back of her mind, Asenna still felt guarded because he was, after all, a stranger. However, the fact that they were getting along so well after less than a day made her feel more hopeful than she had since she had agreed to the marriage, so she allowed herself to let go a little and enjoy the beach with him. Azimar seemed to laugh easily and wasn't afraid to make a fool of himself in her company, which Asenna appreciated because the unfamiliar feeling of the sand and waves made her clumsy.

Once they had exhausted themselves chasing the minnows, Azimar showed her a small recess in the cliff face where there was a haphazard pile of fishing spears that looked like they had been handmade. He picked one up and hefted it, then handed another to Asenna.

"It's been a long time," he said, "but I think I could still catch a few. Want to try?"

"Could be fun," Asenna shrugged and grinned, deciding not to tell him that she had been raised by one of the greatest Ulvvori spearfishermen of all time. Instead, she reached down and pulled her skirt up, tying it into a large knot in front of her so it wouldn't get in the way.

"Carro and I used to do this every day when we would come and stay here in the summers. He was always better at it than me though. More patient, I guess," Azimar told her as they walked back to the water and began scanning the waves for fish.

"You grew up together?" Asenna asked, spotting a target and raising the spear at an angle.

"I met him in training when we were boys. He doesn't have any family, so we sort of adopted him." Asenna threw her spear and watched with satisfaction as it sank into the sand, trapping a wriggling fish on the end. She looked up at Azimar with a triumphant smile and he appeared mildly impressed as he grabbed the fish and tossed it onto the sand.

"You're good!" he laughed, handing the spear back to her, "did your brothers teach you?"

"No, my father did," Asenna watched Azimar throw and miss, "his name was Larke, but he died when I was maybe…nine or ten."

"I'm sorry," Azimar leaned on his spear, watching as she lined up another shot, "what happened to him?"

"He was--" Asenna grunted as she launched the spear again, striking her target, "he was hunting mammoths in the far north." Azimar helped her pull the fish in and tossed it on the beach with the other.

"My father was lost at sea on one of our trading ships," said Azimar quietly. He seemed to have given up on fishing, "I was twelve." Asenna instinctively reached out to take his hand, but she lost her balance in the sand, toppled into him, and they both plunged into the surf. The salt water stung Asenna's eyes and nose and she thrashed around as the waves tugged at her, rolling her backwards so she could not figure out which way was up. Finally, she broke the surface and gasped, just as Azimar came up beside her, laughing and coughing at the same time. Feeling panicky, Asenna pulled herself from the water and they both struggled onto the beach and fell onto the sand.

"Are you alright?" Azimar asked, wiping water out of his eyes.

"I'm fine," Asenna coughed, "I think I swallowed a pound of salt though. Disgusting."

"Your balance is not nearly as impressive as your spearfishing, my lady," Azimar teased. Now that she was safe on land, Asenna allowed herself to laugh a little at the ridiculousness of the situation.

"At least *I* caught something," she shot back at him. They both laid still for a few minutes, catching their breath while the waves lapped at their feet, then Azimar rolled over so he was facing her. His smile faded and he suddenly looked rather serious as he twisted his fingers through a strand of her hair that was coated with sand. Before he could say anything, Asenna blurted out the question that had been burning in her mind for weeks.

"Why did you choose me?"

"I…what?" Azimar looked a little perplexed.

"The day you came to meet with my uncle about the alliance," Asenna said slowly, "and you asked for a Ulvvori bride. You could have chosen any girl in that camp…so why me?"

"Ah," said Azimar, his blue eyes glittering, "you were there in the tent with us, with Tolian and all those Elders and Wolf Riders, and…you stood out to me because you were the only one without the golden eyes. I wondered what a young woman with no magic powers had done to be able to be in that meeting."

Asenna laughed out loud. "I forced my way in," she told him, "my mother and brothers were going, and I told them that if they didn't let me go too, I'd just eavesdrop from outside."

"Well," Azimar murmured, tucking a piece of hair behind her ear, "besides the fact that you are incredibly beautiful, I guess I saw that strength and stubbornness in your eyes, and I need someone strong to sit on that throne next to me. So, I chose you." Asenna had no idea what to say in response, so she simply asked the next question that came to her.

"When will we actually be…married? I don't know how these things work in the south. The Ulvvori don't really have weddings."

Azimar nodded. "My agreement with your uncle was that we would wait until the Wolf Riders have joined my army at Anburgh. I know Tolian is an honorable man, but this is an alliance, after all, and I need to make sure he upholds his end of the deal. I'm not sure how long it will be until I can get away again, but I hope it will give you some time to settle in."

"Do I have to…wear the big white dress and everything?"

Azimar let out one of his barking laughs. "No! Not if you don't want to. It won't be anything like a normal wedding, so you may wear whatever you like, no matter what my mother has to say about it," he ran his hands down the bodice of her dress, brushing sand away from the fabric, "besides, I much prefer this color on you." Azimar leaned in to kiss her and Asenna's stomach flipped over again and again as his hand brushed her cheek, but then she heard a voice drifting down from the clifftops, calling Azimar's name. He pulled away to shade his eyes and look up.

"Come on," he said, standing up and trying to remove the sand from his clothes. It was a futile endeavor, because they were both coated in it from head to toe. "If we don't go up, Carro's liable to come down here and spear *me* like a fish. He gets a bit anxious being away from the camp too long."

"I think your mother might spear me when she sees this mess," Asenna chuckled, untying the knot in her skirt and shaking the sand out, then picking her fishing trophies up by the tails. They were a good size and appeared to be edible.

"Don't let her get under your skin too much," Azimar advised, letting her go ahead of him on the stairs, "she's just a bit puffed up and self-important from spending too much time amongst the *society* women in Ossesh." When they reached the top of the cliff, Asenna saw Carro and a few of the other men waiting for them. There was a nasty bruise forming around the cut on Carro's cheek, but he seemed unfazed by it.

"Very nice, my lady," he said, smirking at the sight of the fish in her hand, "did he catch any or did he make you do all the work?"

"Look here," Azimar pointed a finger at him and laughed, their previous disagreement seemingly forgotten, "if I'd wanted to be a fisherman, I'd have been a fisherman. Now, what's going on? Why did you feel the need to haul me up here?"

"A message from Roeld," Carro said, handing Azimar a piece of folded parchment, "we need to leave as soon as possible." The relaxed and personable Azimar vanished in an instant as he read the message, and he seemed to forget that Asenna was even there as he started walking back toward the house. Asenna felt a wave of apprehension when she realized that she would soon be left at Ilmira's mercy and she followed a little way behind, still clutching the fish by their tails.

By mid-afternoon, Asenna's apprehension was nearly unbearable as she sat on the top step under the portico, watching Azimar and his men prepare their horses to ride to Anburgh. He had changed back into his chainmail, paired with the Sinsayed family colors of gray and red, carried a silver helm under his arm, and the broadsword tied on his belt. Carro came out of the house, twins sabers strapped to his back, and sat at the top of the stairs opposite Asenna to lace up his greaves. He and the rest of Azimar's men wore black uniforms with high necks that made them look to Asenna like a flock of crows.

"Sorry to steal him away from you so soon, my lady," Carro said.

"Are you, Captain?" Asenna sneered, "I thought I was a distraction. Or...was it a liability?"

Carro's face flushed. "You weren't meant to hear that."

"Well, I did. Wasn't this whole alliance *your* idea anyway?"

"The alliance, yes," Carro said, finishing with the greaves and standing up to face her, "the marriage was not. Look, we just can't afford any sentimentality right now, so whatever...feelings he has for you *are* a distraction. Love doesn't win wars."

"But I'm not here for love, am I? I'm here for an alliance."

"That's not what it looked like down on the beach earlier."

"Were you spying?"

"You were spying on us this morning, weren't you?" Carro snapped.

Asenna sized him up and could tell he was easy to irritate, so she needled him further. "A woman's prerogative," she said, "especially when she's in a strange place, surrounded by strange men."

"My apologies," Carro sighed, pinching the bridge of his nose, "I'm sure it's not easy for you to leave your family like this."

"I'd do anything for my family," Asenna said softly, "even if it means being amongst strangers."

"And I'd do anything for *my* family," Carro motioned to the men behind him, "this alliance protects both our families, and I won't let him waste that opportunity chasing a fantasy. When he stands at the edge of the cliff, thinking he can jump and grow wings, it's *my* job to pull him back. Understand?" Asenna saw a flicker of desperation in his dark eyes.

"I'll try to keep the distractions to a minimum, *Captain*."

Carro gave her a stiff bow. "When this war is over, he's all yours." He turned and loped down the steps. Azimar looked up at Asenna and waved for her to come down. She descended the stairs as slowly as she could and he met her at the bottom.

"Did he say something to upset you?" Azimar asked softly, "he didn't support the idea of me getting married, but I won't let him take it out on you."

"Don't worry about him. I can hold my own."

"Yes, you can, and *that* is exactly why I chose you," Azimar smiled, "I'm sorry I have to go. I'm even more determined to end this quickly so I can come back and marry you sooner." Asenna wasn't sure how to respond, but before she could say anything, Azimar kissed her, wrapping his fingers into her hair and around her back. Asenna put her arms around his neck and he lifted her off the step.

"Time to go, Azimar!" she heard Carro shout over the wind. Azimar slowly released her and she sank back onto solid ground, feeling as though she might crumple like a piece of parchment being fed to a fire.

"I almost forgot," he said, fumbling with his gloves and pulling a silver ring set with a pair of tiny rubies from his pocket. He slipped it onto Asenna's finger and then kissed her hand. "I'll be back soon."

"I'll be right here," Asenna said firmly, feeling the pit open back up in her stomach as he turned and mounted his big gray charger, then swung around to face his men.

"Tell me you're with me!" Azimar cried, raising his fist in the air.

"We are with you!" came the response.

"'Til when?"

"'Til death!" The cry built into a rumble and then a roar as the men spurred their horses forward. Asenna watched as they rode off down the dirt track road, following Azimar to the north. When they had vanished over the horizon, Asenna felt a bony hand on her shoulder and looked up to see Ilmira standing there with a tiny smile playing on her thin lips.

"Now we can begin the real work," she said in a smooth but vaguely threatening voice, "of turning you into the queen that my son deserves." All the loneliness and apprehension and bitter anger Asenna had kept under the surface the past few weeks rose up like the waves on the beach below the cliffs. She was drowning, but this time there was no one there to pull her out and she knew that she simply had to swim.

PART ONE

ONE:
THE HEIR

~ Three Years Later ~

The shrill, wavering cry pierced through Asenna's dreams and jerked her out of a surprisingly restful slumber. She forced her body to sit up, feeling around on the bed for the basket where her infant son slept. Once her eyes had adjusted to the moonlight outside the windows, she could see that he had kicked himself free of the swaddling wrap and was flailing wildly. Asenna scooped him up and bundled the cloth back around him, then pulled her shirt up and let him latch onto her breast. He guzzled the milk noisily, but his body relaxed and he melted into her stomach as she leaned back against the pillows, rubbing her eyes to try and stay awake.

"That's the third time tonight, little one," she sighed softly, "if you don't let me rest, I won't be able to make it through your naming ceremony tomorrow." Asenna tilted her head back and looked out the window at the bright, nearly-full moon hovering over the roofs of the city. *One month old today,* she thought to herself. The baby's jaw loosened as he began to drift back to sleep, but Asenna knew better than to try and pull him away and put him back in the basket. Instead, she closed her eyes and tried to practice how she would ask Azimar about taking their son to meet her family. She missed them desperately and the few letters they were able to write were not enough for her. Asenna had continued to write and Ephie had continued to take the letters to the Royal Postmaster, but for nearly ten months they had gone largely unanswered. Azimar assured her that the Ulvvori were safe, there was no news of any catastrophe, but Asenna felt in her gut that something was wrong. The problem was, she had no way of finding out what it was.

Since Azimar had won his war against Rogerin a year before, he had barely allowed Asenna to leave the palace. Her family had visited her only once in the capital, just after the war had ended, but the controversy and chaos caused by the presence of their four adult dire wolves was too much, and Azimar had refused to allow them to return. For the past year, Asenna had barely spoken to anyone aside from Ephie, Ilmira, and Azimar. The ministers and generals and generals who hovered around her husband all but ignored her, the servants merely obeyed, and she was permitted very little contact with the people of Sinsaya, the newly renamed capital city. The crushing isolation had nearly consumed Asenna, until her son had been born. When she saw his deep, golden eyes for the first time, the searing pain of being separated from her family turned into a dull ache that she was able to push aside, at least most of the time.

Asenna had also hoped their son's birth might heal the rift that had developed between her and Azimar since the end of the war, but in this she had been disappointed. When he had come to meet the baby for the first time, Azimar had barely even looked at her.

"The golden eyes, it means he has the Wolfsight, yes?" he had asked, blue eyes sparkling with something that made Asenna's neck bristle.

"Yes, he has it."

"When will the dire wolf find him? How does it happen?" It was a genuine question, but Asenna had let out a small laugh, which died in her throat when Azimar glared at her.

"The wolf doesn't seek the child out," she had explained, softening her voice, "when a child with the Wolfsight is born, their parents take them to a nursing she-wolf and ask her to choose one of her pups as a companion."

Azimar's brow furrowed. "So he will not have a wolf?"

"Not unless we take him to see my family very soon," Asenna had known that her voice sounded too hopeful, because Azimar smirked at her.

"I'm not letting you traipse across the kingdom with my newborn son," he had snapped, "it is no matter. The people will believe what I tell them to believe. He will still be the greatest ruler Esmadia has ever seen and the foundation of the Sinsayed Dynasty." Asenna had kept her silence. After three years, she knew better than to argue with Azimar. While she had first started to see hints of his unpredictable and vicious mood swings when he visited her at the villa during the war, they had only worsened as the conflict dragged on for two years and then ended. The charming young man from the beach, who had seemed to understand and care for her, had been consumed by paranoia, anger, and vindictiveness. Sometimes, Asenna would not see him for weeks at a time, but would hear him shouting at his mother or Carro late at night, and Ephie would slip out of bed to bolt the bedroom door shut. Since their son had been born a month before, Asenna had only seen her husband twice, so the naming ceremony felt more like a confrontation than a celebration.

"I think that's enough for now, little pup," she whispered to the baby, gently putting her finger in his mouth to unlatch him from her breast. She paused for a moment, waiting to see if he would wake back up and cry, but he merely grunted and pulled his tiny body into a ball. Asenna swaddled him again and laid him back in the basket, then took her dressing gown from the foot of the bed and slipped it over her clothes. The sky on the horizon was beginning to fade from black into pale yellow, indicating that the sun was on its way. Yawning and stretching, Asenna went to the antechamber where Ephie slept and gently shook her awake.

"Ephie? Can you start a bath, please?" she whispered. The maid's eyes remained closed, but she nodded and then pulled her hunched body from the bed. Asenna disliked sitting and watching Ephie work, so she went to stoke the fire that had burned to embers during the night.

"Are you ready for the ceremony today?" Ephie asked her.

"I hardly know what it is," Asenna confessed as she tossed a few small pieces of kindling into the fireplace and then went to pick up her son's basket and move it next to the warmth of the flames that slowly flickered back to life. "What can you tell me?"

"I don't know much, either," Ephie replied, setting out a stack of linen towels, "there hasn't been a public naming ceremony for an heir in a long time, but don't you fret. I'll be by your side the whole time. Do you know the name Azimar has chosen?"

"He won't tell me, but I imagine it will be Elijas, after his father," Asenna sighed, "he wouldn't even hear of using a Ulvvori name, which is why I need you to keep a secret for me, Ephie." Asenna went over to her vanity and opened a drawer, pulling out a small bundle of cloth.

Ephie straightened up. "You know I would do anything for you."

"Azimar won't give him a Ulvvori name," Asenna said, her voice wavering as she unwrapped the bundle, "so I'm going to give him one, and I want you to be the first to hear it." Asenna pulled the cloth back to show Ephie the large canine tooth of a dire wolf, which had been carved with Ulvvori symbols and a name.

"'Fenrinn,'" Ephie read, running a shaky finger over the letters.

"I hope you don't mind," Asenna said, "all the things you told me about your son…your little Fen…I hope that my boy can be as loving and kind as he was." A small sob escaped Ephie's mouth as Asenna pulled her into a brief hug before she shuffled away, wiping tears from her eyes while she prepared the bath.

When Asenna finished bathing both herself and Fen, she wrapped him slowly and carefully in the bright red length of cloth that Azimar had insisted she use. Once he was bundled up and asleep again, Asenna took the wolf tooth bearing his name and tucked it firmly into the swaddling at his side, so it would not be seen or felt while Azimar held him. She had no idea what to expect at the ceremony, but it had been months since she had last been presented to the public in her role as queen, so she tried to quell her racing thoughts by making herself look the part. As she sat in front of the mirror letting Ephie curl her hair around a hot poker, Asenna examined her own face, something she usually went out of her way to avoid. Two years of living mostly alone with Ilmira at the villa had strained her, and when she had first arrived in the capital after Azimar's victory, she had heard people say she looked more like a prisoner of war than a queen. However, more distance from her mother-in-law and then nine months of pregnancy had allowed Asenna to put a little weight on, which she didn't mind, even if it felt strange to be soft in places that had always been bony and hard with whipcord muscles. Ephie finished with her hair and dabbed some kohl around her eyes with a small horsehair brush, then smoothed rouge across her cheeks and lips. Asenna was pleased with the effect, even though she knew it would be a task to wash it off later.

Just as Ephie was tying the last of the cords on the bodice of Asenna's gray gown, there was a sharp knock on the door. The sound made Asenna jump and she realized that her entire body was taught like a bowstring, anticipating having to see Azimar and wondering what type of mood he might be in. Ephie went to open the door and Carro stepped into the room, hands folded neatly behind his back. Asenna glanced over and registered that he looked exactly how she felt: exhausted and wound-up. Carro was the one constantly on the front lines of managing Azimar's volatile moods and she did not envy him the task, but her vaguely antagonistic relationship with the Captain had turned downright cold since the end of the war. When Azimar had taken the throne, he had given Carro a position in his newly-created secret police. Officially styled the 'Black Sabers,' they had quickly become hated and feared throughout Esmadia because of the number of brutal, high-profile assassinations immediately following Azimar's ascension. Shortly after announcing her pregnancy, Asenna had also discovered that Azimar had ordered the Black Sabers to intercept and read all her letters, so she turned her back to Carro without a greeting.

"What do you want?" Ephie asked Carro with a vicious bite in her voice. She was the only servant in the palace who could get away with speaking to any Black Saber that way, and Asenna was thankful for her ferocity.

"I was sent to escort Her Majesty and the Prince to the ceremony," Carro replied, averting his eyes from both women and staring at the far wall instead. Asenna stood up and gathered Fen from his basket. When she passed Carro, she could see the deadly twin sabers hanging on his back, but also spotted a long dagger on his belt and boot knife on his leg. *Armed to the teeth for a naming ceremony,* Asenna thought, shaking her head, *what is Azimar thinking?*

"The entire city has gathered," Carro told her as they walked through the warren of hallways that comprised the palace, "they are eager to meet their new prince, and to see their queen again after so long." Ephie glared at him suspiciously.

"I shall be glad to see them too," Asenna gave him a standard, emotionless response. She had learned that it was best not to reveal her true feelings to the people that surrounded Azimar, lest they be used against her later. Carro fell silent until they arrived at the meeting room which led out onto a large balcony where the King gave public appearances and speeches. Asenna could hear the buzz of the crowd outside, and she suddenly felt quite dizzy and anxious at the thought of all those people staring at her. She squeezed her eyes shut for a moment.

"Are you alright, Your Majesty?" Carro asked, "you look…unwell…"

"I'm fine, Captain," Asenna snapped, taking a deep breath and pulling herself together, "surely my husband needs his loyal dog back at his side now?" The level of acrimony in her voice caused Carro to shake his head.

"I didn't read your letters, Asenna," he said quietly, then turned away before she could respond and walked through the curtain that led out onto the balcony, holding it open for her to follow. Ephie gave Asenna a firm squeeze on her upper arm before she stepped out, cradling Fen in one arm and shielding his eyes from the sun with the other. The day was unusually bright and warm for mid-winter and it took Asenna's eyes a moment to adjust. On the balcony stood a number of the kingdom's high-ranking ministers and Lords, alongside Ilmira, who was wearing her usual scowl, and Azimar, who looked resplendent in a simple red shirt covered by a gray velvet waistcoat and black breeches. On top of his deep chestnut curls sat a large golden crown that Asenna did not recognize. The tines were made to look like tiny pikes and they were interwoven with thin rods of gold that had been twisted like ropes. On the front of the crown hung the golden head of a dire wolf, its eyes set with tiny sapphires to mimic the color of Azimar's own eyes. *What a ridiculous, ugly thing,* Asenna thought to herself, but she smiled at him nevertheless and pressed her body against his in a long embrace which drew cheers from the crowd. Azimar kissed the top of her head and when she looked closer at his face, she saw almost no trace of the strain and anger that had covered him like a shroud the last year. Asenna felt both hopeful and suspicious about the sudden change in his demeanor. Experience told her that his good moods were usually a temporary façade to get something he wanted, but she also couldn't help that her heart still skipped a beat when he looked at her the way he used to.

"My darling wife," he purred in her ear, "and my beautiful son. What a wonderful day. Are you ready, my love?" He motioned for her to stand beside him on the balcony and she gave a small wave to the people below, who seemed thrilled to see her. Azimar's chief advisor, a thin and balding man named Bernart Greenlow, held his hands up for silence.

"Welcome, citizens of Esmadia," he called out, "this is a great day in the history of our realm. One year ago today, your King, Azimar Sinsayed and his loyal men freed Esmadia from the tyranny, superstition, and malice of Rogerin Godmere." The people roared their approval and Bernart continued, "he has brought us into a new age of enlightenment, prosperity, and freedom. And now, through the faithful efforts and bravery of Queen Asenna, your King has an heir to carry on his work for generations to come! Today, your Prince shall receive his name and our new age can truly begin. This is a day that will be forever recorded in history books as the birth of the mighty and honorable Sinsayed Dynasty!" The crowd roared again, waving the red, gray, and green Esmadian flags and chanting Azimar's name. He glanced over at Asenna with a satisfied expression and then stepped forward to address the crowd.

"Esmadia! I made an oath many years ago that I would no longer sit by and watch my people suffer under the ignorance and oppression of Rogerin Godmere and his ilk," he turned back toward Asenna and held his hands out. Reluctantly, Asenna placed Fen in his arms and stood to the side, but her heart began to hammer when Azimar untucked the swaddling cloth and started to unwind it from Fen's body. Looking around anxiously for Ephie, Asenna realized that she was still inside and there was nothing anyone could do.

"Today," Azimar continued, pulling the red cloth as he spoke, "I make another oath to my people: that I will leave you in better hands than I found you, and better even than *I* could offer. Today, I give you the flesh of my body, a male heir, with the blood of a conqueror and the golden eyes of a wolf: Prince Elijas Sinsayed!" Dramatically, Azimar held the naked child above his head for all the crowd to see. The applause was thunderous, but Asenna's entire body felt like it was on fire as she watched the spectacle. Her eyes frantically searched the swaddling wrap, which Azimar had dropped beside him, trying to find the wolf tooth that she had tucked next to Fen's arm. She was frozen in place, waiting for a chance to kneel down and snatch the amulet up, but before she could, Azimar held Fen out to her and Asenna had no choice but to take the baby while Azimar bent to pick up the swaddling himself. Asenna watched in horror as the tooth fell out and hit his boot. Azimar picked it up and glanced at it for a moment before straightening up and slipping it into his pocket. His sharp blue eyes looked back at Asenna for a split second and he gave a tiny, almost imperceptible smile.

Asenna felt like she wanted to run or vomit or both. From the day she had realized she was pregnant, Azimar had made it very clear that anything to do with their son, other than day-to-day care, was to remain strictly under his control, and his hatred for superstition and magic had only intensified. Once, soon after their small wedding, Asenna had made a small Ulvvori fertility charm and worn it under her gown, hoping it would help her give Azimar the heir he so desperately wanted. When he had found it, however, he had flown into a rage and left bruises on her arm. Asenna knew that her use of the wolf tooth amulet would not go unpunished and her body began to shake as she wrapped Fen back into his swaddling. Azimar continued his speech for another few minutes, but Asenna could not hear him. Several rogue tears slipped down her cheeks, but she fixed a false smile on her face so anyone who noticed them would assume they were the delighted tears of a mother.

When Azimar finished speaking, he turned and held his arm out, indicating that she should lead the way back into the meeting room. Ephie was waiting to take Fen, but Asenna was too afraid to let him go. Once everyone had cleared the balcony, Azimar's ministers crowded around Asenna, asking to see Fen's golden eyes. They pelted her with questions, which she could barely answer. She tried not to make eye contact with Azimar as he stood in the corner of the room, looking at her like he was a fox and she was the rabbit he was planning on ripping apart for dinner. Luckily, Ephie stepped in between Asenna and the over-eager ministers, insisting that the queen was still in recovery from childbirth and she needed to rest. Azimar only approached Asenna once the gaggle of chattering men had moved away.

"Carro will escort you back to your chambers," he said evenly, "and I will come see you this afternoon. Now that he has his name, we need to discuss his upbringing as a Prince."

"He is far too young, Your Majesty," Ephie said.

"You forget your place," Azimar snapped at her, "if I wanted advice on child-rearing from an old hag, I'd ask my own mother." Ephie's face tightened, but she stayed silent. Azimar leaned in to kiss Asenna and her body flooded with fear when he gripped the back of her neck a little too tightly. She barely remembered the walk back to her chambers, clutching Fen to her chest and fixing her gaze on Carro's twin sabers ahead of her so she didn't stumble. When they were alone again, Asenna placed Fen in his basket and slumped against the bed, sobbing, barely even able to explain to Ephie what had happened.

"It was so stupid," she wept, "why did I do it?"

"Oh, you sweet child," the old woman whispered, hugging her, "don't you worry. We will figure something. You did nothing wrong. Don't you worry." Ephie held Asenna tightly for what felt like hours until her tears stopped, then went to hang a kettle over the fireplace to make tea. Asenna finally pulled herself up into an armchair and put her face in her hands. Over on the bed, Fen had begun to wriggle and fuss, so Asenna picked him up and settled back into the chair to nurse him. He looked at her with his brilliant golden eyes and Asenna felt a wave of despair.

"How could I bring you into this, little one?" she said softly, tracing a finger along his pudgy little arm, "you deserve so much better." Ephie came over and set a tea tray on the desk.

"Don't you talk like that," she scolded, stroking Asenna's hair, "he has a mother who loves him and that's all he really needs." There was a knock and Asenna sucked in her breath, holding it while Ephie went to open the door. Carro stood in the hall again, looking a bit more flustered than before.

"The King is on his way," he said, looking as though he wanted to say more, but stopping himself. Asenna stood up and put Fen in his basket, then tried to wipe some of the smeared makeup off her face. Only moments later, Azimar swept past Carro into the room with Ilmira behind him. Asenna's heart immediately dropped a beat when she saw her mother-in-law wearing a victorious smile.

"Darling," said Azimar pleasantly. He walked over and sat on the bed beside Fen, leaning over to coo and shake the baby's feet around. Asenna tried to give a small curtsey but her legs were trembling so badly that she could not manage it.

"I'm glad to see you," she tried to say, but found her voice catching. Azimar got up and went over to the desk, poured himself a cup of tea, then reached into his pocket and took out the wolf's tooth. He placed it beside the tea tray and sat down, sipping as though it were a garden party. Asenna glanced over at Ephie, who was mouthing the words to a silent prayer.

"What is it?" Azimar asked softly after almost a full minute.

"A dire wolf tooth," Asenna replied, as evenly as she could manage, "it's…an old Ulvvori tradition. For a naming ceremony."

"And what name is written on this tooth?"

"Fen…Fenrinn."

"Is that the name I gave him today?" Azimar set his teacup down a little too hard and Asenna winced.

"He is my son too, Azimar…and he *is* Ulvvori," Asenna breathed, her voice barely more than a whisper, "we were your allies. The Riders fought and died for you to have the throne, and I don't understand why you--" In an instant, Azimar was across the room, backing her up against the vanity, his hot breath suffocating her as she squeezed her eyes shut.

"He is a Prince and a Sinsayed, not some mongrel cave-dweller," Azimar hissed, putting his hand around Asenna's forearm and squeezing hard, "he may have the Wolfsight, but he is *not* Ulvvori and never will be, because he is *mine*. Do you understand me? He will never set foot in those fucking mountains and you will not fill his head with nonsense about moon spirits or magic or the rest of it. I will not have it, Asenna! Belief in magic makes people weak and stupid, and *my* son will not be weak."

"Yes, sir," Asenna whispered. Azimar backed away and composed himself, but Asenna had to lean against the vanity just to continue standing. She felt Ephie's hand on her arm and opened her eyes to see that Ilmira's smirk had widened. Carro still lingered in the doorway, his eyes darting back and forth between Asenna and Azimar.

"Ephie, you will begin packing the Queen's things immediately," Azimar said, sitting back down and picking up his tea, "she will be leaving Sinsaya in the morning."

"I don't understand," Asenna said slowly, "where are we going?"

"*You* are going to the villa, and you will be staying there on a more…permanent basis from now on. My son will remain here." All the fear and sadness suddenly fell away from Asenna's body and she pushed away from the vanity.

"What do you mean?"

"I feel that I can no longer trust you to raise the Prince, Asenna. Your mind has been corrupted by the superstitions and foolishness of your people. I thought you could overcome it, but it has become increasingly clear to me that you still cling to your ways and I won't allow my son to be influenced by such dangerous beliefs. He will remain here under the care of my mother and a few very carefully selected wetnurses."

"No!" Asenna's voice cracked, "you can't do this, Azimar, please!"

"I will bring him to visit you when I see fit," Azimar replied coolly. Asenna felt her body begin to tremble, but this time with rage. She balled her hands into fists and took a step toward her husband.

"No!" she screamed, "you will *not* take him from me!" She managed a few more steps before Carro moved between them, putting a firm hand on her arm.

"Don't," he murmured, shaking his head ever so slightly. Asenna tried to jerk her arm away, but he held on.

"It is done, Asenna," said Azimar, glaring at her over Carro's shoulder, "make your peace with it. You have one more night with him."

"You cannot separate a she-wolf from her cub!" Asenna cried, trying to push past Carro, who grabbed both her upper arms and held her back. Azimar turned and seized her face.

"You are no she-wolf," he let out a cruel laugh, "you are a bitch, only good for one thing. Consider yourself fortunate I don't put you in the kennels with my other dogs." He let her go and turned on his heel, leaving the room with Ilmira behind him, still wearing her satisfied smirk. Carro held Asenna's arms for a few more moments, then released her and backed away as she leaned on the desk, sobbing quietly.

"Did I hurt you?" Carro asked from the doorway. Asenna acted without thinking, seizing the teapot in front of her and hurling it at his face. Her aim was surprisingly accurate and Carro had to raise his arm to block the attack. The teapot made contact with the leather gauntlet on his wrist, shattering and sending scalding tea and pieces of delicate porcelain flying. As Carro ducked out the door and vanished, Asenna was pleased to see a small trickle of blood over his eyebrow. Her chest heaved as she stumbled to the bed and beat the mattress with her fists.

"He can't do this!" she cried to Ephie, who stood behind her, "how can he do this to me? My baby…" Asenna finally fell onto the bed and curled into a ball, sobs racking her body. Ephie took a firm hold of her shoulders.

"Sit up and listen to me, Asenna," she croaked, "I won't allow this to happen. You must listen to me. I will do what I can, but it will require the greatest courage on your part, do you understand?" Asenna sat up and looked into Ephie's deep brown eyes. She knew that if only one person cared about her anymore, it was Ephie.

"What…what can we do?" Asenna asked, wiping her tears away. "I'll do anything. Please tell me." Ephie wiped Asenna's face with her sleeve.

"You need to rest now. Lay with Fen and feed him, then sleep. I'll wake you when I have a plan. We must get the two of you away from Sinsaya."

"Away? Where? What about you?" Asenna's heart dropped.

"I'm not sure yet," Ephie gave a strained smile and Asenna could tell she was lying, "you rest now. Let me do some work." The crash of the teapot had woken Fen and he cried out, so Asenna laid down in the bed with him and tried to distract herself by singing every Ulvvori lullaby that she could remember her own father singing to her whenever she had trouble sleeping as a child. Eventually, she slipped away into a series of nightmares where she was being hunted by men in black wielding fishing spears.

~~~

"Asenna, you must get up now," Ephie whispered urgently. As Asenna sat bolt upright, memories of the previous day flooded back and she felt tears sting her eyes. Fen was, blessedly, still sleeping beside her in the basket. "I have a plan for you, but it must happen now, before dawn." Ephie placed a drawstring sack beside her on the bed and opened it. From within she produced a large piece of parchment which she laid flat so that it was illuminated by the lamplight. It was a detailed map of Esmadia and Kashait, its neighbor to the east. On the upper corner, someone had used charcoal to draw a rough map of the city and the palace complex at its center.

"I need to get home," Asenna said, indicating the location of the Ulvvori's winter settlement in the foothills of the Midwinter Mountains.

Ephie shook her head. "Asenna, I must tell you something," she said, her voice strained, "please forgive me, but your pregnancy was already so difficult and I...I didn't want to cause you any more pain..."

"Ephie..." said Asenna softly, "what is it?"

"The Ulvvori have been driven out of the mountains. They are living as refugees now and traveling toward Kashait to seek asylum there," Ephie's voice was a whisper, whether from secrecy or emotion Asenna could not tell. Her head began to reel as she struggled to understand what Ephie was saying. The Ulvvori had lived in the Midwinter Mountains for as long as there had been recorded history in Esmadia, nearly twenty-five hundred years, and Asenna could not fathom anything that could make them leave.

"How? Why?"

"I cannot give you too many details now," Ephie said, "because you must go quickly, but I will tell you...that it was Azimar. Around four months ago...he ordered a vicious attack on The Den by the Black Sabers." Asenna covered her mouth and choked back a loud sob.

"My family?" she asked desperately.

"I don't know, my sweet girl. I am so sorry, but I am sending you to people who will help you find them, wherever they are," Ephie was crying too, but she put the map in front of Asenna and pointed, "please, you must listen now, because this is the part that will require enormous courage and strength. This spot on the palace wall, near the stables, was destroyed during Azimar's final siege, you remember? They've done a shoddy job rebuilding it, but that is to your benefit, because it was rebuilt with rough stones that are full of handholds." As Ephie explained, Asenna felt a rush of blood to her limbs.

"I have to climb...just like I did at home on the cliffs."

"It's the only way. The guards are posted here on the corners, but they won't be patrolling down the center, especially on the rebuilt section. You must climb to the top and then down the other side."

Asenna swallowed and nodded. "I can do it."

"That's my girl," Ephie put a hand on her shoulder and smiled, "now, once you are in the city, go to Beacon Street and then find the blacksmith's shop with a wolf head on the sign. No matter what time it is, someone will answer if you knock on the door slowly five times. The blacksmith's name is Ferryn and he is my brother. He will help you." Asenna was somewhat startled. In all the years she had known Ephie, she had never mentioned any family other than her sons.

"Your brother is here? In the city?"

"Yes, but it is too long a story for now. Ferryn is a blacksmith, but he also deals in…secrets and information. He knows people who can hide you, move you, and keep you safe. Do *exactly* what he says. I swear on my life that you can trust him and his two daughters, just as you trust me," Ephie's tone was clipped, but Asenna could see tears building in her eyes again. She squeezed the old woman's hand.

"Can't you come with me, Ephie?" she said softly.

"I cannot, sweet girl. I'm certainly no climber, and I might have been able to charm the idiot guards outside your door tonight, but Azimar has the Sabers posted on the palace gate and we both know they would never let me out," Ephie squeezed Asenna's hand back, "now, I have new clothes for you here, and we must tie Fen to your chest." Asenna immediately stripped off her nightdress and put on the too-large black clothes, then grabbed her own riding boots. Once she was dressed and Fen had been changed, Ephie took one of the linen sheets off the bed and used it to tie a sling which held Fen securely to Asenna's chest. Asenna put the bag across her back and then Ephie helped her don a dark, hooded cloak.

"One more thing," Ephie said, taking the wolf tooth amulet out of her pocket and tucking it back into Fen's swaddling. She placed a soft, lingering kiss on the baby's forehead.

"Where will you go?" asked Asenna, her voice cracking again.

"Don't you worry about me, child," Ephie replied, "I'll have those bastards spinning in circles looking for you and then I'll take my rest in the prison block. Three square meals a day and no work!" She laughed, but Asenna could see the lines on her face grow deeper as they walked to the door. Ephie opened it and poked her head into the hall, then she stood back and took Asenna's hands.

"Ephie…" Asenna began to sob, "how can I ever thank you?"

"You can thank me by staying alive and by keeping your sweet son away from Azimar and his pack of bootlickers. That's how you can thank me, by living the life that you and Fen deserve," she leaned in and kissed Asenna on each cheek, then kissed Fen once more, "*Izlani* will keep you safe."

"Goodbye, Ephie." Asenna turned around before she could change her mind and walked as quietly as she could down the empty, darkened corridor.

TWO: COMMANDER

Carro shut the door to his room and took a deep, centering breath. The sun had just come up and it was time to do the task that he had laid awake dreading all night. Putting his fingers up to the small gash above his eyebrow, he winced and sighed. He had obviously suffered worse wounds, but knowing that Asenna was willing to hurl tableware at him made Carro all the more trepidatious as he set out along the corridor. The Black Sabers were housed inside the main palace, near enough to the King's quarters that they could arrive quickly in an emergency. The Queen's rooms were a bit farther away and Carro walked slower than normal, trying to lay out a plan in his head. He resented the fact that Azimar had tasked him with this, but he was far more afraid of Azimar's temper than Asenna's, so he obeyed. At the end of the corridor, Carro met up with two of his men who he had selected for the job the night before, and one Black Saber recruit named Gade who he was trying to train.

"What are we doing, Captain?" asked Gade immediately. Carro rubbed his temples. He hadn't wanted to tell them what the job was, but now it was unavoidable.

"You won't like it," he said, turning to face them, "Azimar has ordered that Prince Elijas be removed from the Queen's care. She's being sent to the villa and the child will stay here with Lady Ilmira." There was not much that shocked Carro and the Black Sabers anymore, but this news had his men glancing nervously at one another. Removing babies from their mothers was not something any of them had signed up for.

"Let's get it over with then," snapped Jesk, Carro's gruff, bald Lieutenant.

"I know it's not our usual fare," Carro sighed, "but Azimar has his reasons. So, three of us will escort the Queen down to the gate, where a carriage is waiting. The other will take Ephie, with the Prince, to Lady Ilmira. Jesk, I assume you would rather avoid another run-in with Ephie?"

"Damn right. That crazy old bitch nearly had my eye out," Jesk laughed. Carro was unamused, but tried to fake a small smile so his men wouldn't see how bothered he was.

"Fine then. Jesk, Gade, and I will escort the Queen. Roper, you take Ephie with the Prince. All good?" The men all nodded their agreement and they continued through the palace. Jesk fell back with Roper and they exchanged theories, but Gade caught up with Carro and walked beside him.

"Can't you tell us anything, Captain? We need to know what we're getting into."

"It's not dangerous, Gade," Carro chuckled, "we might have to keep her restrained while Roper takes the baby, but she's hardly a threat."

"That cut on your forehead says differently," Gade smirked. Normally Carro wouldn't suffer a teenage recruit to talk to him that way, but he let Gade get away with more because he reminded Carro a little too much of himself.

"Who said this came from Asenna?"

"It's alright, I won't tell anyone," Gade winked and Carro raised his hand playfully as if to smack him.

"This is just something he thinks is best," Carro told him gently, "you know I don't get involved with their…personal issues." Gade nodded as if he was experienced in these things and Carro shook his head and smiled. At only sixteen, Gade hadn't even fought in Azimar's rebellion, but liked to pretend he knew what the older men were talking about. They reached the corridor where Asenna's rooms were and Carro pushed his hair back anxiously.

"Let me go in first and see if I can talk to her," he told the men in a low voice. Steeling himself for the assault, Carro knocked on the door and heard Ephie's voice call for him to enter. His men hung back slightly as he walked in and looked around. The room was empty, save for Ephie, who was sitting in an armchair next to the window with a resolute expression on her face. Asenna and the baby were nowhere to be seen. Carro's stomach twisted into furious knots as he approached Ephie. When she looked at him, the hatred burning in her eyes was almost unbearable and he had to look away.

"Where are they, Ephie?" he asked.

"Don't insult me by pretending like we're friends, *Captain,*" the old woman spat, "in fact, I'd be grateful if you'd cut my throat now and get it over with."

"You know I won't."

"Why? Have you grown a heart overnight? Or is it rather that I'm the only person who knows where she is? Don't think I'm going to tell you. I'd rather throw myself out that window."

"Your loyalty is admirable," Carro said, "but you and I both know it won't get you anywhere with Azimar. Besides, I can find them even without your help." Ephie looked away from him again. Carro's men entered the room and their faces fell as they realized what was going on.

"She wouldn't dare…" Jesk breathed.

"Roper, Gade, take this woman to the prison block and tell them not to let her go for anyone other than myself. Jesk, you're with me," Carro snapped. As Roper and Gade escorted her from the room, Ephie turned around.

"When they kill me, Captain, tell them to do it under the full moon," she called to him, "so my spirit can be carried up to *Izlani*." Carro couldn't look at her. Once she was gone, he swept out into the corridor with Jesk on his heels.

"What the fuck is an *Izlani*?" asked Jesk.

"It's the Ulvvori's moon goddess," Carro muttered, walking faster. Even though Jesk was a full head taller than him, the older man struggled to keep up.

"Where are we going now, Captain?"

"To see the Boss. He needs to know about this before we begin searching."

"Do you think she's still in the city?"

"Asenna is too naive to plan something like this on her own, but Ephie is no fool. She will have told Asenna about the Ulvvori already, so she won't run north. She'll go to someone who can help her find them and this city is rife with smugglers who could do that. We just need to figure out which one Ephie sent her to." Carro stopped suddenly and Jesk nearly ran him over.

"Captain?"

"Jesk, I need you to go to the Master of the Household, Mr. Anslo. He'll be in the kitchen right now. He keeps records of all the servants who work in the palace. Tell him I need all the information he has about Ephie, especially anything about her family or any next-of-kin. Bring it to me in the council room," Carro said, his mind working quickly. Jesk saluted and turned back the other direction toward the kitchens. As Carro walked, he tried to plan how to break the news to Azimar, but he knew that no matter what he said, the outcome would be the same and he just hoped that it wasn't bad this time. He didn't want to face his men with a black eye again. Outside the King's chambers, there was a double guard posted, who Carro waved away.

He knocked three times and called his own name.

"Enter," came Azimar's voice. Carro stepped into the room and shut the door behind him. Azimar's rooms were normally cluttered and dark, but today he had thrown the curtains open and was standing at his desk reading a piece of parchment. He seemed to be in good spirits, but there were particularly dark circles under his eyes and a small bottle of clear liquor on the desk beside him. Carro's body tensed up even more at the sight of the bottle.

"Sir," Carro said, approaching slowly, "we have a problem." Azimar looked up, his blue eyes digging into Carro, who tried to hold the piercing gaze but couldn't.

"What problem?" Azimar's voice was deadly quiet and calm.

"It's...the Queen. It appears that she's taken the Prince and...escaped...in the middle of the night," Carro waited for the explosion and it came swiftly. Azimar roared and then reached down and overturned the entire desk, spilling papers and empty teacups onto the floor. Carro flinched and took a few steps back.

"What the fuck do you mean she escaped?!" Azimar snarled, coming around the overturned table and backing Carro up against a dresser. "How? Where is she?"

"We don't know yet," Carro turned away from Azimar's breath, which was hot and heavy with alcohol. "I'm going to send search parties into the city. Please, Azimar..."

"How could you let this happen?!" Azimar's fist slammed into the dresser, inches from Carro's face, sending tiny droplets of blood flying, "why wasn't there a guard posted?"

"There was, but they left--"

"Idiots and traitors!" Azimar bellowed, stalking back across the room and kicking a chair, sending it flying into the opposite wall, "*you* will pay for this if she isn't found! *You* were the only one who knew! I swear...everyone is against me..."

"Azimar," Carro moved toward him, trying to steady his voice and breathing as he felt panic rising up in his chest, "I need your permission to start searching the city."

"Do it!" Azimar cried, "you have full command of the Black Sabers. Just find her and do *not* come back here until you do, Carro, or I swear..." Suddenly, Azimar lurched sideways and leaned on the wall, his body starting to shake violently. He looked back, eyes glassy as he slid onto the floor and Carro ran to catch him.

"Everyone against me..." Azimar groaned, his body contorting.

"No one's against you. Come on," Carro begged, "I need you to get up. Azimar..."

"You have...to find my son. Please find my son, Carro."

"I will, I'll find them, but first you need to get up!" Carro put his fingers in his mouth and whistled for the guards, who entered cautiously. "Go and get Lady Ilmira! Now!" Carro barely managed to pull Azimar up by his arm and move him over to the bed.

"Tell me you're with me," Azimar whispered, grabbing Carro's shoulder and holding it with a surprisingly strong grip.

"I'm with you," Carro murmured, "I'm right here. I won't leave." Azimar's eyes were still focused elsewhere, like he was seeing people who weren't in the room, and he continued to twitch and writhe as Carro sat beside him. A few minutes later Ilmira appeared, her face a mask of alarm and fear. She closed the door on the guards.

"When did it start?" she asked, rushing over and feeling her son's forehead.

"Just a minute ago," Carro replied as he stood back, "he's been drinking again, Ilmira. I told you he needs to stop. I can't watch him kill himself like this!"

"As if I can control every single thing he does!" Ilmira hissed back at him, "you think I want this to happen? He is my son! My only son!"

"And I'm the one who takes the brunt of this!" Carro said, coming around beside her, "you don't stay with him when it gets bad. You have no idea. He has to stop! He can't even go a day without a fucking bottle in his hand and the doctors have all said that's what's causing this! His temper is one thing, Ilmira, but this is something different and dangerous and you know it." Ilmira sat down on the bed beside Azimar and pushed his hair away from his face. He was still muttering to himself and twitching.

"It's not just the drink," she insisted softly, "there's always something else that makes this happen. What did you say to him?"

"Don't you *dare* blame me..." Carro breathed, "I tell him what he needs to hear, even when it sets him off, and then I suffer the consequences, not you!"

"What did you say to him?" Ilmira cried, standing up and facing him with tears running down her wrinkled cheeks.

"I told him about Asenna and the Prince..." Carro couldn't think straight and regretted his words immediately.

"*What about them?*" Ilmira moved toward him like a cat stalking her prey.

"They...they ran from the palace in the middle of the night."

"That little bitch! I knew she would do something like this!" Ilmira screeched, "why are your men not out looking for her, Captain?! Go! Now!" Without another word, Carro left the room as quickly as he could, chest heaving. Once he was away from the guards and in a corridor by himself, he stopped and leaned against the cool stone wall, trying to stop the pounding in his chest and the trembling in his hands. As long as Carro had known him, Azimar had been temperamental, but these episodes, which had begun when they were teenagers, were becoming more frequent and destructive. Mostly he yelled or threw things or rambled incoherently to himself while Carro sat with him, but sometimes it was all Carro could do to keep Azimar from throwing himself off the balcony or cutting his own wrists. During these times, Ilmira would send the guards away and Carro would be left to care for his friend alone, sometimes for days at a time. Over time, Carro had noticed that the episodes seemed to be linked to Azimar's drinking habits, but Ilmira had refused to take any action to get him to stop. Carro had been the one left trying to manage the situation as best he could, but it was starting to take a toll. Slumping against the wall, he put his face in his hands. He knew he had to focus, but couldn't shake the quivering panic that had overtaken his body. Carro took a few deep breaths, then imagined wrapping the entire scene up in a neat bundle. He placed the bundle into an imaginary box and then pictured locking it and shoving it under his bed. Once he knew it was gone, he was able to steady his breathing and continue walking.

When Carro made it back to the Black Saber's block, he found that Roper and Gade must have roused the men, because dozens of them were waiting in the corridor outside the council room where the Black Saber Captains met to plan missions. They all snapped to attention when Carro appeared.

"At ease," he told them, "you'll have orders soon." He walked into the council room, where his fellow Captains were already waiting for him. There were eleven of them all together, each commanding a company of one hundred men. At only twenty-eight, Carro was the youngest of the group, but now he suddenly found himself in command.

"What's happened?" several men asked as he fell into his chair.

"The short version," Carro began in a shaky voice, "is that Queen Asenna has taken the infant Prince and somehow left the palace in the middle of the night. The King is…in bad condition and has placed me in command for the time being." It spoke to his own merits and the implicit trust that existed between the Black Sabers that not a single man at the table questioned this sudden promotion. They all simply looked at him expectantly, awaiting orders, and then Jesk burst into the room carrying a stack of papers.

"I have the information you asked for, Captain," he said, setting the papers in front of Carro and giving a clumsy salute.

"Thank you, Jesk." Carro surveyed the information and smiled to himself, feeling pleased with the situation for the first time all morning.

"Well?" asked one of the other officers.

"It appears that Asenna's maid, Ephie, has family in the city. A brother and his two adult daughters. The brother owns a blacksmith shop on Beacon Street and it seems that he sometimes runs with…an unsavory crowd," Carro pinched the bridge of his nose for a moment as he thought, then slapped his hand on the table and stood up. "She had to have left sometime in the middle of the night, so she will either still be in the city, laying low until we stop searching, or she is already on the road, trying to find the Ulvvori. Given the information here, I'm willing to bet that she will have some kind of mercenary protection. I want armed search parties to start sweeping the city immediately. While they search, I'll take a hunting party to Beacon Street and see what information I can get from this blacksmith. If she's already left the city, we'll go after her. Listen closely though, I will *not* have this become a circus. You search thoroughly, but you do it respectfully and quietly. We don't need a riot on our hands right now. Understand?"

"We'll organize the search parties," one of them said, "what else do you need, Commander?" Carro thought quickly, planning the pursuit in his mind.

"I'll need a hunter," he said at last, "someone who can track and someone who knows the Ulvvori and where they might be. Someone who won't talk."

"I know of someone," said another officer named Sirota, who was actually a Lieutenant filling in for his indisposed Captain, "I'll send for him, but I know he doesn't come cheap."

"I don't think Azimar will put a price on finding his son," Carro assured him, "bring him to me as soon as you can, Lieutenant. I'll choose my men for the hunting party. Everyone clear on what's to be done?"

"Yes, Commander!"

"Dismissed," Carro called, and they scattered instantaneously. Once the room cleared, Carro went and stood in the hall, surveying the men walking by and calculating whose skills he might need. It was what he did before every mission, and it was this aptitude for choosing the right people that had gained him the trust of both his men and Azimar. He treated it like a puzzle, matching the requirements of the job with the talents of the individual Black Sabers.

"Roper, Jesk!" he called out, "you're with me." He indicated the council room and they went inside, "Vaylen, Tarett…Blight…Walcott…Sly, Daine…and Ilar. With me." Once he had everyone he needed, Carro followed them into the council room. The eager buzz in the air was palpable. It had been a long time since they'd been on a proper mission outside the city, but Carro knew he needed to impress upon them how different this was.

"When do we leave, Captain?" Jesk called down the table.

"He's the Commander now, you idiot," Tarett laughed, "show some respect!" Jesk made a rude gesture back.

"When do we leave, *Commander?*" he asked again in a sing-song voice.

"Listen to me, all of you," Carro tried to keep his voice as even as possible, "this is not a game. We are not tracking some criminal or failed assassin that we can kick around a little to soften them up. We must be…delicate. If anything happens to the Prince, we would be better off taking poison than facing Azimar. The information I have indicates that Asenna may have protection. Given her's and Ephie's background, it's likely going to be Ulvvori hiring themselves out, and where there's Ulvvori, there could eventually be dire wolves." A hush fell over the room. Every man present had fought alongside the Wolf Riders during Azimar's rebellion, and it was impossible to forget the carnage they had visited on Rogerin's forces.

"We aren't going after the Ulvvori though, are we?" Roper asked.

"No, but Asenna will be trying to find them. I'm sure by now she has been made aware of the attack on her people, but they are her only family and she will seek their protection. If she finds them before we get to her, we *will* have to deal with the Wolf Riders, and they will certainly not deal lightly with us…after what we've done to them," Carro said.

"Well, what are we waiting for then?" Jesk asked.

"I'm waiting for our tracker," Carro told him, "Sirota is bringing him here, so I want you to go pack your things and get your horses ready. Roper, you'll need your bow. I'll meet you down at the stables."

"Yes, sir," Roper replied as they all stood up, looking at him expectantly.

"Tell me you're with me," Carro said, lifting his voice a little.

"We are with you!" The men pounded their fists on the table in unison, creating a single loud *bang* that shook the windows.

"'Til when?"

"'Til death!" *Bang.*

"Dismissed," Carro waved his hand and they were gone.

When he was alone again, Carro collapsed into his chair again and squeezed his face with his hands. He had been a soldier for as long as he could remember, but he had never been asked to pursue this type of quarry and he wondered if his men were even capable of such a sensitive operation. Azimar had chosen most of the Black Sabers solely for their ruthlessness and loyalty, not necessarily intelligence or subtlety. The council room door opened and Carro looked up to see Gade peering at him. He smiled and waved for the boy to come in.

"Can't I go with you, Captain?" Gade asked, "I promise I won't get in the way. I want to earn my sabers."

"No, Gade. Not this time. I need men who have…been around longer," Carro didn't say it out loud, but he knew that the fierce protectiveness he felt for Gade would be a liability on this mission, because if it came down to it, he would put the boy's safety before almost anything else.

"Isn't there *something* I can do?" Gade begged. Carro considered him for a moment, then leaned forward.

"Yes, actually," he said almost in a whisper, "but it's something only for me and you must not tell anyone else. I want you to make sure that Ephie is looked after. Whatever she's done, she's an old woman and I won't let her die alone in a filthy prison cell. Promise me that you'll check on her, make sure she has food, and if anyone gives you grief, tell them you're there on my orders. Can you do that for me?"

Gade's face became serious. "Isn't she accused of treason?" he asked timidly.

"Not officially, not yet. And the Boss doesn't even know she's down there, because I didn't tell him yet. I won't let you get in trouble. Do you trust me?"

"Of course," Gade chewed on his lip as he considered Carro's words, "I'll do it, I promise. But how long will you be gone?"

"I'm not sure this time. It could only be a few hours, or a few weeks. Can you go and get Badger ready for me? I'll be down soon." Gade saluted, then bounced out into the corridor.

"More enthusiasm than sense, that boy," remarked Lieutenant Sirota, coming into the room accompanied by a middle-aged man whom Carro could only describe as 'feral.' He was dressed all in animal skins, with greasy grayish-brown hair hanging around his shoulders and several small dangling hoops in one ear. His fingers were covered in tarnished silver rings and on his exposed arms, Carro saw neat rows of small scars, at least several hundred, like soldiers in formation. They started at his shoulders and reached all the way to his wrists, seemingly covering every inch of available skin. Carro had seen ritual scarification before, but he thought this was rather excessive.

"Commander," Sirota said, "this is Gaelin…" He looked inquiringly at the man, as though he expected such a person to have a last name. Gaelin merely grinned, showing off yellowing teeth that had been filed into sharp points, and Carro shuddered.

"No surnames amongst the Ulvvori, boy," the hunter growled.

"You're Ulvvori?" Carro asked.

"Half-breed, if you believe a word my mother said, but not been back in a good long while," Gaelin examined Carro's face in a way that made him feel quite exposed, "and you, Captain? Where'd you come from? I like to know the men I work for."

"I don't make a habit of exchanging personal information with petty back alley criminals who will use it to try and blackmail me later," Carro retorted, folding his arms. Gaelin let out a horrible, guttural laugh and clapped his hands together.

"Oh, this one's got claws on him! Alright, boy. I'll play your game. What's the job?"

"You will address him as Commander--" Sirota began with his teeth gritted.

"It's alright, Lieutenant," Carro said, "please, Gaelin, sit." Gaelin threw himself into a chair, propping his filthy boots up on the table. Sirota made a noise in his throat, but Carro shot him a warning glance. He needed Gaelin more than he needed a clean table.

"A proper gentleman," Gaelin laughed, "I'll bet you were raised by a good family, hmm?" His light gray eyes bored into Carro and a tiny smile played on his lips.

"We find ourselves in need of your…skills," Carro told him.

"What've you Bloody Sabers lost this time what needs findin'? Hmm?"

"A Queen," Carro said, "and the infant heir to the throne."

"Sounds expensive," Gaelin's face spread into a greedy smile.

"The King will pay handsomely for your services," Sirota snapped.

"What exactly's the job?" Gaelin asked, "I'll warn you, I'm no fighter." Carro paused, wondering how much information he should divulge to this man.

"We believe," he said slowly, "that she will be searching for the Ulvvori. You know the people and their habits, perhaps even their current location. You can help us find her before she reaches the protection of the Wolf Riders." Gaelin sucked on his cheek for a moment, still staring hard at Carro, then reached out his hand.

"I'm in. When do we leave?"

"Right now," Carro said, shaking Gaelin's hand and wondering if he might come to regret this deal. Carro and Sirota escorted Gaelin to the Black Saber's supply room and told him to select what he wanted from the array of weapons lining the walls.

"I told you I'm no fighter, boy," Gaelin said, but Carro saw his eyes glittering as he surveyed his choices.

"I can't afford to take a man into the field unarmed," Carro replied. While Gaelin took his time looking, Sirota pulled Carro aside.

"Sir, I have to question hiring a Ulvvori tracker for this mission."

Carro laughed. "You brought him to me, Sirota."

"I was not aware of his…background. Don't you think he might harbor some sympathies? Resentment toward the Black Sabers? He could lead you straight to the wolves."

"I know you fought in the war, Sirota. Have you already forgotten that the Ulvvori fought with us?"

~ 40 ~

"Of course not, Commander, but things have…changed since then," Sirota's brow furrowed, "the Ulvvori are no longer our allies and I'm wary of trusting them, even if this one appears to have left their pack mentality behind. They're dangerous people."

"*We're* dangerous people, Sirota, and things are always changing. Men like Gaelin always change with them, and you can trust that, if nothing else."

"I suppose our motto of 'loyalty forever' seems a bit foolish then."

"Not at all, Lieutenant, because *we* aren't men like Gaelin. You should go see to your search parties. I think I can handle him on my own," Carro said.

"Good luck, Commander," Sirota threw a quick salute and left.

"Have you decided yet?" Carro asked Gaelin, who was spinning a dagger quite skillfully in his hand. *That's exactly what I thought,* Carro told himself, *a fighter* and *a liar.*

"You're a bit young to be a Saber Captain, ain't you?" Gaelin said, sticking the dagger back into its sheath and tying it to his belt.

"And you're a bit indiscreet to have survived this long in your line of work," Carro shot back, "answer me this though, since you're so keen on us getting to know one another: why did you leave the Ulvvori?" Gaelin studied him as they left the armory and walked down the corridor.

"I like money," he said lightly, "the way it feels in my pockets. I like the noise it makes, and the power it brings. The Ulvvori don't use it. So…I left."

"That's it? Money?" Carro frowned.

"That's it, boy. What, did you think I had some kind of tragic history like the rest of you wretched creatures?" he laughed and put on a high, mocking voice, "*'ooooob me Mummy didn't love me enough and I had to prove I'm a man so I joined up to kill people!'*"

"That's not…" Carro started to say, but thought better of it, "you know, most of us were recruited from the regular army units. Azimar took who he wanted and he didn't exactly give them a choice."

"Yeah, but why join the army in the first place unless you got somethin' to prove?" Gaelin asked, "they ain't conscripted anyone except Ulvvori boys for awhile now. You made that choice. Why?" Carro was silent, suddenly regretting the conversation.

"Not many other options where I'm from," he answered at last.

"You going to tell me some of that tragic history now?" Gaelin wheedled, "I promise, blackmail is well outside my skill set."

"Nothing to tell," Carro said, "so stop asking or you'll lose your tongue." Gaelin seemed unfazed by the threat, but he pinched his lips together to indicate that he understood. Feeling annoyed, Carro led him down to the stables, where his hunting party were packing their saddlebags. Gade was there too, feeding sugar cubes to Carro's horse, Badger.

"Don't give him too many. He'll never listen to me again."

"Badger deserves them because he's a good boy," Gade grinned, stroking the broad white stripe on the horse's otherwise black face that had earned him his name. "I put a few extra in your bag in case he gets out of line though." Carro grabbed Gade by the shoulders and held him at arm's length. He was scrawny and a bit ungainly, like a colt still growing into its legs, but Carro had seen potential and pulled him from the army to train as a Black Saber. He didn't regret the decision, but he hadn't anticipated that he would end up caring for Gade so much, and now he felt constantly anxious about the boy's safety.

"Behave yourself, alright?" Carro told him, "do what I asked, and I promise I'll take you along on my next mission so you can earn your sabers."

"Yes, sir," Gade saluted him, "loyalty forever!"

"Alright, alright," Carro rolled his eyes, "go back inside. I'll see you." Gade said goodbye to the other men, then headed back toward the palace while Carro checked Badger's tack. A stablehand brought out an extra horse for Gaelin, but the hunter eyed it rather skeptically.

"Won't bite, will she?"

"That depends on how nice you are," Carro needled, "her name's Kleo. Try telling her she's pretty and she might let you stay on longer."

"Ah, just like my first wife," Gaelin muttered.

Carro snorted as he swung up into Badger's saddle. "And that's how I know you're a liar, Gaelin. There's no world where I'd believe you've convinced *multiple* women to marry you."

"For a few extra coins, I'll teach you all my secrets, boy," Gaelin winked, lifting himself clumsily onto the horse. "You seem like you could use a good--"

"We're ready, Commander!" Jesk called from across the yard.

"Let's move, then," Carro called back, leading them toward the only gate out of the palace complex. By now, the news of Asenna's flight must have spread, because servants and valets and stablehands leapt out of their way, whispering to one another as they passed. Carro ignored it, his mind singularly focused on the task ahead of him. Everything else had been locked away in the imaginary box beneath his bed.

THREE:
THE TWINS

Luckily for Asenna, the moon was still bright and it shone through the palace windows, lighting her steps as she went. She knew exactly where the spot on the wall that Ephie had marked was. Azimar had used one of his mighty war machines to break through during the final stage of his war against Rogerin, but Asenna had not seen it since it had been rebuilt and she prayed that Ephie was right about the texture. A smooth wall would be a death sentence. Reaching an exterior servants' door, Asenna opened it carefully and checked her surroundings before exiting. She slipped along the side of the palace, trying to stay in the shadows, until she reached the stables, which were built up against the outer wall with paddocks and training corrals in front of them. She saw no soldiers about, so she skirted along a fence line and then pressed herself up against the outer palace wall. Ephie had been correct. The wall had been rebuilt using rough, uncut blocks of stone. It would be tricky, especially since Asenna had not climbed in years, but there was too much at stake to go back now. The moon was at precisely the right angle to give her a good view all the way up.

"*Izlani* is helping us, little Fen," she whispered, placing her hand on one of the blocks and pulling herself up. It was desperately hard. The sling and bag and cloak hindered her movement and there was no joy in this climb as there had been in others. Asenna was driven only by fear and anger and desperation, but it was those feelings that finally propelled her to the top. She paused to catch her breath, hunching up against the battlements to hide herself. Fen was still sleeping, but she knew that the longer she took the more likely he was to wake. Sliding up and over the side of the wall, Asenna carefully lowered herself down and found a foothold. This side would be harder because the moon was no longer lighting her way, so she was extra careful when testing where to place her feet. As she moved further down, Asenna felt Fen beginning to stir in the sling and she paused, silently begging him with every fiber of her being not to wake up, but it was no use. He squirmed and then began to grunt and mewl. Asenna tried to shush him, but hearing her voice only made him more agitated and he let out a single loud wail. Suddenly, she heard boots on the wall above her and tried to press her body as flat as she could against the stone without crushing Fen, who was still searching for his midnight meal.

"Thought I heard something over here," said the voice of a guard.

"Like what?" came the reply from another man.

"Dunno…like a cat…or a baby?"

"You idiot," said his companion, "a damned cat?!" Asenna willed them to leave, but Fen let out a choked, wavering cry and Asenna knew she had to do something.

"There it was again!" said the guard, moving closer to where she was hanging. Asenna steeled herself and tightened her grip on the stone with her left hand. With her right, she reached into the sling and pulled down her shirt. Now she understood why Ephie had given her one that was too large, and she silently thanked the old woman for her foresight. Fen greedily began to nurse while Asenna moved her right hand back to its position and then listened intently for the guards. Every nerve in her body was on fire and she could feel herself beginning to shake, but she tried to control it by holding her breath and pressing her cheek up against the cool stone.

"It's just some brat screeching in the gutter down there," said the second guard, "they don't pay us enough for this shit." He walked away and the other guard lingered only for a moment before following. Asenna released the breath she had been holding and began to move herself down the wall again. When she reached the bottom and felt the cobblestones beneath her feet, she let out a small sob and fell to the ground. Fen unlatched and stared up at her with his big golden eyes as if he was just now noticing her distress.

"You almost got us caught, little one," Asenna laughed quietly, tapping his tiny nose with her finger, "you must be more patient." He yawned and spit some of the milk back up. Asenna wiped it with her sleeve and then reached around and pulled the map out of her bag, folding it so that only the part with the city sketch was visible. Seeing that they were not far from Beacon Street, she set out through the streets of Sinsaya with her hood pulled up. It would be morning before Azimar realized she was gone, and Asenna knew she had to reach Ferryn's shop quickly before the Black Sabers were sent out. She pictured them like a giant flock of crows descending on the city and blotting out the sun, making her shiver and walk faster.

When Asenna reached Beacon Street, she searched each building carefully until she found the shop with the wolf's head sign and then knocked slowly. *One. Two. Three. Four. Five.* It was only around thirty seconds before she heard footsteps and the door opened. The man behind it, illuminated by an oil lamp in his hand, looked like a hunk of leather that had been magically brought to life. His skin was a deep brown and cut with so many creases, wrinkles, and scars that Asenna wondered how he did not simply fold in on himself. His eyes were barely visible under bushy gray brows and his gray and black streaked hair stuck out at odd angles around his face. Even though it was the middle of the night, he wore a blacksmith's apron and carried a pipe in one hand. Despite his haggard appearance, Asenna could tell he was careful and intelligent from the way his eyes scanned her.

"Are you Ferryn?" she asked.

"You're Asenna," he replied, opening the door wider, "did Ephie send you here?"

"Yes, please, we need your help," Asenna leaned forward slightly so he could see Fen, who was still wide awake and babbling happily in his sling. Ferryn craned his neck to see the child and when he got a glimpse, his eyebrows shot halfway up his forehead. He ushered her inside and shut the door, bolting it three times.

"Come with me, and keep that hood up," he said gruffly, leading her to the back of the workshop and through a door to a small living area. They passed through and out into a courtyard that sat in the center of the buildings. Across the courtyard was a large lean-to shed that looked like it would topple over at the slightest breeze, but Ferryn opened the door and motioned for her to go inside. The shed was full of horse tack and a variety of blacksmithing tools that Asenna could not identify. Ferryn followed her inside and shut the door behind him, then locked it too. In the darkness, he began tinkering around and moving some of the tools and tack and Asenna wondered if he hadn't gone mad since the last time Ephie had seen him. But then there was a *click* and a hidden door that appeared to be part of the wall of the building swung inwards, revealing a well-lit spiral staircase descending straight into the ground. Watching her feet on the narrow stairs, Asenna followed Ferryn down and they emerged into an underground chamber with rough, whitewashed walls and oil lamps burning in sconces every few feet. It appeared to Asenna like any other typical tavern you would see in a city, with tables and stools, a bar, and a long fireplace whose chimney she could only assume went through the ground above them. Seated at the tables were a dozen or so men and women, all of whom looked like they had seen battle at some point in their lives. The red-haired woman behind the bar was the only one who was not missing a digit or an eye or an entire limb. As they walked toward the bar, she saw them and went to open another door, ushering them into a small private dining room where a pleasant fire was already crackling.

"Thank you, Careen," said Ferryn, "would you find the twins for me? Tell them it's urgent." The woman nodded and shut the door. Ferryn untied his apron and hung it on a hook beside the fireplace, then turned to Asenna and folded his arms. "So…you're Azimar's 'Wolf Queen'…"

"I'm not…what's a wolf queen?" Asenna asked, taking a chair without asking. Her legs and arms were burning from the climb and her back was beginning to ache as well.

"That's what people down here have been calling you," Ferryn shrugged and sat down at the table, "so, what's Azimar done now that you have to flee from? Surely he would never harm the child…his only heir…"

"He wants to separate us," Asenna explained, "he was going to send me to the south under house arrest and have his mother raise our son. Please, I just want to get away from him and find my family. I'll do anything." Ferryn tapped his empty pipe on the table absentmindedly.

"Once my daughters arrive we will think of something. I suppose…Ephie told you about the Ulvvori?" he said quietly.

"Yes, but she didn't have time to give me details," Asenna replied, "she just said it was Azimar…" Ferryn gave a long sigh and pushed his masses of hair back from his face. She could tell that the subject was painful for him, but she needed to know.

"I suppose we have a little time while we wait, and it's best that you know what happened. It started just a few months after Azimar won the throne," Ferryn began, "he went back to the Ulvvori. Of course, the Wolf Riders were key in his victory, but after Rogerin was defeated, they went home. Everyone knows that Riders don't leave the pack. Well, Azimar decided that they owed him, right? After all, he had stopped the conscriptions, stopped the raids and attacks, and he wanted something more in return than just a throne and a bride. He wanted Riders for himself, for his army."

"But…Rogerin tried that and it didn't work…"

"No, because Rogerin had no relationship with the Ulvvori before he started demanding our service. Azimar thought that because of the alliance, and your marriage, that they would join up willingly. He asked for a small corps of adult Riders and their dire wolves, already trained and battle-tested. But Tolian refused, and the Riders refused and…Azimar wouldn't stand for that. He pretended to accept their refusal gracefully, but then only a few weeks later, he began sending miners and soldiers to the mountains, ostensibly trying to dig up more of that black rock he uses to fuel his war machines. He sent so many that eventually they came to blows with the Ulvvori, because they were hunting the deer and mammoths, poisoning our water, and moving onto our land. Once first blood was drawn…well…"

"What happened?" Asenna could scarcely breathe, imagining the worst.

Ferryn's voice was full of emotion and Asenna saw a few tears slip out from under his eyebrows as he spoke. "About four months ago, Azimar sent the Black Sabers to ambush them at The Den. It was early morning and they were underground, in the caves, with no way out. The wolves are too big to maneuver and fight in the tunnels, and the bastards used some kind of poisoned smoke. I don't know how many were lost, but the rest were driven out of the mountains and forced to march east. The last I heard, the survivors are heading for Kashait as refugees. Even if I could get you up there, there's nothing and no one left to go back to." Asenna bent forward and a strangled sob broke through her lips. She clutched Fen and rocked herself back and forth, trying not to scream. Her entire family could have been dead for months and she would never have known. Now all her unanswered letters suddenly made sense and she felt like there was a new darkness swallowing her whole. After a few minutes, she sucked in a few ragged breaths and dried her eyes to look up at Ferryn, who was watching her and looking concerned.

"What about Tolian?" she asked, "my mother, Elyana? And my brothers?"

"Tolian and his wolf survived, I know that much, but I cannot say about your mother or anyone else. My own two daughters barely made it out alive. I'm sorry I cannot tell you more," Ferryn said, his voice softening.

"I don't understand," Asenna breathed, "the Black Sabers and the Riders fought together in the war, in nearly every battle. How could they suddenly turn on each other like that? They were allies...friends...I saw it with my own eyes..."

"I can't say for certain," Ferryn sighed, "but the rumor is that Azimar lied to the Black Sabers, that he told them the Ulvvori had betrayed him somehow and that's why he was ordering the attack. I imagine those brutes didn't think too hard about it. They're all too easily led by him for whatever reason." As he spoke, the door opened and two impossibly tall women came into the room. They were older than Asenna, she guessed in their mid-thirties, with identical, angular faces and long black hair that had been braided and twisted into ropes and decorated with beads or metal cuffs that glinted in the firelight. They both wore short swords on their belts, and one had a swirling black tattoo along the shaved side of her head, while the other bore a deep scar along her jawline. Asenna immediately felt quite small and intimidated by them, but she hoped they were willing to help her.

"Pa," said the one with the scar, kissing Ferryn on the cheek, "what's got you calling us up in the middle of the night?" She glanced suspiciously at Asenna as the two of them went to stand behind their father.

"These are my daughters. Talla," Ferryn motioned to the one with the tattoo, "and Tira. Girls, this is Asenna, daughter of Elyana, and she needs our help." Asenna appreciated him using the Ulvvori form of address rather than introducing her as Azimar's wife, but she could tell that the twins knew who she was anyway from the looks of mistrust stamped on their faces. Ferryn stood up, pulled a large rolled up piece of vellum off the mantle, and set it on the table. Asenna saw that it was a huge map showing Esmadia and Kashait in extreme detail.

"What kind of help?" asked Tira skeptically.

"Help to escape from Azimar, get to the pack, and get to Kashait before the Black Sabers find her."

"You want us to escort a refugee queen and the royal heir to a foreign country while Azimar's dogs come after us?" Talla rounded on her father, "are you insane?"

"How old is the child, Asenna?" Ferryn asked.

"One month…"

"Show them his eyes," Ferryn instructed her. Asenna paused, but then pulled the side of the sling down so that Talla and Tira could see Fen's face. They both leaned over and gasped.

"What is it?" Asenna asked, a little defensive, "he has the Wolfsight. Why does it matter? I thought you were Ulvvori?"

"We are…" said Tira slowly, "but there hasn't been a baby born with the Wolfsight since we were forced out of the mountains. Four months now, they've been driven from place to place, half a dozen or more babies born, but none with the Wolfsight."

"So, Fen…is the only one?" Asenna said quietly.

"Yes," said Ferryn quietly, "the only child born with Wolfsight outside of our home. Which is why we must get you to Kashait as quickly as possible. I believe that is where the Ulvvori are heading. Talla, Tira, you will do this for me, and for your people."

"She's not our people!" Talla said angrily, "she married Azimar! He's the one who did this to us! He killed Flint and Frost!"

Tira nodded along with her twin. "And Aija…" she added softly.

"Shame on you both!" Ferryn slammed his fist on the table and Fen let out a small wail, "she agreed to marry Azimar to stop the conscriptions, to stop exactly the thing that happened to our own family, just as you both volunteered to fight his war! Would you dishonor the memories of your loved ones by allowing this child's sacred gift to be abused by Azimar? The boy is *our* flesh and blood as much as hers! That is the meaning of the pack!" Asenna rocked Fen slowly and watched the confrontation, feeling more like a burden every minute. Tira and Talla fell silent and Ferryn turned back to the map. He began to trace a route with his finger in silence, but Asenna was watching the twins' faces. She had not noticed before in the dim light, but now that they were standing closer to the fire, she could see that their eyes were a pale yellow color, like the last of the autumn leaves to fall from the trees. In the Ulvvori language, the word *'ialas'* meant 'yellow,' but it also referred to a Rider who had lost their Wolfsight because their dire wolf had died. The creatures naturally lived longer than humans, but were still subject to disease, accidents, and attack. Many *ialas* ended up leaving the Ulvvori because it was too painful to stay, and Asenna guessed that was why the twins were in the city with their father now.

"I'm sorry," she said softly in Ulvvori, "about your wolves." The twins stared at her as if she had cursed at them.

"Don't be," Talla spat back, "they died defending their pack." Tira put a gentle hand on her sister's arm.

"Focus," said Ferryn sternly, and he proceeded to explain the route they would take toward Kashait. Asenna leaned back in her chair and found herself drifting into sleep, but she was not able to rest for long before Ferryn gently shook her.

"The twins have gone to pack their things, but we'll have to cut your hair," he said, pointing at a pair of shears sitting on the table, "it's not the most effective disguise, but it will help. Now, I can do it or I can get Careen."

"I think I'd prefer Careen," said Asenna warily.

"Smart choice," Ferryn went to the door, "I suppose you saw the scar on Tira's chin?"

"You did that…cutting her hair?" Asenna gulped, but Ferryn gave her a wicked smile.

"No, but that's what I like to tell people. The real story is far more heroic and she needs to be brought down a peg sometimes." Careen came in and frowned at the shears but began combing out Asenna's hair with her fingers anyway.

"What did happen?" asked Asenna, who found herself desperately curious about Ferryn's pair of fearsome daughters. She tried to ignore the *snick snick* of the shears behind her.

"Something about a cave bear," Ferryn answered wryly, "I wasn't there though. I'm sure Ephie told you that she and I came here together many years ago after our sons were conscripted, but my girls had their wolves, so I couldn't bring them. They were old enough and safer with the pack anyway." Asenna was silent for a few minutes before Ferryn stood and walked over to look at Fen, who was sleeping in the sling, shielded from the falling hair by Asenna's cloak.

"His name is Fenrinn," said Asenna quietly.

Ferryn glanced at her, a sad smile on his lips. "Like Ephie's boy…" he murmured, "sweet little Fen. Oh, he was a wonder."

"All done," said Careen, "I'm sorry I couldn't do better."

"I don't suppose you have a mirror?" Asenna laughed, running her fingers through the cropped strands.

Ferryn shook his head. "No one in this place wants to look themselves in the eye. Stay here. You'll leave as soon as the twins get back." He left the room and Asenna tried to shift the sling to make it more comfortable. She waited only a few minutes before the twins came back, both dressed for traveling with saddlebags slung over their shoulders. In addition to their short swords, Tira now carried a crossbow on her back and Talla wore a large hatchet at her belt, which also appeared to carry several small glass bottles. Asenna was curious, but afraid to ask what they were.

"Are we riding?" she asked instead, eyeing the saddlebags. It had been over a year since she had been on a horse.

"Walking first," said Talla, "we'll get horses once we're out of the city. Can you ride?"

"Well enough." Asenna watched them go over the map one more time and then at last Ferryn reentered the room.

"Time to go," he said. Asenna stood up and wrapped her arms around Fen. Talla and Ferryn walked in front of her, with Tira at the rear, back through the tavern, up the spiral stairs, and through the shed. Once they were in the blacksmith's shop, Ferryn turned around.

"Be safe, Asenna, daughter of Elyana," he said, touching the tips of his fingers to his lips, "I hope we meet again someday. And you, little Fenrinn, you be safe as well."

"Thank you for everything, Ferryn. I can never repay your kindness," Asenna told him. Ferryn turned and ducked out the back of the shop again, leaving Asenna alone with the twins. Talla unbolted the door and leaned out carefully to check the street.

"You stay with us," Tira instructed Asenna, "you don't speak to anyone, keep your hood up, and keep the kid quiet. Got it?" Asenna nodded and swallowed as they stepped out into the street. The gentle fade of dawn was starting to appear over the rooftops and her stomach dropped, knowing that they would only have a few hours head start before the Black Sabers were after her.

~~~

Asenna could not remember the last time she had walked this much. It had to have been before she went south to marry Azimar, when the Ulvvori moved from their winter home in the Valley to their summer home at The Den. That was at least three days of walking on steep mountain trails with a large pack on her back. Somehow though, this felt harder. Maybe it was the stress of the last few days, or maybe it was the knowledge that they were being hunted, but she felt a deep exhaustion overcome her after only two hours on the road. She tried not to complain to the twins, who only spoke to her as much as necessary, but she knew she would need to stop and rest soon. The two women were not unkind to her, but Asenna knew they were not her friends and she wanted to avoid angering them. They would not tell her where they were going either, so Asenna had to simply follow along. She was just about to open her mouth to ask for a break when Talla held up her hand.

"Wait with her while I go check the farm," she said. Tira nodded and sat down on a large rock by the side of the road while her sister walked ahead and then disappeared behind a small hillock where the wide dirt track bent. Asenna took that to mean she could sit down too. Fen had just woken up, so she nursed him while she removed her boots and stockings and let her feet rest in the soft grass. The road ran northeast from Sinsaya toward Ossesh, the largest port city in Esmadia, and in the early morning it was already busy with people, carts, and carriages. The twins had assured Asenna that no one outside the city likely knew she was missing yet, so it was only people coming up the road from the south they needed to worry about.

"What's the farm?" Asenna asked.

"Just a place to stop and get horses. We won't stop moving until we can get across the river, tonight or tomorrow," Tira kept her pale eyes fixed on the road behind them as she spoke.

"The Southrun River?" Asenna asked, frowning.

"Yes, and then through the Forever Forest," Tira answered, taking a drink from a large water flask and then handing it to Asenna.

"How long will it take us to get to Kashait that way?" Asenna asked, closing her eyes and picturing the map of Esmadia. The Forever Forest stretched for hundreds of miles between the Southrun River and the Kashaiti border, and there were no roads running through it.

"Ten days at least, maybe longer," Tira stood up, "since we might be dodging Black Sabers the whole way and you've got the kid."

Asenna's stomach dropped. "How do you know they'll find us?"

"You do ask a lot of questions, don't you," Tira remarked.

Asenna felt her face burn. "I'm just…trying to figure out the plan"

Tira's eyes swept over Asenna's face before she answered. "They might already know where we are and they're just waiting until we're alone so they don't have a public scene on their hands. They're unpopular enough as it is. But we have a decent lead, and if we can get horses and get to the river, we might be able to lose them there."

"All clear," said Talla as she rejoined them. The three of them walked around the hillock, then turned off the main road to follow a cart track that wound off a few hundred yards to a squat stone farmhouse with outbuildings scattered around it. Asenna saw three big horses tethered to a fence outside and a pack of young children working in a field behind them. The children stopped and waved at the twins as they approached and a thin, worn-out looking woman met them at the door of the house.

"Got your message," she said, "that's all the horse I can spare today."

"Draught horses?" said Tira incredulously, "we're not plowing a damn field, Lusie. What are we supposed to do with those? They don't even have saddles!"

"Take them or leave them, Tira," Lusie sighed, "I said that's all I've got today." Tira grumbled a little, but went over to the horses and began to assess the blankets that were hanging on the fence in front of them. Asenna held back, having little experience with horses, but she marveled at how large the beasts were, nearly the size of a full-grown dire wolf. She listened to the twins bicker for a moment, but they stopped suddenly as a small plume of dust appeared in the direction of the main road. It was obviously a rider approaching the farm quickly. Fear gripped Asenna's chest as Tira swung the crossbow around and loaded it with a bolt, moving to stand in front of her. The lone man on the horse was not a Black Saber, however. He had messy, straw-colored hair that was pulled back in a ponytail, and looked more like a farmer than anything else. He leapt down from his horse before it even fully stopped and ran over to the twins, who seemed to recognize him.

"Andros, what is it?" Talla asked as he caught his breath.

"The Sabers," he gasped, "they were at your father's shop, and now there's eleven of them leaving the city. They don't seem to be in a hurry, so you have a few hours, but I got here as fast as I could to warn you: they've got Gaelin with them." Tira let out a string of curses in Ulvvori and put the crossbow back on her back.

"We need to go," Talla snapped, "now! Andros, help me."

"How will they know we're here?" Asenna asked.

"Gaelin will know," Tira said, "damnit! We should have guessed they'd hire him!"

"Talla, there's something else too," said Andros, taking one of the horse blankets out of her hands. Talla stopped, recognizing the seriousness in his voice. "The Sabers were at your father's shop trying to get information from him, about whatever…whoever it is they're searching for. I'm so sorry, Talla, but…he's dead." The air suddenly felt heavy as Tira let out a rabid scream and Talla turned to kick a fencepost, which snapped clean in half when her foot made contact.

"*Bastards!*" she howled, "I'll kill every last one of them!"

Andros took her arms and shook her slightly. "No, Talla! You need to finish whatever job this is!" He motioned toward Asenna and Fen. "That's what he wanted you to do, isn't it? It must be important or they wouldn't be after you, right?" Talla balled her fists up and didn't respond, but she nodded to Andros and then to her sister. The three of them finished fixing the blankets on the backs of the enormous horses using long leather straps, then Andros waved Asenna over.

"I don't think we've met," he said in a soft voice that barely matched his rough-looking exterior, "I'm Andros, and you met my mother, Lusie. Those are my brothers and sisters." He waved over at the children working in the field.

"Thank you for helping us, Andros," said Asenna quietly.

"Do you ride?" he asked, taking the reins of the largest horse, a black monstrosity that towered over Asenna.

"A little, but never like this."

"It helps if you know their names," Andros told her, "Talla's is Dimple. Tira's is called Candle. The kids named them."

"What's mine?" asked Asenna, eyeing the horse.

"Pandemonium, or just Pan," said Andros, a small smile creeping across his face, "don't worry though, he's actually the easiest of the three. That's why he's yours." Talla and Tira hoisted themselves up with ease and Asenna remembered that they were used to riding male dire wolves, which were often larger than the largest draught horses and didn't wear saddles. Andros helped Asenna up onto Pandemonium and then she tightened the sling where Fen was sleeping. Asenna took the reins and tried to squeeze her legs, but it was like sitting on a table. She was already dreading how sore she would be that evening, if she even made it to the evening.

"We're going to the river and riding it up," Talla explained to Andros, "then we'll have to take the old bridge over the bluffs. After that it's the forest and, if we can make it through, Kashait. Once we've found the Ulvvori, I promise I'll come back."

"You do what you need to, love. I'll be here," Andros told her.

"Swear you won't do anything stupid if they come here looking for us. Please, *lai'zhia*?" Talla said, putting her hand on his shoulder.

"I'll stall them as long as I can *without* being stupid," Andros said firmly, standing on his toes to kiss her as she leaned down. Asenna couldn't help but watch the way he cupped her face in his hands and the pain that clouded his eyes as Talla moved her horse away. Some kind of new ache opened up in Asenna's belly and her mind flashed back to the first time that Azimar had kissed her like that, on the edge of the cliffs in what felt like an entirely different lifetime. She shook off the feeling and turned to face east. Lusie came out of the house with another set of saddlebags and swung them across Pan's withers.

"I've packed extra swaddling for the baby, and as much food as I could," she said.

"You are too kind, Lusie," Asenna replied. Lusie simply patted

Asenna's leg and then went to stand with Andros as the three of them began riding across the field behind the house.

Asenna liked the rhythm of the horse beneath her and she soon fell into a more comfortable position, holding the reins with one hand and rubbing Fen's back with the other. Talla rode ahead, attempting to goad Dimple into a lazy trot, while Tira rode at the back, singing under her breath in Ulvvori and periodically turning to look behind them. As the day wore on, it became unusually warm for mid-winter and Asenna eventually pulled her hood down when they had been riding for several hours without seeing another person.

"What bridge are we using to cross the river?" she asked Tira, pulling her reins so Pan fell back level with Candle. "I thought there was only the stone one near Ossesh."

"This one isn't anything special," Tira assured her, "I'm not even sure who built it or why because it doesn't seem to be connected to any road we know of."

"I've only crossed the Southrun on the ice at The Den..." Asenna remarked. Each spring, the Ulvvori moved from their settlement in the foothill valleys south of the Midwinter Mountains up to The Den, which sat in the heart of the peaks. They had to arrive before the winter ice pack that covered the Southrun began to break up, so that they could cross safely. The summers at The Den were then spent cutting trees and constructing large rafts that could carry them back down the river when the weather began to turn cold again. The rafts were loaded with the deer, mammoth, and salmon that they spent the summers hunting in the mountains and then the wood would be dried out and used to heat their tents for the winter in the valleys. The first time Asenna had seen a real bridge was when she had traveled south to marry Azimar.

"Ah, there she is!" said Tira, pointing ahead of them. Over a rise Asenna could see the top of a tall, rocky bluff capped with trees. As they rode closer, she started to hear the loud rush of the Southrun. On the western bank, where Asenna and the twins were, the ground sloped gently toward the water, changing from hard packed earth into a loose sandy gravel at the river's edge. On the other side, however, the bluff rose straight up at least a hundred feet out of the water. It was imposing and it made Asenna nervous because the sheer cliff face ran as far north and south as she could see. Tira hopped off Candle's back and then walked around to help Asenna down.

"Will they follow us this way?" Asenna asked, glancing behind them.

"Unfortunately, they've hired Gaelin. He's a good tracker, but he also knows us and he knows about the farm. He'll be able to track us to the river too, and their horses will certainly be faster than ours. If Andros can stall them, we might be able to cross the bridge first and burn it. Then they'll have to go all the way up to the Ossesh bridge and back down. If they catch up with us before the bridge though, I want you to ride as fast as you can and we'll hold them off," Tira explained as they led the horses up to the water's edge to drink.

"And we'll kill as many of those fucking monsters as we can," Talla hissed, looking back toward the farmhouse and squinting.

Tira shook her head. "That's not what we're here for, Tal. Our priority is getting Asenna and the baby to the pack as quickly as possible and then helping them all get to Kashait."

"You do what you want," Talla snapped, leaping back up onto Dimple's back and jerking the reins around, "I'm cutting some Saber throats if it's the last thing I do." She finally got the big horse to gallop and they moved north, kicking the river water into a halo of spray around them. Tira came over to hoist Asenna back onto Pan's back and then remounted Candle and the two of them followed Talla, riding in the shallows of the river.

"It's been harder for her," Tira said in a softer voice than Asenna had heard her use all day, "she still has Andros and Lusie and the kids to worry about." Asenna saw an opportunity to try and befriend at least one of the twins and she took it.

"Back in the city, you said you lost someone named Aija during the attack on The Den." Asenna watched Tira's face to make sure she wasn't angry, but she gave a sad smile.

"My…wife, for lack of a better word. We were together since we were about nineteen, just never really got married."

"I'm so sorry," Asenna murmured, "I feel awful that you were dragged into this, after everything you've both been through…and now your father…"

"Don't be sorry. That's what our father loved to do: help people. I know it probably looked like he was some criminal with shady connections, but he used all those connections to help people who needed it, even when there was no benefit for him. That's why Ephie sent you to us. They both knew what the consequences might be, especially with the Sabers involved."

"Well, I'm forever in debt to your family," Asenna said, looking down to check on Fen, who was awake again and gurgling softly.

"What's his name, by the way?" Tira asked, clearly trying to change the subject, "I heard that Azimar named him Elijas, but…that's awful…"

Asenna laughed. "Fenrinn, or just Fen."

"After our cousin? Ephie's son?"

"Yes," said Asenna, "she talked about him all the time and I wanted to honor her…somehow. She's been my only friend since I came down here."

"I wish I could see them again. We were all so young when…"

"Ephie said your father came south with her to find your brother?"

"Yeah, Issi," Tira grinned, "he was a little terror! He was born about five years after me and Talla, and he gave our mother such a hard time until she got sick and died. He was the same age as Ephie's second boy, Yolan, and her eldest, Kavan, was the same age as me and Talla. Little Fen was the youngest of all of us. Talla and I were about thirteen when they took him, so Papa and Ephie came down here and we stayed in the mountains." Asenna was silent for a while as they rode along in the water. She couldn't imagine all that Tira and her sister had endured, losing their family one by one like that, and then their dire wolves. Looking up at the moon, which was barely visible above them in the blue sky, Asenna said a silent prayer that her own mother and brothers had survived. She could not bear the thought of going through everything she had for three years only to find them gone.

When the sun was directly overhead, the bluffs on their side of the river began to rise and they could not ride in the shallows anymore. However, the twins determined that they were likely far enough ahead of their pursuers to take a short break under the sparse cottonwood trees that grew along the riverbank. The horses munched grass nearby and Asenna felt almost peaceful for a while, taking Fen out of his sling and laying him out on her cloak to get some fresh air and clean clothes. She noticed Tira looking intently at him as he chewed on his own fingers.

"His eyes…" she said at last, "what do you think it means, that he was born with the Wolfsight down here and the other children weren't?"

"I'm not sure," Asenna admitted, "but I know it would have been dangerous for him. Azimar wanted to use it for his own ends somehow, even though he doesn't really believe in it."

"How can he not believe in it? We fought with him in that damn war!" Talla cried suddenly, catching Asenna off guard with her harsh tone.

"He thinks that the wolves are just domesticated and trained…like war horses or those cave bears in the circus. He doesn't really believe in the…connection between the Riders and their wolves, that they can talk to each other and feel each other," Asenna told them.

"He's a fool," Talla snorted, "it's not just training. I can't explain it, but I could hear Flint in my head and we could speak to each other. I knew his voice and he knew mine, even if I didn't say anything out loud."

Tira nodded. "Yes, we could hear them. It's not the same as with a horse or a dog, even a good one. I wonder how he wanted to use Fen's Wolfsight then, if he doesn't believe."

"A lot of people in the south think that the Riders can command the wolves and call them up, like an army," Asenna told them, "it was the power of it, the symbol. Azimar thinks that believing in magic makes people weak and stupid, but he was always willing to use other people's beliefs to control them. I guess if people really believed that Fen could command armies of dire wolves, they would think twice before challenging him. It was part of his plan for a Sinsayed Dynasty."

"Men," Talla rolled her eyes, "too preoccupied with how many sons they can father and how strong they can be, but no concern about how they're raised. That's how Andros' father is too. He got as many boys as he could from Lusie and then abandoned them all for brothels and taverns in the city. Yet he'll boast to anyone in earshot that he has six healthy boys working his farm. Tira was the smart one, finding another woman."

Tira laughed and threw a chunk of jerky at her. "You're right, I am the smart one, and yet for all your complaining here *you* are, betrothed to a man."

"Andros is different," said Talla, her demeanor softening a little. Tira smirked and drifted off into thought while she chewed on her jerky. Asenna picked Fen up and looked at his big golden eyes, which were beginning to focus more easily on her face. He spit up a little milk and just as Asenna put him on the cloak to clean him, Talla sat up and tilted her head.

"What is it?" Tira asked, jumping to her feet. Asenna glanced over at the horses, who had stopped grazing and were twitching their ears nervously. She scooped Fen up and tucked him quickly into the sling.

"They found us!" Talla cried, pointing beyond the trees. There was a plume of dust coming up the river from the south and Asenna could barely make out the rumble of hoofbeats in the distance. Panic gripping her body, she got up and swung the reins over Pan's neck, using a jagged stump nearby to scramble onto his back. They urged the three horses into an impossibly slow gallop, heading north along the riverbank. Asenna held Fen's head with one hand and the reins with the other, squeezing her legs around Pan's enormous body as hard as she could manage to try and lessen the impact of the gallop on Fen. Riding beside Asenna, Tira released her reins and swung her crossbow around, notching a bolt onto it, while Talla slid the hatchet from her belt and glanced behind them. Asenna thought about the hunting knife that Ephie had put in her bag and wished she had taken it out, but then they came around a bend in the river and she saw the bridge. The eastern bluffs had slowly been falling away as they rode, while the western side rose higher. The spot where the bridge sat was nearly even on both sides, but it was still at least fifty feet above the rushing, churning water and it looked impossibly old and rickety. Asenna urged Pan on, knowing it was their only chance.

FOUR: HUNTER

Every street in the city was buzzing with gossip and nerves as the Black Sabers searched block to block. Carro and his party headed straight for Beacon Street, but stopped two streets over to leave their horses. They were greeted by another Black Saber Captain, Roeld, who took them around the buildings and pointed.

"The blacksmith's shop is just there," Roeld said, "we already searched and didn't find anything except the old man."

"Good work," Carro said, moving toward the street. Roeld grabbed his arm.

"Hang on, Commander," he said, and Carro saw the worry in his eyes, "a neighbor told us that the blacksmith, Ferryn, is harmless, but there's two daughters and…they're Wolf Riders." Carro's stomach twisted again.

"Surely there's no dire wolves in the city," said Jesk quietly, glancing behind him.

"Wolves are dead," said Gaelin casually, "I've known Ferryn and his girls a long time, and the twins showed up here 'bout three months ago as *ialas,* 'yellow.' Means their wolves died. Probably you boys what killed them in the attack on The Den, yeah?" Carro began to shuffle the information around in his head with the rest of the puzzle pieces. A Wolf Rider was one thing, but a vengeful Wolf Rider was quite another. Even without the dire wolves, they were a force to be reckoned with, highly skilled in combat and probably the only fighters in Esmadia who could match the Black Sabers for sheer ruthlessness.

"This changes things," Carro said, "we didn't plan for Wolf Riders, even without their wolves. If they're the ones escorting Asenna and we go after them head-to-head, we'll lose too many men and the Prince too. We need information before we go any further. Jesk, Daine, with me. Roeld, you and your men guard the door." Carro walked down the street and knocked at the blacksmith's shop. A wizened old man answered it, clutching a large hammer in his hand. Carro jerked his head and Daine immediately pushed into the shop and seized the man's arms, forcing him to drop the hammer. Closing the door gently, Carro turned to face the blacksmith. This was the part of the job he hated most.

The old man spat at him before Carro could speak. "Get out of my home, filth."

Carro resisted the instinct to draw his saber and tried to keep his voice placid. "If you can give me the information I need, I will see that your sister is released from our custody immediately."

"You have Ephie? She's alive?" Ferryn breathed. Carro was satisfied to see his expression almost immediately shift from defiance to fear.

"Yes, and if you are cooperative, she will not be harmed. Are your daughters escorting the fugitive Queen to find the Ulvvori?"

"No fool, are you Captain?"

"Do they know where the Ulvvori refugees are now?"

"You're a butcher," Ferryn whispered, "all that Ulvvori blood on your hands. It's a wonder every single one of you hasn't taken his own poison."

"Which route are your daughters taking?" Carro continued.

"I've had enough," Ferryn said, throwing his head back, "do what you want to me and my sister. We did the right thing and we'll pay for it."

"Just tell me which way they're going," said Carro softly. He could see Daine getting more and more angry and knew that he needed to wrap this up quickly to avoid violence, but Ferryn suddenly lunged forward with a fierce growl and tried to drive his head into Carro's stomach. Carro side-stepped the attack, but Jesk, who was standing behind him, kicked out and caught Ferryn hard on the side of the head with his boot. The old man hit the floor with a thud and rolled slightly, blood pouring from his ear and mouth.

"Damnit, Jesk!" Carro cried, kneeling beside Ferryn and searching for a pulse.

"Dead?" the Lieutenant asked. Carro dropped his head into his hand, seething internally.

"Good one!" Daine laughed, "he wasn't talking anyway, Commander. Let's just go get the queen and the prince and be done with it. They've got to still be on the main road." Carro stood up and drew a saber from his back, feeling a sudden surge of overwhelming anger. He pressed the blade into

Jesk's neck and backed his Lieutenant up against the wall. Jesk's eyes grew wide with terror, even though he and Daine could have easily crushed Carro.

"Commander...what..." Jesk muttered.

"Shut up!" Carro growled, "this is not a joke! Jesk, you were trying to defend me, but this mission is not a lark. You have both been left on too long a leash and I am about to tighten it. Are we clear?" Both men nodded in tacit agreement. Carro stepped back out into the street and saw that a small crowd had gathered.

"Do any of you know the man who owns this shop?" Carro asked them. A teenage boy wearing a blacksmith's apron stepped forward.

"I...I'm Ferryn's apprentice," he said timidly.

"I'm very sorry," Carro told the boy, "but your master is dead. Captain Roeld here will send some men to help you with the body." The boy's face fell.

"Murderer!" another young man screamed at Carro, and several people in the crowd echoed the cry, but he walked back to his men as Roeld stepped in to diffuse the situation.

"You didn't have to kill him," Gaelin muttered when Carro came around the side of the building, "Ferryn was a good man."

"I'm sorry, Gaelin," said Carro in a stiff voice, "if you still want the job, it's time to earn your keep." He pulled out his map of Esmadia and laid it on a crate nearby. Gaelin hesitated for a split second, his eyes flicking over to the shop and back, then he knelt down beside the crate.

"The last information I had said the Ulvvori are north of the forest, movin' east toward Kashait," the hunter said, "your girls might cross the river here at the old bridge on the bluffs, and then through the forest so as to try and give you the slip. They could find the Ulvvori on the other side. Or they could just as easily go up and cross at Ossesh and then try to catch up to the pack on the plains. But they know you'll be on their tail, and the forest is easier to disappear in. Too many eyes on the road."

"So we need to stop them before they cross the bridge?"

"If you don't, they'll burn it and you'll be the one havin' to go up and around," Gaelin said, "but I'll warn you now, you don't want to go up against Talla and Tira if you don't have to, especially not after you what you done to them."

"There's two of them!" laughed Roper, "we can catch up to them on the road right now and be done with it!"

"How well do you know them?" Carro asked, ignoring Roper.

"Well enough," Gaelin shrugged, "Tira's a bit on the softer side as far as Riders go, but Talla'll cut you open and make you say please before she stuffs your guts in your mouth."

Carro grimaced. "An unnecessary amount of detail, Gaelin, but thank you. That's helpful," he murmured, still studying the map, "I don't want a full-out battle on the road. We need to track them and be patient, but there's no way to know if they're on foot or riding at this point. Gaelin, is there somewhere they'd go to get horses?"

"Aye," Gaelin said, "there's a little farm between here and the river. No guarantee they'll get horses there, but if they're headin' for the forest anyway, they'd go to the farm first."

"We'll start there. With any luck, we can catch them resting at the farm. Asenna won't be able to travel that long without needing to stop and that's to our advantage," Carro said, folding the map up and stuffing it into his pocket, "if they've already left the farm, at least we'll know which direction they're headed and whether or not they're riding." Once they were back on their horses and riding toward the city gates, Gaelin moved up beside Carro.

"This is where I'll be askin' you for somethin', Commander," he said in a low voice.

"What is it?"

"Your men don't touch a single hair on the head of anyone what lives on that farm," Gaelin said, "it's just an old woman and a bunch of kids anyway. Nevermind their connection to the twins or anyone else. Yeah?"

Carro looked over at him. "In spite of what you might believe, Gaelin, I'm not a monster. You have my word, no one on the farm gets hurt. And I'm sorry about Ferryn. I didn't order it." Gaelin grunted and then pulled his horse back a little. No matter what people thought of the Black Sabers, Carro did try to do his job in a civilized way. He wasn't interested in causing mayhem or terror if he could avoid it, but the doubts about whether or not his men could carry out this sensitive mission were growing by the minute. His mind felt like it was at a breaking point with all the different pieces being added to the puzzle, knowing that he had an obligation to at least try to keep his men safe, but also that getting to Asenna now meant going up against two hostile Wolf Riders. However, if he failed the mission, Azimar would have something much worse than a public execution waiting for him, so Carro steeled himself as they went through the gate and pressed ahead out into the open air.

~~~

It took the hunting party no time at all to reach the little farm, since the sight of eleven Black Sabers was enough to clear a path along the main road, allowing them to ride faster. When Carro dismounted in front of the house, a pale, exhausted-looking woman came out the front door and then immediately ran back inside. Looking around, Carro saw only a small barn, a chicken coop, a shed, and a well, but not much else except a single gray pony tethered to the fence. He could tell by the sweat stain on its back that it had been running hard fairly recently, but had since been unsaddled. When Carro turned back toward the house, a large blonde man was standing outside with his arms folded.

"What do you want?" he called out as Carro's men approached.

"Just information," said Carro, holding his hands up a little, "we're looking for three fugitives and have reason to believe they came this way."

"Criminals?" the man asked. Carro saw movement behind him and noticed several young children watching them from the doorway of the farmhouse. The older woman stood with them, looking fretful.

"Three young women. One is carrying an infant," Carro told him.

"An unusual quarry for the Black Sabers," said the blonde man evenly, "aren't you normally in the business of killing people in their beds while they sleep? Or dragging them out to be hung from the walls?"

"Listen here, you fucking--" Roper started toward the man, but Carro flung his arm out.

"Stand down!" he hissed at Roper, then turned back, "I'm not here to play games and I'm not going to hurt anyone. I just want information and then we will leave." Carro saw the man's eyes darting around, probably trying to figure out how many of the Black Sabers he could take.

"I haven't seen any fugitives, but you're free to search the house or the barn," he said at last, "as long as you don't hurt my family or our animals."

"Search the barn, then the house," Carro said to his men, "do *not* damage anything and do not touch anyone." The men broke their formation and flooded into the barn with Carro walking behind them and the blonde man following. There were four horse stalls inside, each with fresh hay and droppings on the floor.

"What's your name?" Carro asked. He was standing closer to the man now and realized that he looked vaguely familiar.

"Andros."

"Do you keep horses, Andros?" Carro could immediately tell that he had made the farmer nervous by the way he kicked the dirt with his boot and twisted his hands behind his back.

"Yes, but we've loaned them out right now," he said. *Liar,* Carro thought.

"I see. Plow horses?"

"Yes."

"And the pony?" Carro waved back at the animal tied to the fence, "where did he go today?" Andros finally looked up at him and Carro realized where they had met before. When he had left Ferryn's shop on Beacon Street, Andros was the one who had called him a murderer. The pieces of the puzzle fell into place in Carro's head and he whistled for his men.

"Commander?" said Jesk as he came out, "what's wrong?"

"We're being stalled," Carro said quietly, staring at Andros, whose face suddenly became defiant like Ferryn's. "They're heading for the bridge and they have horses now, albeit slow ones." Jesk lunged forward and grabbed Andros by his hair, shoving him to the ground, and Carro heard the woman and children in the farmhouse cry out.

"What do we do with him?" Jesk growled.

"Let him go," Carro said sternly, "I said release him, Jesk! We don't have time for this." Jesk let go of Andros, but he was glowering. Carro stalked back over to where Gaelin was waiting with the horses and mounted Badger again. The rest of the men followed and Carro led them away from the farm at a faster pace.

"I don't understand, Commander," Jesk said, riding beside him.

"That man was on Beacon Street. He must know the twins somehow," Carro said, "my guess is that he passed us on the road to warn them. They've got a bigger head start than I'd hoped."

"If we have to go around, can't Gaelin track them through the forest?"

"If it was just Asenna on her own, I'd say yes," Carro said, "but these other two...I get the feeling they know how to disappear. We have to catch up and face them out in the open. There's no other way now." Jesk nodded and fell back with the other men. As they rode east away from the farmhouse, Carro's ears picked up some disgruntled muttering from behind him.

"They were probably right under our damn feet in that barn," Vaylen was saying angrily, "why would they ride straight into a cursed forest? Makes no sense."

"Wasn't the Commander given free reign for this?" Sly agreed, "what's he playing at, listening to that little Ulvvori freak?"

"He has a plan," Jesk admonished them, "don't question it."

"Well, I say we should have torched the barn to make an example," Vaylen spat.

"Save it," Roper said to them, "you can teach these two wolf bitches a lesson when we catch up with them." There were a few dark chuckles and Carro tried to ignore it, knowing that he did not have time to dole out reprimands. They rode hard until they finally reached the Southrun and had to stop to let the horses drink. While his men waded into the river to fill their own water flasks, Carro scanned the horizon to the north, but saw no telltale dust cloud indicating that Asenna and the twins were ahead of them.

"They must be riding in the river," he muttered to himself. His most pressing concern was the fact that the sun was slipping into the western half of the sky. Badger nudged his arm and Carro pulled out a few of the sugar cubes that Gade had packed for him. Once the horse had gobbled them up, Carro put the rest in his pocket and swung back into the saddle. They rode in the shallow water so as not to give away their own position, but it also slowed them down and Carro found himself becoming impatient. After a while, he looked up and saw Ilar's keen blue eyes watching him as they rode side-by-side. Ilar was the oldest member of the Black Sabers at nearly sixty, but you would never know it from his strength and nimbleness, and Carro often found himself seeking the older man out for advice.

"What is it, Ilar?"

"If you don't mind, Commander," Ilar said quietly, "I can't help wondering why this all happened. Why did she run in the first place? It's an awful risk for her to take with a baby that young." Carro hesitated before answering, but he knew that Ilar was not one to gossip.

"The Boss was going to…separate her and the child," Carro told him, "he was sending her to live at the villa and Ilmira was going to raise Elijas."

"Hmm, well I can't say I blame her in that case," Ilar mused, "when the war started, Azimar got the support of the Ulvvori because he promised to *stop* separating them from their children. Now he's run them out of their home too. Kings shouldn't break promises to their allies…or their wives."

Carro raised his eyebrows. "I believe you just committed some very light treason, Ilar," he chuckled, "but…do you really think she was right to run? Seems like she's put herself and the baby in far more danger this way."

"It's not my job to think," Ilar smiled, revealing the gaps in his teeth, "but sometimes I do it anyway. And I *think* that if a man makes vows to his wife, and then does something like that, she has every right to protect her child, especially from someone like Ilmira. But you know the Boss better than any of us do." There was something about Ilar that made him feel less guarded, and Carro looked around to make sure the others were riding farther back.

"I don't know anymore," he confessed, "Azimar's changed so much since the war ended. When we were younger, I'd have followed him anywhere. I'd have done anything for him because I trusted his judgment, but now…everything feels different. He's different." Ilar simply nodded. Carro had always appreciated that the older man knew when to speak and when not to. Roper and the rest of them never shut their mouths and he didn't want to deal with that at the moment, so they continued riding along the river in silence.

In the back of his mind, Carro knew that Ilar was right. Azimar had broken his promises to the Ulvvori. He had sworn they would be able to live undisturbed, then he had sent miners and soldiers onto their land. He had mistreated the Ulvvori bride he had sworn to honor and cherish. Then he had sent the Black Sabers to attack them in their own home and turn them into refugees. Carro felt a cold chill come over his body and tried to shake it off like Badger was shaking away the flies. He had never questioned Azimar's orders before, even when it involved violence, but he had meant what he said to Ilar: everything felt different this time, and it had since the attack on The Den, when Azimar had lied to him about why they were there. Before Carro could even begin to grapple with the overwhelming thoughts, Gaelin pulled his horse up and pointed ahead of them. On the horizon was a very faint plume of dust.

"The bluffs on this side are gettin' too high for them to ride in the river anymore," Gaelin said quietly, "that means they're almost at the bridge. You'll want your archer out in front. Tira's usually got a crossbow on her and her aim is damn good." Carro turned in his saddle to face the men, who had gathered up behind them.

"Alright, this is it. The bridge isn't much farther and they haven't crossed yet. Roper, you're in front with me. Aim for the woman with the crossbow first, but don't hit Asenna or her horse. If the child gets hurt, we're all dead. We have to stop them from reaching the bridge. Understood?" They all nodded their assent.

"Tell me you're with me!" Carro called out.

"We are with you!" the men replied, their voices lower and more serious than they had been back in the council room. Carro turned back around and goaded Badger into a trot, staying in the shallows to try and retain the element of surprise. His mind focused and narrowed until all he could see was the old bridge across the bluffs. It had been years since he had been to it, and he couldn't imagine it was in any better condition. Carro half expected an ambush, but none came and soon the bluffs on the western riverbank were rising up beside them, indicating that they were close. Leading his men from the shallows, Carro kicked Badger into a full gallop. Beside him, Roper had dropped his reins entirely and rode with no hands, an arrow already nocked on his bow. As they came over a rise, a small patch of trees came into view, and Carro could see the three huge draught horses running ahead.

"Go!" he called to Roper, who kicked his horse harder and stood up in the stirrups to fire a warning shot. It landed exactly where it needed to, in between the two horses running in the back. Carro watched as Asenna and the woman with the crossbow, Tira, turned around and yelled something to one another. Their horses were big and slow and Carro could feel the gap between them closing. Roper loosed another arrow and it whizzed past Asenna's head, striking the flank of Tira's horse. The animal cried out and lunged to the side, but Tira managed to jump clear of its enormous body as it fell.

"Watch your fucking aim!" Carro bellowed at Roper. He watched as Tira rolled onto her feet and sprinted toward the bridge, keeping pace with Asenna's horse and using it as a shield to dissuade further arrows. The other twin, Talla, had already reached the bridge and her horse was refusing to cross, so she jumped down and drew her short sword, calling out to her sister. Carro watched in desperation as Asenna approached the bridge, but her horse also balked and reared. She had to clutch his neck to stay on, her left hand cradling the baby in the sling on her chest. Tira seized the reins on Asenna's horse, pulling him onto the bridge. Carro's stomach dropped as he watched the animal step onto the planks and begin moving across. Suddenly, Tira whipped around and fired a bolt from her crossbow directly at him. Carro jerked on his reins, but Badger could not react in time and the bolt struck him in the chest.

"Badger, no!" Carro cried as the horse stumbled and fell, throwing him forward and then landing on his legs. Jesk and Ilar stopped and were able to push Badger's body off him.

"Are you alright, sir?" Jesk asked.

"I'm fine. Go!" Carro yelled at the others, "don't let them cross!" Ahead, Sly, Vaylen, and Walcott finally made contact with the hatchet-wielding Talla in front of the bridge. As soon as Carro had determined that he really wasn't injured, he drew his sabers and ran with the rest of the men behind him. Tira was still firing bolts at them from the center of the bridge, but she was using them sparingly. Roper stopped at the edge of the bluff to fire back at her, but he could not get a clear shot with Asenna in the way. Talla was still fighting, snarling at the men as they attacked and swinging her weapons with a wild sort of precision.

"Come on!" she screamed at them, backing toward the bridge and laughing. Sly lunged at her, but Talla's sword swept across his throat first and Carro saw a bloom of bright red splatter her face and arms. Sly fell to the ground and Talla used Vaylen and Walcott's temporary distraction to land her hatchet in Vaylen's thigh, then kick Walcott in the chest so that he stumbled and fell over Sly's twitching body. Yanking the hatchet from Vaylen's leg, Talla retreated onto the bridge and walked backward as Tira fired more bolts. At last, Carro reached Vaylen and saw blood pouring from the wound on his leg.

"Go get that bitch!" Vaylen cried, trying to staunch the bleeding with his hands. Walcott, Ilar, and Tarett were already almost in the center of the bridge, approaching Talla slowly with their sabers raised. Tira fired another bolt from the eastern side of the river, striking Blight in the eye just as he reached the bridge and causing him to topple off the bluff. Tira and Asenna had made it across the river. Carro turned toward the bridge, but as he did, Talla stepped off the other end, knelt down, and struck the pommel of her sword against the blade of her hatchet. Carro watched in horror as it sparked and turned into a roaring stream of flame that shot down the length of the bridge toward his men.

"Get out of there!" Carro yelled, taking a few steps forward. Walcott,

Tarett, and Ilar turned to run, but the flames engulfed their legs and they fell before they could reach the riverbank. Then Carro noticed the small dark bottle with a cloth stuffed into its neck that was lying just behind Ilar on the planks. Gaelin had seen it too and he threw himself to the ground, covering his head, just as an almighty explosion ripped through the air, sending huge spears of wood flying past their faces. Carro ducked, dropping his sabers and covering his face. When he raised his head moments later, he choked on the acrid smoke filling the air. Stumbling to the edge of the bluff where the bridge had been anchored, he waited for the air to clear.

When it had, Carro saw Asenna sitting on her horse at the edge of the forest, her hand still cradling the baby's head as he wailed, frightened by the strength of the blast. She should have looked triumphant or happy, but all he saw in her face was sadness and fear. Carro felt the desperation bubble up inside his chest and he doubled over, letting out a scream of rage that reverberated around the bluffs. As he straightened up, Asenna turned her horse and vanished into the sea of trees behind her. Carro's head was still spinning and aching from the force of the explosion, so he moved away from the edge. He had seen bridges and buildings set on fire using lamp oil before, but never anything like this. Feeling unsteady, he walked back to where Jesk was sitting beside Vaylen, trying in vain to stop the bleeding from his friend's leg. Roper was trying to help Daine work a large splinter of wood out of his arm. Sly's body was still bleeding out on the grass nearby, covered in pieces of the shattered bridge, with some of his skin seared away from the proximity of the explosion. The smell of burning flesh reached Carro's nose and he turned to vomit into the grass. Ilar, Walcott, and Tarett had all simply vanished into thin air, as though they'd never been there. Carro heard a groan and a creak behind him and turned to watch as the eastern half of the bridge collapsed and fell into the river. Vaylen suddenly cried out and Gaelin came to stand near Carro.

"He's not goin' to make it," the hunter said quietly, "if you Sabers have anything like last rites, give them now." Shaking a little, Carro walked over and sat beside Vaylen.

"Vaylen, look at me. Tell me you're with me," he said, his throat raw. Vaylen's eyes, wide and fearful, began to glaze over as he looked up at Carro.

"I'm...I'm with you..." he stammered, then his body shuddered and fell still.

"Damnit!" Jesk cried, standing up and kicking a chunk of wood into the river, "how the fuck did that happen?! What was that?!"

"Kashaitis call it 'sunfire'," said Gaelin, "comes from one of their universities."

"Magic..." Jesk hissed, "evil magic..."

"Hardly," Gaelin laughed at him, "it's made from rocks mined right out of the earth, just like Azimar's precious blackstone." Jesk started toward Gaelin with a murderous look in his eye, but Carro stepped between them.

"It doesn't matter what it is!" he yelled "we underestimated them to our own detriment. Those two women just took out six of us on their own! We need to rethink our plan."

"If you don't get after them soon, they'll disappear forever," said Gaelin, "you've got no time to wait."

Carro paced back and forth, his mind racing and his head pounding. "Gaelin, if we can get to the other side of the river, you can track them from where they entered the forest, right?"

"Aye, as long as it don't rain too heavy."

"We need to get to the Ossesh bridge as soon as we can then. We'll lose time that way, but it's better than losing them completely," Carro looked around for the horses, but most had either died or scattered during the blast. There were four still standing off in the distance.

"I'll walk," said Gaelin, "never did like riding anyways." Jesk and Roper went to grab the horses while Carro went up the river a little way to get away from the smell and the voices. Crouching down on the edge of the bluff, he allowed his head to fall into his hands and felt himself trembling. As a Black Saber Captain, he only had two mandates: protect his men and finish the mission, and now he was failing at both. To make matters worse, he could feel more doubt creeping into his mind with each minute that passed. Half his men had just died before his eyes, and yet the image he couldn't shake was the fear on Asenna's face when she looked at him. He heard Azimar's voice in his head screaming "how could you let this happen?!" and the trembling grew more intense as he imagined his fate should he go back empty-handed. *Maybe I should just throw myself off the bluff,* he thought, *it might be less painful.*

"Commander!" Jesk's voice carried up the riverbank and snapped Carro back into his body. He stood up and pushed his hair back off his face, pretending as though he hadn't just considered hurling himself into the river.

"What is it?"

"It's Gade," the lieutenant panted, "he's here. He rode from Sinsaya with a message from the Boss." Carro felt even more terror and confusion seize his body. He couldn't have Gade getting tangled up in this.

"What message?" He began walking back toward the bridge with Jesk.

"We didn't read it. He said it's only for you." When Carro saw Gade, he started to panic in earnest. The boy was wearing the uniform of a fully initiated Black Saber, a pair of curved blades hanging on his back, and a sleek white horse standing nearby bearing Azimar's crest. Gade gave Carro an enthusiastic salute.

"Gade! How the fuck did you even find us?" Carro yelled at him.

Gade's face fell. "Captain Roeld said that you--"

"Nevermind. Give me the message and then I want you back on that horse and gone," Carro snapped, holding his hand out. Gade pulled a small piece of parchment from his pocket and handed it over.

"Commander…" he began, but Carro waved him off and turned around to open the letter. In Azimar's stilted handwriting were words that made Carro feel as though he might vomit again:

Kill her and bring me my son, or the boy's life is forfeit. Loyalty forever.

He's making me choose, Carro thought, *Asenna's life or Gade's.* The stone that had been sitting in the pit of his stomach since the beginning of the mission suddenly dropped out, leaving a painful and gaping wound. Carro motioned for Gade to come over to him and once they were only inches apart, he grabbed the boy's head.

"Get back on the horse right now," he whispered urgently, "don't go back to Sinsaya, don't go anywhere near Azimar. Find somewhere safe where no one knows you and stay there."

Gade backed away, looking hurt. "I was given strict orders to stay with you, Commander, until the mission is finished."

"I don't fucking care what he told you!" Carro bellowed at him, "look around, Gade! We just lost six men within a matter of minutes! I need you to trust *me*!"

Gade lifted his chin defiantly. "I won't disobey a direct order from my King," he said. Carro could feel the other men watching him intently and he realized that he was beginning to lose his grip on the situation.

"We're wastin' time," Gaelin barked, "let the boy make his own choice."

"It's my job to protect him!" Carro shot back, "this isn't your concern, Gaelin."

"I'm going with you!" Gade cried, "I promise I won't do anything stupid." Carro turned on his heel and seized the reins of the nearest horse, hauling himself into the saddle.

"Let's go then," he said quietly. Without a word, the rest of the men mounted their horses and Gaelin trailed behind them on foot.

They moved north along the river for hours in silence. Carro could feel Gade's eyes on the back of his head, but he couldn't help but be furious with the boy for his eagerness to fight and to kill, even though that was exactly why Carro had chosen him for the Black Sabers. *The same reason Azimar chose me,* Carro told himself, *he used me and now he's using Gade too.* He suddenly felt a surge of anger toward Azimar that he had never felt before and a deep exhaustion washed over his body, as though he had been holding an anvil and was suddenly able to put it down. With the sun finally starting to set in earnest, he held up his hand, indicating that they should stop for the night.

Wordlessly, Carro skinned the rabbit that Roper shot for their supper, but as it cooked on a spit made from the arrow that killed it, the sight of the burning flesh made his stomach writhe. All he could see was Sly's face, bubbling and red and raw, and he had to excuse himself to go down to the water and vomit again. When he was finished, he drank from the rushing river and then sat back on his heels and tossed a few pebbles into the shallows. There was a crunch behind him and Carro turned to see Gade walking down.

"Are you alright?" the boy asked, sitting beside him.

"Fine," Carro murmured, "I'm sorry about earlier. It was a hard day…"

"Jesk told me," Gade picked up a smooth, round rock and skipped it across the water, "why did you tell me not to go back to Sinsaya?"

Carro hesitated. "Azimar is…not himself right now…"

"He's worried sick about the Prince."

"Yes, but this is something else. Gade, do you trust me?" Carro looked over and met Gade's big blue eyes. He could tell the boy was searching, trying to understand.

"Of course, Captain…Commander…sorry." Carro waved it off and reached into his boot to pull out Azimar's letter. Gade read it slowly, his eyes growing wide with fear.

"That's why," Carro said, "because his judgment is…compromised, and I won't risk your life if I fail. If it comes down to it, I need you to leave when I tell you to and don't try to argue with me. Alright?"

Gade nodded. "I don't understand though," he said, "why me?"

"Because Azimar knows how much I care about you. Because he used to feel the same way about me. Or at least…I thought he did."

"I'll leave now," Gade said softly, "if you want me to."

Carro shook his head. "No, you're safer with me. You'll stay and I'll think of something. Now, go eat and then get some rest."

"I *am* starving," Gade said, hopping up and giving Carro a salute before jogging back to the camp. Carro stretched himself out on the riverbank and stared up at the moon, hanging above him like an apple on a tree. He closed his eyes and let the light wash over him like the river was washing over the stones at his feet, and after a few minutes his heartbeat slowed and his breathing became more steady. The brief moment of relative peace was interrupted by Gaelin throwing himself down on the riverbank too.

"What do you want?" Carro asked.

"The moon might make you start howlin'," Gaelin said, "*awwwooooo!*"

"Gaelin, have you been drinking?"

"You ever talk to Her? *Izlani?* She might just listen to you…" Carro opened one eye and saw Gaelin looking at him with what could only be described as hunger on his face. He sat up, feeling uneasy.

"Go to bed," he told Gaelin, trying to stand and walk away. Gaelin suddenly reached out and grabbed Carro by the front of his shirt, jerking it to the side and knocking him back down. Carro's elbows hit the rocks hard and he kicked out at Gaelin, who had already let go and was standing over him.

"What the fuck was that?!"

"I knew it…" Gaelin breathed. He was pointing at Carro, who looked down at himself and realized that his shirt had ripped and was hanging over his right shoulder, exposing the large, mangled scar in the shape of a U that sat just beneath his collarbone. Gaelin's expression was almost gleeful, but Carro yanked his shirt back up and rolled away.

"Get out of here, Gaelin," he barked.

"Why hide it?" the hunter asked, moving around in front of Carro and blocking his escape from the riverbank.

"I'm not hiding anything," Carro insisted, "it's just an old scar."

"If you think I ain't seen that same exact scar on a hundred other men, you're a fool," Gaelin said, his voice deadly serious, "do your men know? Does Azimar know?"

"No one knows!" Carro nearly shouted, but he caught himself at the last second and covered his own mouth until he had regained his composure, "no…one…knows, except Azimar, and I swear Gaelin, if you tell anyone…It doesn't matter anyway."

"Doesn't matter that you're Ulvvori? Doesn't matter that you were ripped from your mother's arms and branded like livestock and turned into a child soldier? Doesn't matter that you were forced to kill your own people at The Den?" said Gaelin, his voice becoming more intense and emotional with every word. Carro straightened up, drawing a saber and resting it against Gaelin's throat.

"I'm *not* Ulvvori," he hissed, "and if you tell *anyone* about this, I'll put my sword through your fucking skull and throw you in the river." Carro turned and tried to walk away, but Gaelin put a hand on his shoulder.

"You're Ulvvori whether you like it or not, boy," he told Carro, "and no matter what you've done in Azimar's service. You can't just take it off like you take off those sabers and pretend to be somethin' else."

Carro paused for a moment. "I've been pretending for twenty-three years. I think I'll be alright," he murmured, walking back toward the campfire and leaving Gaelin standing on the riverbank alone.

FIVE:
THE FOREST

Asenna's eyes and throat burned when she turned back toward the smoking wreckage of the bridge. Tira had warned her to cover her ears and she had, but the sound had been louder than anything she'd ever heard and the thick smoke filling the air made her gag and cough. She tried to comfort Fen as best she could, but he was inconsolable. Talla appeared suddenly out of the black clouds with a vicious grin on her face.

"Got four of them, probably five if that fucker with the leg wound dies," she said to Tira.

"Only one today," Tira replied, "but I knocked another one off his horse. Does that count?" The two of them turned toward the woods and began to walk, but Asenna sat still on Pan's back, trying to see across the river. She saw movement through the smoke and picked out a few men standing near the bridge with two bodies on the ground, bloody and burned. Then she saw Carro, standing on the very edge of the bluff and watching her with a wild expression in his eyes, his hands balled into fists. He looked panic-stricken, like she had seen him during the war when something had gone horrifically wrong and Azimar had blamed him for it. Fen continued to wail as they stared at each other for a moment, then Carro bent over and let out an agonizing scream. Asenna's head was swimming and she couldn't watch anymore, so she jerked on the reins and rode east into the forest.

The trees enveloped them like a thick blanket, blocking out the sound and smell of the destroyed bridge as if it hadn't happened. Asenna had never been into a forest like this one. The piney woods of the Midwinter Mountains were sparse and rugged, the ground rocky, sloped, and inhospitable to most undergrowth. But here, the trees remained lush and green even in the middle of winter. Their trunks were impossibly tall and thick, with canopies so broad they blocked most of sunlight and cast dappled patterns onto the ground that swirled and danced in the soft breeze. Beneath their feet was a soft carpet of grass, which broke only for tree roots and rocks. Small streams flanked with moss and patches of wild thyme and oxlips seemed to bubble up from under the ground at every turn. Every so often, they passed by glens and meadows blanketed with rainbows of wildflowers, and everywhere Asenna could see small animals, birds, and insects busy at work. The entire place made her feel like she had been pulled into some kind of spirit realm.

The uncanny feeling was magnified by the fact that Fen settled down as soon as they had crossed the threshold of the forest. His wide golden eyes darted around at the canopy above them and a tiny smile flashed across his face every now and then. Asenna had never seen him so quiet and alert for so long, and after at least thirty minutes riding with no signs of trouble, she felt safe enough to pull him out of the sling and hold him in her arms so that he could look around properly. Even when she dropped Pan's reins, he dutifully followed the twins through the trees. The tension that had hung over them since leaving the city quickly dissipated and Asenna could even hear the two sisters laughing and joking, albeit about their slaughter at the bridge, but the feeling of lightness and relief that had washed over her when they entered the forest became more pronounced as they went. Eventually, Asenna found herself so content that she was almost sleepy and she put Fen back into the sling just in case. After an hour or so in the forest, they encountered a small herd of deer like Asenna had never seen. Unlike the giant deer roaming the mountains, which stood taller even than an adult dire wolf and whose single antler could cradle a full-grown man, these were small and lithe, with white speckles splashed across their backs. Their antlers fanned out into delicate cups and they simply watched the humans and horse pass by with a mild, detached interest.

"What kind of deer are those? I've never seen them before," Asenna leaned down to ask Talla, who looked up and frowned.

"You haven't heard of the *no'shela skana*?"

"'Star deer'?" Asenna translated the words from Ulvvori, "I guess I haven't."

"Oh, here we go!" Tira laughed, "Papa was a bit of a storyteller and he taught Talla everything. Now you've gotten her started, she'll never stop." Talla nodded and smiled, but Asenna could see a bit of sadness in her yellow eyes and she knew that Talla was thinking about Ferryn.

"My father might have told me, but I was so young when he died, and my mother was never the storytelling type, especially after he was gone," Asenna said, "tell me, please."

"It's not a well-known one, so don't worry," Talla said, "you know that the *rani no'shela* were Izlani's first children, but do you know how they got into the sky?"

Asenna thought hard, trying to remember what her father had told her. "Izlani created the *rani no'shela* first, and they were made of pure light. When she started to make more children, the animals, it got crowded and the *no'shela* found that they couldn't live with the animals because they burned too bright. They asked Izlani to put them in the sky to help her other children find their way and mark the days…right?"

"Close," Talla said, her voice taking on a sort of musical quality as she began the tale. "Izlani asked all the animals if they could help her move the *no'shela* to the sky, and they all made excuses why they couldn't do it. Finally, she asked the *skana*. She asked the *dria skana* from the mountains first and they said no. Then she asked the *cyn skana* that lived in the hills and the plains and they were eager to help. They gathered up the *no'shela* in their cupped antlers and then bucked their heads and threw them up into the sky. As the *no'shela* flew up to their new home, they dropped some of their sparks of light down over the *cyn skana's* backs. That's how they got their speckles. As a reward for their help, Izlani gave them a new name: *no'shela skana,* and a home in the Forever Forest, where they would be safe from predators."

"It's a beautiful story," Asenna murmured, "could you tell me more tonight?"

"As many as you want," Talla grinned, "*this one* has no appreciation for them at all." She jerked her thumb at her sister.

"I appreciate them!" Tira insisted, laughing, "but you used to make me stay awake all night so you could practice memorizing them and I was tired!" Talla just rolled her eyes.

When dusk began to close in through the trees, they stopped at the edge of a small meadow. Lusie had packed several large pieces of fresh flatbread in Asenna's saddlebags and Tira dug up some edible mushrooms, which they cooked on a flat rock over their fire. Combined with the wild thyme that was growing on the banks of a stream, it felt like one of the best meals Asenna could remember having. In fact, they all began to feel rather sleepy and complacent afterwards and decided not to move on until morning. Asenna left Fen laying on her cloak next to Talla, who was sharpening her hatchet on a whetstone, and went to help Tira gather up some sticks, feathers, and pine sap to make new bolts for her crossbow. When they got back to the little camp, Tira pulled a delicate knife out of her boot and handed it to Asenna.

"You remember how to use it, right?" she smiled. Asenna took the knife and weighed it in her hands. It had been a long time, but surely she had not spent twenty-two years learning the skills of the Ulvvori just to forget them when it was most critical. It took her a few tries, but she finally found the muscle memory that she had used as a child to make fishing spears with her father. Carefully and slowly, she cut the bark off the sticks, then straightened and sharpened them to a deadly point, then cut notches for the fletching, which Tira secured into place with the tree sap. The three of them worked in silence, with only Fen's babbling and the sounds of the birds to disturb them. Eventually, they began to lose the last bit of light that filtered through the trees, and the small fire did not provide enough to keep working, so they began to settle in for the night.

"Do either of you feel…strange?" Asenna asked the twins, "but in a good way? Like you could just stay here and sleep forever? I can't remember the last time I felt this relaxed."

"It's the forest," Tira said in a cryptic tone.

Asenna looked up at her. "What do you mean?"

"You know how when you stand in a canyon and shout, and your voice hits the walls and comes back to you over and over?" Tira asked, sitting down cross legged on her own bedroll across the fire, "this forest does it too, but with your emotions. Whatever you're feeling in here is exaggerated and intensified until it overwhelms you. If you're a little nervous, you'll start to feel complete panic and get lost and never make it out. If you're too complacent, you'll start to feel lethargic and you'll just lay down under a tree and never get up. That's why it's called the Forever Forest."

"I thought it was called that because the leaves don't change," Asenna said, suddenly feeling more apprehensive as she glanced around, "is it some kind of magic?"

"Another story I'm assuming your parents didn't tell you," Talla said, "about the sacred springs?"

Asenna spread her arms out and shook her head. "My family are fighters and hunters, not storytellers," she chuckled. Talla settled down on her blanket with her arms behind her head and Asenna leaned in a little.

"The story says that spread throughout the world, there's sacred springs," she started, "the water in the springs is magic, but each one is a little different. They say that's where we got the Wolfsight from: a sacred spring in the Midwinter Mountains."

"I know *that* story!" Asenna piped up, "a long time ago, the dire wolves needed help to protect the mountains from humans, so they asked Izlani to make companions for them. Izlani created us under the earth and brought us up to the surface for the dire wolves."

"Whenever I made Frost mad, he said he was going to ask Izlani to drag me back down and send up a new girl for him," Tira laughed.

Talla nodded and picked the tale back up. "...and the wolves showed the first Ulvvori the springs and when they drank from it, they were given the Wolfsight. The story about the springs says that the water is Izlani's lifeblood. It soaks into the land around it, making everything just a little different, special, or magical. Whatever you want to call it."

"So, there's a sacred spring in this forest then?" Asenna asked.

Tira shrugged. "Maybe, or maybe it's the story that creates the feelings. People experience what they already believe is true."

"How do we find our way out then?"

"Stay on your toes," Talla answered, "stay alert, but don't let your feelings get the best of you. You have to treat them like waves. They come and they go on their own and you just have to hold your breath sometimes and wait for them to pass. Sometimes people think too hard about it and start to panic if they feel anything at all though, so be careful. We're with you and we can guide you out if you start to lose it. We've been in here a few times."

"What will happen to the Black Sabers if they follow us?"

"I guess it depends," said Talla, "how well they can control their emotions, and whether they really trust each other. If there's any doubts or bad feelings between them at all, those will become much worse, and they'll start to see one another as enemies. Maybe they'll just kill each other and we won't have to worry about it." She gave a harsh laugh and Tira grinned.

"That's the dream," she agreed. There was another long silence and then Asenna thought of something.

"Do you think that's why the Ulvvori children aren't being born with Wolfsight?" she asked, "because they aren't living on the land that's fed by the magic spring?"

"I guess it's possible," Tira said, "but the springs are just a story. No one has ever found any kind of sacred water up there, and plenty have looked for it. Besides, that doesn't explain how Fen got it."

"No, I guess you're right," Asenna frowned, "but how else do you explain the Wolfsight? And the way this forest is?"

"We don't need an explanation for everything," Talla said quietly, "sometimes…things just are what they are and we don't need answers, because even if we got them, nothing would change. Why worry about it?"

"Curiosity?" Asenna suggested.

Tira laughed out loud. "Curiosity is for people whose basic survival is guaranteed. I don't have time or energy to be curious about how the enchanted forest works when there's half a dozen men following me through it, trying to kill me."

"That's fair," said Asenna, pulling the cloak tighter and rolling over, trying to push the burning questions out of her mind and sleep.

~~~

The following morning they woke up to a light rain coating their skin and it cast a dismal feeling as they packed up their camp to continue. Asenna opted to walk because of the soreness in her legs and buttocks from riding so much the day before, but she was struggling by midday when they stopped to rest and attempted to dry themselves off. Once they were moving again, the rain picked up, with fat raindrops hitting the canopy above them and then cascading down in rivulets onto their heads. Asenna decided to ride Pan again so that she could hold a large piece of oiled deerskin that Talla gave her over Fen's head. The skin smelled atrocious and Asenna spent most of the day feeling nauseated, but there was no choice except to keep moving. By the time they stopped in the late afternoon, however, the rain had eased and there was a soft golden light filling the air above the wildflower meadow where they camped.

"That rain should help cover some of our tracks, so we can stop earlier tonight and dry off," said Talla as they shook out their cloaks and blankets and hung them over bushes and tree branches while Asenna sat down to change Fen.

"Gaelin can still track after rain," Tira warned, "it's just harder, but he can."

"How do you know this Gaelin anyway?" Asenna asked, "is he Ulvvori?"

"Gaelin's half Ulvvori. His father was some kind of trader from Ossesh, and his mother obviously wanted to save him from being conscripted, so she sent him to live there when he was little. He came back after his father died when he was a teenager. Him and Pa were friends when they were younger, but Gaelin hated living in the mountains, so he would go out and find work and come back every now and then. He's actually the one who got Pa and Ephie jobs when they moved to the city, but then he started doing things that Pa just couldn't understand and they had a falling out."

"What things?"

"Working for Rogerin," Talla spat, "even after everything he did to our people."

"I guess he thought he could redeem himself by taking Azimar's side during the rebellion," Tira continued, "we all made that mistake, but now he's working for the Black Sabers like the greedy, two-faced sack of shit he is."

"Did you both fight in the war?" Asenna asked softly.

Tira's eyes dropped to the ground. "Yeah, the whole thing."

"What was it like?"

Talla raised an eyebrow. "We don't really have a basis for comparison, but it was terrible," she said, laughing under her breath.

"It was a stupid question, sorry," Asenna admitted, "I know it was terrible. I just...sometimes I wish I'd been at home while it was happening so I could have helped, instead of sitting in that awful empty house with Ilmira yelling at me every day."

"Is she as miserable as she looks?" Tira smirked.

"Worse," Asenna groaned, "far worse. Whenever we were alone she treated me like a naughty child. There were so many times I wanted to just...steal a horse and run back home, but I didn't want to cause any problems between Azimar and the Riders."

"What's *he* like?" Talla asked, her voice low, "I never met him during the war."

"Tal...I'm sure she doesn't want to talk about it," Tira muttered, but Asenna shook her head and fidgeted with the torn-up beds of her fingernails.

"It's alright. At first...he was wonderful. He listened to me. He was charming and sweet and thoughtful, but he was never around. He would come back for a week or so and then leave again to go fight. After the first year or so, he started to become angry and paranoid and...cruel, even though he was winning. I guess it wasn't the real him at first, or maybe the war just...changed him too much."

"Don't give him so much credit," Talla scoffed, "plenty of men and women fought in that war and didn't turn into bloodthirsty maniacs. It sounds like you got a bad one from the start and he was just good at hiding it. He even fooled Tolian into thinking he was trustworthy, and that's not easy."

"Do you ever hate them?" Tira asked, "your family? For giving you away to him? I'd have been furious with Pa if he'd ever tried something like that." Asenna thought for a moment, unsure of how honest she should be in the midst of an enchanted forest that toyed with her emotions. She took a deep breath and tried to control the hard knot forming at the back of her throat as she spoke.

"Sometimes, yes, but I did agree to it. At first, he was so sweet that I thought I'd gotten lucky. But when he was gone, and then after he started to...change, I guess I was angry that they didn't try to find another solution, that they didn't try to negotiate more. He chose me specifically and I said yes, but what else could I do? How could I sit there and let my entire family go off to war and not do the one thing anyone was asking of me? It's not as if I could fight, but I thought if I could just help somehow..." Tira was taking the short sword off her belt and she paused, then held it out a little.

"Do you want to learn to fight?" she asked Asenna.

Asenna was nursing Fen, but she looked up eagerly. "Really? You'd teach me?"

"Why not?" Tira shrugged, "it'll give us something to do in the evenings while we're traveling, and it would be good for you to be able to at least hold your own for a few minutes, in case we run into trouble." Asenna looked down and realized Fen was asleep, so she gently unlatched his mouth and put him down on her cloak.

"Whatever you think would be best," she said, her chest filling up with excitement as she stood and took the sword Tira was holding out for her.

"Your family really never taught you *anything*?" Tira asked, putting her hands on her hips and looking perturbed, "that doesn't sound like Tolian at all. He was always so strict with the Riders, making sure we all knew what we were doing."

"They never imagined I'd need to fight," Asenna said as she carefully drew the sword, "I was just one little girl in a whole family of Riders. My father thought it was more important to teach me how to hunt and fish. He said I was much more likely to get lost in the mountains alone than I was to be fighting."

"Well, I can at least show you some basics," Tira replied, "Tal, pass me yours." Talla picked up her short sword and tossed it to Tira, who caught it and pulled it from the scabbard in one deft motion. They practiced for an hour or so and Tira showed Asenna how to stand, how to hold the sword, and a few small defensive moves. She tried to focus more on how to dodge an attack and disarm an opponent without too much swordplay, but Asenna found that she actually enjoyed the part where the blades met and scraped against each other. It made her feel more powerful than anything in her life, and the magic of the forest made that small amount of confidence go to her head. By the time they finished when it was growing dark, she felt like she could take on the entire world, and the delusions of grandeur made falling asleep rather difficult.

On the third day, the sun had come back out and Asenna was able to walk again. Even though the soreness in her limbs had only worsened after practicing with Tira the night before, Asenna noticed herself feeling happy and content as they wove through the trees. The twins were in a better mood as well and the three of them felt comfortable enough that they began to sing some of the Ulvvori's call and response songs that were used to keep everyone together during their long treks between settlements. The songs made Asenna feel at home, but they also brought some of her anxiety about her family to the surface, which she tried to tamp down. Not knowing whether they were alive or dead was almost unbearable, but she tried to remind herself of what Talla had said: having answers would not change a situation. She tried to let the feelings of anxiety and helplessness wash over her and then fade away, just like the feelings of pride she felt when she was able to learn one of the moves Tira was teaching her, and just like the feelings of terror and fury that bubbled up every time she imagined Carro and his men following them through the forest.

That evening when they stopped, the twins put on a small mock battle to show her some of what they were teaching. They leapt and spun around the trees like dancers, laughing whenever one of them narrowly missed the other. Asenna held Fen in her lap, leaning him back a little on her stomach so that he could watch too. The flashing blades seemed to particularly catch his attention. When they were finished, Tira picked him up and held him in the air.

"I think he liked it!" she crowed, "I'll start training him as soon as we get to Kashait!"

Asenna giggled. "Maybe he should learn to walk first," she said, watching as Tira made faces at Fen while he kicked his little legs and squealed.

"He needs a dire wolf before anything else," Tira said, putting him back into Asenna's arms and then collapsing on the ground to catch her breath.

"Do you think he could?" Asenna asked, "he'll be nearly two months old by the time we arrive. Isn't that too long to wait?"

"I think it's probably up to the she-wolf," Talla mused, "they're the ones who give us their pups as companions. I think any of them would be willing to make an exception for your son, especially now that we don't know what will happen to the Riders. He could very well be the last one."

"If he could have a dire wolf…" Asenna trailed off, thinking hard. A small bubble of hope formed in her chest, then almost instantaneously expanded into an overwhelming surge of happiness and optimism and Asenna found herself crying.

"What's wrong?" Talla asked, looking alarmed.

"I…I don't know," Asenna half-laughed and half-sobbed, "I just felt so happy and then…the forest made me cry!" Tira cackled and even Talla cracked a wide smile and before long all three of them were laying on their backs on the forest floor, almost hysterical with laughter. Tira finally managed to get enough of a grip on herself to roll over and pinch her sister on the leg, which brought Talla back down and then finally Asenna was also able to pull herself together, wiping tears from her face.

"Ohhh," Tira sighed, still chuckling, "don't do that again!"

"What? Feel happy?" Asenna giggled.

"Yes!" Tira playfully threw a piece of bark at her, "no joy allowed on this trip!" By the time they settled down for the night, Asenna had allowed the waves of exhilaration to wash over her and move away, but she held onto the small, shining flicker of optimism in her as if her life depended on it.

On the evening of their sixth day in the forest, Asenna and Tira wandered away from the camp to gather firewood, leaving Fen laying on a blanket beside Talla while she dug a fire pit. Asenna was humming softly as she picked up sticks when she heard something move on the other side of a large flowering bush. She froze and her hand went to the dagger that she had been carrying on her belt. Tira was nowhere to be seen and Asenna's body was gripped with panic when she realized that she was alone. As she was contemplating whether to run or fight, one of the beautiful, delicate speckled deer stepped out from behind the bush. Asenna relaxed and smiled, then let out a quiet gasp when she realized that the animal was completely white from nose to tail, instead of brown with white speckles like its fellows. The stag stared at her for a few moments, twitching its big ears back and forth, then its entire body flinched and it ran the opposite direction. A deep feeling of dread overtook Asenna and she turned to see Tira standing stock-still behind her.

At the exact same moment, they heard Talla screaming their names. Asenna's feet began to run without her even realizing it, scattering the firewood onto the forest floor as she reached for her dagger. When they arrived at the small glen where their camp was, Asenna's terror instantly turned to blinding rage. The Black Sabers had found them. Talla was backed up against a large tree, standing over Fen, brandishing her hatchet and sword and spitting profanities. Before the men could even register their arrival, Tira seized her crossbow off the ground and fired a bolt, striking a tree beside Carro's head. He turned and held up one hand as they approached.

"Asenna, please!" he cried, "we don't want to fight!"

"Fuck that!" yelled the bald man next to him, lunging at Talla.

"Jesk, no!" Carro barked, the same moment that Asenna cried out. Talla and Jesk stepped over Fen and then lurched to the side. Tira dropped the crossbow and ran in front of the tree, drawing her sword. Asenna was able to go behind her and scoop Fen up, then back away, holding her dagger in one hand. Carro's eyes were darting between Asenna and the twins and she could tell he was looking for a way to end it quickly. As Talla struggled against Jesk on the edge of the glen, the other two Black Sabers closed in on Tira. She slashed down with her blade, catching one just above his knee. He fell backwards and she landed a vicious kick to his face, rendering him unconscious, then she turned to face the remaining man, who was impossibly large. Carro was slowly moving around the edge of the trees toward Asenna as Tira engaged the giant Black Saber.

"Get away from me!" Asenna hissed at Carro, holding the dagger in front of her and desperately wishing she had the crossbow so she could put a bolt between his eyes.

"Asenna, I don't want to--"

"You think I won't kill you? Get! Away!"

"No, I know you will," Carro pleaded, "so please just listen to me and no one has to get hurt!"

"Go fuck yourself," Asenna spat at his feet. Suddenly, Talla slid in between them, having badly wounded Jesk.

"Let's go!" she snarled at Carro. He shifted his eyes from Asenna and drew his sabers, spinning the blades in flashing circles and baring his teeth back at her. They circled one another, looking like a pair of wild animals with their hackles raised, then Talla lunged in, her hatchet meeting Carro's sword with a loud scrape. Carro swiped at her leg with his other saber and caught her on the thigh. Asenna saw blood on Talla's leg and began to feel the overwhelming dread rising in her throat, but she pushed it down and backed away from the fighting toward the tree where Pan was tethered. Tira was still struggling against the enormous Black Saber while Carro and Talla spun around each other. The wound on Talla's leg slowed her down, but she was still more than an equal match for Carro, who seemed to be fighting exhaustion as much as he was fighting her.

Asenna stumbled over something and looked down to see Tira's crossbow lying on the ground, right next to the quiver of bolts. She crouched behind a tree trunk, slipped Fen into the sling that was still on her chest, then put the dagger away and picked up the crossbow. Once she had it loaded, Asenna turned the weapon on Tira's opponent and fired. The bolt struck him on the upper arm just as Tira lunged and knocked him off balance. He crashed backwards onto the forest floor, then Tira drove her sword through his neck with a loud cry as Asenna loaded another bolt. Carro stopped moving just long enough for Asenna to aim and fire the crossbow directly at his chest, but he turned at the last second and the bolt barely grazed his shoulder. He whirled around to look at Asenna, and Talla managed to sweep his legs out from under him with her foot. He fell hard on his back, dropping both sabers, and the twins moved in with their weapons raised, but then Asenna felt a cold blade slip around the front of her throat and a hand gripped her upper arm.

"Drop the crossbow," said a voice in her ear. Asenna complied.

"Gade, no!" Carro shouted. Talla and Tira spun around, realizing that they hadn't accounted for all Carro's men. Asenna couldn't see her attacker, but he felt smaller than the others and she could hear quick, panicked breathing in her ear. She cast around in her mind and remembered that Gade was the young recruit who was always trailing Carro like a shadow.

"I've got them, Commander!" Gade called out. Carro leapt up, leaving his swords on the ground and putting his empty hands out in front of him.

"Gade, don't! They will kill you!" Carro was begging now, his face contorted into a mask of desperation and terror. The twins had their weapons raised, but there was little they could do without spooking the boy.

"You said it was my life or hers!" cried Gade.

"No! No, I didn't say that!" Carro seemed to be breaking down as he pleaded, "I will fix it, Gade! You don't have to do this!" Asenna felt the knife press into her flesh and looked down at Fen, who was awake and squirming in distress.

"Alright, wait!" she said, slowly pulling Fen out of the sling and holding him out in front of her "please, just don't hurt me. Tira, take him." She tried to tell Tira what she wanted with her eyes but had absolutely no idea if it would work.

"Asenna, no…" Tira said. She was shaking her head, but Asenna saw the tiny curve at the corners of the twins' mouths that told her they understood exactly what she was asking.

"Please, Tira! Just give him to them!" Asenna cried. Her eyes met Carro's and his face drained of all color. Tira moved forward slowly, extending her arm as if to take the baby. As soon as she touched Fen's swaddling, however, Talla dropped both her weapons, lunged forward, and seized Gade by the hair, jerking him backwards and wrapping her own hand around the blade of the knife to push it away from Asenna's neck. Tira grabbed Fen while Asenna ducked away and turned to climb onto Pan's back. Meanwhile, Talla wrestled Gade underneath her and slammed his head into the ground several times, then scrambled backwards to retrieve her hatchet and sword, reaching out to slash at Carro, who jumped backwards. Tira passed Fen up to Asenna while Talla used a nearby rock to pull herself onto the horse, then they goaded Pan into a gallop and moved away with Tira sprinting behind them. Asenna glanced back, expecting to see Carro pursuing, but instead he was standing in the glen with his hands at his side, looking like he had seen a ghost.

SIX: DESERTER

Carro watched Asenna ride away, feeling just as rooted to the spot as the trees around him. He heard Jesk and Roper's voices as they recovered from their encounters with the twins, and then he suddenly remembered Gade and jerked himself out of the fog. The boy's face was bloodied and his nose looked broken, but he was still breathing when Carro flipped him onto his back.

"What the fuck happened?!" Jesk yelled from where he was sitting and examining a nasty cut that ran across his entire chest. Roper tried to stand up, but Tira had kicked him so hard that he was still dizzy and fell back, cursing as he examined the shallow slash on his knee.

"You let them go," Roper said, his voice deadly quiet. Carro stood up and faced him.

"I didn't let them go. Gade didn't follow my orders to stay behind with Gaelin. I had no choice." Roper hauled himself up and squared his body with Carro's. They were roughly the same size, but Carro knew that even when Roper wasn't nursing a head injury, there was no match.

"That's not what I saw," Roper sneered, "I've watched you hit moving targets half that size with a knife like the one on your belt right now, *Commander*. But you just stood there…and let her go. Why?"

Carro turned away angrily. "You took a kick to the head. I wouldn't expect you to know what you saw."

"Carro?" said Gade softly, raising his head.

"Are you alright?" Carro asked, kneeling to help the boy sit up.

"I think so…"

"You idiot!" Carro grabbed his shoulders, "I told you to wait with Gaelin. You put everyone else in danger, including yourself!"

"I wanted to help! I had her! She was handing the baby over!"

"No she wasn't, you snivelin' whelp!" Gaelin appeared behind them, "it was a trick! She wanted you to let your guard down so the twins could take you out. Seems our little queen has been learnin' a thing or two from Ferryn's girls."

"You were watching that whole time and you couldn't help?" Jesk said to Gaelin.

"I get paid to hunt, Lieutenant, not to fight. You wouldn't've even found them if it weren't for me," Gaelin laughed, "I'm happy to critique your performance afterwards though. You seem to've lost another man." He pointed to Daine's body.

"*You jumped-up little freak--*" Jesk hissed, moving toward Gaelin with his fist raised. Carro got between them and put his hands out.

"Enough!" he shouted, and they all fell silent. He couldn't tell if it was the stress of the last few days or if he had fallen harder than he thought, but Carro felt like there was a rabid creature trying to claw its way out of his chest and his head was reeling.

"Sir," said Jesk, "we *need* reinforcements. We should send Gade–"

"No!" Carro snapped, "no reinforcements. Gade isn't going anywhere."

"No reinforcements?" Roper muttered, his eyes narrowing with suspicion, "and what did the boy mean about his own life or hers? You're hiding something and I'm not going anywhere until I hear it!" Jesk was looking between Roper and Carro nervously. He had always followed Carro's lead, but even he knew that something was off.

Carro sighed, realizing that he had no other option but to tell them. "The message that Azimar sent with Gade…it ordered that we kill Asenna, and if we don't, Gade would die in her place."

"So? Kill her…" Roper scoffed, "what's the problem? You're really going to sacrifice one of your own to save that girl from her own stupid decision? I knew you were soft."

"I made an oath to protect her! So did all of you!" Carro looked around desperately, but their faces were hard. He felt like everything was spinning out of control, just like it had at the bridge, but this time it was so overwhelming that he could scarcely breath.

"Is that why you let her go?" Jesk asked, "some oath you made years ago? We all swore oaths to Rogerin too and look what we did to him!"

"That was different!" Carro protested, "we were ten years old when we made those! You expect me to kill an innocent woman that I swore to protect?"

"Innocent? She committed treason against your King! Your friend!" Roper was seething, his hands clenched into fists, "'Loyalty Forever!' How can you question that after everything Azimar has done for you? We are supposed to be your brothers! Innocent or not, how can you put *her* life above Gade's? Above ours?"

"Why can't I protect both of them?!" Carro was almost screaming now, his throat raw and burning, "how can you all follow his orders so blindly when you know it's wrong? Don't you see what he's become? *Think* about the things we did for him after the war was already over, and the things we did at The Den! There were women and children in those caves! How can you even live with yourselves after that?" Roper shrugged and spat on the ground.

"The Ulvvori deserved what they got." He said it so casually that something inside Carro snapped and he found his hands around Roper's throat, squeezing harder and harder until they fell to the ground. Roper scrambled at Carro's hands and chest and face, desperate for air as he started to shake, but Carro stared into his eyes, watching them roll back, and he did not want to stop.

"Commander, no! Carro! Stop!" Jesk seized Carro under his arms and ripped him away from Roper. Carro fell backwards onto his elbows, chest heaving, and watched Roper gasp and cough as he tried to crawl as far away as he could. Jesk turned, his face harder and angrier than Carro had ever seen it.

"I am relieving you of duty, Commander," he said, "you've betrayed your men and let us die because you didn't have the courage to follow your orders, and now you've attacked one of your own. The King will decide what to do with you." Blind panic engulfed Carro's body as he imagined what Azimar might do to him. He scrambled to his feet and drew his sabers as Jesk began to move toward him.

"One more step and you're dead, Lieutenant!" Carro snarled, crossing the blades in front of him. Jesk paused, knowing that it was not an empty threat. Carro glanced at Gaelin to see if he would receive any backup, but Gaelin was simply watching with a smirk on his face.

"I knew you were hiding something!" came Roper's cracked voice from across the glen. It took Carro a moment to realize that Roper was pointing at his shoulder, which had been exposed when Jesk had wrestled him away. Jesk's eyes flickered over the U-shaped brand and then widened.

"Ulvvori..." he breathed, "I don't understand...you never told me..."

"We can't trust him!" Roper croaked, "he's leading us straight to the wolves! Kill him, Jesk!" Seeing that his Lieutenant was frozen with shock and indecision, Carro sheathed one of his sabers and turned to Gade. The boy's eyes were wide with confusion and alarm.

"Gade, please come with me," said Carro, putting his hand out, "Azimar will kill you if you go back. Please…"

"*Kill him, Jesk!*" Roper screeched, but Jesk was still paralyzed.

"You lied to me," Gade whispered, taking a step away, "all those things you told me…where you came from, about your family…none of it was true…was it?"

"Yes, I lied to you, but it doesn't matter now! I am trying to save your life!" Carro implored.

"Like you saved your men at the bridge?" Gade yelled, suddenly angry, "like you saved Daine? Jesk is right! You could have saved all of them by just doing what you were ordered! You put her life before ours, before *mine*!"

"No! I can save you both, Gade, please! I need you to come with me!"

"I'd rather take my chances with Azimar than with you," Gade spat. Carro could feel the hatred in the boy's voice like a flame too close to his skin and he winced. Stepping away, Carro waited to see if they would come after him, but they didn't move, so he slipped away between the trees.

Carro ran until he couldn't run anymore and he stumbled over a root, sprawling out face down in the grass and remaining there until his ragged breathing slowed. He reached up and tore the twin sabers off his back, throwing them against a nearby tree and screaming at them as they clattered to the ground. Everything building up inside him burst out and Carro found himself on his knees, sobbing with his head in his hands. His whole body shook and his throat burned and he pounded the soft earth with his fists, but eventually the rage and despair ran its course and he lay on his back, staring up at the canopy, unable to focus his eyes. When he finally raised his head, he realized that he wasn't sure how far he had run or in what direction, so he hauled himself to his feet and over to the nearest tree. Scrambling to the top to get a look at the sky, Carro saw that it was dusk and he couldn't yet make out the edge of the Forever Forest, which meant that Asenna and the twins still had several days of walking to make it to the open plains, and then at least one more day to the Kashaiti border. Carro knew that if Roper and Jesk decided to go back to Sinsaya for reinforcements, they could skirt the forest using Azimar's fastest horses and cut Asenna's party off before they reached Kashait. He was determined to reach them before that to deliver his warning, even if it meant getting his throat slit. When he landed back on the ground and stood up, Carro saw Gaelin sitting at the base of the tree, picking his horrible pointed teeth with a twig.

"What are you doing here?" Carro snapped, surprised to see the hunter, but also somehow not. Keeping his eyes trained on Gaelin, he walked over and picked up his sabers, sliding them one by one back into place and adjusting his torn shirt to cover the brand on his shoulder. Carro found himself desperately wanting to leave the blades behind, to shed that part of his life and leave it to rust here under the trees, but he also knew he couldn't go on unarmed.

"Your boys decided that us Ulvvori can't be trusted and they drove me off. I came to find you to make sure I get paid," Gaelin said and Carro stared at him, a bit dumbfounded.

"You are…something else, Gaelin," was all he could say, "you can come, but I think you know you won't be getting any coins from me now."

"You can pay me in entertainment value, then," said Gaelin, standing up and beginning to walk east, "I'm goin' to enjoy the show when we finally catch up with the twins."

Carro jogged after him. "How did you know that's where I was going?"

"You people are so predictable with your drama and heroics," Gaelin waved him off, "I knew you'd wanna try and help them, and it so happens I've got more information than you do because I hung around a bit to hear your boys make their plans."

"Where are they going?" Carro asked, "back for more men?"

"Aye, they're plannin' to cut around north of the forest."

"That's what I thought," Carro's mind began to race again, trying to find a solution to the new puzzle in front of him, "do you know where the Ulvvori are? Could you go to them for help?"

"By my estimation, they could be in Kashait by now or they could be camped out on the coast. Either way, I can find your women before I can find the Ulvvori, so you'll just have to tell them what you've gotta say and hope they decide you're worth the trouble of keepin' alive." Carro fell silent as they walked. His mind was still attempting to do calculations, but now instead of tactical decisions, he was trying to work out what he could possibly say to these women to keep them from simply cutting him to pieces. He was normally quite skilled at talking his way out of bad situations, but this was different.

"How do you know they won't kill you too?" he asked Gaelin after they had been walking for a while, "you've been helping us hunt them…"

"I've known Talla and Tira since they was pups," Gaelin answered, "they know when to trust me and when not to."

"That makes no sense. They either trust you or they don't."

"Eh," Gaelin flashed a smile at him, "sometimes things ain't so black and white, boy. You're about to learn that the hard way."

"What does that--" Carro started to say, but then he felt something hard strike the back of his head and everything went dark.

When Carro woke up, everything was still dark. He panicked for a moment, thinking that he had lost his vision, but then realized he was blindfolded and his hands were bound behind him, he was sitting on the ground, and leaning against what felt like a tree trunk. His sabers were gone and it was deathly quiet.

"Gaelin?!" he called out.

"Shut up," growled a voice to his left. Carro turned his head and could just barely make out the shape of a person standing beside him through the blindfold.

"Gaelin?" Carro asked, shifting himself slightly. Suddenly the person was far closer, breathing into his ear.

"You're going to wish I was Gaelin when I'm through with you," said the distinctly female voice in a threatening whisper. "Gaelin only takes coins. I'm going to take a lot more than that."

Carro pulled his face away. "Please, you have to let me talk to Asenna," he said loudly, hoping she might be nearby.

"You have nothing to say to her," said his captor, landing a hard punch to the side of his head. Carro groaned and leaned over onto the tree roots.

"You don't understand!" he started to beg when his head stopped spinning, but then the blindfold was suddenly and painfully ripped off and Carro waited for his eyes to adjust. It was bright outside, daylight, which meant that he must have been unconscious for an entire night. He couldn't see any sign of Asenna, the twins, or Gaelin. His captor had vanished. Carro struggled to see if the ropes binding his hands might give, but they were tied well. He tried to twist his body and look around, but saw only trees and some birds. Before he could even begin to formulate a plan, Gaelin appeared around the side of the tree.

"Right where I left you."

"What's going on?" Carro asked, "where's Asenna?" Gaelin reached back and grabbed Carro's bound hands, hauling him onto his feet and marching him away from the tree.

"Gaelin, wait!" Carro dug his heels into the ground and flipped around to face the hunter.

"Come on, don't make this harder than it should be, boy."

"I need you on my side. Just convince them to hear me out. Please."

"I'll do what I can, but I sure hope you talk prettier than you look," Gaelin shrugged and pulled Carro back around, pushing him through the trees until they reached a spot where a large boulder sat between two trunks. An underground spring bubbled up from beneath the rock, creating a small pool surrounded by moss and flowers, and Carro suddenly realized how desperately thirsty he was. Talla stepped out from behind the rock with Tira beside her, each wearing one of his sabers tied to their belt. Carro winced when he saw the bloody bandage around Talla's leg where he had cut her. Gaelin shoved him onto his knees as the twins approached, both looking quite pleased with their catch.

"Please, I want to help. You have to listen to me--" Carro began.

"Why?" Tira spat, "why would you even want to help us now?"

"I...I can't explain it to you. I need to talk to Asenna."

"You can talk to us first, but Gaelin's already told us everything we need to know. Your men went back for reinforcements and they're going to cut us off outside the forest. Or was there something else you've been holding onto to try and save your worthless life?" She drew his own saber from her belt and rested it on his shoulder.

"You have to send Gaelin to find the Ulvvori," Carro told her, "the rest of you need to stay while he takes the horse and goes for help. I wouldn't put it past Azimar to send every single Black Saber after Asenna and the child. You can't fight them and you can't get to Kashait fast enough to outrun them, not with one horse and an injured leg and a baby."

"We don't even know where the pack is right now," said Tira, "how is Gaelin supposed to find them within the time it'll take us to pass through the forest?" Carro looked to Gaelin for some kind of support.

"I may or may not be able to find them," the hunter shrugged, "boy's right though, it could be worth a shot. Maybe we keep him? He knows their tactics and capabilities, and he knows Azimar's mind." Tira looked from Carro to Gaelin and back again, then she squatted down in front of him, sliding the tip of the saber to his throat.

"I have a few questions first, and if you lie to me, I *will* know," she said, so quietly that Carro could barely hear her.

"Anything," Carro swore, trying to hold her gaze even though he found the pale-yellow color of her eyes disquieting.

"Did you kill our father?"

"No, and I didn't order it either. I *never* wanted it to happen," Carro wanted to tell them the entire story, but his instinct told him that shorter answers were better with these two.

Talla let out a snarl. "I don't believe a word out of that wretched mouth. Cut his tongue out, Tira."

"Hang on," said Tira, holding her hand up.

"I'm telling the truth," Carro said softly.

"Were you at The Den?" Tira murmured. Carro's stomach dropped, but he knew there was no point in trying to lie or even twist the truth, since he had a feeling she already knew.

"Yes, I was there."

"Did you fight?"

"No, I was with Azimar as a bodyguard."

"Liar!" Talla cried, stepping forward, but Tira stood up and gently held her back, keeping the sword trained on Carro's neck.

"Did you know about the poisoned smoke?"

"I didn't know about any of it until I arrived," Carro tried to keep his voice even, but the memory of the battle distressed him. "Azimar told me we were going to do a survey of a new mine. When we got there and I realized what was happening, I…I should have done something. I'm sorry." Carro looked away from Tira's unearthly eyes.

"How convenient for you to grow a conscience now, when it's your life on the line and not ours," Talla sneered, "do you have any idea how many Ulvvori died that day? How many wolves we lost? Women and children! You're pathetic. Just kill him, Tira. Better yet, let me have him and I'll make it nice and slow like he deserves." Carro's eyes flicked between the two women. Talla was chomping at the bit to flay him, but Tira seemed to be considering his words more carefully.

"I say keep him alive, if anyone's countin' my vote," Gaelin said lightly.

"Don't think you're off the hook either, Gaelin!" Talla barked, "I can continue your little scar project someplace other than your arms."

"Tira?" came a softer voice from behind the twins. Carro looked up and saw Asenna standing beside the boulder, "what's he saying?"

"Lies and more lies," Talla told her, "that's all his kind know how to do." She turned and stalked away through the trees and Tira went over to consult with Asenna. They spoke quietly for a few moments, then Asenna came and knelt down in front of him.

"Why are you here, Carro?" she asked, her voice calm but firm, "in all the years I've known you…you'd never leave your men."

"You'd better hope he has an abridged version ready, cause it's a whole fuckin' saga," Gaelin said, rolling his eyes. Carro shot him a warning look and then turned back to Asenna, trying to somehow impart to her everything he had been feeling since the day of the naming ceremony and even before. He knew she would understand if he could just find the right words.

"I can't trust Azimar anymore," he started, "I used to believe in him and what he stood for, but now he's changed. I know you've seen it too. He's asked me to do things I can't…I won't…do."

"Like what?"

"He ordered me...to kill you, in order to get the baby back." A look of horror passed over Asenna's face and she closed her eyes for a moment as he continued speaking, "and he told me that if I didn't do it, he would kill Gade instead. I thought there was a way I could protect both of you, but...I was wrong. Look, in my boot there's a letter that will show you I'm telling the truth." Asenna looked back at Tira, who nodded, then she reached into his boot and pulled out the message from Azimar. As she read her husband's words, she covered her mouth and turned away from Carro for a moment to compose herself, handing the message to Tira.

"That's Azimar's writing," she murmured, "I...I can't believe he would want me dead. But why would you even want to protect me, Carro? Surely Gade is more important to you?"

Carro took a deep breath. "Azimar swore never to separate mothers from their children again, didn't he? And I swore an oath to protect you and your children. For me, those weren't just words. He can break his promises, but I won't break mine."

"What about your oaths to your men?" Asenna asked.

"I gave them a choice, and they chose Azimar," Carro said quietly. "Look, just let me help you get past whatever reinforcements they send and then you can kill me, ok? Let me do this, and then the wolves can tear me apart."

"An excellent idea," said Talla as she walked back toward the rock, "although they do prefer their meat tenderized, so maybe we'll drag you behind the horse for a bit first."

"Talla, stop," said Tira suddenly, "I think...we take him with us. Gaelin might be able to find the Ulvvori, but this one knows the Black Sabers. He can help us avoid them and if we can't avoid them, he could help us fight. He's more useful alive. What do you think, Asenna?" Carro watched as she considered him, willing her with everything he had to allow him to live, at least long enough to make this one thing right. After what felt like an eternity, Asenna nodded.

"Alright, but he stays restrained and he goes nowhere near my son," she said. Carro let out a loud sigh of relief, Talla scoffed and walked back behind the rock, and Gaelin just flashed his horrible teeth in a grin. They untied Carro and allowed him to wash his face off and drink from the pool at the base of the rock, with Tira's sword on his neck, but then Gaelin bound his wrists and ankles and sat him under the tree where the horse was also tethered. The animal looked down at him with big curious eyes.

"Fancy meeting you here," Carro said quietly. The horse just snorted in his face and turned away to graze. Carro watched out of the corner of his eye as the twins and Asenna began preparing food. He was desperately hungry, but didn't dare ask to be fed and he eventually fell asleep against the tree with his stomach growling. When he woke up, it was to Gaelin kicking his boots and then hauling him onto his feet.

"Up," said Gaelin, bending down to untie Carro's legs, then attaching another rope to his hands and tying it around the horse's neck. Once they had packed everything, Talla swung herself onto the saddle blanket and took the reins, giving Carro a fiendish smile.

"You best hope he doesn't spook and run," she whispered, "I don't know if I have the strength to stop him. You know, with my injured leg." Carro just nodded, trying his best to ignore her murderous jibes. The party set off with Tira and Asenna walking in front, Talla following them on the horse, and Carro shuffling along beside her. Gaelin walked with Tira for a while, but then dropped back next to Carro.

"How are we doing?" he asked cheerfully.

"I've been better," Carro replied.

"Well, whenever you've had enough, I'm sure Talla would be more than willin' to grant you the sweet release of death."

"There will be *nothing* sweet about it," Talla assured him. Carro tried to focus on walking, even though his legs were starting to shake from hunger and exhaustion and nerves, but the longer they went on the more he stumbled. Eventually, he collapsed onto the forest floor. Talla dragged him a good twenty feet, nearly pulling his shoulders from their sockets, before alerting the others.

"Perhaps we should feed it," she laughed.

"Talla, come on," said Tira, frowning, "Carro, when was the last time you ate?"

"I don't remember," he groaned. They paused for a small meal of hard biscuits and wild apples, and then it was Asenna's turn to ride the horse. Carro said nothing as he walked along, feeling somewhat steadier after the meal, but he could feel her eyes on the back of his head.

"How did you figure out where to find us?" Asenna asked him suddenly. Carro looked up at her. The stress of the last week was evident on her face, but Carro could still see the fierce pride and stubbornness that had been there before, even when Azimar was at his worst.

"Ephie's records, in the palace," he said carefully, "they listed Ferryn as her next-of-kin. Gaelin did the rest."

"What about the farm? Gaelin said you barely touched it. That doesn't sound like the Black Sabers."

"A farmhouse full of kids? Come on. I'm not a monster." Carro let the corner of his mouth pull into a tiny smile. "Can I ask you a question now?"

"That depends..."

"How did you get past the guards and out of the palace?"

"Ephie bribed the guards somehow, and I climbed the wall," Asenna suppressed a small smile too, "the spot where they rebuilt it after the siege."

Carro nodded. "Clever."

"It was Ephie's idea." Suddenly she pulled the horse up and Carro had to stop. She was looking down at him with an intense expression. "What happened to her? Is she alive?"

"I…I don't know," Carro admitted, "when I went to your room that morning, she was there alone. I had her taken to the prison block and then…Azimar sent me after you." A pair of tears fell from Asenna's eyes and she kicked the horse to keep walking.

"You're right about Azimar," she said after a few minutes, "that he's changed. It started after the war, but he would never talk to me about it. I saw how thin he was getting. He was erratic and angry and…violent. He was never like that before. At least…not as often…"

"He was always violent," Carro said quietly, and Asenna's brow furrowed when she looked at him, as if she were concerned.

"I just don't understand what happened," she said, "was it the war?"

"No. During the war he was…happy," said Carro, "look, when I met Azimar, he was thirteen and I was ten. He was supervising my group's training for the army. He helped me when I was struggling, made sure I moved up with him every time he was promoted, but…he was always fighting someone. The generals, the instructors, the other students, his mother, Rogerin, everyone. He could never just…live. There always had to be a conspiracy to uncover or an enemy to defeat. Then he became one of Rogerin's top generals, almost like his son, and there was no one left to fight but the old man himself, so he did, and he won. When he made himself King, and all his detractors had been, well…conveniently assassinated, who was there left to fight? He started seeing threats everywhere, even when they didn't exist. It was the Ulvvori, or the Kashaitis, or me, and then it was you." Carro glanced up and saw Asenna nodding.

"That's what it felt like, yes," she said sadly. "I was so naive. At first I thought he would get better after the war was over. Then I thought he might get better after Fen was born, but…" She turned her face away.

"Fen?" Carro asked, trying to steer them away from talking about Azimar, as he could tell it was upsetting her.

"Fen. Fenrinn," she said, nodding toward the baby in the sling, "that's what I named him, after Ephie's son who was conscripted."

"I didn't know that about Ephie…"

"She had three boys," Asenna told him, "all taken. Ferryn had one too. That's why they moved down here, to find their sons."

"Do a lot of Ulvvori do that?" Carro asked, his heart suddenly marching double-time in his chest, "try to find their boys?" He didn't dare look at Asenna in case she saw how badly he needed to hear the answer.

"Some do," she replied in a bitter voice, "of course, no one ever finds them. Rogerin made sure of that. He had his agents give them new names and beat the memories out of them early on. After they branded them...like cattle." Carro turned his head away and squeezed his eyes shut, trying to block out his own memories of exactly what she was talking about.

"'Forget your family and your name, but never forget what you are,'" he murmured under his breath, then cleared his throat and looked back up at Asenna. "Well, Fen is a good name." He fell back a little, attempting to end the conversation, and Asenna seemed to get the hint, so they walked in silence again. When dusk began to settle in around them, Tira chose a spot to stop and this time when they ate, they gave Carro a bit more food. He was still left tied up beside the horse, but Gaelin was kind enough to remove the saddle blanket and toss it over him this time. It took Carro a long time to fall asleep, between the hard tree root he was using as a pillow, the ropes chafing at his wrists and ankles, and the woolen blanket scratching him everywhere else. When he did sleep, he saw Gade's face and heard the boy's voice repeating over and over: "*I'd rather take my chances with Azimar than with you.*"

The next day when Carro woke up, Gaelin was the only person nearby. The twins and Asenna were nowhere to be seen. He tried to stretch, but having his arms tied behind him made it difficult and Gaelin was no help, just chuckling as he watched Carro struggle.

"Hungry?" Gaelin asked, holding up a hard biscuit. He walked over and untied Carro's hands, then gave him some food and sat down while they both ate.

"Where is everyone?" Carro asked.

"Water," Gaelin grunted with his mouth full of biscuits, "when are you plannin' on tellin' them about that?" He reached over and tapped Carro's shoulder, where the brand was still hidden by his shirt.

"Are you insane?" Carro laughed, "you don't think everything I've done is just a little bit worse when you consider where I came from?"

"In case you ain't noticed, boy," Gaelin growled, "Ulvvori tend to be far more forgivin' of their own than of strangers. You don't see me with ropes around my ankles. Why do you think that is?"

"Because the twins know you? And you've somehow convinced them that you're trustworthy?"

"Don't Asenna know you?"

"No, she doesn't. We've just been...existing near one another for three years. The only thing she knows of me is what she's seen: her husband's loyal dog." He repeated the words she had said to him before the naming ceremony, which admittedly had stung.

"Then maybe you need to let her see a bit more, yeah? Maybe she understands you a little better than you think, and maybe you could use someone other than me on your side."

Carro snorted. "If *this* is you being on my side, then I don't want to know what it looks like when you're against me."

"What can I say?" Gaelin chuckled, "you remind me a bit of my younger self. Just not nearly as good-lookin'."

"If this is the future I'm looking at, I'd better let Talla go ahead and put me out of my misery now," Carro waved his hands vaguely at Gaelin just as the twins reappeared through the trees with Asenna behind them. Tira handed Carro a flask of water, which he tried to conserve despite his desperate thirst. They were up and moving again soon, but Talla was riding the horse today, so Carro tried to distract himself from her constant stream of quiet verbal abuse by considering Gaelin's words.

When he had left, it had not been with the intention of earning anyone's forgiveness. His only thought had been to help get Asenna and her son to Kashait safely, and he had intentionally avoided considering anything beyond that. It had always seemed pointless before, but now Carro allowed himself the briefest moment to imagine what a life away from Azimar and the Black Sabers might look like. As he turned the possibility of surviving, of actually *living*, over in his head, he slowed his pace too much and Talla jerked the rope. The savage glare she shot in his direction made Carro reconsider his chances of survival, so he put the idea back into the locked box in his mind and kept walking.

SEVEN:
THE LULLABY

The trek through the forest had suddenly become far more difficult and Asenna could feel it wearing her thin with each passing hour. With the intensity of their emotions magnified by whatever mysterious force lived in the trees, it seemed that every day was destined to begin and end with some kind of verbal altercation between Talla and Carro, with Tira intervening. The fact was, with Talla's injured leg and Asenna having to care for Fen, they occasionally needed Carro's help setting up and breaking down their small camp. They had to release him from the ropes for this, but Talla found any excuse to remind him that he was living on borrowed time. Carro, for his part, was clearly trying to take her abuse in stride but sometimes he snapped back and it was all Tira could do to prevent Talla from slitting his throat. The atmosphere was dour and Asenna found herself having more and more difficulty controlling the formidable waves of emotion that shifted rapidly from optimism to despair to anger and back again. Focusing on caring for Fen and training with the twins was all that kept her from tearing her own hair out as they walked east day after day.

One night the tension and fear caught up with her. They had stopped for the evening and Asenna had laid Fen out on her cloak as usual. After eating, Tira got up and wiped her hands, then picked up one of Carro's sabers from where they were sitting against a tree.

"I had a thought," she said to Asenna, "you should probably practice against these since that's what they'll be carrying." She handed her short sword to Asenna and then drew Carro's sabers one at a time.

"I can barely defend against one blade yet," Asenna muttered. Her body felt hotter than usual and it was making her irritated. Tira hefted the sabers and examined them carefully.

"Maybe Talla should do it," she said, "it's a bit closer to what she does with the hatchet and the sword." Talla jumped up eagerly and took the sabers from her sister, then scraped the blades together like a cricket rubbing its legs and Carro winced. Tira came and stood behind Asenna and tried to show her how to stand and how to move the single sword to block Talla's slow, false attacks with the sabers. Asenna found it extremely difficult to track what was happening with two swords coming at her, especially with how heavy and slow her body felt and how fast her head began to spin as they practiced.

"This is not working!" she cried after the fifteenth time she made a mistake, allowing Talla past her defenses.

"It would be easier to learn if she was actually teaching you the right way," Carro said from behind Talla, where he was peeling the shells off some nuts they had found. Talla spun around and took a threatening step toward him.

"What the fuck did you say?"

"Your form is terrible. You're all over the place," Carro told her, "you're fighting like a Wolf Rider, not a Black Saber."

Talla let out a low growl. "And how the fuck would you know the difference? Have you killed enough of us to understand how we fight?"

"I spent two years fighting alongside the Riders during the war," Carro said, lifting his chin a little, "you think I didn't pay attention? What kind of officer would I have been if I didn't use everyone's strengths to my advantage?"

Tira let out a loud scoff. "There is no way you were old enough to be commanding soldiers in that war," she said, coming over to stand beside her sister and giving Carro a suspicious look.

"I'm going to take that as a compliment," Carro laughed darkly, "Azimar trusted me, remember? He gave me a command." The twins glanced over at Asenna, who nodded, but even just that small movement made her muscles burn and she realized that she was starting to feel a little unsteady on her feet as the argument continued.

"Fine, *Captain*," Talla snorted, "what am I doing that is so offensive to your sensibilities?"

Carro held out his bound hands. "I can show you."

"Do you think I'm stupid?" barked Talla, "just call it out and I'll fix it." She turned back and held the sabers up. Asenna lifted her sword, but the dizziness was rapidly overcoming her.

"Wrong!" Carro called, his voice flat but slightly amused. Talla was seething and she turned back to yell at him, but Asenna threw the sword down and put her hands on her head.

"Can you all just shut the fuck up for a minute?!" she cried. Everyone fell silent, then Asenna's vision went black and she stumbled to the side. She felt Talla catch her and heard Tira call her name, but everything was blurry as she sat down hard on the forest floor, heart hammering.

"What's wrong, Asenna?" Talla was saying in her ear.

"I…I don't know," she murmured, "I think I just…need to lie down." Tira came over and helped her over to her cloak.

"*Izlani*, please help her…we don't need this right now," Tira whispered. Dizziness, nausea, and fever rapidly overcame Asenna's body, and there were shooting pains in her breast when she tried to nurse Fen. As the evening progressed, her body was wracked with chills and she found herself trembling and sweating, lying on her cloak while Tira sat beside her, wiping her head with a wet cloth. Gaelin and Talla tried to figure out how much time they could spend resting before they were in danger of being found, but Asenna found that she could barely focus on their voices. Fen slept beside her, blissfully unaware as Asenna drifted in and out of consciousness.

"It's nursing fever…" she told Tira during a lucid moment, "I had it once before…just after Fen was born, but it wasn't this bad."

"What can we do?" Tira asked softly.

"We need to bring down her fever and she needs to nurse the kid as much as possible," Gaelin said, "I know somethin' that could help, if I can find it." He turned and set off into the forest and no one dared to question how he knew so much. The fever made Asenna's vision blurry and she slept for tiny stretches of time before the pain roused her. When she slept, her dreams were nonsensical and fragmented. She was barely awake when Gaelin returned and started stripping the leaves off the plants he had found, giving them to her to chew on one by one.

The leaves helped ease the pain and fever enough for her to sleep more soundly, but in the middle of the night Asenna's dreams turned from vague shapes and shadows to fully fledged nightmares. She was lost in the forest, carrying Fen, and they were surrounded by monsters she couldn't quite see. The creatures seemed to be formed of darkness, flitting between the tree trunks, their foul and rattling breath nipping at her neck as she ran. Then suddenly her father, Larke, was there beside her, holding the monsters at bay with his great longbow. He was exactly as Asenna remembered him, his black beard streaked with gray and kept in a neat braid for her mother's sake, golden eyes dancing as he fired his arrows into the dark corners of the dream-forest. He looked back at Asenna and smiled, then put his hand on Fen's cheek and began to sing an old Ulvvori lullaby:

Little one,
Don't you fear,
As you dream, I will hold you.
Always here,
Forever near,
Through the storm, my love is true.

His gentle voice calmed Asenna and Fen, but the shadowy creatures around them crept further out of the trees, reaching out their long, spindly fingers and wrapping Larke in a shroud, pulling him away. Fen began to wail and Asenna held onto her father's hand tighter.

"Please don't go!" she cried.

"You'll be alright, little Senna," Larke called, still smiling as he was consumed by the blackness and Fen continued to bawl in her arms.

"Please, Da! You have to sing to him!" Asenna begged, "please! Please…you have to sing! Please! It's the only thing!" She could no longer see her father's face, but a soft voice drifted over her ears again, singing another verse of the same lullaby:

Sleep my son,
Safe and sound,
We shall never forsake you.
Lost or found,
Free or bound,
Our love will ever see you through.

The song soothed Fen's crying and calmed Asenna so that she was finally able to roll her body over and open her eyes. But it was not her father sitting there, holding Fen's little hand. It was Carro. A sudden jolt of anger gave Asenna the strength to sit up on her elbow and reach for the dagger she kept under her cloak.

"Get away from him," she whispered, pressing the blade hard against the veins on Carro's forearm before he could react. In the same moment, Talla managed to limp over and put the tip of her sword against his neck. Carro pulled his bound hands away from Fen and pushed himself backwards.

"You said to sing to him…I thought…I didn't mean to--" Carro stuttered. Asenna sat up, realizing that her fever had finally broken and feeling the strength rush back into her limbs.

"I was dreaming," she said, "it was my father…not you…"

"I'm sorry. I didn't mean to scare you."

"Wait a minute," Talla said, pushing the tip of the sword further into

Carro's neck, "how did *you* know that song?"

Carro's face drained of color. "I...I don't know...I must have heard Asenna singing it before..." Asenna sat on her knees and picked Fen up. He was calm and happy, not a sign of the distress from her dream.

"I *never* sing that verse..." she said softly, questions tumbling wildly through her aching head. She almost felt like she hadn't quite left the dream-forest behind.

"Because that verse was added later," Talla finished the sentence for her, "for the boys who were conscripted...like my brother. We taught it to them so they wouldn't forget their families." Her voice had woken Tira and Gaelin, who both stirred and sat up.

"What did he do?" Tira asked, scrambling for her sword.

"He was singing, but he shouldn't know those words, unless..." Asenna felt a small pit open up in her stomach as she realized the only possible answer and wondered how she had never noticed it before. She slowly leaned toward Carro, who turned his head away, but did not try to stop her as she pulled the neck of his shirt back, revealing the ugly pink scar on his right shoulder. Tira let out an audible gasp and Talla squatted down and grabbed Carro's face, turning it back toward them.

"What was your name? Before they took you?" Talla demanded, her voice suddenly high and thin as her yellow eyes desperately searched his face. Asenna could not read Carro's expression, but she saw his hands start to shake and he clenched them, then jerked his face away.

"Why the fuck does that matter?"

"Tell me!" Talla snarled. Tira came up behind her.

"I don't remember!" Carro's eyes darted between the two of them, alarmed at the line of questioning, but Asenna was holding her breath, remembering what Talla had said about their younger brother.

"Do you remember anything at all? Your mother's name?" Tira asked, voice wavering with emotion. Carro glanced between them again and seemed hesitant to answer.

"Eirini. Her name was Eirini and she had sort of...reddish hair. That's all I remember, besides the song..." he said at last. Talla let out a strangled sob as Tira grabbed her shoulders.

"It's not him, Tal, come on." Tira pulled her sister away from Carro, then went back and sat on her knees in front of him.

"Why didn't you tell us?" she asked.

"Why does it matter? Would it stop you from killing me?"

"Yes..." Tira said earnestly, "Ulvvori don't kill one another. Everyone knows that. It's the whole reason Rogerin started the conscriptions in the first place, so we couldn't fight back without killing our own sons or brothers. Eventually we got so desperate...we had no other choice." Carro looked around and they all nodded. Asenna's head was still spinning, but she turned to Gaelin.

"Did you know about this the entire time?"

"I had my suspicions from the start and then I confirmed them, aye," he admitted, "but it was the boy's secret to tell or keep, not mine."

"Why keep it hidden? What were you playing at?" said Tira. Carro answered her, but looked directly at Asenna when he did.

"I wanted you to see me for what I am now, not for something that happened to me a long time ago that doesn't matter."

"Did Azimar know?" Asenna asked. She suddenly wondered how many times her husband might have wielded this secret to manipulate Carro and she felt a stab of pity, but quickly brushed it away.

"Yes, he knew," Carro said, "he was the only one."

"He knew…and he still made you stand there and watch what he did to us at The Den?" Tira asked breathlessly.

"He was punishing me," Carro hunched his shoulders and shook his head, "when he started sending soldiers north to open the mines, I questioned him. I thought we were close enough that he would listen to me, that I could make him see it was a bad idea, that he was breaking his promises to the Ulvvori. He saw it as disloyalty. When we got there and I realized what was happening…"

"Why didn't you stop it?" Talla spat, angry again, "you could have killed him. Just like you killed Rogerin and all those other people. Isn't that your job?"

"Talla…" said Tira quietly, "it wouldn't have made a difference. By the time Azimar got there, the Black Sabers already had their orders."

"I never would have been able to touch him," Carro said to Talla, "I would have been executed on the spot just for trying."

"Then you would have at least died with some kind of honor!" Talla's voice was harsh, but Asenna could also hear deep sadness, "just like our wolves and our friends! Just like Aija!"

"Don't you *dare* use her name to condemn him," Tira hissed at her sister, "you've had the privilege of never having to make such a difficult choice, Talla! Be grateful for that!" Talla's eyes widened in shock and she turned, disappearing into the trees again. Tira wrapped her own arms around her torso and Asenna could tell she was holding back tears. Suddenly, she leaned forward and seized Carro's bound feet. In one swift motion, she yanked a knife from her boot and cut the ropes away, then freed his hands and threw herself back down on her blanket.

"I still don't understand why you didn't tell us," Asenna said to Carro, lowering the dagger that was still clutched in her hand.

"Well, first off, I didn't realize the Ulvvori had a law against mistreating one another. If I'd known it could make Talla leave me alone, I'd have led with it," Carro snapped, "and second, I don't understand why it matters so much. I'm still the one who's been hunting you. I'm still the one responsible for Ferryn's death. I'm still 'your husband's loyal dog,' right?"

Asenna looked at Carro and she could all but see the anguish in his eyes.

"Are you?" she asked quietly, holding his gaze.

"No," he replied, "I seem to have slipped my chain and run away."

Gaelin snorted. "Dogs'll do that when you kick them one too many times. How about you all shut up and go back to sleep now?"

"I don't want anyone's sympathy, Asenna," Carro told her, his voice softening a little.

"It's not sympathy, trust me," Tira said, "it's our laws. I won't be taking my eyes off you until we find the Ulvvori, but I can't keep you prisoner any more than I could keep Talla, and I can't stop you from leaving either."

"You would just…let me go? How do you know I wouldn't go back?"

"If you did, then maybe I'd get to kill you in a fair fight," Tira said with a wry smile.

Carro hesitated. "I'll get you to Kashait, and then you'll never have to see me again. That's the least I can do."

"Fair enough," Tira said. She turned her attention to checking Asenna's fever and getting her water, but Asenna was watching Carro as he slid back down in the notch between two tree roots and draped a hand over his eyes. Achy and exhausted from the fever, she could not find her way back to sleep as her natural curiosity took over and she felt compelled to talk to Tira about what had just happened.

"Did you know Carro's mother? Eirini?" she whispered.

"No, I didn't. But I don't think it would help either way. Seems like he's got it pretty heavily repressed."

"Can you blame him? Everyone knows what they did to those boys, and Azimar wasn't any kinder to him, if we're being honest. I can't imagine that kind of life…" Tira frowned at her.

"My sympathies are *extremely* limited considering the situation. He's still a Black Saber more than anything else. Just…keep him at arm's length from that bleeding heart of yours, alright? This doesn't change anything."

"My bleeding heart," Asenna laughed softly, "you're probably right."

The next day, Asenna's fever had vanished and the pain in her breast was minimal enough that they decided to keep moving, calculating that reinforcements could be riding along the northern edge of the forest already. The plan was for Gaelin to take Pan and ride to try and find the Ulvvori once they got close enough to the plains that stretched between the forest and the border. The rest of them would press on and try for Kashait, assuming that

Azimar's forces did not find them first. The twins made the decision to allow Carro to walk without binding his hands or even tying him to Pan's neck. Instead, they made him walk at the front of the group and Tira kept her loaded crossbow aimed lazily at his back the entire day. None of them spoke until they stopped at midday. Asenna could tell that the tension between the twins had not yet broken and she was loath to get in the middle of it. It was an awkward silence, only broken by Fen's occasional babbling or crying and the sounds of the forest.

As the rhythm of Pan's easy gait and her own exhaustion lulled Asenna into a sort of trance, she watched Fen sleeping and could not help but imagine what Carro and the other boys like him had endured. The Ulvvori had many names for the particular days that made up their calendar, names that marked the cycle of traveling, hunting, fishing, harvesting, and building. Giving a name to a certain day meant that it was important, that it was something to be celebrated, or a time to make a transition. But the day that the men arrived each year was The Day With No Name. It was a day that most of the Ulvvori could not even speak about, so intense was the pain. Every spring, just before they moved to their summer home at The Den, the men would come up from the south in wagons and fan out through the camp, taking any boy who had turned five during the previous year. Any resistance to the conscriptions was swiftly punished. Asenna's immediate family had always been shielded from it by their Wolfsight, but her aunt, Dirye, had been killed while trying to escape with her own son. The boy had been loaded into a wagon still covered in his mother's blood while Asenna's parents had held Tolian back so he wouldn't be lost too.

After decades of this genocide, when Azimar had come to them and promised an end to the suffering, they had seen the offer of an alliance as a blessing from Izlani herself. When Asenna had agreed to Azimar's offer, she had been thinking only of her cousin Kirann, and the light that had left her uncle's eyes that day. As Asenna recalled everything that had driven her to agree to her ill-fated marriage, a small seed of sympathy for Carro took root in her mind. She tried to bury the feeling, but by the time they stopped that evening she was desperate to talk to someone about it. The twins went to find a rabbit for their supper, since they were running low on supplies, so Asenna nursed and changed Fen, then approached Gaelin while he was attempting to clean Pan's hooves.

"Are you leaving soon?" she asked. Gaelin dropped Pan's massive foot to the ground and the horse's long tail flicked him in the face.

"Tonight or tomorrow. If this blockhead will cooperate," he panted, sweat pouring from his face, "but he'll barely let me pick his hooves, never mind ride him, so I guess we'll see." Carro walked over and held his hand out.

"I can do it," he offered. Gaelin hesitated for a moment, then handed the knife over and stepped back. Asenna watched Carro lift Pan's feet one by one and carefully chip the dirt, moss, and rocks out. The giant animal held perfectly still for him, without so much as a twitch.

"Well, I'll be damned," Gaelin laughed, "at least someone here likes you, boy."

"Oh, he doesn't like *me*," Carro flipped the knife and held it out for Gaelin to take, then reached into his pocket and pulled out a handful of melted and broken sugar cubes. Pan licked them greedily from Carro's palm and then nibbled his sleeve, looking for more.

"Ah," Gaelin said, "bribery. Very effective. I'll make a dishonest man out of you yet!" He slapped Carro on the shoulder and then went to lay out his blanket on the ground near the firepit. Carro wandered off a little way to continue pulling bark off a fallen tree limb for the fire, while Asenna sat on her own cloak next to Fen, who had his foot in his mouth.

"Do you think we can trust him after you leave?" Asenna asked Gaelin.

"You've known him longer than any of us, girlie. You tell me."

"Well, obviously I didn't know him *that* well. Besides, just because you know someone doesn't mean you can trust them. I trusted Azimar and look where that got me," Asenna gestured around at the forest.

"Sounds to me like you both trusted the wrong person," Gaelin said flatly, "and you'll spend the rest of *your* life makin' that up to your son. Who's Carro got to make it up to except you and the Ulvvori? From where I'm standin', two of you got more in common than not."

"So you're saying we should trust him?" Asenna ran her hands through her cropped hair, thinking hard. It wasn't beyond her to forgive, but she also wasn't sure if she could trust herself to make that kind of decision, and she had to consider Fen's wellbeing.

"I'm not the one to tell you who to trust. Maybe you just need to see it with your own two eyes. But I was there when he left his men. What I saw is that he's all twisted up and don't even trust himself. He still went against twenty-some-odd years of whatever they did to him and came to find you, knowin' the twins would probably kill him on sight. He could've just run north…disappeared, left you to your fate. Well…that's not nothin'."

"He doesn't get a pass for making *one* good decision."

"You people know I charge extra for the advice, right?" Gaelin grunted.

"I'll remember next time," Asenna laughed, "thank you, Gaelin." Before Asenna could think about anything else, the twins returned with two large rabbits and she realized that her stomach was growling. Asenna could tell that the twins had managed to work out their disagreement and they even decided lighten the mood with a few stories as everyone sat down to help start a fire and prepare the food. After they ate, Gaelin offered to regale them with a story about one of his smuggling jobs, which turned out to be far more lewd than they had bargained for. By the end they were all laughing and pleading with him to shut up. Asenna knew that the good feelings were only being magnified by the magic of the forest, but she tried to enjoy it all the same, grateful for the distraction from whatever might be coming.

Once the sun set, Tira told Gaelin that he needed to leave. They had decided it would be safer for him to travel at night, and Carro had fashioned a makeshift torch out of a branch wrapped in cloth, which Talla then soaked with some of the clear liquid from the bottles she carried. Gaelin's face twisted in discomfort as he swung onto Pan's back, but he took Tira's crossbow and quiver full of bolts without complaint.

"I hope you're keepin' a tally, boy," he growled at Carro, "because I'm startin' to think I ain't gettin' paid for this job."

Carro laughed and his face relaxed slightly. "Gaelin, if you can find us a miracle, I will work off the debt every day for the rest of my life. Just find the Ulvvori and don't get killed," he said, then added more quietly, "thank you…for everything."

"Be careful," Gaelin said, looking at Talla specifically. She nodded as he tugged on Pan's reins and rode away into the darkness of the forest. The four of them watched him go in silence, but Fen started whimpering and Asenna went to go nurse him. Talla and Tira settled down on their cloaks as well, and Carro took a blanket that Gaelin had left behind and pulled it over to a nearby tree, away from the fire. Once Fen had finished and fallen asleep, Asenna set him down and wrapped one side of the cloak around him.

"I can take the first watch," she said to Talla, who was sharpening her hatchet again even though she had barely needed to use it. Asenna guessed it was some kind of nervous habit.

"Are you sure?" Talla asked, "I don't mind watching him."

"I'm not tired," Asenna assured her, "just leave me your sword?" Talla shrugged and passed it over, then wrapped up in her blanket and rolled over. Once Asenna was sure that the twins were asleep, she went and sat in front of Carro, who was whittling away at a stick with the sharp edge of a rock. He looked up warily as she sat down.

"Perfect time to kill me," he remarked, "while they're both asleep."

"I'm not going to kill you," Asenna said, holding her hands up, "I just want to talk. Three years we knew each other…why didn't you ever just tell me? I know we never really got along, but…"

Carro raised his eyebrows. "Azimar made it very clear I wasn't allowed to tell *anyone*, but especially not you."

"Why me?"

"He had this…fear, I guess, that if I got too close to the Ulvvori, I would leave and try to go back. That's why I wasn't with him the day you met, when he came to ask for the alliance."

"I wouldn't have told him I knew," Asenna said quietly. Carro looked up at her with a strange expression.

"You're right, we never got along," he said, "but…I always respected you for the way you could stand up to him…completely unafraid."

"I think it's easier to not be afraid when you have a family of Riders at your back. I knew he would never *really* hurt me because he was too scared of them."

"See…I never had that," Carro muttered, "there was nothing and no one standing between me and him if I said the wrong thing. That's why I never told you, or anyone else."

"I'm sorry," Asenna murmured. "Especially for the times I said something that got you in trouble. I know there were a few."

Carro waved his hand. "It doesn't matter now."

"When we find the Ulvvori," said Asenna softly, "maybe…I could help you look for your family. Your mother." Carro winced.

"No," he said firmly. Asenna was surprised at the ice in his voice.

"You…you don't want to know what happened to her?"

"She didn't care what happened to me…"

"What? Why would you think that?"

"Asenna…not every mother is as devoted as you," muttered Carro. "Why do you even care so much? Why would you want to help me?"

Asenna shrugged. "Call it my 'bleeding heart,' or maybe I'm just nosy and stubborn."

"I'm going to go with nosy and stubborn," Carro said, setting his stick down, "look…if I tell you, will you stop asking me about it? All of it?"

"Yes, I promise."

"Fine…" Carro took a deep breath, "The day they came to take us, I saw other families, mothers, parents, siblings, and they were fighting, struggling, screaming…*begging* the men not to take their sons. They tried. Even if they failed, even if they were injured or killed, they *tried* to stop it from happening. They were desperate and scared and sad. My mother…took me up to the wagons, told me to be brave, and then just…walked away. Like I was…a dog she didn't want anymore." Asenna could feel his discomfort in telling the story. He refused to look her in the eye and she could see his hands trembling even though he was squeezing them together so hard the blood was draining away.

"I'm so sorry," Asenna whispered, "what about your father?"

"Never had one. It was always just me and her."

Asenna finally understood what had happened back in the glen. "Is that why you let us go? Because you thought I was giving Fen up to save myself?"

Carro nodded. "After everything else I've done, I couldn't be the one who forced a mother to make that kind of choice." He finally met her eyes and Asenna felt every ounce of his agony come down over her like a fog. She knew it had to be the magic of the forest, but the tears filled her eyes anyway and she tried to blink them away.

"I won't mention it again."

"Thank you," Carro said, picking his stick back up.

"But you should know," Asenna said, "I understand the feeling. Not exactly the same, but, when my family agreed to Azimar's terms…the marriage, I was so afraid and confused. I didn't understand why he had chosen me, why it was on my shoulders. I only agreed to it because I couldn't stand the thought of letting everyone down that way, of throwing away an opportunity to end everything we had been through. During the war, when I wouldn't hear from anyone for months, I hated them because it felt like they didn't care what happened to me. I felt alone and unwanted and…angry."

Carro seemed genuinely surprised. "I know it was part of the deal, your marriage, but…I always thought you wanted him. You seemed so in love at first."

"I was young and naive, and he was so charming," Asenna laughed bitterly, "I *wanted* to love him, and I wanted him to love me, because I thought that would make me forget about everything else. But I learned that you can't rely on other people to love you, because most of the time they won't…or they can't. You have to just…carry yourself."

Carro studied her face for a moment. "And what if you can't?" he asked, "what if you can barely even stand to live in your own skin minute to minute?" Asenna looked around, trying to find a way to explain what she wanted to say, and her eyes landed on a small green snake that was making its way through the grass a few feet away. She leaned over and scooped it up, then handed it to Carro, who raised his eyebrows, but took the creature from her carefully.

"You shed the skin and start over," she said. Carro watched the little snake twist itself around his hands for a few seconds and nodded. Sensing that the conversation was over, Asenna went back to sit beside Fen. She watched Carro out of the corner of her eye as he let the snake wrap around his wrist a few times, looking at it as if he had never seen one before. Eventually, he placed it back in the grass and laid down between the tree roots, falling asleep quickly. Asenna dug through her bag and found a needle and thread that Ephie had hidden at the bottom, then set about sewing up a hole in her cloak. She had always liked sewing because it kept her hands busy while allowing her mind to wander. Tonight, her mind had so many places to visit that by the time she woke Tira up to take over, she had patched or mended her own cloak, an extra shirt, several of Fen's swaddling blankets, and the trousers she was wearing. Tira eyed the neat little pile as she took her position beside the dying fire.

"Busy little bee," she remarked, "are you nervous?"

"Maybe a little…about making it to Kashait," Asenna admitted.

"Well, get some rest," Tira said, "my guess is that tomorrow we'll start seeing the trees thin out and that means we're getting close."

"And then what?"

"We head for Kashait as fast as we can, hope that the Black Sabers don't catch up with us, or that Gaelin doesn't just run off and sell the horse."

"Is that…a possibility?"

"Anything's a possibility with that one, but he did owe Pa a favor, so maybe he'll follow through. If not, are you ready to fight?" Tira's face became serious.

"I may not have a choice," Asenna answered, looking over at Fen, "and I'd do anything to protect him. But I don't have my own sword and Gaelin took your crossbow."

"We still have his sabers," Tira suggested, waving over to where Carro's blades were lying next to Talla, "I can use those and you'll take my sword."

"If they find us, Carro will need them, won't he?"

"You trust him enough to give them back?" Tira furrowed her brow.

"It's not that I trust him, but I don't know that we really have a choice, do we? If the Sabers catch up to us, he has to fight."

"And what if he turns right around and fights for them? He hasn't tried to attack us yet because he's been outnumbered, but that could change when he has backup."

"What's the bigger risk? That we have one extra opponent or that we have one fewer defender?" Asenna pointed out.

Tira weighed the options. "I hope it doesn't come to that," she said finally, "get some sleep, Asenna." Feeling the heaviness of midnight in her body at last, Asenna curled up next to Fen and closed her eyes.

EIGHT: DEFENDER

Carro woke up to a sharp boot kick from Talla. He sat up, rubbing his eyes, and realized that for the first night in a very long time, he had not dreamed. Not about his mother, or The Den, or the explosion at the bridge, or Gade, or Azimar or anything else. His mind was completely blank. It felt strange to wake up without his heart already racing and body tensed. *Am I...well-rested?* He wondered, *is this what it feels like?* Talla and Tira were packing their things into the one set of saddlebags that they still carried, while Asenna was sitting and nursing Fen. He clearly remembered their talk the night before, but was determined not to mention it because he felt strongly he might have hallucinated the entire thing. Once they had eaten and were nearly ready to leave, Asenna beckoned him over to where she was standing and held out a long length of cloth.

"Can you help?" she asked, "the twins have their hands full."

Carro didn't move. "Uh, what is it...that I'm helping with?"

"It's a sling, for Fen," Asenna said, "just put it around him and then tie it on the middle of my back. It's simple, I promise." She held the front of the cloth around Fen on her chest, then draped one end around her shoulder and the other around her hip. Carro took the two ends and pulled them behind her, then tied a firm knot.

"Perfect! Shall we?" Asenna set out toward the east and the twins followed, indicating that Carro should walk in between them. He couldn't help but notice that they did indeed have their hands full of weapons. Talla wore her sword and held her hatchet, while Tira carried her sword and had a long hunting knife stuck in her boot. They also each had one of his sabers still hanging on their belts.

"Will I be getting those back if we're attacked?" he asked Talla, "what do your laws say about allowing me to defend myself?"

"We'll cross that bridge when we come to it," she snapped at him.

"Yeah, or you could just blow it up," Carro muttered under his breath. Tira actually heard him and laughed out loud. Talla glared at her.

"Come on, Tal, you set yourself up for that one," Tira chuckled, but Talla just rolled her eyes. As they walked, Tira started up quietly singing a song that felt familiar to Carro, but he couldn't place it, and he couldn't understand the Ulvvori lyrics.

"What is it? The song? I've heard it before," he asked, moving up beside Asenna with the twins flanking them.

"A Song for Moving Day," she said, "it's the one we sing when we're going north in the springtime. You never walk with your family, only your friends, and all the children beat on their little drums to keep the pace." Carro felt a memory break into his mind of walking up a rocky mountain path holding a small drum in his hand and beating it with a bone.

"I...think I remember that...," he said slowly, "and everyone picked wildflowers and threw them onto the path?"

"That's right! It was always my favorite day," Asenna said, but her face fell a little bit.

"What's wrong?" Carro asked.

"I wish we could go back. Kashait is friendly...but it's not home."

"We'll go back," said Talla behind them, "if it's the last thing I do, we'll go home again. After the attack on The Den, all the Riders swore we wouldn't rest until it was done...someday."

"Do you think the Kashaitis would help?" Carro wondered.

"They don't like to get involved in our messes," Tira told him, "so I doubt it. Still, if we can make it there and they let us stay long enough, maybe we can rebuild our own forces enough to go back."

"The trees are thinning. Look," said Talla, pointing to the ground just ahead of them. She was right. Instead of the dappled sunspots they had been getting used to, they were starting to see larger patches of light coming through the canopies. The grass was not nearly as green and lush, and there was less moss growing around the trunks of the trees. Everything was drying out from contact with the direct sunlight.

"Alright," Tira said, coming around to face Carro, "time to work. What are we looking for? We know they'll be coming from the north, but how many? And what kind of soldiers?"

Carro squeezed his eyes shut so he could think. "Azimar has no way of knowing whether we've found the Ulvvori yet," he said slowly, "but he knows that the Wolf Riders will wreak havoc on any force, especially out here in the open. He'd send a larger company of cavalry, with mounted archers, and Black Sabers as scouts. If the Black Sabers find us first, and there's no wolves, then we're fair game. If there *are* wolves, then they know at least one of them could probably get back to the cavalry and lead them to us."

"How many cavalry?"

"I can't say for sure," Carro answered, "at least a few hundred. A smaller force can move faster, but a larger one stands more of a chance against the wolves."

"We held off four hundred of Rogerin's cavalry with only a hundred Riders at Hallow Hill," said Talla, "remember, Tira?"

"How could I forget?" Tira murmured.

Carro cleared his throat. "I was at Hallow Hill too," he said in a low voice. The twins both stared at him and he suddenly felt quite self-conscious.

"I don't remember the Sabers being there."

"We weren't 'officially' the Black Sabers yet," Carro explained, "but we were there, right alongside you. We lost a dozen men taking that damn fort, and then two more in the storm after. It was so cold we couldn't even drink without freezing our mouths." The twins glanced at each other and Carro could tell they finally believed something he was saying.

"We only survived that storm because of our wolves," Talla's voice was absentminded.

"A lot has changed since then," Tira said quietly. Carro reached out and put his hand on her elbow, knowing that he was risking having it sliced off. He saw Talla raise her hatchet, but did not move his hand as he tried to hold Tira's gaze, praying that he could get through to her.

"I was on your side then, and I'm on your side now, alright?" he said. After a few moments, she nodded and turned to keep walking. Carro followed suit, noticing with some relief that the twins were now allowing him to walk beside them.

It took a full day of travel to reach the part of the forest where the trees spaced out enough that they could see the open plain before them. It seemed like it stretched on forever, marked by low rolling hillocks and scraggly trees. They camped just inside the tree line, forgoing a fire and carefully rationing what little food they had left, their eyes constantly trained on the northern horizon. The rather upbeat mood from the morning had turned tense and Carro kept himself busy sharpening the end of a stout branch with his rock, just in case the twins did not see fit to return his sabers during an attack. When he finished the crude weapon, he tried throwing it like a javelin a few times to make sure the balance was at least halfway decent, then leaned it up against a tree and returned to his blanket. Asenna was looking up at the sky when he sat back down. It was a clear night, but there was only a tiny sliver of the moon visible above them and the deep crease between Asenna's eyes told him that she was worried.

"What's wrong?" he asked.

"She's turning her face away from us," said Asenna quietly.

Carro looked around. "Who is?"

"Izlani..." said Asenna, glancing over at him, "the moon?"

"I know the name, but what do you mean about turning away??"

"I guess they wouldn't have taught you anything about the Ulvvori, would they?" Talla said in a bitter voice.

"I asked about it once and got a nasty beating. Never did it again," Carro shrugged and then saw Asenna looking at him, completely horrified. "Sorry, you didn't need to hear that."

"Alright, where do I start?" Talla sighed. Carro shifted so that he could face her and listen. "Izlani is our Mother. The earth, *Kharia,* is her body and the moon is her shining face. When she turns it away, she's turning her attention to the stars, *rani no'shela,* the 'light before people,' her first children. Izlani created the *no'shela* first, then the animals, but the *no'shela* moved into the sky when *Kharia* became too crowded. I'll tell you that one another time. Izlani loved the animals, especially the *ulvvia,* dire wolves, but she also wanted to create children who were more like her. She made the first humans, *shela,* under the earth and then brought them up to the surface, into the sunlight. They scattered to every corner of the world and many of them forgot about their Mother, like children tend to do. The Ulvvori still remember her because we were created later, as companions for the dire wolves." The steady cadence of Talla's voice had pulled Carro into something that felt like a trance, and when she stopped suddenly he blinked as if he was just waking up.

"The Ulvvori were created *for* the wolves?" he asked.

"Yes. To help them protect the mountains from other humans."

"Why would the dire wolves need help from humans?" Carro laughed.

"Frost, my wolf, used to tell me that humans respect other humans more than they do animals," said Tira, "so the dire wolves asked Izlani for their *own* humans."

"That makes sense," Carro murmured, "but why do only some of the Ulvvori have the Wolfsight? Why not all of you?"

"Us..." Tira said, looking up at him, "you count too...whether you like it or not. That's how the pack works."

"Us..." Carro repeated under his breath, feeling a little disoriented at the thought that he might be able to belong anywhere.

"When Izlani brought us up from under the earth," Talla explained, "she gave the first Ulvvori a choice to drink from the sacred springs that supposedly flow through the mountains. She told them that if they drank, they would have a bond with the wolves, but it meant they would have to be fighters and protectors. Some Ulvvori chose not to drink. It's impossible to build a society with only warriors, and Izlani wanted us to have the bond of a family...a pack, where we each have our own strengths and we take care of each other."

"Tell me more," said Carro eagerly, leaning forward.

"Alright," Talla gave him the first genuine smile he had ever seen and leaned back on her elbows, "what would you like to hear? How the Midwinter Mountains were created? Or maybe the story of Seren, the girl who became the Northern Star?"

"Maybe...just start with the basics?" Carro said, smiling back.

"Fair enough. Izlani's lover is *Kusa,* the Sun, whose light helped create their children. It's Kusa who feeds and warms us, and lights our way in the daytime. Izlani gives us the nighttime to love each other and tell stories and dream. The reason Izlani shines so brightly, even during the day, is because of how strong Kusa's love for her is. It lights the entire world, day and night." Carro felt his mind suddenly flooded with all the questions he had always wanted answers to but had held back for fear of punishment or discovery.

"During the war, some of the Riders told me that the Ulvvori used to have rulers, monarchs, of their own," he asked, "is that true? What happened to them?"

"Yes," Talla nodded, "they were called the Midwinter Kings and Queens. The Riders chose from amongst themselves and at first, it was just the Rider who was the most senior, the strongest, the wisest, you get the idea. Sort of like what Tolian is for us now, but far more powerful. They would rule until they died or stepped down, and then the Riders would choose the next King or Queen. From what we know, over time it became too focused on passing the crown through families. The Riders would arrange marriages between their children to try and create bloodlines that were the strongest in terms of the Wolfsight. The dire wolves didn't like it, because it was too much like what the *shela* in the south did, so they put a stop to it. They banned the practice of arranging marriages and the last Midwinter Queen stepped down voluntarily maybe...five hundred years ago. We had peace amongst ourselves since then, until Rogerin."

Carro shook his head. "Five hundred years of peace. I doubt the rest of Esmadia will ever see that. Seems like we have another civil war between generals or kings or princes every generation. If people could just--"

"People are too busy trying to survive to do anything about who is sitting on the throne," Tira said, "even though it's the people on the throne who are making it so hard for them to survive. It's all just a vicious cycle they can't break themselves out of."

"Well maybe someone should help them break it," Carro replied.

Talla snorted. "Good luck finding someone. The Kashaitis will do just about anything to stay out of our wars, even building that ridiculous border wall, and all the other countries overseas have no stake in it. Esmadia has to figure out how to help itself." Tira responded to her sister, but Carro's mind drifted off elsewhere and he looked over at Asenna again, wondering why she was so quiet. She was still sitting in the same spot, holding what looked like a large tooth in her hand and turning it over and over.

"Are you ok?" he whispered, trying to ignore the twins' debate, which was becoming quite heated. Asenna looked down at the tooth.

"It still feels like everything is on my shoulders sometimes," she said in a melancholy voice, "all I want to do is keep Fen safe, but Tira's right about Esmadia. It's a vicious cycle and there's no one there to break it. Maybe…I have an obligation to try."

"I think," said Carro, choosing his words carefully, "it's too much for one person to fix an entire country that's had what? Twenty-five hundred years to fix itself. I think you *feel* an obligation to take care of everyone…because you're a good person, but you shouldn't confuse that with an *actual* obligation."

Asenna gave him a weary smile. "I guess you know me better than I thought," she said, laying down and pulling Fen under her arm. "Don't let those two kill each other, alright?" She waved her hand at the twins, who were still arguing.

"Oh, you couldn't pay me enough to break up one of their fights," Carro laughed.

~~~

The next morning, the four of them tried to decide if they should stay put and wait for Gaelin, but the twins decided that, in the absence of any Black Saber sightings, they should press on toward Kashait. There was a chance they could make it to the border wall before midnight if they just kept walking. Carro didn't like it, but he had little choice in the matter. By late morning, he was practically walking backwards so he could watch for an attack. At midday, they came across a small, abandoned village, only a dozen or so buildings scattered along the remnants of an old road, and decided to rest and eat inside the crumbling ruins. One of the walls had fallen away on the side, allowing a perfect vantage point for Carro to sit and watch the northwestern horizon. Just as they were beginning to pack up to leave, he sat bolt upright and squinted. The twins came over to his position and crouched down, looking to where he was pointing just north of the tree line where they had come from.

"Dust," he said quietly, "a lot of horses."

"We can't run. They'll catch up with us," Tira put a hand on the hilt of her sword, "we have to hide and hope they don't search the village."

"No!" Talla hissed, "we make a stand here!"

"Are you insane? There's three of us!"

"Asenna has to take Fen and run," Carro said, "we stay and fight. We can slow them down at least."

"How do you know they'll come through the village?" Tira asked.

"Because that's what I would do," Carro said. The twins looked at one another and nodded. Tira turned to Asenna, who was watching them all with wide eyes.

"You have to run, Asenna. We'll stay and try to give you time."

Asenna shook her head, tears welling up in her eyes. "No! I can fight!"

"Asenna, I am not giving you a choice!" Tira slammed her fist against the wall of the ruin, "our job is to protect you and Fen! *You must run.*"

"What if they see her?" Talla asked.

"They shouldn't...if she leaves right now," Carro stood up and held his hand out to Asenna, "come on." She stared at him for a moment and he could tell she was debating whether or not to trust him, but she let him pull her onto her feet and held onto his hand tightly. Her unexpected display of faith startled him, but now it only made Carro more determined not to let her down as they walked east down the faint trail of the road.

"Carro, please," Asenna begged, the desperation in her voice making his stomach churn, "the three of you against who knows how many Black Sabers and cavalry? You know you can't win this!" They arrived at the edge of the buildings and Carro swung her around so they were face-to-face, close enough that their breath mixed together. She still had a vice grip on his hand.

"It's not about winning," Carro said as gently as he could, "it's about giving you and Fen enough time. That's what I promised and that's what I'm going to do, even if it kills me." He pulled his hand away and stepped backwards. Tears spilled out of Asenna's eyes and Fen let out a tiny cry.

"Carro!" one of the twins called from back in the ruins.

"Please go, Asenna." He turned and walked away, gripping his sharpened stick and clenching his jaw. When Carro glanced back, he saw her hurrying in the opposite direction and he jogged back to the spot where the twins were still crouched, watching the cloud of dust on the horizon grow closer with every passing minute.

"They'll funnel through on the road, then dismount and fan out to search the buildings," he told the twins, "Talla, you don't happen to have any more of that Kashaiti sunfire, do you?" A wanton smile crossed Talla's face as she pulled a bottle of clear liquid from her belt.

"I don't have any more of the black powder, but I've been saving something else just for these bastards," she purred as she uncorked it. Carro watched as she ripped a small strip of fabric from the bottom of her shirt and stuffed it into the mouth of the bottle. "Once I light this and throw it, we may not even have to fight. The horses will panic and the fire will take care of the rest." Carro swallowed and silently reminded himself to never get on Talla's bad side again.

"We should spread out," he said, "each hide in a different spot."

"Wait," said Tira, putting a hand on Carro's arm, "I need you to tell us something. You said you didn't kill our father, so who did?"

Carro looked between them and sighed. "It was Jesk. The one Talla cut across the chest back in the glen."

"If he's with them, he's ours, alright?" Talla said. Carro nodded and the twins glanced at each other. In unison, they reached down to untie his sabers from their belts. As they passed the blades over to him, Talla hesitated.

"On our side?" she asked, searching him with her sharp yellow eyes.

"On your side," Carro said, feeling the decisiveness in his own voice. It felt good to have the sabers on his back again, but he knew that using them on the men he had called his brothers just over a week ago would not be easy. He took the thought and locked it in his imaginary box, then skirted the ruins and moved east, selecting a building with an attic and a collapsed roof so he would have a higher vantage point, while the twins positioned themselves on either side of the entrance to the village. As he waited, watching the dust cloud, Carro also checked the plains to the east where he could see Asenna moving away.

"Please protect them...*Izlani*," he whispered, looking up at the moon, which was very faintly visible in the clear blue sky. Suddenly, he heard a whistle from one of the twins and turned his attention back to the approaching soldiers. They were visible on the horizon now and he estimated at least fifty, dressed in black and riding quickly. His instincts had been right about the Black Sabers being sent out first as a scout. Carro shifted and pulled his sabers out of their scabbards, laying them on the floor of the attic in front of him so they wouldn't flash in the sunlight and give away his position. Then, he waited. The riders drew closer and closer and his body became more and more tense as they did. When they were less than a hundred yards out, Carro felt his heart drop violently into his stomach as he recognized Jesk and Roper riding behind Captain Roeld at the front. Behind Jesk was Gade.

"Damnit, Gade. Why?" Carro groaned, but it was too late now. As the party slowed from a trot to a walk just outside the village, Carro steeled himself, trying to control the jumpy, anxious feelings coming up into his chest. He gritted his teeth and waited until Roeld and Roper had passed before picking up his sabers and leaping from the attic.

As he did, a large flame came arcing out of one of the buildings to the west and landed in the midst of the Black Sabers. There was a sound of breaking glass, and then nothing but fire and chaos. Horses screamed and bolted in every direction, throwing their riders and slamming into one another. Carro landed and had to roll in order to break his fall, almost finding himself trampled under the stampede. He ducked around one of the horses, swinging his blades upwards and slicing the throat of the rider, who almost fell on top of him. Dodging out of the way, Carro moved through the melee, cutting into the men's legs and arms as they tried to defend against his attack, and staying low enough that he could not see their faces. He wove in and out of the panicked horses and heard his name being shouted all around him as he went. Catching a glimpse of Talla through the flames, hacking and swinging with her hatchet, he turned back toward the lead riders just in time to see Gade calling out to Roper. He was pointing to the east, where Asenna was still barely visible on the horizon, and Carro's heart dropped even further. Roeld shouted an order and Roper, Jesk, and Gade pulled away from the group, galloping out of the village toward Asenna.

"*No...*" Carro breathed. Looking around and grabbing the saddle of the nearest horse, he swung up behind its rider and without hesitation, held the man's head back with the hilt of one saber and ran the other one across his throat. Carro felt the blood spray into his mouth, but he shoved the body to the ground and pushed the horse as fast as it could go. The three men were gaining on Asenna, who had seen them coming and was running as fast as she could, clutching Fen to her chest. Suddenly, Carro heard hoofbeats behind him and whirled around to see Talla riding hard on his flank. They exchanged a look and she pulled ahead. Carro moved his horse so that they could get on either side of the three riders and try to cut them off, but then two things happened at once. Roper lifted his bow, aiming directly at Asenna, just as Talla pulled her horse up behind Gade and raised her hatchet to strike. Feeling as though he was being ripped from his own body, Carro made his decision.

"Roper!" he screamed as loudly as he could, standing up in the stirrups to make himself an easier target. Gade's strangled cry as Talla buried the hatchet in his back hit Carro only a moment before Roper's arrow did. The searing pain shot through his left shoulder and spread to his chest and ribs. Carro managed to stay on the horse long enough to watch Talla swing the hatchet into Jesk's neck, before a second arrow buried itself into his hip and he couldn't hold on any longer, toppling off the horse and hitting the ground hard. The shaft of the second arrow snapped and Carro felt the point push deeper into his body as he rolled. The pain was overwhelming, pulling him into a rushing current of darkness and drowning everything else. Before he blacked out, Carro swore he saw a great shadow with white fangs standing above him, and he was almost sure he could hear the blood curdling cries of the Black Sabers in the village as they were torn to shreds. The last thing he felt before being sucked under the surface was a pair of warm hands on his chest and neck, frantically feeling for a heartbeat, and a strangled voice calling out a name that could have been his, but felt foreign somehow.

"I have to go now…" he mumbled, letting himself slip beneath the waves.

~~~

Carro was absolutely certain he was dead. He couldn't imagine being in this much pain and still being alive. As he fell in and out of consciousness, he smelled blood, wet fur, dirt, wood smoke, and meat cooking. There were so many different voices that his mind could not distinguish who they belonged to. Some of them sounded like they were completely in his head and not drifting through his ears at all. Some spoke in a language he could not comprehend. Some were light and welcoming, like the celebratory bells that rang every Winter Solstice in the city, and some were deep and rumbling like a rockslide. He felt himself being jostled and lifted and carried and dragged and he couldn't be sure who was doing it or why or even where he was, but he had no strength to open his eyes and find out. Every movement, every breath was excruciating, sending violent spasms through his hips and legs and chest. Finally, blessedly, the movement and the voices stopped and he felt a soft warmth and light envelope him. *I'm definitely dead now,* he thought, *that was all just the journey and now I'm gone.* Carro checked his body, moving his toes, his legs, his hands, and fingers in succession, without opening his eyes. He could feel everything, which meant he could also still feel the agony radiating from his shoulder and hip. When he finally got the nerve to open his eyes and look around, he saw that he was lying on a cot in a small tent, his naked body wrapped in a massive animal pelt. It was light outside and he could hear muffled voices, footsteps, and children's laughter. He tried to pull himself onto his elbows, but the pain was too intense and he let out an involuntary cry, falling back onto a rolled up blanket behind his head.

"This is a terrible fucking afterlife," he groaned, trying to keep still.

"Well, I'm not sure you quite deserved a good one," said a sharp voice from the other side of the tent. Carro twisted his neck and saw Gaelin standing there with his signature smirk.

Relief flooded his body. "Gaelin!" he breathed, raising a hand.

"You know, it's generally frowned upon to survive your heroic self-sacrifice," the hunter teased, taking his hand and shaking it a little.

"I'll make sure to die next time, don't worry," Carro found that he couldn't laugh, so he let out a few wheezing breaths.

"I don't think your friends would let you, to be honest," Gaelin glanced back at the tent flap, then grinned again, "they made great efforts to keep you alive for some fuckin' reason."

"My…friends?" Carro asked softly, squeezing his eyes shut and opening them again to make sure he wasn't dreaming.

"Of course, it was through my own heroic efforts that *any* of you survived, seein' as how I brought the Riders to your rescue, but you can thank me later," Gaelin moved aside as the twins came into the tent, followed by Asenna. Carro was relieved to see that they looked none the worse for wear, save for a few bruises and cuts on Tira and Talla. Asenna knelt beside the cot and Carro saw tears gathering in her eyes.

"Fen?" he asked, "is he alright?"

"Yes, he's perfect, thanks to you. But you nearly died. You were shot twice and would have been again, if the Riders hadn't come."

"It was quite unnecessary, actually" said Tira, smiling at him, "we had it under control."

"Well, mostly…" Talla grinned.

"Where are we? What happened to the Black Sabers?"

"The Riders showed up just in time," Asenna told him, "they wiped out the rest of the Sabers and then brought us to Kashait. We're safe now, just over the border…with the Ulvvori." Carro allowed himself a small smile, but he felt his nerves roar back to life as he imagined the reception he might receive.

"Good," he closed his eyes again, "that's good."

"Let's go," said Tira quietly, "let him rest." Carro heard them leave, but when he opened his eyes, Asenna was still there, looking nervous.

"What is it?" he asked.

"It's Gade. He was killed…"

"I know," Carro whispered, "I saw…I watched it. But I had to choose and…I chose you and Fen." He felt tears burn his eyes, but held them back.

"I know he was like your brother, and I'm so sorry, but…I'm also very grateful for what you did," Asenna was twisting her hands together anxiously.

"I'm just glad you're all safe. Even Gaelin, I guess," Carro gave her a weak smile.

"Are you hungry?" she asked, standing up.

"Starving. How long was I out?"

"A few days. Wait, I'll bring some food, and there's someone I want you to meet," she ducked out of the tent and came back a few minutes later with a small bowl and a woman who Carro guessed could only be her mother, since her face was so much like Asenna's, but with more lines. Her chestnut-brown hair was streaked with gray and tied into a long braid that hung over her shoulder, and her face was twisted into a wary frown.

"This is my mother, Elyana," said Asenna, putting the bowl on a stump beside his cot. Carro could not sit up, so he only nodded.

"Thank you for allowing me to recover here," Carro said to her. Elyana moved to stand next to her daughter and Carro noticed her pale-yellow eyes, exactly like the twins'.

"If we're being honest, it wasn't my decision," she said in a cold voice, "my brother has a softer heart than I do, because I would have left you to die on the plains."

"Mama," Asenna said through gritted teeth, "I told you what happened."

"Yes, you did," Elyana didn't take her eyes off Carro and he found that he couldn't hold her gaze, "and taking a couple of arrows doesn't erase what else he's done. I'll reserve my judgment until he's no longer reliant on our hospitality and forgiveness." She swept out of the tent and Asenna sighed.

"I'm sorry. It's been so hard for her…since the attack."

"She lost her dire wolf?"

Asenna nodded and picked up the bowl. "It's not much, but they only just crossed the border a few days ago so food has been a bit scarce, but apparently the Kashaitis are sending supply wagons."

"It's plenty, thank you," he told her, reaching over with his good arm, "go be with your family. Please. I'm alright." Asenna hesitated for a moment, but then stood up and left the tent. Carro tried to roll onto his side, but Roper's arrows had hit him in the left shoulder and the right hip, so no matter which way he turned it was excruciating, but he finally managed to find a position where he could tip the bowl into his mouth without spilling too much broth. It barely touched the hunger that was making his entire body ache, but he didn't want to ask for more considering the situation.

After a short time he drifted back to sleep and when he woke up again it was pitch black inside the tent. Carro tried to adjust his body into a more comfortable position, but groaned in pain and frustration.

"Need a piss?" came Gaelin's rough voice from a few feet away, making Carro startle.

"No, just trying to move."

"I wouldn't recommend it," Gaelin's face was suddenly illuminated by the flame of a small candle, "those ain't just some cat scratches you got."

"The sooner I can move, the sooner I can leave," Carro grunted.

"Why would you do that?" Gaelin lifted the edge of the animal pelt to check on the wounds, which had been covered with a thin green paste and some bandages.

"I'm just making things worse for Asenna. For everyone, probably."

"Yeah, Elyana gave me quite the dressin' down too. Don't worry so much about her. She's always been a bit frosty."

"What about Tolian? I met him once, during the war, but I doubt he'll remember me. Probably better if he doesn't."

"Aye, Tolian's got a more forgivin' spirit. It's him and the council who'll have the final say on what to do with you."

"What are my options?"

"Hmmm," Gaelin pretended to think, scratching the stubble on his chin. Reflexively, Carro reached up and felt his own face. It was strange and disconcerting after so many years of being clean-shaven to find hair growing there. "Ulvvori justice is a strange thing. There's been other conscripts what have returned and been welcomed with open arms, even some what fought for Rogerin. But your situation is…different, so I can't say."

"I'd heard some of them come back after their service is up," Carro said, "but you're right…it's different for me."

"Yeah, and no point thinkin' about it now, so go back to sleep. You already woke me up once and if you do it again I'll give you a matchin' wound on the other hip." Gaelin went back over to where he had some blankets rolled out on the ground and covered himself up, blowing out the candle, but Carro had a hard time falling back asleep. His mind was racing, thinking about the other conscripts Gaelin had mentioned.

He had met others during his time in the army, of course, but he had never revealed his own origins to them. Some men talked about it openly and made plans to return to the Ulvvori when their thirty years of service were finished. A few even deserted, but were usually caught and punished. Others, like Carro, hid it from everyone, fearing the bigotry and harassment that Ulvvori conscripts often faced. Knowing that there might be other conscripts in the camp made Carro feel less alone, but he knew that a warm welcome was likely not in his cards. He lay awake until dawn, imagining every possible outcome of the judgment he was to receive. When the camp began to stir outside the tent, Gaelin woke up and went to get water.

"Where are we exactly?" Carro asked, wiping his mouth after drinking clumsily.

"Just across the Kashaiti border. The camp is temporary until we hear if they'll allow us to stay on a more permanent basis. I heard tell that Queen Selissa herself is on the way here to meet with Tolian and the council."

"The Kashaitis are friendly to the Ulvvori though, yes?"

"Relatively," Gaelin shrugged, "at least they ain't gatherin' forces to drive us out. They let us through the wall quick enough."

"How much longer until I can get up?" Carro asked.

Gaelin lifted his bandages. "Maybe a few more days. How's the pain?"

"Worse in my hip."

"They thought that one might've hit the bone, since you fell off your horse like an idiot and pushed it in further," he prodded the area around the hip wound.

"Damnit, Gaelin!" Carro yelped, smacking his hand away.

"That's what I thought," Gaelin pulled the bandages away and used the fresh water to clean the area. Just as he was finishing, Asenna came into the tent carrying a small basket. Carro could smell fresh bread and his mouth began to water.

"Good news!" Asenna said brightly, "the Kashaiti wagons arrived last night. I took what food I could, but there's clean bandages and some balm made from beeswax. They said it might help with your wounds." She pulled a small ceramic jar out of the basket.

"Best get it on quick," Gaelin said, "I'm goin' to see about that food." He left the tent and Asenna knelt by the cot.

"Not to be rude," Carro said, "but is that bread?" Asenna reached over and took a small brown loaf out of the basket. She broke off a piece for him and Carro nearly swallowed it whole. He had never been so hungry in his entire life.

"Is it ok if I..." Asenna held up the jar and indicated his shoulder. Carro nodded, and she lifted the bandages off, wrinkling her nose as she did, and began slowly spreading the balm on top of the wound. "Just tell me if I'm hurting you, alright?"

"How's your family?" Carro asked, trying not to let on how much it actually did hurt.

"Oh..." Asenna paused and Carro could tell that her initial cheerfulness had been a facade, "they're alright. All of this is so difficult for them."

"I'm sure your mother was happy to meet Fen though."

"Oh yes," Asenna laughed, "she hasn't let him out of her sight except when he needs to nurse. It's been rather nice, if I'm honest, to have a break. I forgot what it was like to be able to rely on people."

"And the rest of your family?" Carro was careful not to pry too much, but he was hoping she might give a hint as to how Tolian was feeling toward him.

"My uncle and brothers and their wolves are here too, thank goodness," Asenna carefully placed a clean bandage on Carro's shoulder. She reached down and started to lift the blanket off his hip, but she didn't realize he was naked underneath, and Carro slapped his hand down over the blanket, accidentally hitting his own wound. He rolled onto his side, doubling over and gasping in pain as tears filled his eyes.

"Oh, I'm so sorry!" Asenna cried, "I didn't realize..." She looked upset for a moment, but Carro started to wheeze with laughter and she cautiously joined in. After a few seconds they were both giggling like children and couldn't stop. Carro laid back flat on the cot, covering his own mouth and trying to take deep breaths because it hurt so badly to laugh, but then Asenna let out a loud snort, causing both of them to double over again.

"Maybe I'd better do that one," Carro puffed after a few minutes, finally able to measure his breathing. Asenna wiped tears from her face and nodded, handing him the jar. Gaelin suddenly reentered the tent, holding a few apples and a small bag.

"What in the world…" he looked between Asenna and Carro, who both burst out laughing again at the confusion on his face.

"I have to go," Asenna said, still chuckling softly, "I hope the beeswax helps." She ducked out of the tent and Carro had to take a few more deep breaths to calm himself down.

"The fuck was that all about?" Gaelin tossed Carro an apple, which he caught with his good arm and shoved into his mouth.

"Just something stupid," he said, smiling as he chewed and relived the moment in his head, feeling a small bubble of optimism in his otherwise aching stomach.

NINE:
THE PACT

Asenna was still smiling as she walked back through the Ulvvori camp to her own family's tents. It hadn't taken her long to feel at home again, although it was strange to be camped out on the dry, flat plains of Kashait rather than the foothills of the Midwinter Mountains. Many things were still the same as she remembered, however: the large round tents flanked by smaller square ones, sledges made from the antlers of giant deer, children dodging in and out between the tents and campfires, and the dire wolves. Asenna had forgotten how huge and terrifying they appeared at first sight, even though she knew them to be gentle and family-oriented. They were everywhere in the camp, napping in the sun, carrying their Riders through the rows of tents, pulling sledges loaded with firewood, or caring for their own litters of pups. The largest of them stood at least six feet at the shoulder, with some growing even larger. Tolian's pitch-black wolf, Echo, was at least seven feet tall from her massive claws to the tips of her ears, which were larger than Fen's entire body. Their presence made Asenna feel safer than she had in years, and her heart swelled when a group of young children ran past her with their wolf pup companions nipping at their heels.

Stopping outside her family's tent, Asenna paused to take a deep breath before entering. The interior was sparse, since the refugees had not been able to carry much in their escape, but Tolian was not one for luxury anyway. He and Elyana and Asenna's two brothers, Haryk and Ivarr, were seated on stumps around a firepit that had been dug in the center of the tent, eating the thin soup and brown bread that the Kashaiti supply wagon had brought. Fen was sprawled out on a blanket behind Elyana, kicking his legs while Ivarr's dainty black dire wolf, Nettle, napped beside him. Nettle was still relatively young and still only the size of a large cart pony, but Echo, her mother, was so large that she could no longer fit comfortably inside the tent and Asenna knew she was probably sitting outside somewhere nearby, supervising the activity in the camp. Asenna could feel her mother's eyes searching her as she sat down and tore a piece of bread off the loaf that was sitting in a basket at Ivarr's feet.

"How is Juniper?" Asenna asked Haryk casually, avoiding her mother's gaze. Her eldest brother's dire wolf was expecting her first litter of pups any day and Asenna was anxious for them to arrive. The day after she had arrived in the camp, Tolian had consulted with the Elder Council and they had decided that she should attempt to bond Fen to one of Juniper's pups as quickly as possible after they were born. It was exactly what Asenna had hoped for, but she still couldn't help feeling apprehensive about whether or not it would even work.

"She's doing well," Haryk said, eyes darting between Asenna and Elyana, "Nikke and Ash are with her right now. She's got to be close."

"That's wonderful, Haryk," Asenna tore into her bread and continued to try and look anywhere but at her mother or uncle.

"There's something else too, that I wanted to tell you," her brother said slowly, "Nikke and I are going to be married. We aren't sure when, but it'll be soon, once we're more…settled somewhere."

Asenna nearly choked on her bread. "Why?" she asked loudly.

"Why? Because…we want to…" Haryk replied, looking a little perplexed, "look, Senna, I know you aren't great friends with Nikke, but--"

"No, I mean why get *married*? That's not something we do. Mama and Papa never got married, neither did Tolian and Dirye."

"That was our decision," said Tolian quietly, "Haryk and Nikke have made their own, and we should support them in it."

"Just because *you* had a bad experience--" Haryk started to say, but Asenna stood up, throwing her uneaten bread back into the basket.

"*A bad experience?*" she hissed, "is that what you think I had? Like I ate some rancid meat and spent the week in bed?"

"No, I know it was hard, but…you agreed to it."

"Of course I fucking agreed to it!" Asenna shouted, "how could I not, with thousands of eyes on me all wondering if I would sacrifice myself to save their sons? I didn't grow up like all of you, with a wolf behind me at every step! What else was I supposed to do when the only thing standing in the way of our freedom was me and my own selfishness? And none of you said a word, did you? No one even tried to find a solution that didn't involve selling me off!"

"Don't you dare pretend like it was all on you!" Haryk spat, putting his plate down, "you didn't have to fight a war for two fucking years and watch your friends and their wolves die!"

"The only reason you even had the opportunity to fight was because of me! Because I was willing to put *my* body on the altar in the first place!" Asenna felt tears sliding down her face and Ivarr suddenly stood up and moved between them, pulling her into a tight hug.

"Both of you sit down! This is ridiculous," said Elyana stonily, "everyone in this family has sacrificed or lost something these last three years, and we shouldn't be arguing over whose loss was the greatest."

"I agree," Tolian said, "we have far more pressing issues right now."

"Yes," Elyana murmured, yellow eyes shifting over to her brother, "like the fact that *you* are allowing that man to be anywhere near our family after what he's done." Ivarr finally let go of Asenna and stood back.

"He will stay for now," Tolian answered slowly, not looking at them, "because, Ely, we do not kill our own and we do not leave them to die. Captain Morelake poses little threat so long as he is under guard at all times."

"And you think that *Gaelin* is a trustworthy guard?" Elyana laughed, "that man would sell his own soul if it wasn't so tarnished and worthless."

"My deal with Gaelin will hold for now," Tolian said, finally looking up, "have some faith in me."

"Am I the only one who sees the danger here?" Elyana barked at them, "that man was like a brother to Azimar. He chased my daughter and grandson, hunted them through the forest for weeks. He nearly killed them, and I am expected to just accept his presence amongst my people? My family?"

"For the time being, yes," Tolian repeated, "Asenna, would you be willing to forgo your visits until your mother feels more comfortable?"

"Why can't you trust my judgment?" Asenna asked her mother, "especially after everything I've seen, shouldn't it be my decision? I am not a naive little girl anymore!"

"Your judgment is completely clouded by your damned bleeding heart," Haryk muttered. Asenna opened her mouth to retort, but Elyana overrode her.

"Would you allow your son to pay the price if you're wrong about him?" Asenna ignored her, walked over, and picked up Fen from the floor, then went to the tent entrance and turned around to face them.

"For the last three years, I've paid the price for the faith that you two placed in Azimar. It seems I can't trust you to make good decisions on my behalf, so I will be making my own from now on," she said, trying desperately to keep her voice steady. Feeling satisfied at the look of shock on her mother's face, Asenna turned and stalked out of the tent, clutching Fen to her chest.

She was barely away when she heard footsteps coming after them, but it was only Ivarr and Nettle. He had always been her best friend since they were so much alike, and Ivarr was not as deep in their mother's pocket as Haryk was, but she could tell from his frown that she had crossed a line.

"Senna, that was uncalled for," he said softly, walking beside her, "none of us could have known what Azimar would become. We're all paying the price for trusting him."

"I know, but I can't stand her still treating me like I'm a child. She has no idea what I've gone through to protect Fen. I'm more than capable of making my own choices now, even if she doesn't like them."

"Of course you are, but…it's hard for her, for all of us, to watch you defend him." Asenna stopped and faced her brother. It was almost like looking into a mirror now that her hair had been cut short, except for Ivarr's sparkling golden eyes and neatly trimmed beard.

"I'm not defending *anything* he's done before," she sighed, "I'm defending what he's done since he left. There was absolutely no reward for him when he took those arrows for me, Ivarr. Not only did he nearly lose his own life, he had to watch someone he loved die in order to do it."

"You're right," Ivarr said, reaching out to rub Fen's back, "we just don't want you to put yourself in harm's way unnecessarily. Can't you just…be grateful from a distance or something? To make Mama happy? What do you think the chances are that he'll stick around after he's recovered anyway?" Ivarr's big, doleful eyes were silently pleading with her. He was always the one trying to keep the peace in their somewhat volatile family and Asenna felt a little guilty for causing him more strife.

"I don't care if he sticks around or not, but at the very least I won't let him be mistreated while he's here," Asenna said, taking Ivarr's hand, "I just need you to trust me. Please?" Nettle took a step forward and nudged Ivarr's shoulder with her muzzle. They looked into each other's eyes for a moment and Asenna knew they were sharing their thoughts. While she had never particularly wished to be a Wolf Rider, Asenna had always been jealous of the power to hear their voices, longing for the implicit understanding and connection that you didn't have to use words for.

"Well?" she asked, "what does Nettle think?"

"Nettle says that I should trust you, and that you should take her next time you go visit because she will be able to smell any dishonesty on him," Ivarr laughed.

"Thank you, Nettle," Asenna scratched her under the chin, "but I'd better hold off a while to let Mama settle down. Let's go back to the wagons and see what's left for supper tonight."

"When you do go and take Nettle, I'd like to come along too," Ivarr told her as they walked east through the camp, "I was hoping to meet the twins anyway. Haryk said they used to train together, but we've never really been introduced."

"Oh, no. They're far too mean for you, Ivarr," Asenna punched his arm playfully, "you need someone sweet and kind to balance out the rest of the pigheaded idiots in this family, especially now that Nikke is coming on."

"Senna, I know you think Haryk's only with her because their wolves mated, but I think they actually do love each other...in their own strange way," Ivarr said quietly, "maybe give her a chance?"

"For your sake, *lai'kheri*, I will, but not for Haryk's," she agreed. As they walked, Ivarr filled Asenna in on some of the gossip that had occurred in the years since she had left. He intentionally steered away from more difficult topics, but Asenna could still hear the sadness in his voice when he mentioned friends that had been lost in the war or the battle at The Den.

Within hours of arriving in the camp, Asenna had learned that at least a third of the Ulvvori had been killed that day. For such a relatively small group, the numbers were devastating. More Riders and wolves had been lost in the attack than in two years of Azimar's war, and now there was a new fear that the Riders would be even more reduced in number since the Wolfsight had apparently left them. Asenna was reminded of this daily by the fact that she could not walk more than twenty feet through the camp carrying Fen without someone stopping her. They kissed the baby's forehead and whispered blessings and the dire wolves licked his face and toes, making him smile and coo happily. It was disconcerting, but Asenna understood that if the Wolf Riders died out, the Ulvvori might cease to exist altogether. Returning to their land was no guarantee that the problem would be fixed, since they could not definitively say what had broken the connection in the first place. Tolian had said that the dire wolves could not tell them either, since the knowledge of the magic had been all but lost to them over time too. Asenna thought about the sacred spring that the twins had told her about in the forest, but she knew that it was more than likely a myth and not a solution to their very real and immediate problem.

"You could have left him with Mama," said Ivarr gently after the third time they were stopped so that someone could see Fen, "I know you don't like all the attention."

"I won't give her the satisfaction of knowing I need her right now," said Asenna, "besides, I--" She stopped mid-sentence and froze when a chorus of dire wolf voices split the air: two short yelps followed by a single long howl.

"Visitors?" Asenna turned back toward the main camp.

"It could be Queen Selissa. They said she was on her way."

"Should we go?"

"Probably. She might want to meet you, right? I mean...aren't you technically still a Queen as well?"

"I...have no idea..." Asenna realized that she had not even considered this question and she suddenly felt anxious at the thought of having some sort of expectations placed on her. In the three years she had been married to Azimar, she had played little to no role in his court, other than appearing silently by his side when he called for her. Now that she thought about it, Asenna realized that she was not even sure what the legal status of her marriage was, and she couldn't imagine there was anyone in the camp who could tell her. She pushed the thought away to deal with another time.

"We should go back and see what Mama wants us to do," Ivarr said softly, sensing that Asenna was a bit stuck and putting his hand on her arm. When they got back to their family tent, it was indeed buzzing with activity. Echo, Tolian's massive black dire wolf, was stationed outside the tent entrance. She greeted them with a small yip and Nettle nuzzled the corners of her mouth just as Elyana emerged from the tent and set her sights on Asenna and Ivarr.

"There you are!" she hissed, "where were you two? Nevermind, just get in here. Selissa and her entourage have arrived. Ivarr, you and Haryk will stay. Asenna and Fen will come with us." They followed her into the tent and once Asenna had put Fen back down on the blanket, Elyana threw a bundle of clothing at her. Since arriving in the camp, she had been wearing her brothers' old clothes, but her mother had somehow managed to scrounge up a worn-out brown smock dress.

"A dress?" Asenna asked skeptically, holding it up, "*you're* not wearing a dress."

"Riders don't wear skirts, Asenna," her mother snapped. Asenna had to resist the cruel urge to remind her mother that she was, technically, no longer a Wolf Rider. Instead, she went behind a curtain that was set up on one side of the tent to change, then ran her hands through her short hair, trying to make it lay flat. When she finished, she went outside and found Tolian and Elyana talking to a tall, bald man with a pointed gray beard who was dressed in white robes embroidered with the Kashaiti crest, a golden dolphin leaping over a sunburst, and trimmed with golden thread. Asenna felt it was in poor taste to wear such finery to a refugee camp, but she reminded herself to reserve judgment since the Kashaitis were providing them safe harbor and supplies. Accompanied by Echo, they followed the bald man through the camp. Some of the Ulvvori stopped to watch them as they went, greeting Tolian or whispering behind their hands while pointing at Asenna and Fen.

At the eastern edge of the camp, a three-sided white tent had been erected on gold posts close to where the Kashaiti supply wagons were sitting.

The open side was covered by a translucent veil, so its occupant was not visible as they approached, but the man motioned for them to wait. Two dozen soldiers in white uniforms and golden helms stood at attention around them, carrying large pikes. As Asenna examined them closer she realized that they were all incredibly tall women, with long braids down their backs and heavily muscled arms. Asenna had thought the twins were fierce, but Selissa's guards were in a class by themselves and she could not help but stare as they walked by. When they passed under the veil at the front of the tent, Echo had to remain outside due to her size, so she laid down and stuck her snout into the tent. The Kashaiti valet looked quite alarmed, but apparently decided that it was not worth saying anything.

Queen Selissa sat before them on a simple wooden chair. Asenna had never seen anyone so regal in her entire life. She was quite tall and older than Asenna had expected, at least in her late sixties, with long ropes of white hair that fell around her shoulders, decorated with small golden cuffs and beads like the twins'. Her sable skin was smooth and almost luminous with the way that the tent glowed in the sunlight and she wore a simple white gown embellished with a golden belt and golden bangles on her arms. A delicate crown that looked almost like a bird's nest fashioned from golden twigs laced with pearls sat on her head.

The bald man cleared his throat. "May I present Queen Selissa Holdenmoor, the Pearl of Kashait, Our Most Judicious and Noble Citizen, Mother of Our Nation. Your Majesty, I present Tolian, Head Wolf Rider of the Ulvvori, as well as his sister Elyana, and her daughter, Asenna, Queen of Esmadia and mother of Prince Fenrinn." Asenna opened her mouth to protest at her own title and Fen's, but her mother glared at her. Selissa smiled and stood up, spreading her arms.

"Welcome," she said in a warm voice marked by a thick Kashaiti accent, "I am so sorry for your troubles. Please know that you are safe here and I will do all in my power to defend and assist you."

"Thank you, Your Majesty," Tolian said, bowing, "we are extremely grateful for your assistance and hospitality. I hope that it is not too much of an inconvenience. I have been made aware of the situation beyond the wall with Azimar's troops." Asenna looked at him, startled, since she had not been told of this yet. She knew it was not the time to ask, however.

"Not at all, my friend," said Selissa, putting a hand on Tolian's arm. She had an air about her that felt comforting, like she was a trusted confidant rather than a monarch, and Asenna's anxiety lessened slightly. "Kashait is always ready to welcome refugees, and we are dealing with the situation you mentioned. I hope that we can discuss an arrangement to benefit us both, but first, I had hoped to meet the little one." Her deep brown eyes fell onto Fen and she smiled.

"May I?" she asked, holding her arms out. Asenna hesitated, but then passed the baby to her. Fen slipped easily into her arms and she made faces at him while he grabbed at her hair. "Goodness, I do miss them at this age. All of mine are grown, but my youngest granddaughter, Marik, is just a few months older than your Fenrinn. You are very lucky."

"How many children does Your Majesty have?" Asenna asked in her politest voice.

"Twelve," Selissa gave her a broad smile, "and now twenty-six grandchildren and three great-grandchildren. I have been very blessed."

"Indeed, you have," said Elyana.

"Would you all mind very much if I spoke to Asenna alone for a few minutes?" Selissa asked, looking around as though she was worried about causing offense. Tolian and Elyana bowed again and exited the tent, leaving her alone with Selissa, who sat back in her chair, still rocking Fen.

"Please, Your Majesty," Asenna said quickly, "what exactly is the situation…beyond the border wall? I haven't been informed yet."

Selissa surveyed her for a moment. "I do not wish to worry you," she said, "but Azimar has sent a small number of cavalry units to harass our border. They have not engaged our soldiers yet, but…I believe it is only a matter of time. We are quite capable of holding them off, never fear."

"I-I'm so sorry," Asenna murmured, "we never meant to cause you any trouble by coming here." Selissa shook her head.

"No, child. It is no trouble. I was told of your escape from Sinsaya," said the Queen softly, "but my informants could not give me many details of what transpired afterwards. I would very much like to hear it from you. Although, I understand if it is too difficult a tale to tell." Asenna swallowed and then began to tell Selissa about her escape from the palace, the twins, Ferryn, and the trek through the forest. As she spoke, she wondered if she should mention Carro, unsure what Kashait might do with him if they found out that one of Azimar's most trusted men was inside their borders. However, she suspected that Selissa already knew, so she did not leave him out. Selissa listened carefully and when Asenna finished, she frowned.

"Goodness. I cannot imagine the fear you must have felt, but I am glad that you found some protection from your new friends, however dubious their motives."

Asenna felt safe in Selissa's presence and suddenly decided to take a chance. "My mother and uncle don't trust Carro," she said slowly, trying to gauge the queen's reaction.

"Hmm," Selissa slipped a golden bangle from her arm and held it out in front of Fen, who closed his tiny fist around it, "I suppose you can't really blame them, can you? I'm sure they are quite concerned for your safety."

"Well…no, I can't blame them," Asenna admitted, "but they weren't there. They didn't see what I saw. If they had, I think they would feel differently."

"You cannot make them see something they refuse to see, Asenna. That is the truth of the situation. You can advocate on the young man's behalf, certainly, but you cannot change people's minds. You may have to allow him to make his own impressions. If he is what you say he is, then you should trust that he will be able to show others too."

"Isn't the Queen of Kashait sometimes called the 'Judge of Men's Hearts'?" Asenna asked, trying to keep her voice a little aloof.

Selissa gave her a knowing smile. "Yes, that is true. The Queen of Kashait is elected by the people as a figurehead, because we believe our ruler should be valued for her moral character and wisdom. Because of this, I am often asked to provide guidance and perspective on judicial or political decisions. My judgments are hardly binding though, and are meant merely as…strong recommendations."

"Perhaps, I could ask you to meet Carro yourself and then give my uncle and our Elder Council your 'recommendation,'" Asenna's heart was pounding as she made the request, "I understand that this is not a Kashaiti matter, but…I would be remiss if I did not at least try to help the man who saved my life, and my son's." Selissa stood and handed Fen back to Asenna, then walked around behind her chair and placed her hands on the back, drumming her long, elegant fingers on the wood.

"I admire your strength and conviction, Asenna, and your willingness to put your faith in people, in spite of all you have been through," she said, "I will do this for you, if you promise me something in return."

Asenna felt wary, but her instincts said that she could trust Selissa. "What is it?"

"As long as Azimar is alive, you must *never* take your son back to Esmadia," Selissa's voice was suddenly hard, "I am sure I do not need to tell you that angry men are like wildfires: they will consume everything in their path and still seek more. They must be starved and deprived of fuel if they are to be stopped. You have his eldest son, his only living heir, the future of the dynasty that he so desires. You must starve the wildfire by keeping the boy away from him. Do you understand?"

"Yes," Asenna nodded. She had no intention of ever taking Fen back to Esmadia if she could help it. "But you know he could have more sons, right? He could already be married again for all I know."

Selissa's eyes wandered around the tent. "I have agents in Esmadia to deal with that possibility," she said in a faraway voice.

"What do you--" Asenna started to say, but she was interrupted by the valet, who re-entered the tent with Tolian and Elyana. Selissa began chatting animatedly with Tolian, as if her conversation with Asenna had not happened at all. It was startling to think that Kashaiti operatives could have been in Esmadia all along and Asenna wondered why they hadn't acted before. She turned all the new information over in her mind as Selissa and Tolian spoke, hardly hearing what was being said. Eventually, she came back to the conversation and realized that Selissa was making an offer of land to the Ulvvori.

"I understand that your preference is to return to Esmadia, especially given the situation with your children and the Wolfsight, but I would like for you to stay here as long as you need to and consider the land your own. It is quite a splendid place, along the river, with plenty of resources for you to build a new life," Selissa was saying, "I have been authorized by my government to offer it to you free of conditions, since the area is so sparsely populated at the moment."

"I will have to consult with my Elder Council," said Tolian, "but after what we have endured, I am sure that my people are not interested in moving on anytime soon. Your generosity will not be forgotten, Your Majesty." He gave a deep bow.

"One more thing," said Selissa, "I would very much like to stay here one night and meet some of your people. Particularly, this young man who Asenna says saved her life. I understand that he is one of the children who was stolen from your people by Rogerin many years ago?" Tolian glanced at Asenna and she avoided his eyes.

"Yes, Your Majesty, he is. It is a…special circumstance, however. We are reserving our judgment until he has recovered from his wounds, according to our laws."

"Nevertheless, I should like to meet him. The courage required to leave behind everything you have ever known, fully aware that there is likely to be only rejection and ridicule waiting on the other side, is no small thing," Selissa said, lifting her chin.

"Yes…very well, Your Majesty," Tolian bowed again and then Selissa walked them out and called for her valet. As soon as they were once again concealed by the Ulvvori tents, Elyana rounded on Asenna.

"How *dare* you try to undermine your uncle! We should be grateful that she even agreed to let us across her border, and you ask her for favors to influence this matter which should remain among our people?"

"Ely," said Tolian calmly, "Asenna is perfectly within her rights to ask for outside judgment on Captain Morelake. His crimes against her and Fen occurred beyond our territory."

"She's asking for outside defense! She wants Selissa to take his part and advise you to let him stay here!" Elyana threw her hands up.

"I do understand that," Tolian gave her a look, "but once again, she is within her rights. I see no harm in allowing Selissa to speak with him. She was, after all, elected for the soundness of her moral judgment and for being able to 'see into men's hearts.' Perhaps she will be able to tell us what is in the Captain's heart."

"Mama," said Asenna quietly, "I'm not asking you to love him or accept his presence in our lives or even *speak* to him again. If he recovered and left and never came back, that would be fine, but you've both told me that many of our people want to see him executed and I can't let that happen. I only want him to be given the same second chance at life that he gave to me and Fen. I owe him that, if nothing else." Elyana scoffed and walked away. Tolian and Asenna went to follow her, but then Asenna heard someone shouting her name through the camp.

"Mama! Asenna! It's happening!" It was Haryk, running toward them between the tents with a wild look on his face.

"Juniper?" gasped Asenna, "is she having the pups?" Haryk nodded, smiling, and they all ran through the camp back to the small tent that had been set aside for Juniper and Ash, just behind their family tent. Nikke and Haryk went inside alone to assist with the birth and Asenna bounced Fen anxiously in her arms as they waited by the entrance. Ivarr and Tolian sat nearby and Elyana paced back and forth, chewing her fingernails. As they waited, the news seemed to spread throughout the camp, and a small crowd gathered outside the tent. Asenna could feel the apprehension in the air as everyone waited to see whether the bond between the Ulvvori and the dire wolves had truly been broken. Just as the sun began to set, Haryk and Nikke emerged from the tent, grinning from ear to ear.

"Three pups!" Haryk whooped, "all healthy and beautiful!" Asenna leapt up and hugged her brother, then Ivarr and the rest joined in. When they broke apart, Haryk turned to Asenna.

"She wants to see you and Fen," he said quietly.

"Are you sure?" said Asenna, not wanting to overstep, "now?" Haryk nodded and led Asenna into the tent while Nikke and the others stayed outside. It was dark and warm, lit by only a few short candles. Asenna could see Juniper curled up at the back with three tiny bundles of fur at her belly. Her huge golden eyes glinted in the firelight as she watched them approach. Juniper's coat was a dusty brown except for the rich black fur lining her neck and ears. Her mate, Ash, Nikke's dire wolf, was only slightly larger, with sleek black fur and a white streak on his chest. He sat behind Juniper, licking her ears gently and watching Asenna with the same golden eyes. Asenna gulped as she stepped closer and placed Fen on the ground a few feet away from the she-wolf, then knelt beside him.

"Juniper," said Asenna, reciting the words that her mother had taught her only a few days before, "daughter of Echo. I come before you today and humbly ask you to honor the Wolfsight born in my son, Fenrinn. I ask that you take my son as your own and give me one of your daughters as my own, that our children be raised together as one, that they fulfill the ancient pact between our people, and that we live out our days together as one family." Asenna dropped her head and waited for a response from Haryk, who would have to relay Juniper's answer to her, but the she-wolf raised her body off the ground and stepped over her newborn pups. Asenna held her breath as Juniper pushed her muzzle into Fen's belly, sniffing him and allowing him to grab at her nose and whiskers. Then she turned toward Asenna, who felt a strange sensation come over her, like she was floating and could no longer feel or see her surroundings, only the she-wolf's piercing golden eyes. Asenna heard a deep, purring voice in her head, making her jerk in astonishment.

You have brought me one that is too old, Asenna, daughter of Elyana. Asenna tried to move, but her body was held in place by some force she could not see.

I don't understand, Asenna thought to herself, *what's happening?*

You have brought me one that is too old, came the reply, *why?*

Juniper? Asenna tried to form the thought as she would a sentence and push it out toward the she-wolf, *how is this possible? I don't have--*

The Sight merely acts as a bridge between our people, so that we may stand in the center of a river and speak with little effort, Juniper's voice told her, *even without a bridge, I could stand on the other side of a river and shout to you and you might shout back, but our voices would be lost in the rushing of the river or the call of the birds. I am shouting to you across the river now, Asenna, and I have little strength to continue. Why have you brought me one that is too old?*

He was not born in the pack, Asenna tried to answer.

Then Izlani has granted him The Sight.

What do you mean?

If he was not born in the pack…in the mountains, then surely it was Izlani who gave his Sight, Juniper murmured, *she always has her reasons, Asenna, and you may not know them until she wants you too, but you must embrace your son's gift nonetheless, since it was given so generously.*

Of course I will, Asenna replied, *but he can only learn to embrace his gift if he has a companion. It is not his fault that we had to run and find you.*

We also had to flee our home, Juniper said, and Asenna felt the she-wolf's despair wash over her.

I only wish for my son to have his birthright, and the same for your daughter. Asenna tried to impart her own emotions to the she-wolf. All the apprehension and fear of not belonging. Juniper considered her for a moment, tilting her head slightly to the side.

There is only one daughter, she finally said, *and if you will uphold the pact, they will be bonded. But I warn you, Asenna, do not tell anyone that I have spoken to you this way. Not even Haryk. I love him as my own, but he is a stupid boy. Do you understand?*

Yes, anything you ask. Asenna nodded and felt her body release from the hold Juniper had on it. The tent came back into focus and Haryk was still standing, looking at the she-wolf and waiting for her response. Juniper turned around and padded back over to her pups. She nosed all three in turn, then picked up the smallest one in her mouth, turning to deposit the tiny creature next to Fen. Then she glanced at Haryk, whose eyes glazed over a little as he listened to her voice in his head.

"Juniper says that they are bonded, and that her daughter's name is Sage," he grinned. The tiny female puppy, with fur like polished silver, scooted her body up beside Fen, who rolled onto his side and put his arm around her. The two of them fell asleep in unison and their breathing began to synchronize. Asenna, still feeling a bit dizzy, looked at Juniper and bowed and the wolf leaned forward and licked Asenna on the face. Haryk walked over and helped Asenna up off the ground, giving her an excited hug that lifted her off her feet. Asenna could tell that her brother had absolutely no idea what had just transpired, and as shaken and confused as she was by it, she was not about to break her promise to Juniper and tell him. The two of them walked out of the tent and were greeted by a rather large crowd who was waiting with bated breath. Asenna saw her mother and the twins and even Gaelin standing perfectly still, all eyes trained on her face.

"The pact is complete," Asenna told them, and suddenly she was engulfed in a sea of hugging and cheering and shouting. She could not help but smile as everyone within arm's reach congratulated her. It was the most joyous Asenna had felt in a very long time, knowing that Fen would be accepted and that they had a future with her people, no matter where they had to go and no matter where his Wolfsight had come from. There was finally a small voice in her mind, telling her that against all odds, maybe things would finally be better now.

TEN:
VIKMIRI

Carro pulled himself off the cot slowly, an inch at a time, allowing a few seconds in between movements to recover from the shooting pains that radiated out from his hip and shoulder every time he moved. The pain had dulled slightly, but it still took his breath away if he moved too quickly or in the wrong direction. Once he was sitting up, he swung his legs around so his feet were on the ground. After a few deep breaths, he pushed off and managed to stand for a few seconds, but his entire right hip and leg felt like they were on fire, so he sat back down and punched the rolled-up blanket that served as his pillow.

"Damnit!" he gasped, as much in pain as in frustration.

"Everything alright?" Tira asked as she came into the tent.

"I can't stand for more than a few seconds."

"There's always that," Tira indicated the dubious-looking crutch that Gaelin had made for him, leaning in the corner of the tent.

"I'm not using a fucking crutch to meet this woman."

"Queen. She's a Queen. And there's no shame in it. You were wounded."

"I'm not using it," said Carro flatly, "I'd just as soon lie on my back."

"You know that whatever she says, it's not a final judgment. Tolian and the Council will decide what happens to you."

"I know, but how can they not take the advice of a woman who is allowing them to stay in her country and not asking anything in return? Especially a woman who was literally chosen to lead because she can accurately 'judge men's hearts,'" Carro ran his hands over his face.

"If you really believe in her ability to judge your heart, then why are you so worried? It'll be the same whether you're standing or sitting or using a crutch," Tira sat cross-legged on the floor in front of him, "wait...is this some kind of...masculine pride thing?"

Carro shot her an annoyed look. "No, it's just a normal *human* thing. I believe it's called dignity. Maybe you've heard of it?"

"It *is* a man thing!" Tira laughed and rocked backwards, "you are such strange creatures, aren't you?"

"Can you just shut up and help me, please? I think if I stand a little longer every time I'll at least get used to the pain," Carro snapped. Still chuckling to herself, Tira stood up and held her hands out so Carro could grasp her wrists and pull himself up. The agonizing burn shot through his hip again and he closed his eyes, trying to push through it. After twenty seconds, he fell back onto the cot, breathing hard.

"That was good!" said Tira, "I can't imagine that judging a man's heart could take longer than that. Not much there, after all, right?"

"Hilarious. Can you go see if they're on their way?" Carro asked. Tira poked her head out of the tent and called to Talla.

"Yeah, they're almost here," Tira told him, "do you need help?" Carro was struggling to put on the clean shirt that Asenna had brought him the night before when she came to tell him about Fen's wolf pup. His hip wound hurt the most due to the arrow having struck bone, but he had also lost range of motion in his shoulder and the shirt was difficult to manage. Tira came over and jerked it down over his head, then held the sleeves so he could get his arms in. Carro groaned again as he put his arm down.

"Oh, stop," Tira told him, "during the war I had an arrow in my leg for two days and didn't moan as much as you are now."

"Horseshit," Carro laughed.

"Yeah, it is," Tira said, giving a guilty smile, "I'll go see how close they are." She left the tent quickly and Carro shook out his hair, which was getting far too long for his taste. Feeling a bit inspired, he took the jar of beeswax balm that Asenna had left and rubbed some onto his palms, then used it to smooth his hair back, the same way he had always worn it as a Black Saber. There was nothing he could do, however, about the nearly three weeks of stubble covering his face. Most of the Ulvvori men he had seen wore beards, so Carro knew he might have a hard time finding a razor if he wanted to get rid of it.

"As good as it's going to get," he mumbled to himself, trying to straighten the blankets behind him on the cot. Gaelin stuck his head into the tent with a pointy smile.

"Alright there, pretty boy? How's the hip?"

"It hurts, Gaelin. Are they here?"

"Aye, and I tell you, this queen is somethin' else. *Stunning* woman. If I'd had a bath in the last month or two I might feel brave enough to kiss her hand. As it is, I'll leave that to you."

"You're disgusting," Carro breathed, grateful for the small distraction. Gaelin disappeared and Asenna came in, accompanied by her mother and uncle. Carro tried to stand, but Tolian put a hand on his shoulder.

"No need," he said gently, "I don't suppose you remember me?"

"Yes, sir, but I believe we only met once, at Anburgh."

"Indeed," Tolian's golden eyes raked Carro over with a sort of polite curiosity, "a great deal has changed since then, but I hope you know how grateful my family is for what you did for Asenna and Fen."

"And I'm very grateful to--" Carro started to say.

"Can we get this over with?" Elyana cut him off.

"We can," said the imposing woman standing in the tent entrance. Carro stood up a little too quickly and let out a quiet gasp when the pain flared back up in his hip. Asenna flinched as though she wanted to help him, but she did not move and Carro swayed on the spot, trying to bow.

"Your Majesty," Carro gasped, "I'm sorry, I'm not--"

"Please do not apologize, Captain Morelake," the Queen said, holding up her hand, "you were wounded in service to your friends." Carro barely caught the eye roll Elyana gave.

"Your Majesty," he said, fighting against the waves of pain, "I would prefer not to use that surname anymore. It was given to me…against my will." Selissa nodded, running her eyes up and down his body and making him feel like he was naked again.

"As you wish, Carro. They tell me that you were Azimar's closest friend since boyhood, almost like a brother. Is this true?"

"Yes, Your Majesty," Carro answered, trying desperately to hold her penetrating gaze.

"Such a strong bond could not have been easy to break," Selissa murmured, "I appreciate that these things are rarely simple, but I would like for you to explain to me in your own words why you are here." Carro took a deep breath and looked at Asenna, who gave him a tiny nod.

"Azimar was my friend, like my brother, and I trusted him. I believed in the world he wanted to build, but it started to change during the war and after he took the throne. He began asking me to do things that I knew were wrong, and if I questioned him…" Carro paused, searching for a civilized way to explain the things Azimar had done to him, "…I was punished. When Asenna ran, he sent me after her and…ordered me to kill her, to get Fen back. He threatened the life of someone I cared about if I failed. I couldn't make that choice, so I left."

"But you did not *just* leave," Selissa said gently, "you went to Asenna and her protectors and begged to help them, knowing they would likely kill you on sight. Why? Why not simply vanish, board a ship, and start over somewhere far away?" Carro paused and considered her words. He had not imagined there would be an interrogation involved and it was difficult to think through the pain.

"They were still in danger, and I knew I could help. I couldn't live with myself if I'd allowed them to walk into it alone."

"And can you live with yourself now?" Selissa asked. Carro finally had to look away from her and his eyes fell back on Asenna, who was watching him with a strange expression. His legs were beginning to shake from the effort of standing upright, but he swallowed and looked back at Selissa.

"I can't answer that question, Your Majesty," he said, "since I haven't tried yet." Selissa gave him a gentle smile and dipped her head.

"Well?" asked Elyana from the corner of the tent.

"Reading a heart is not a science, Elyana. I do not receive some kind of divine message telling me whether or not this man will ever again make a mistake. All I can see is how much he *wants* to make things right, and that is what matters the most," Selissa folded her hands in front of her and turned back to Carro, who was struggling to continue to stay upright.

"Forgive me, Your Majesty..." he gasped and collapsed onto the cot, not waiting for her permission.

"Certainly, I am sure you must be exhausted. Please rest," Selissa put her hand gently on his shoulder, "Tolian, I will speak with you outside." Tolian and Elyana followed her out of the tent and Carro dropped his head into his hands, fighting back a breakdown.

"You're shaking," said Asenna softly, kneeling in front of him, and Carro realized that his entire body was, indeed, trembling violently.

"What are they saying?" he asked, "please, I need to know." Asenna crept over to the tent flap and put her ear up to it. Carro could only hear a few snatches of conversation here and there, but he caught Elyana's icy tones, Tolian's more measured delivery, and even Tira and Talla's aggressive voices in the mix. It could only have been five minutes, but to Carro it felt like hours before Tolian reentered the tent, his face looking a little strained. Asenna moved around to stand beside Carro, who desperately wanted to get back up, but his heart was beating too hard. He wanted to speak, but it felt like there was no air in his lungs.

"Carro," Tolian began, folding his hands behind his back, "your presence here has caused a great deal of tension in my family, as well as in the camp. Many of my people are asking me to break our laws and have you executed for your crimes against us. As a leader, I try to listen to my people and do what is best for them. However, I cannot deny the fact that *you* are also one of my people, by birth if nothing else. I will not dishonor myself or this family in order to punish you. Whatever you might have done in Azimar's service, it seems that Queen Selissa and others here, including my own niece and two of my most trusted Riders, believe your heart truly has changed and that you mean us no harm."

"I would never--" Carro began, but Tolian held up a hand.

"Therefore, I have decided to give you a choice: I cannot keep you here against your will, so you are free to leave whenever you wish. No one will stop you. However, if you choose to stay with us, you will be accompanied by one of my Riders at all times for a period of one year. You will also be expected to contribute to building a new settlement on the land the Kashaitis have granted us. If you do these things, and you can show me what is truly in your heart, then I would be willing to offer you the same reinitiation into the Ulvvori which has been given to other returned conscripts," Tolian fell silent, waiting for a response, and Carro felt his head spinning. It was far better than he could have possibly hoped.

"Yes," he gasped, "of course I...I'll stay. Thank you, sir." He stood just long enough to shake Tolian's hand, then waited until he left and collapsed back onto the cot, tears stinging his eyes. Asenna opened her mouth to speak, but was interrupted by the twins barging into the tent.

"I told you!" Tira crowed, slapping Carro on the leg.

"Were you eavesdropping?" he laughed, sitting up on his elbows.

"What else are ears for?" Talla smiled. Gaelin came in behind her wearing his usual grin and carrying a small flask.

"I was a bit disappointed they didn't clap you in irons, but this'll do," he said, offering Carro a drink. It tasted like vinegar and dirt, but it helped clear his head.

"Thank you," Carro said, his voice cracking from emotion, "I...I don't deserve this, but I'm grateful anyway. I just...want you to know how sorry I am, especially to you...Tira, Talla, for your father's death. I hope you know I'd do anything to change it."

"We know," said Tira quietly, "but anyone who says you don't deserve this doesn't know what they're talking about. They weren't there and they didn't see what you did for us."

"You should rest now," said Talla, "we'll celebrate later." As they all began to leave, Carro reached out and grabbed Asenna's hand.

"Can you stay for a minute? I need to ask you something."

Asenna came back over. "Just me?"

"I don't need the...commentary from those three," Carro told her, twisting his hands together. He didn't dare look up at her for fear he might lose his nerve. "I wanted to wait until Tolian made his decision, because I didn't want you to think I was only doing this to get your support. I know it might seem stupid and unnecessary at this point, but telling you how sorry I am doesn't feel like enough. I'm in your debt, Asenna, and if you'll accept it, I want to make a new oath to you and to Fen. Not as someone's wife or Queen, but just as...yourself." Carro could feel her eyes searching him as he waited for an answer.

"Of course I'll accept it," she said quietly. Carro heaved his body off the cot and dropped onto his knees in front of her.

"Asenna, daughter of Elyana, I hereby pledge myself to the defense and service of you and your son, Fenrinn. I will go where you go, obey your commands, and give my own life for yours if necessary. I will never forsake nor betray you. I freely and gladly make this oath without reservation and will be bound by it until death or release by your hand." Asenna reached down and pulled his chin up so he was looking at her.

"I freely and gladly accept your oath of service, Carro, son of Eirini, and I swear in return that I will never ask something of you that I would not be willing to give myself," she smiled and then held out her hands to help him stand up.

"You added that last part," Carro pointed out as he sat back down.

"I thought it was only fair, considering how your last few oaths have turned out," Asenna grinned and the bridge of her nose scrunched up. Carro suddenly caught that she might be teasing him.

"Well...thank you," he breathed, trying to let himself smile and laugh too. After she was gone, Carro realized he was still trembling and he pressed his hands together, trying to make it stop. As he laid down and closed his eyes, he tried to think of the last time he had felt such acceptance, but nothing came to his mind. He reveled in the feeling all night, not knowing how long it might last.

~ *Two Months Later* ~

Thunk. Carro pulled his ax out of the stump and tossed the split pieces of wood onto the pile nearby, then grabbed another log. *Thunk.* Another swing of the ax and two more pieces of firewood tumbled to the ground, then were added to the pile. He dropped the ax and picked up his shirt to wipe the sweat away. It was early summer now and even waking up at dawn to chop firewood offered little relief from the relentless Kashaiti heat. Carro glanced over at his guard, a young Wolf Rider named Linn who was clearly not taking her job seriously. She was napping against her dire wolf's shoulder while the animal, Thorn, kept his golden eyes fixed on Carro.

"I'm done," he called out to Thorn, guessing that the wolf understood him, because Linn suddenly stirred and sat up.

"Finished?" she asked, coming over to inspect and giving a sideways glance at the ax he had left leaning on the stump.

"Yes, can we go?" Carro grabbed his water flask and took a long drink, then began walking back through the little village. The land Kashait had given to the Ulvvori had turned out to be beautiful and welcoming. While they were still out on the vast, dry plains, there was a spot along the Oragos River where the ground fell away into tall sandstone cliffs with the river running along the base, creating a miles-long strip of greenery and fertile soil. It was here that the Ulvvori had spent four months building their new settlement, far enough away from the riverbanks that they would not be threatened by annual flooding, but close enough that they could grow crops in the partial shade. It was an ideal spot and many of them seemed pleased enough to stay there permanently.

Shortly before the Ulvvori had moved from the refugee camp, however, Talla and Gaelin had decided to return to Esmadia alone. Carro and Tira had stayed and set up tents on the outskirts of the village, rather than building the little sandstone cottages that comprised the rest of the settlement. Tira still planned to return eventually to find her sister and Carro had not argued with this plan because he did not want to put down roots when most of the Ulvvori were still relatively unwelcoming, if not overtly hostile, toward him. Because of this, Carro spent most of his time with Tira, and sometimes Asenna or Ivarr, when they could get away from Elyana. But with the border skirmishes between Azimar's troops and the Kashaitis becoming more frequent, many of the Wolf Riders had gone to help. Tira had taken to filling in for them on her horse, going out nearly every day on patrols or hunting trips. This left Carro alone by the fire at night more often than he would like, whittling random objects from chunks of wood to try and stop his mind reliving the moment Talla had sunk her hatchet into Gade's back.

When he and Linn reached the edge of the village, Carro ducked into his tent and grabbed a small bag of his dirty clothes. Tira was just emerging from her own tent beside his, looking a bit drowsy.

"You didn't come back last night," Carro said to her, "what happened?" As he said it, Carro saw movement inside the tent behind her and a man emerged, pulling his shirt on. Carro's eyes widened as he recognized one of his regular guards, Ekhan, who shot him a guilty look and walked away. His dire wolf appeared from behind the tent to follow.

"What?" Tira asked, giving Carro a shameless grin, "I'm not breaking any rules."

"I'm fairly certain Tolian didn't even think he would *need* to make a rule about this!" Carro said loudly. Tira shrugged and then looked over at Linn, who shouted at her.

"What is wrong with you?!"

"Why don't you come and find out, Linn?" Tira called back, winking. Carro shook his head, but couldn't help laughing.

"Settle down," he chuckled, "I'm done for the day and I'm going to get cleaned up. Are you going back out tonight?"

"I think so," Tira replied, "they're so short on Riders now, they need all the help they can get. I'll stop and see if Asenna or Ivarr could keep you company though, if you want? I know you hate being here alone."

"I'll be fine. Don't worry about it," Carro murmured as he started toward the river with Linn and Thorn behind him.

"How long is this going to take?" Linn sighed when they approached the cottonwood trees that were scattered along the riverbank.

"Do you have somewhere to be?" Carro asked, struggling to keep the annoyance out of his voice. Linn was not as antagonistic as some of his other guards, but her constant sighs and eyerolls grated on his nerves.

"If I did, I wouldn't tell you, *vikmiri*," she snapped back, using the Ulvvori word which Carro had quickly learned meant 'a diseased animal' or, in his case, 'pariah.' The epithet stung, but Carro let it go and kept walking. When they reached the water, he went to his favorite spot, where the riverbed opened up into a shallow, slower pool shaded by trees. Stripping down and tossing his clothes into the water, Carro waded in, not bothering to check if Linn had turned around yet. He had all but gotten over his obsessive need to cover himself, which had come from a lifetime of trying to hide the brand on his shoulder, especially living next to Tira, who had absolutely no compunction when it came to privacy. Once he felt clean enough, Carro took his time washing his clothes, drying off, getting dressed, and hanging his clean laundry out on the tree branches to dry. Linn watched him from a short distance, looking sour. Carro had to admit that he got a little pleasure from stalling when she was around, just to irritate her.

Once he was finished, he went back to the tents and found that Tira had already left. As the sun began to set, he built a small fire and ate a few handfuls of nuts, dried berries, and bread, then sat down to continue carving a small block of wood he had been working on turning into a cave bear. Another Wolf Rider arrived to relieve Linn, but Carro barely acknowledged the man as he settled down near the main road. When the sunlight had all but faded, Carro heard someone approaching and looked up to see Asenna, who was carrying a short sword in each hand. Feeling a little apprehensive at the sight of her armed, he set his whittling knife aside and stood up.

"Is everything ok?"

"Well," Asenna said, grinning, "Tira told me that she's been called off on another patrol, and Fen is in bed, so I thought I'd keep you company."

"With…swords?" Asenna held one out to him, but he didn't take it.

"If Tira can't keep training me, then I thought you could do it."

"Hey!" called the guard, "he isn't allowed a weapon!" Asenna rounded on him and took a few steps.

"Well then, you'd better go and report me to Tolian. Go on!" she sneered. The man looked startled and didn't move. "That's what I thought. Shut up and mind your own business." She turned back to Carro and shoved the sword into his hand, then drew hers.

"What was that?" Carro asked, slightly amused, but also grateful that she was willing to stand up for him.

"That was me being sick and tired of everyone telling me what I can do. Now, are you going to fight me or not?"

"Honestly? I'm a little afraid to right now, but…if you insist, we can start with your grip."

"What's wrong with it?"

"It's just a little…sloppy. Here, can I?" Carro asked, reaching out. Asenna nodded and he gently adjusted her hands. Once she was ready, he moved back, drew the other sword, and they faced each other. Carro looked over at his guard again and saw that the young man was watching him closely and toying with a small throwing knife. He knew he needed to be careful and avoid sudden movements, so he coached Asenna through a few drills where she was the one attacking and he was merely blocking her. From the way she gritted her teeth and the noises she made when she swung, Carro could tell she was working out some sort of frustration, but after nearly an hour, his bad shoulder was aching. He dropped the blade into the dirt and held up his hands.

"I yield, my lady," he said, smiling and tapping his shoulder, "I'm hurting." Asenna looked a little abashed and lowered her sword.

"I'm sorry," she sighed, "I forgot you've been splitting wood all day."

"It's alright," Carro assured her, "I can tell you needed it. You can stay…if you'd like." He motioned to the other stump beside the fire and she came to sit with him as he picked his whittling project back up.

"What's it supposed to be?" she asked.

"Ah…well, it was supposed to be a cave bear, but now you've got me questioning myself."

"I mean…" Asenna giggled, "have you ever even *seen* a cave bear?"

"Once…maybe. It could have been an exceptionally large badger though," Carro replied, feeling an involuntary grin cross his face. Asenna leaned over and took the carving from him, turning it in her hands.

"The snout should be shorter, and cave bears don't have tails. This *might* be a…very fat dire wolf…if you squint…" Carro looked at his guard again and noted that the man was smirking, making him suddenly feel quite self-conscious.

"It's late," he said, "shouldn't you get back?"

"Don't you start telling me what to do too," Asenna groaned.

"I wouldn't dare. I just...don't want to cause problems between you and your family, and I have a feeling *that* one is reporting my every move back to your mother." He flicked his eyes over to the guard.

"Oh, I don't need your help to cause problems with my family, trust me. But I probably should get back." Asenna stood up and grabbed the swords. "Tomorrow?"

"Whenever you want. You know where to find me," Carro told her. She held out the carving for him to take, but he shook his head. "Give it to Fen. He won't know the difference." Asenna smiled and pocketed the little creature, then walked away, leaving him alone with the guard.

"You think you're clever?" the man called out. Carro didn't look at him. "That horseshit might work on naive little girls like Asenna, but the rest of us know better. We know what you are, *vikmiri*."

"Go fuck yourself," Carro called back, going into his tent without bothering to wait for a reply.

~~~

Carro's evenings continued this way for at least two months. After Fen was asleep, Asenna would come to keep him company for a few hours, always bringing the swords with her. Sometimes the weapons ended up going unused while the two of them sat by the fire and she tried to teach him a few words of Ulvvori, or critiqued his wood carvings. Other nights, Asenna seemed to be full of rage, and Carro let her take it out on him with a blade in her hand until he could barely move his arms.

One night, however, she didn't bring the swords at all, and showed up at his tent wearing a long skirt paired with a beautifully embroidered, fitted bodice, rather than her usual tunic or smock dress, and a crown of small blue flowers perched on her head.

"What's the occasion?" Carro asked.

"It's the summer solstice," Asenna said, "Tira didn't tell you? There's a bonfire and a party."

Carro looked over at the Wolf Rider assigned to him that night, who simply shook her head. "Yeah, I don't think I'm invited to that."

Asenna's face fell a little. "Are you sure?"

"Don't worry about me, please" Carro told her, "go and have fun." They both looked up as they heard the squeal of a fiddle starting to play, keeping time with a quick drumbeat.

"One dance first?" Asenna asked, holding her hand out.

Carro shook his head and held his hands up. "I *don't* dance."

"It's not hard, I promise. Come on."

"Your toes will regret it,' Carro said, looking down at her bare feet, "trust me."

"If I can learn to fight, you can learn to dance," Asenna sighed, reaching down and grabbing his hand to pull him off the stump. Carro let her lead him away from the firepit and when she placed his hand on her waist, he felt something shift in his stomach. His face started to burn as she looked up at him and he suddenly felt completely off-kilter. The sensation was intensely distracting and Carro barely heard her explanation as she slowly led him through the steps.

"See?" she said, spinning away from him and then finishing with a bow, "you're really just moving in a small circle, except it's a group dance, so everyone does this and goes around the bonfire in the middle."

"Alright," Carro said, trying to shake off the strange feeling that was still making his heart flip over in his chest, "I'll try, but just one." Asenna pulled him into the reel, spinning them around to the beat of a new song. Carro knew he was thinking about it too hard and he kept stumbling, but she managed to keep them on track, twirling around the firepit and howling with laughter at his inability to keep the steps until the song finally ended. Carro's hip was already aching, but he found that he didn't want to stop.

"How can you be so good at swordplay and so *bad* at that? It's almost the same exact thing," Asenna let out a breathless laugh and pushed her hair off her face.

"Trust me, I wish I knew," Carro replied, leaning over and bracing his hands on his knees. Despite his misgivings and aching body, Asenna somehow convinced him to dance a few more songs, and then to Carro's relief the drums stopped and the fiddle let out a long, high note. He heard a woman's voice begin to sing in a wavering tone and he closed his eyes, trying to see if he could understand any of the Ulvvori lyrics.

"How do we dance to this one?" he asked Asenna.

"*We* don't," she said softly, coming to stand next to him, "this one is only for lovers. The words…well, she's telling her love that, if she dies first, she'll wait for him in the next life…and she wants him to know how thankful she is for him. She says…ah, it's hard to translate, but something like 'when I'm lost in the storm clouds, you pull me back to the ground,' and that…uh…" Asenna looked down and blushed.

"That what?"

"…when they make love it feels like the stars are raining light down onto them, washing them clean of…everything that came before that moment," Asenna murmured, her face still bright red, "that's why she calls him *lai'rani,* 'my light,' because he saved her from…some kind of darkness. That part is hard to translate too. It's like…the darkness that was inside of her." Carro stood perfectly still and soaked in the sound of the song, then glanced over at Asenna and felt his heart start to skip again. He had never allowed himself to really look at her before, but now the way the firelight was dancing on her skin and hair made it seem like she herself was made of flames. Suddenly, Carro had the same irrepressible urge to reach out and touch her that he felt when he looked into a campfire, but he resisted, knowing that he was sure to be burned if he did. The song ended and Asenna cleared her throat, breaking through the daze she had put him in.

"I'd better go, before my mother sends out an armed search party."

"Yeah," Carro cleared his throat too and took a step away from her, "I'm sure you have a dozen young men waiting to *not* step all over your feet during the next song." He forced himself to smile and Asenna laughed.

"Doubtful," she said ruefully, "according to Ivarr, they're all a little afraid of me. Something about my temper."

"Can't say I blame them there," Carro teased, and Asenna looked a little surprised that he was joking with her, but then she smiled too.

"See you tomorrow?" she asked.

"I'll be here," Carro replied, spreading his arms out to indicate that he rarely went anywhere else, but Asenna seemed to misunderstand the gesture and wrapped her arms around him in a brief embrace. Carro was too startled to return it, and by the time he even realized what had happened, she was walking away.

The next morning, Carro woke up and came out of his tent to find that Tira had already caught Pan from the field and put a bridle on him. Linn and Thorn were back on guard duty, waiting impatiently by the main road. Carro took the reins from Tira, making sure to give Pan a few light kisses on his velvety nose since he was all out of sugar cubes.

"How was the party?" Carro asked, peering into her tent, "no surprise visitors this morning?"

"You just missed her," Tira laughed, "and the party was fun. Asenna was a bit late showing up though. You want to tell me about that?" Carro raised an eyebrow at the look on her face.

"She was trying to teach me to dance so I wouldn't feel left out."

Tira threw her head back and let out a howl. "*You* danced? Don't you have to pull the stick out of your--"

"Alright! Thank you!" Carro said loudly, rolling his eyes, "I actually did alright for a while."

"She's been keeping you company an awful lot," said Tira pointedly.

"Well, you're never around anymore. She's just trying to pick up your slack and supervise me."

"Hmm…yeah…supervise," Tira nodded, yellow eyes glittering. Carro ignored her and led Pan over to a stump to climb on his back. "Do you want some help with the firewood today? I've got nothing else going on and I can tell you're hurting…you know, from all that dancing."

"I'm fine," Carro insisted, even though his hip really did hurt, "it's not that bad." Ignoring Tira's smirk, he set off back through the village toward the wood pile with Linn and Thorn in tow. When he reached the woodpile, Carro slid down from Pan's back and led him over to the giant antler sledge that he used to deliver firewood every morning. He backed Pan up to the sledge and fitted the harness around his body, then began to toss the logs he had split the previous afternoon into the center cup of the antler. As he worked, Linn settled down against Thorn's flank and pulled out a whetstone to sharpen the long dagger she carried. Carro had the sledge almost completely full when he heard voices approaching. It was a group of eight Ulvvori boys that Carro estimated were probably in their late teens. He noted that they all had golden eyes, but didn't see any sign of their dire wolves nearby. They were, ostensibly, there to collect firewood for their families, but it was earlier than people normally started coming and Carro froze with a log in his hand. He had become all but deaf to the verbal harassment that was thrown at him daily, but many of the Wolf Riders were particularly belligerent and Carro knew better than most how aggressive young men in a group could be. As they approached, one of them spotted him and grinned, then elbowed one of his friends.

"Got any firewood for us today, *vikmiri?*" he said, voice dripping with scorn. Carro straightened up and tossed the log he was holding onto the sledge.

"This is spoken for," he said steadily, "but you're welcome to split more yourselves." Carro motioned to the ax that was still leaning against the stump.

"But you're already here," said another boy with a laugh, "go on, we can wait."

"Split it yourselves," Carro repeated in a low voice. A few of the boys exchanged looks and Carro took a deep breath, trying to maintain his composure. He stalked over to the woodpile, grabbed the largest unsplit log he could find, and placed it in the center of the big stump. Picking up the ax with his good arm, he swung it up and single-handedly brought it down on the center of the log, sending the two halves flying several feet and burying the blade deep into the stump. He looked back at the young men, relishing their slightly crestfallen faces as he yanked the ax out, then held it out.

"See," he said lightly, "it's easy. Even for twats like you." The boy in front took a step toward him, face twisted in anger, and the others tensed up as well. Carro noted that several of them were carrying weapons and he tried to calculate his odds, then glanced at Linn, who was sneering and hadn't moved a muscle. Carro tightened his grip on the ax handle, knowing he didn't dare move first.

"You have one more chance, *vikmiri*," growled the young man in front, "or I'll make sure you never leave this woodpile. Trust me, no one would miss you." Carro willed himself not to give in to the fury rising in his chest and the voice in his head, which sounded remarkably like Azimar, screaming at him to bury the ax in the young man's face.

"I have work to do," he said calmly, "and I don't want to fight."

"I thought you were a Black Saber!" one of the boys scoffed, "are you afraid of a little fight?"

"No," Carro answered, "but you should be. Last chance to walk away." Several of them inched closer and Carro raised the ax slightly just as the first boy lunged at him, fist closed. Carro sidestepped and his attacker fell to the ground and rolled, but he felt a wild rush bubble up in his stomach as the other young men approached. Another one charged and Carro managed to kick him to the ground, but not before a fist made hard contact with his ribs. Ignoring the shooting pains start up in his hip, Carro flipped the ax in his hand and dropped to his knees, driving the base of the handle into another man's foot until he felt a crack. Before he could stand up, a boot made contact with the side of his head and he tumbled onto his side, the pain now extending down his arm from his shoulder. Carro groaned and tried to pull himself up, but the kick had dazed him and he felt them closing in. The blows started landing one after another, from all sides, sparing no part of his body.

Carro tried to block them, but he finally felt the rage that had been building inside him for months break like a river through a dam, pouring into his chest and head and setting his limbs on fire. Rolling onto his knees, Carro lunged at the pair of legs closest to him, tackling the young man to the ground and trapping his arms against his body. He managed to land at least half a dozen hard punches to the young man's face before he felt a massive, furry body slam into him and he was thrown clear of his attackers. Linn had finally joined the fray and Thorn now had Carro pinned underneath his huge paws. The wolf bared his fangs just inches from Carro's face and he could feel the hot breath in his own throat as he squeezed his eyes shut.

"Get out of here, and take him with you!" he heard Linn shout at the other men, "are you trying to make my job harder?" Carro opened his eyes and saw her glaring at him as she came around to Thorn's side and pulled a length of rope off her belt.

"I didn't mean--" Carro started to stay, lifting his head to see the young men dragging their friend away, his face bloodied and his body limp.

"Get up!" Linn snarled, "hands behind you." Carro complied, his heart hammering and his whole body aching. *Let's see how Tolian feels about executions now,* he thought bitterly as Linn tie his hands behind his back and shoved him forward. They walked through the village and Carro could see the whispering and looks of disgust as he passed. Those didn't bother him as much as the expressions of smug satisfaction, as if all their worst fears about him had been confirmed. When they arrived at the central plaza of the village, Carro spotted Asenna and her mother talking to a few other women near the council house. She looked so happy, holding Fen in her arms while Sage laid at her feet, and Carro's heart sank when he thought about how she might react to his newest transgression. She looked up as people around her started to whisper and point, and Carro saw her face shift from confusion to horror before she handed Fen to Elyana and ran over to him.

"Carro, what happened to you?" she asked, "what's going on, Linn?"

"Get out of the way, princess," Linn growled. Asenna stepped aside, but followed them into the council house where Tolian was sitting at a low table with a few members of the Elder Council.

"Linn? What's happened?" Tolian asked, standing up. Linn shoved Carro forward and he lost his balance, falling onto his knees in front of the table. Blood dripped onto the floor from his face and mouth, and every part of his body was in so much pain that he could not even look up.

"Some men came to get firewood and he got into a fight with them," Linn explained, "he beat one of them nearly to death."

Tolian came around the table and squatted down. "Is that true, Carro?" he asked. Carro raised his head and swallowed the blood that was pooling in his mouth. Tolian's impassive face was swimming in front of his eyes and he felt like he might vomit if he stayed upright much longer.

"Yes," he coughed, "but I did *not* start that fight, Tolian."

"Liar!" Linn spat at him.

"Thank you, Linn, you may wait outside," Tolian said.

"I was the only witness!" she protested, "I saw what happened!"

"And you did nothing to protect the man in your charge, did you?" said Tolian, raising his voice ever so slightly, "you and Thorn could have ended it before it even began. Is this the honor of a Wolf Rider? You should be ashamed of yourself! I will deal with you later." Carro waited until Linn was gone, then slumped to the side and coughed up a mixture of blood and spit.

"Don't believe a word he says, Tolian!" came Elyana's voice from behind him. "We all knew this would happen eventually."

"Carro," said Tolian slowly, ignoring her, "I need you to tell me how badly you are injured, and then I need you to tell me exactly what happened." Carro took stock of his body and decided that the worst was probably some cracked ribs, although his head was still swimming.

"I think...I'm alright," he murmured, "and yes, I did beat that man, but I *swear* to you Tolian, I did not start it. They asked for firewood and I told them they could split it themselves."

"And then they attacked you?"

"Well, I...I may have been a little rude about it..." Carro admitted.

"Do you know the man you injured?" Tolian tugged anxiously at his short gray beard.

"No, I've never seen any of them before," Carro told him, "they were all Riders, but their wolves weren't around. That's all I can tell you."

"Please stay here for now," said Tolian, "I will see what I can find out from Linn. Elyana, if you would please come with me." She looked like she wanted to argue, but handed Fen off to Asenna and followed her brother outside. Carro moved to sit up against one of the large posts that supported the roof and Asenna untied his hands, then sat next to him. He could see the elders gathered around the table whispering and looking at him, some with pity and some with contempt. Fen, however, was reaching out for him and squealing loudly. The child's emotions seemed to transfer to Sage, who wandered over and began licking a cut on Carro's arm. He reached out and scratched the pup behind her ears.

"Is that really what happened?" Asenna sighed, pushing Carro's hair off his face and wiping the blood with her sleeve, "if they attacked you for no reason..."

"You have too much faith in people," Carro tried to laugh, but groaned instead as the pain shot through his ribs, "I was not completely innocent."

"As if rudeness deserves a beating," she said softly, tilting his face back to see his injuries better. Her hand brushed against a fresh cut on his cheek and Carro instinctively reached up, covering her fingers with his. Their eyes met for a split second before Asenna yanked her hand away and blushed.

"Pan is still down there alone, hooked up to the sledge," Carro looked away and tried to change the subject, "someone needs to go get him and take the firewood today."

"Don't worry about Pan and the firewood. I'll make sure someone takes care of it." She put Fen down in front of her and he sat up straight, leaning slightly against her leg. He was nearly six months old now, with a thick head of dark curls, and he reached out for Carro, who offered the baby his undamaged hand.

"Sorry, he's getting a few teeth," Asenna laughed as Fen clamped his gums down and Carro squeezed his cheeks together, making him giggle.

"It's alright," Carro said, "he's a bit more gentle than Pan when he wants a piece of me." He leaned his head against the post and stared up at the beams and thatched roof above him.

"I wish I could do something," said Asenna with an edge in her voice, "I wish I could make them stop."

Carro looked back at her. "You are too good, Asenna. By all rights, you should be treating me the same way." They were both silent for a few minutes before Tolian re-entered the council house, accompanied by one of the boys who had attacked Carro.

"I have spoken with this young man and he has confirmed your story. He is deeply apologetic for the cowardly behavior he and his friends displayed, and as a punishment they will be taking over your woodcutting duties for the time being. The boy you injured will recover and be no worse for wear aside from his broken nose." Tolian waved and the boy left the council house quickly.

"Thank you, sir," Carro said, "I'm sorry to have interrupted your meeting." He started to try and pull himself up, but Tolian approached and put a hand on his shoulder.

"Asenna, could I have a few minutes with Carro, please?" he said. Asenna looked nervous, but she picked up Fen and walked out, Sage trotting behind her. Tolian indicated that Carro should sit on one of the low stools beside the council table, and the elders who had been watching the scene play out stood up to leave them alone as well. Once they were gone, Tolian sat down and laced his fingers together.

"Why do you stay here, Carro? I don't mean that as an implication that I would like you to leave, but four months ago, Selissa asked if you would be able to live with yourself going forward. You told her you had not tried yet, so now I would like to ask you again: Are you able to live with yourself?"

"No…I'm not," Carro traced the whorls on the table with his fingertips, "but I made a promise to stay with Asenna and Fen. I'm not going to break it, even having to put up with…this every day." He waved a hand over his face.

"You know, I've seen you leave firewood out for Asenna every day," Tolian said, his voice measured and his golden eyes trained on Carro's face. "Of course, you know she could get it herself, or her brothers could bring it, but you make sure it's you who does it. She comes home in the evening and has one less thing to worry about, one less concern for the well-being of her son. I know it might seem small to you, especially when you compare it to all the bad choices you've ever made, but every stick of firewood you leave outside her door is a fulfillment of the oath you made…and an act of love."

"Yes, sir," Carro murmured, digging his fingernail into the table.

"Then why are you still unable to live with yourself?"

Carro took a deep, shaky breath and finally met Tolian's eyes as he spoke. "When I was ten, I had just started my formal training in the army, and I was smaller and quieter than all the other boys in my group, so I became a target. They came after me all the time and no one stopped them. The officers said it would toughen me up, teach me how to fight back. One night, I was sent…to pick up firewood…and some of them followed me out of the barracks. I think they meant to kill me. Azimar happened to be walking by and he quite literally saved my life, then he made sure no one ever touched me again. After that, I did what he told me to do because I knew my life wasn't worth anything, but I owed it to him anyway. I trusted him so much, I...stopped thinking for myself. So today, when they attacked me, all I could hear was his voice...telling me to just bury that ax in their heads and be done with it. I don't want to be that person anymore, but...who else am I?" Carro pushed a little too hard on the crack in the wood and split his fingernail.

"Your life is worth a great deal to us," Tolian said softly, putting his hand on Carro's, "and I admire your devotion to the promises you've made, but I wonder if you make them in order to avoid having to rely on your own judgment? Maybe you are seeking atonement by allowing others to make decisions for you."

"Well...making my own decisions hasn't gotten me very far."

"I do not agree with that at all. It was your own sense of justice that led you to abandon the Black Sabers rather than kill Asenna, and it was your own decision to nearly give your life for hers."

"To be honest," Carro said slowly, "I didn't exactly plan on surviving when I made those decisions, so maybe my judgment has a bit of a death wish. It all just feels like...I'm trying to build a roof while it's pouring rain. How am I supposed to live a life I never planned on having?" Tolian was silent for a moment and Carro saw something shift in his face.

"As it happens," he said quietly, "I do know something about that. I imagine that Asenna has told you what happened to my family. My wife, Dirye, and our son Kirann."

"Yes, she told me."

Tolian nodded and his eyes drifted away. "I wanted to die that day. I actively chose it, desperately tried to throw myself on their swords. But the people who loved me most would not let it happen. I was lost...for so long, and sometimes I even hated Larke and Elyana for not letting me go. I had to learn how to live a life I never planned...nor ever even wanted." He paused and Carro had to look away.

"What happened?" he asked softly, "how did you...come out of it?"

"I didn't," said Tolian, looking back at Carro, "I still have to wake up every day and make a choice to stay, and I don't do it for myself. For as long as my family still needs me, I'll stay here for them."

"I don't think I can let myself rely on other people that way anymore," Carro said slowly, "even people who...love me. I need to find out what I am when I'm *not* beholden to anyone, out of fear or love or anything else."

"I am proud of you, Carro," Tolian said, "and I will support you in anything you decide. But whatever that is, I must ask you to be gentle when you tell Asenna. She has lost enough, and she cares for you...very much."

Carro felt his face burn, but he nodded in agreement. "Of course, sir." Feeling every agonizing movement painfully in his ribs and hip, Carro left the council house, but did not see Asenna in the plaza. He limped back to the woodpile, determinedly ignoring the stares and whispers from all sides as he went. Someone had unhitched Pan from the sledge and taken it out, leaving the horse tethered to a nearby fence. He tossed his head and stomped when he saw Carro.

"I'm so sorry, Pan," Carro breathed, pressing his face against the horse's cheek and wrapping his arms around his neck, "I know that probably scared you to death." He slowly led Pan back to his tent, where Tira was sitting by the firepit alone making crossbow bolts. She jumped up when she saw his face and bloodied clothing.

"What happened to you?" she cried, "who--"

"It was nothing, Tira. Just a stupid fight."

She followed him into his tent. "A fight? With who? Are you in trouble?" Carro sat down hard on his cot.

"Are you still planning on going back?" he asked, "to Esmadia?"

"Well...yes, eventually, but..." Tira stammered, "but I thought you were staying...you made a promise to Asenna."

"Let me worry about Asenna," Carro told her, "can I come with you?" Tira sat beside him and put a hand on his shoulder.

"Carro, you don't have to leave. People are stupid. You don't need everyone's approval to stay here and be happy."

"Can I come with you or not?" Carro snapped, avoiding her eyes.

"Of course you can. I'd be glad of the company," Tira said softly, standing up and going to leave the tent.

"Good, I want to leave as soon as possible."

After the two of them finished eating that evening, Carro went back into his tent to pack the rest of his things. He had only been there a few minutes when Asenna came in carrying Fen in her sling.

"Sorry I disappeared earlier. Fen was--" she started to say, then she saw his half-packed bag, "what's going on?" Carro faced her and ran a hand nervously through his hair. He had been trying to plan what he would say all afternoon, but now that she was standing in front of him, all the words he had come up with seemed horribly inadequate.

"I'm leaving," he murmured, "I'm going back with Tira."

Asenna took a small step backwards. "I don't understand..."

"Remember in the forest when you told me I had to shed my skin and start over?"

Asenna let out a small gasping laugh. "I was just...it was a metaphor,

Carro! I thought things were getting better…today was just a bad day. You didn't do anything wrong!"

"Why do you--" Carro started to shout, but then brought his voice down so as not to scare Fen. "*Why* do you keep defending me?"

"Because you're the only one!" Asenna cried, "you're the only one who understands what it was like with him…what I went through. *I trust you*, so why can't they?"

"I don't even trust myself, Asenna! You don't know what this is like," Carro tried to soften his voice this time, but it still came out harsh with emotion, "whatever problems you might have with your family…they love you endlessly, and you had that your whole life before you met Azimar. You had their voices in your head, reminding you of how loved you are, even when being with him was fucking unbearable. But…the only voice I have *ever* had in my head is his. Even now, halfway across the world, I can't silence it. I have to spend all day, every day reminding myself that my life is still worth anything, because he told me so many times it wasn't, and that was the only thing I ever heard from *anyone* who claimed to love me."

"I know, but that doesn't make it true…"

Carro found he couldn't stop and let the words pour out of him like a waterfall. "And even after all that, I woke up every damn day for eighteen years and made a choice to obey him. I hurt…*killed* people for him, and I watched him hurt people and didn't stop it because at least he wasn't hurting me. I chose him, over and over and over. What kind of person does that make me? How am I any better than him?" Carro felt himself shaking and sat down on his cot, hoping she wouldn't see it.

"You are *nothing* like him…" Asenna's voice wavered and Carro looked up at her, unable to understand for a single second why she wanted to be anywhere near him.

"I don't know how you can believe that," he sighed, "I want to believe it too, but this is the only way I can find out. I need to know who I am without Azimar, the Black Sabers, the Ulvvori…and without you. I'll always be in your debt after the way you've stood up for me, but…I need you to release me from the oath I made that day."

"Debts and oaths? Is that really all this is to you?" murmured Asenna, her eyes becoming hard even though they were glittering with tears. Carro stood up and turned away from her so he wouldn't see them fall.

"That's all it can be, Asenna."

"I won't--" she started to say, but he turned back and dropped onto his knees in front of her. Carro knew it was dramatic, but he needed her to leave so he could stop second guessing himself.

"I humbly beseech you to release me from my oath to serve, protect, and obey. I do not ask this lightly and I beg your forgiveness for violating the trust you have placed in me," he recited the words by rote, struggling to remove any hint of what he was really feeling.

"If I release you, do you promise to come back?"

"I need to stop making promises I can't keep."

"Alright," Asenna's voice finally broke, "Carro, I release you from your oath. Go where you will...with my forgiveness." Using the cot to stabilize himself, Carro stood up and faced her. Tears were rolling down her cheeks now and he desperately wanted to wipe them away, but instead he leaned forward and kissed Fen softly on the side of his head. The baby whipped around and stared at him with a tiny smile, his big golden eyes shining.

"Take care of your mother for me, little prince," Carro whispered in his ear. As he straightened up, Asenna put a hand on his shoulder, where he had been struck by Roper's arrow.

"If you can't promise to come back, at least promise me you'll stay safe?" she asked. Carro felt himself trapped between knowing that he needed to end the conversation but also wanting nothing more than to stand in that spot with her all night. He reached up and slipped his hand into hers, pulling it away from his body. The same unfamiliar feeling that had first come over him while they were dancing suddenly began to overwhelm all his senses at once, making it impossible to let go of her fingers.

"Asenna...please don't make this harder than it already is," he whispered. Their eyes met and Carro felt his resolve starting to leave him. Wavering for a few seconds longer, he squeezed his eyes shut and finally managed to pull his hand away from hers, then went back to where his bag was sitting on the cot. Behind him, Asenna let out a sob, but when Carro turned around she was already gone.

PART TWO

ELEVEN: THE RESISTANCE

~ One Year Later ~

Asenna looked up from the hole she had been digging and squinted. The summer sun beating down on her little garden made it difficult for her eyes to adjust as she scanned the sandstone cliffs above the village, but she eventually managed to spot a dire patrolling along the top, which she knew to be Nettle, with Ivarr on her back. She looked back down and jumped as a small green snake came out from between the leaves and slithered across her foot. Asenna picked it up and let it twist around her fingers for a few moments, then released it in another part of the garden. As she stood up, she realized that Fen had half-buried himself and Sage in black dirt.

"Fen!" Asenna called to him, "stop please! You're both filthy!"

"Mama!" the boy squealed, "lookit Sage!" He roared with laughter as Sage jumped up and shook herself, sending the dirt flying everywhere. The two of them ran back across the garden toward her and Asenna stepped out of their way as they passed. Nothing made her happier than seeing Fen with his little wolf, but she could certainly do without all the dirt they tracked into her cottage. They ran back around again and Asenna stopped them, then pointed at the hole she had been working on.

"Sage, dig?" she asked. Fen looked at the wolf and Asenna could tell they were communicating wordlessly because Sage leapt forward and began to dig, furiously throwing chunks of earth and rocks out behind her. She was about the size of a small hound now, while Fen was a year and a half old and already coming into the power of the Wolfsight. His bond with Sage was one of the strongest Asenna had ever seen between a child and pup, and even Tolian agreed that the way they communicated was years ahead of where most children would be at his age. Asenna had still not told anyone what Juniper had said to her about Fen's Wolfsight, but she knew that the strength of the connection between them must have something to do with it. In spite of her joy at seeing Fen and Sage together, Asenna sometimes felt sad that he might grow up without Wolf Rider friends his own age. Even now, nearly two years since the Ulvvori had been forced out of their home in the mountains, Fen remained the only child who had been born with the power. The dire wolves themselves had even chosen to stop having more litters, since they knew their pups would have no children to bond with. The situation cast a dark pall over their otherwise tranquil life in Kashait, since many of the Riders still clung to the oath they had made to go back, especially since the raids along the border wall had stopped and Azimar had withdrawn his troops for reasons that none of them could understand.

"What are you planting in the middle of summer?" Elyana asked as she walked up to the garden patch and leaned on the fence.

"Yellow squash. I know it's late, but I just want to see what happens." Asenna pulled a few seeds out of her apron pocket and dropped them into the hole Sage had dug, then covered them up. Sage tilted her head and whined, as if to say *'Hey, I worked hard on that hole, why are you filling it in?'*

"Optimistic," said Elyana, smiling, "come on, let's get these little monsters cleaned up and start a fire. Ivarr will be finishing soon and he promised to make more of his famous fish stew." Asenna wiped her hands on her apron, then took Fen's hand and led him and Sage out of the garden. Elyana had relaxed considerably since they had moved into Kashait and Carro had left them, but Asenna still occasionally felt the tension in their relationship, which had been exacerbated by Haryk's marriage to Nikke. The wedding had taken place six months before, and at least once a week since then, Elyana slipped into a casual conversation how much she would like to see *all* her children happily settled down. Asenna tried to ignore it, but it had reached a boiling point when her mother had tried to introduce her to a young Wolf Rider named Varin and it had gone disastrously wrong. Since then, Elyana had focused her attentions on Ivarr, but Asenna still avoided spending long stretches of time alone with her mother.

"I'll take Fen to Juniper if you want to go get more firewood," Elyana said when they reached their little family plot. There were three small cottages in a row, with larger wooden structures built onto the back of two of them to accommodate the family's dire wolves. Tolian, Elyana, and Ivarr occupied one house with Echo and Nettle. Haryk, Nikke, Juniper, Ash, and Sage's two brothers lived beside them. Asenna, Fen, and Sage lived in the last cottage on the row, and Asenna's garden was set behind it in a large field where it could get the most sunlight. In front of the homes was a courtyard space surrounded by trees, with a large fire pit and a long wooden table where the family prepared and cooked most of their meals together. As they came up to the houses, Sage's brothers, Fennel and Hazel, saw them coming and raced out. There was a flurry of whining and tail wagging and yipping as they all ran back to their mother, who was stretched out in the afternoon sun.

"Be back in a bit," Asenna said, waving to her mother and Fen. Thankful for the alone time, Asenna walked down the little path that led to the main road through the village. Most of the houses had been arranged in small family groups on either side of the track, and there was a greenbelt between the houses and the river where they had groves of trees and where some of their small livestock like chickens and pigs were kept. The Ulvvori had never kept livestock before and it had been a learning experience for all of them. Asenna particularly hated the chickens because they were loud and smelled terrible, but she had to admit that collecting their eggs was far easier than the cliff-climbing she had done as a child. The massive woodpile sat on the outskirts of the village. Since there were few trees on the plains, other than the ones by the river, the Kashaitis brought them a shipment of whole trees twice a month, which they exchanged for bison pelts and horns, then the Ulvvori had to strip and cut the trees themselves.

There were several men working on this task when Asenna arrived and they greeted her warmly, but Asenna barely responded. The sight of the woodpile just reminded her of the day Carro had left and she hated it. She waited patiently while one of the men loaded a large sack with split firewood and helped her tie it onto her back, then she set off again down the road to home, reliving the day in her mind as she often did. After she had left Carro's tent that night, Asenna had sat awake trying to think of what she might be able to say to him and Tira to change their minds, but she had come up empty. Deep down, Asenna had known nothing she could say would be able to heal whatever wounds Carro was still carrying, but the desperation to make her friends stay had kept her up until dawn, when she had hidden herself in the trees to watch them ride away. Asenna had not even said goodbye to Tira, with whom she had become exceptionally close, because she had been afraid of breaking down and shamelessly begging them not to leave. The pain of it had stayed with her for months, making it difficult to focus on her daily work and hard to get out of bed some mornings. Even now, it still felt like a dull ache behind her heart.

"Asenna, wait!" called a voice behind her. It was Ivarr, walking beside Nettle and carrying his long hunting spear. "Let me take that." He reached for the firewood and Asenna passed it over.

"Mama said you're making fish stew tonight," Asenna said to him, "did you know that?"

Ivarr laughed. "As long as we have the fish, I'll make anything. I'm starved." They made their way back to the family's little courtyard and began unloading the firewood beside it. One by one, the others joined them. Tolian and Haryk cleaned the table and collected the stools, while Elyana and Nikke cut up some of the summer vegetables from the garden and Asenna and Ivarr prepared the fish. The wolves gathered around too, telling each other about their days with yips and barks and whines. By the time they sat down to eat, the sun was just beginning to set and Asenna realized how hungry she was, but before she could even take her first bite, there was a chorus of short yelps from the wolves on top of the cliffs, followed by one long, single howl. Every pair of dire wolf ears around the firepit perked up and the pups began to whine and wag their tails.

"Strangers?" said Tolian quietly, "we weren't expecting anyone from Sciala, were we?" Elyana shook her head and stood up a little. They all stayed still and listened for another signal, which came shortly: one short howl, two yips, and a longer howl.

"Ulvvori?" Nikke said, looking confused, "there's no hunting party out right now. Who could--" Asenna was already on her feet, racing down the path to the main road and ignoring Elyana's calls for her to stop. She made it to the road and then ran until she had left the sandstone cottages behind. Once she was clear of the village, she stopped to watch the tops of the cliffs, willing the sun to set slower so she could see the road, which wound down along a ridge from the cliff tops before it leveled out and crossed the river at a small bridge. After a few minutes, she saw several Riders escorting two people on horseback onto the ridge.

"Please, *Izlani*...let it be them," she whispered, glancing up at the moon, which was hanging full and bright in the sky. Asenna stood as still as she could while the party descended the ridgeline. By the time they reached the bottom, the light was fading painfully fast, but once the Wolf Rider scouts turned back, the two horses broke into a gallop and Asenna found herself running toward them.

"Tira?" she shouted as they got closer, "Carro?" The response came in the form of a wild whooping cry that Asenna immediately recognized. Finally, she could see their faces, smiling and laughing as they raced each other down the road, Tira's long braids whipping out behind her.

"Asenna!" she heard Carro's voice and felt tears in her eyes. Pan was so large that he could not easily be slowed down when he was charging, so

Carro rode straight past her and then slid out of the saddle before the horse had even stopped. He whirled around, catching Asenna in his arms as she reached him, then she felt Tira grab them both from behind and squeeze.

"You're back!" Asenna found herself sobbing, "you came back!"

"Of course we did!" Tira laughed, breaking away from the embrace, "we had to save you from this terrible drudgery!" Asenna let go of Carro and stood back so she could see his face in the dimming light. He was almost unrecognizable from the man she had watched ride away a year ago. His eyes no longer carried that distant look and when he smiled at her, it felt genuine and warm, rather than guilty or strained. It was clear that a weight had lifted from him, because he somehow seemed younger and taller than before. He had let his beard grow and his hair was long enough to be pulled into a tight braid along the crown of his head, the same style that many other Ulvvori men wore. Asenna also noticed that he was carrying a new pair of curved sabers on his back, with swirling blue stones set in the pommels and grips wrapped in deep blue leather.

"It's so good to see you," Carro said softly, touching the tips of her hair, which now barely brushed her shoulders, "*zai hana eilli*."

Asenna blushed and looked down. "You learned more Ulvvori?"

"Still learning," Carro laughed, "but I had to know when they were talking about me behind my back." Tira grabbed Asenna and turned her around to give her a proper hug, lifting her completely off the ground. Her hair had been shaved on the sides, so she looked even more like Talla now, but the scar on her jawbone still distinguished her, and she had earned a new one along the hairline above her ear. Asenna saw that both Carro and Tira's skin also looked darker, as though they had been spending a lot of time in the sun, and she sensed that they would have plenty of exciting new stories to tell.

"Your hair is so long! You look amazing!" Tira cried, "but where is that baby? I need to see him!"

"He's with my family, and he's not a baby anymore, he's walking *and* talking!"

"No! I don't believe that," Tira cried, wrapping her arm around Asenna's waist as they started back. Carro took the horses' reins and walked on her other side.

"How is Talla? And Andros and Lusie and the children? And Gaelin too, I suppose. Where is he?" Asenna asked.

"They're all fine. Talla couldn't bear to leave them again so she stayed behind. We aren't sure how, but Azimar never found out about our connection to the farm, so it's still safe there. Gaelin even managed to make some new friends and he's with them. That's a story all by itself. Oh, we have so much to tell you! I can't wait!"

"I want to hear everything! Come on, it's too late to put up the tents. You can stay with me and Fen." Asenna led them back through the village, pointing out all the changes that had happened since they left. As they walked, Carro kept taking her hand and squeezing it, then letting go again. He didn't say as much as Tira, who had a hundred questions and two hundred stories spilling out of her, but Asenna could see how much happier and more relaxed he was. Even the limp in his right leg was less pronounced than before. No one in the village even seemed to recognize him as they walked, most of them focusing their greetings on Tira and Asenna. When they reached the path up to the houses, Tira went to tie the horses to a nearby tree and Asenna turned to look at Carro.

"I don't know how my mother will be," she told him quietly, "but I promise I'll--"

"Don't worry about her. I can handle it," Carro put a hand on her arm and Asenna shivered involuntarily, "I'm just happy to be back." Asenna was glad to see that someone had lit the small oil lanterns that hung in the trees and flooded the little courtyard with light. She loved the way it looked, but tonight it also allowed her to gauge exactly what her family's reactions were. Everyone else seemed thrilled at Carro and Tira's return, but just as Asenna had predicted, Elyana all but refused to acknowledge him as she greeted Tira warmly.

"Where is the baby?" Tira cried as she hugged Elyana.

"He fell asleep and I put him to bed already," Elyana replied, "he will be so happy to see you in the morning, Tira. I'm glad you're back safely."

"Please, join us!" Tolian offered, "there is plenty of food and we are all eager to hear what you've been doing." Everyone moved to sit around the fire, but Elyana quickly excused herself and went to bed, which allowed Asenna to breathe easier.

"Thank you for the hospitality," Tira said to Tolian as she finished her first bowl of stew, "we can't tell you how good it is to be home."

"Are you staying long?" Haryk asked.

"Well, that depends. It can wait until tomorrow, but we have news from Esmadia that we need to discuss with you all." Asenna's heart dropped a little and she glanced at Carro, who was intently focused on his food.

"What have you been doing?" asked Ivarr eagerly, "we want to hear all of it."

"A bit of everything," Carro told him, "we started in Sciala and worked on a trade ship all the way around the coast to Ossesh, stayed there a few weeks and worked on the docks, then took another ship back to Kashait. Turned out that one was smuggling illegal plants or something, so we spent two nights in a Kashaiti jail cell, which was actually quite nice." Everyone laughed and Tira eagerly jumped in to finish the recap of their adventures.

"We came back on another ship that went all the way around to Anburgh, and then we went up and down the western and southern coasts with a caravan selling precious jewels to all those rich bastards in their oceanside villas. Then we spent some time up north on a mammoth hunt. We tried to avoid Sinsaya as much as possible, but Talla is right there, and too much of Gaelin's work was in the city for us to stay away the entire time."

"You went back to Sinsaya?" Asenna asked, suddenly alarmed.

Carro grinned. "You think they'd recognize me like this?"

"We walked *right* past a squad of Sabers and they didn't even blink!" Tira howled with laughter and the others joined in. Asenna felt a bit disquieted, but said nothing. She listened to the stories for another hour while her family pelted them with questions, but eventually the oil in the lanterns began to run out and everyone realized how exhausted they were from such an emotional reunion. Tira went to bring the horses up so they could be turned out in the field and Asenna began to pick up some of their bowls, watching and listening from a distance as Tolian approached Carro.

"You look quite well," said her uncle, "did you find what you needed?"

"I did. Thank you, Tolian. Not only for the many chances you've given me, but for your guidance too. I hope we can talk more tomorrow about what's been happening in Esmadia."

"Yes, yes, tomorrow. Welcome home." Tolian went back to his own cottage with Ivarr, while Asenna let Tira and Carro into her home, which consisted of a living area and makeshift kitchen with two small bedrooms. Tira poked her head into Fen's room and cooed over how sweet he and Sage were, snuggled in bed together, before tossing her bedroll into Asenna's room.

"I'll bunk with Fen, if that's ok?" Carro asked.

"Yes, of course," Asenna told him, "he'll be so excited to see you in the morning."

"If he even remembers me. Goodnight, you two. Don't stay up too late." He went into Fen's room and closed the curtain that separated it from the living space. Asenna went into her own room, pulled her apron and dress off, leaving on only her shift, and crawled into bed while Tira stripped off her clothes and boots, piling her small collection of hidden knives in the corner as she undressed.

"So," she said, sitting cross-legged on her blankets, "tell me *everything*."

"Everything?" Asenna laughed, turning over so she was laying on her side, "uh...I've been planting a garden...Haryk and Nikke got married...that's really all there is to tell. It's a slow life here, which is good for us. I hope it's ok for you two after all your wild adventures."

"I'm sure we'll adjust," Tira smiled, "at least, Carro will. He hasn't shut up about the idea of building a house since we started the trip back."

"Oh?" Asenna asked, feeling her heart drop a little bit, "for...the two of you?" She began kicking herself for not noticing before how close Carro and Tira had been sitting, or the way they laughed together, or the looks they exchanged, but then Tira let out a loud cackle.

"You think I'd voluntarily live with a *man*?! I'd sooner be tossed into a viper pit. Asenna, you should know by now that men are only good for two things, and that is *not* one of them."

Asenna laughed. "You know, Ephie told me the exact same thing the first day I met her."

"Where do you think I learned it from?" Tira winked.

"So, you two aren't..." Asenna began to say, but cut herself off because she wasn't sure if she wanted the answer.

Tira made a face as if she had eaten a worm. "I only sleep with men when I'm desperate, and I've certainly never been *that* desperate," her tone softened a little, "besides...I'd have to be blind not to see the way he looks at you." Asenna felt her heart start to race and her face burn in the darkness.

"I think you may need your eyes checked," she breathed.

"That's definitely a possibility," Tira said, pulling her blankets up and yawning, "or maybe I'm the only one not deliberately ignoring what's right in front of me."

Asenna tried to sleep, but she tossed and turned for hours before finally getting up and walking out to her garden. Ivarr had built a small bench outside the fence so she could rest while she worked, and Asenna fell onto it with a deep sigh, leaning back against the fence post. It was a bright, full summer moon and even in the middle of the night, the warm air enveloped her like a blanket. The sounds of the rushing river and the field crickets had once kept her awake at night, but now they felt just as familiar as her brothers' voices or the smell of Sage's fur. Asenna couldn't deny the peace she had found in the little village, something that only two years before she could have never imagined, but there was still that tiny, nagging voice in the back of her mind, telling her something was wrong. It was something she had brushed off as the part of her that still feared Azimar, but now she began to wonder if it wasn't something else. Maybe it wasn't a lurking sense of unease that kept her up at night. Maybe it was the absence of something that she had never even imagined was a possibility.

"Asenna?" said a voice behind her. She whipped around and saw Carro standing on the other side of the garden, "I heard you get up. Is everything ok?" Asenna stood up and put her hands on the fence, digging her nails into the wood.

"Uh, no, I'm fine. I couldn't sleep. I just needed...some air." She tried to disarm him with a small smile, but she could tell he wasn't buying it.

"Plenty of air out here," he said awkwardly, waving his hand around. They stood for a moment with the strangeness of the night hanging between them.

"That's enough air, I think," Asenna muttered, walking around the garden toward the houses. Carro followed her. Before she opened the door, Asenna turned and faced him and he stopped a few feet behind her. "I'm just happy, that's all. It's good to have you both back."

"It's good to be back," he took a few steps forward, his dark eyes scanning her face. "Asenna, I have to tell you…I'm so sorry for the way I left things that night. I should have come after you, but I didn't know what to say or how to explain why I needed to leave."

"I understand why," she swallowed hard, choking back the lump in her throat, "I was just being selfish trying to get you to stay."

"I didn't mean what I said, about debts and oaths being the only thing," Carro's voice was steady and calm, as if he had practiced what he would say to her, but Asenna felt her own knees shaking. "I made that oath because of how much I care about you and Fen, and those feelings didn't just disappear the moment I left. I thought about you every day."

"I thought about you too," she whispered, "and I'm sorry I ran. I couldn't face you leaving, or Tira. It was too hard." Carro's hand moved and Asenna felt his fingers graze her shoulder, but Fen suddenly began to cry inside the house and she automatically turned to go inside. It only took a few minutes of sitting beside Fen's bed, stroking his hair and singing softly, before he fell back asleep on Sage's belly. Carro was sitting in the living area when Asenna came out, leaning his head against the wall with his eyes closed.

"Everything alright?" he whispered.

"Yes, he just wakes up sometimes. You look exhausted. Go get some rest, because he gets up at the crack of dawn and you'll be his first target."

"Looking forward to it," Carro smiled and Asenna sensed that he wanted to say more, but he went into Fen's room instead and pulled the curtain closed.

The next day, Asenna was awoken by the sounds of laughing and barking. She got up to find Carro lying on his back and holding Fen in the air, swinging him around while Sage tugged on his sleeve with her teeth.

"Mama, fly! Fly!" cried Fen.

"You are flying!" Asenna laughed, sitting down beside them and trying to pull Sage away from Carro's arm.

"He's so big now," Carro said, putting Fen down and sitting up, "and talking!"

"Did he remember you?"

"I'm not sure, but I think Sage let him know that I'm safe. She's a smart one," he leaned over to playfully grab Sage's paws and she leapt back, nipping at him and barking.

"She's a blessing, that's for sure," Asenna smiled at the little silver wolf pup.

"What happened to her two brothers? The ones who weren't paired with a kid?"

"Fennel and Hazel. They're still with Juniper, and we aren't sure what will happen," Asenna told him, "if we were at home, they would go live with the wild packs in the mountains, but here…"

"There's wild dire wolves?" Carro asked as he picked Fen up and flipped him upside down while the boy squealed with delight and his curly black hair stuck out on all sides.

"Yes," Asenna tilted her head a little, "I thought everyone knew that. There's always been a few wild packs. When one of our wolves loses their Rider, that's where they go, or if there are more pups than children born in a season, they'll leave after they've been weaned."

"Can they communicate with the Riders like your wolves can?"

"Yes, but they keep to themselves. It's not very common to see them," Asenna said, wondering what had suddenly gotten him so interested in the wolves. Just as Fen started enthusiastically showing Carro his collection of wooden toys, they heard Tira get up.

"Where is he?" she called, poking her head into the room. Fen stared at Tira for a second, looking unsure, but Sage nudged his hand and then he squealed and ran to her. She scooped him up and spun him around. "My own sister *refuses* to give me *any* nieces or nephews, so I have an inordinate amount of gifts for you, little pup. Do you want to see?" Fen clapped his hands wildly and Tira whisked him into the other room.

"Speaking of gifts, I have something for Fen too," Carro said, picking up the saddle bags he had taken off Pan the night before and pulling out a small replica of a sailing ship complete with real cloth sails and a tiny metal anchor. "It actually floats too. I thought he could take it out on the river."

"It's wonderful. You didn't have to do that."

"Oh, it's nothing compared to what Tira brought him," Carro laughed, reaching back and pulling out a long thin object wrapped in a blanket from under his bedroll, "but this one is for you."

"What's this?" Asenna asked as he set it on the floor between them.

"Well, I wasn't sure how much you've been able to keep training since we left, but I wanted you to have it anyway. If you don't want to use it, I understand," Carro said, unrolling the blanket to reveal a beautiful short sword in a deep blue scabbard. A large black onyx was set in the pommel, the grip was wrapped in soft blue leather, and the cross guard was set with tiny obsidian flecks that sparkled as Carro drew it. It was polished to a gleam and

Asenna gasped when she saw her own name etched into the blade.

"Carro..." she said softly, taking the sword from him, "this is incredible."

"I made it myself. Well, with *a lot* of help, but I did a lot on my own."

"You *made* this?"

"When we went back to Sinsaya, the twins wanted to visit their father's shop. His apprentice, Isulf, has taken over and he helped me design it and make it. I wanted you to have something that's just for you, not a blade that was made for someone else. It should be the right size." Asenna stood up and measured the sword against her arm.

"How did you get it so perfect without me there?" she laughed. Carro looked down and Asenna swore she saw him blush.

"I just remembered the way our arms fit together...when we were dancing," he said, and Asenna inexplicably felt tears sting her eyes.

"Thank you," she mumbled, as he cleared his throat and turned away, pulling out a small cloth bag from behind him.

"I hope you never actually have to use it except to practice," he said, "if it ended up only hanging on the wall, I'd be happier with that, but I brought you something else that I hope you'll get slightly more use out of." He opened the bag and pulled out a long necklace strung with delicate beads made from lapis lazuli, onyx, pearl, and what looked like polished bone or tusk. None of them were exactly uniform in shape or size, but the effect of the way they had been strung together in a pattern was beautiful.

"Oh..." Asenna gasped as she took it from him and ran her fingers over the beads.

"I started collecting the pearls when we first got to Sciala," Carro said, pointing to each one in turn as he explained, "and then the lapis and onyx are from the caravan we traveled with. Gaelin said they're both stones that come from the Midwinter Mountains, and I made these from mammoth tusks when we were on that hunt."

"You were collecting beads that whole time to make this for me?" Asenna murmured.

Carro dropped his eyes to the floor. "Well...yes. I told you...I was thinking about you every day, and I just wanted you to have a few little pieces of home, here in Kashait." Asenna leaned over and wrapped her arms around his neck, burying her face in his shoulder so he wouldn't see her tears. Carro hesitated for a moment, then wrapped his arms around her back and pulled her closer.

"Thank you," Asenna whispered, "this means the world to me." She looped the necklace around so it made two strands, then put it over her head just as Tira pushed the curtain back and told them breakfast was cooking outside. Asenna hopped to her feet, but noticed that it took Carro a few seconds longer to stand up.

"Does it still hurt?" she asked, pointing to his hip.

"Yeah, but only when I move," he chuckled. They came outside into the bright morning sunlight and saw that Asenna's family was already awake, chatting with Tira and playing with Fen as they fried eggs and strips of bison meat. Sage, Fennel, and Hazel were behind the houses, running circles around their parents and Echo, who had brought a few large hares in from the field for them to eat. Carro immediately jumped in to help Nikke peel the pile of oranges on the table, and they all listened intently to Tira recount more of their travel stories while they cooked. As soon as everyone had gathered at the table to eat, however, Tolian's face became more serious.

"You told us you had news from Esmadia," he said, "I would very much like to hear it." Carro swallowed the bite of egg he had just taken and Asenna could tell he was nervous.

"I think it would be good for everyone to hear it," said Tira quietly, "as it directly involves this family." A bolt of anxiety shot through Asenna's chest as Tira glanced at Carro, indicating that he should speak first.

"In the year and a half or so since Asenna escaped, Azimar has become…completely unhinged," Carro began, folding his arms, "I saw hints of it before of course, but it was always directed at individual people, like me, or Ilmira or his ministers. This is something different and very dangerous. After he stopped the attacks at the Kashaiti border six months ago, he began sending the Black Sabers systematically throughout Esmadia looking for Asenna and Fen, even though he *knows* they're here. He's…burned entire villages and killed innocent people simply for refusing to let their homes be searched. Lusie's farm was even searched, but of course they didn't find anything, and none of the men who were with me are still around to tell him about Talla and Andros, so they're safe. But he persecutes anyone he suspects of connections to the Ulvvori or Kashaitis, including his own ministers and even merchants. There's a great deal of unrest now because his actions have started to disrupt food supplies and trade. People are starving and afraid of what might happen if it gets worse."

Haryk suddenly slammed his fist down on the table. "So no one batted an eye when *we* were being slaughtered and forced out of our home, but now that it's them and theirs, suddenly there's unrest and fear? Why should we care?!" Asenna was shocked at her brother's outburst, as he was normally so measured. Nikke looked distressed too and put her hand on his arm.

"I understand your anger, Haryk," Carro said, "but the news we wanted to share is that an organized resistance to Azimar's rule has been forming. Andros and Isulf, Ferryn's apprentice, had connections to it. They introduced us to people who hope to eventually depose Azimar. Gaelin has been working with one of their leaders, a woman named Key, using his…skills to help them get supplies and information."

"Gaelin is putting his neck on the line for someone other than himself?" Elyana snorted, "have saber-toothed lions also sprouted wings and begun to talk?"

"Gaelin has earned my sincere admiration for what he's done in Esmadia, and he ought to have yours too, Elyana," snapped Carro, looking her directly in the eye. Elyana gaped at him like a fish out of water and Asenna had to fake a cough to hide her involuntary laughter. Ivarr and Haryk also hid their smiles of amusement behind their hands, but the mood turned serious again when Tira began to speak, looking at Asenna.

"The thing is…this resistance…" she said slowly, "they want Fen." Asenna felt her heart drop into her stomach and she looked at Carro, but he couldn't meet her eyes.

"On the throne?" she whispered, and Tira nodded.

"Absolutely not!" Elyana cried, "what foolishness! He's just a child! And how do they think they will even win a war against Azimar? The only reason he was able to defeat Rogerin is because a third of the army backed him, *and* he had the Riders. What army does your 'resistance' plan to use?"

"The Kashaiti army," Carro answered quietly, "Key sent Tira and I back to ask Selissa if she will intervene with her government on our behalf. We plan to request a small invasion force, and whatever other assistance they're willing to provide." The pit in Asenna's stomach opened even wider, feeling more like the gaping, smoking chasm that had been left when Talla destroyed the bridge over the Southrun. Carro had not returned because he missed her or cared about her, or even because he was ready to be part of the Ulvvori. He had returned to raise an army and wage a war that would pit her son against his own father.

"I see," Tolian folded his hands again, "and what of the Ulvvori?"

"We'd be grateful for any Riders that would be willing to join," said Tira, "but Tolian, if we're successful, think what it could mean. We could go *home.*" The silence was deafening as they all looked at one another. The settlement in Kashait was a paradise. It had served them well and kept them safe, but it was not their home, and every last one of them knew it. Asenna suddenly felt an intense surge of guilt, but underneath there was a burning anger that made her want to scream and throw things.

"I won't risk Fen's life," she said loudly, trying to speak with some conviction even though she was shaking, "not even to take us home. And I swore to Selissa that he would never go back to Esmadia while Azimar is alive. I don't intend to break that promise after everything she's done for us."

"You wouldn't have to. You and Fen would stay here until it's safe."

"What makes you think Selissa will even take up this cause?" asked

Ivarr in his placid voice, "what does Kashait gain from it?"

"Stability," Carro replied, "their trade has been disrupted too and there's growing concern that Azimar could even try to invade Kashait in a misguided attempt to get Fen back, or just to have his revenge. It would benefit Kashait to have Fen on the throne, considering that they sheltered him when he was in danger." Elyana snorted again and rolled her eyes, but stayed silent.

"How organized is this resistance, Carro?" asked Tolian, appearing unfazed, "Azimar's rebellion was highly coordinated and well-supplied, as you are obviously aware. This sounds more like a mob of farmers with pitchforks, scattered across the country."

"Many of them are scattered, yes, but they are more organized than you might think. If they know the Kashaiti army is approaching to back them up, they *will* gather to help. Key told us there are even some inside the army who might be able to convince them to stand down or defect, and let us deal with Azimar and the Black Sabers directly," Carro explained. His voice was calm and even, but Asenna saw his eyes darting around the table, calculating who was buying into the plan and who was not. When he finally looked at her, she tried to make sure he saw that she was not only opposed, but also furious and hurt.

"What is it you need from us at the moment?" Tolian's golden eyes were narrowed slightly, and Asenna knew he was carefully weighing his options.

"For now, just to get a message to Selissa as quickly as possible. We would also be grateful for your support if and when she will meet with us."

"What about the Riders?" said Ivarr, "you said you wanted Riders."

"It would certainly be helpful, considering how much Azimar fears them," Tira responded, "but we'll move forward anyway if the Kashaitis give us their support."

Ivarr stood up and Nettle scrambled to her feet. "I want to go."

"You're an idiot," Haryk spat.

"You swore!" Ivarr cried, turning on his brother, "all the Riders swore after what happened at The Den that we wouldn't rest until every single one of us is home again! They're offering us the best chance we've seen and you won't take it?" Haryk stood up and faced his brother and Asenna stood up too in case she needed to get between them, even though she was still holding Fen.

"It's a suicide mission," Haryk said in a deadly quiet voice, "and I will *not* allow anyone in this family to participate in it. We already fought a war for Esmadia. Why should we do it all over again?"

Ivarr laughed out loud. "You won't *allow*--"

"That is enough, boys!" Elyana stood up suddenly, "no one is going anywhere. This is insanity, Tolian! Will you risk the safety of your entire remaining family just to see Azimar deposed?"

"If my family chooses to risk their lives, I will not stop them," Tolian stood up too and they faced each other down across the table, "and I would never force them to go if they did not want to, but Ivarr is right. We all swore an oath, including you, Ely."

"My sons will not be sent to die in the streets of Sinsaya! I have lost enough!" Elyana shrieked at him, pounding the table with her fist and startling Fen. She turned and walked away, but no one followed her.

"Asenna?" said Carro gently, "what do you say?" Asenna's heart began to hammer as she felt everyone's eyes on her. She tried to steady her breathing and, even though she wanted to scream at all of them, she managed to speak through gritted teeth.

"I need time to think."

"Mama is right though, Fen is still so young," Ivarr pointed out, drawing everyone's attention to him instead, "there would need to be a Regent."

"Yes," Carro replied, "someone who can stabilize the country and rule until Fen comes of age." He looked back at Asenna.

"Me? I'm not...I couldn't..."

"Do not discount yourself so quickly, Senna," Tolian said, "you are far more capable than you think, and I believe you share Selissa's gift for reading hearts."

"I'm not so sure about that," Asenna said stonily, glaring at Carro until he looked away.

Tolian nodded slowly. "I will send a Rider to Selissa with the message. If she agrees to hear your petition, I will support you, but only as your friend. I cannot offer you any official support without the approval of the Elder Council and the Riders themselves. You understand, I'm sure."

"Thank you, sir," said Carro and Tira together.

"Now, we all have a lot to think about and there is still work to be done. Let's not sit idly," Tolian clapped his hands and everyone dispersed from the table, faces set in masks of grim determination or worry. Asenna picked Fen up and began walking back to where Juniper and her pups were playing in the field, but Carro caught up with her behind the house.

"Hey, I'm sorry I didn't tell you last night, I just..." Asenna put Fen down beside Sage and then rounded on him.

"You should be sorry!" she hissed, and he took a step back, "once again, you are trying to take my son from me!"

Carro's face fell. "Asenna...that's not what this is. You and Fen would stay here until it's safe, and then you would be with him every day when you come back. I would *never* ask you to be away from him for any reason. Surely you know that by now."

"And what about the rest of my family?" Asenna stormed, "I just found them again and now you want to send them all back to war?"

"They aren't doing it for me, they're doing it for themselves and they know the risks. Don't you want Fen to grow up in the mountains? In your home? Don't you want to see more children born with the Wolfsight? This might be the only way."

"Did you come back just to ask Tolian and Selissa for help?" Asenna asked, folding her arms, "or because you missed me?" Carro's expression shifted to one of vague irritation, but he took a step closer to her, folding his arms too.

"Don't do that, Asenna. You know it can be both. I missed you every minute of every day, but I also found something that could help your people…*our* people regain everything they've lost. Isn't that what you want?"

Asenna choked back a sob and leaned against the side of the cottage, her body suddenly feeling heavy. "I'm just so sick of it all. The war, the conscriptions, the orphans, parents burying their own children, Riders and wolves losing one another. My whole life…that's all there's ever been. And now, once again, it's all on me. How am I the one who decides if we go back to war? It's not fair. I just…I wasn't made for this, Carro."

Carro leaned on the wall beside her. "You're right. It's not fair that it has to be you. I'd do anything to change that, but I hope you at least know that there is *no* world where I'd be angry with you for refusing. And you know your family will still love you no matter what, but if we can end this now, maybe we can build something better for Fen and the other children, right? The kind of world they deserve?"

"I'm sorry," Asenna wiped her eyes, "how selfish I must sound. I just…don't want any of this fear and uncertainty for Fen. He deserves to grow up safe and happy, no matter where we are." Carro leaned over and put a hand on her cheek.

"Asenna, I will never let anything happen to the two of you. Oath or no oath, I will *always* put you and him before anything else." Their eyes met and Asenna felt something tugging deep in her chest as everything else around her seemed to fade away for a moment.

"There you are!" Tira called, coming around the side of the house. Carro dropped his hand, but her face split into an impish grin.

"What is it?" Carro asked, moving away from Asenna, who suddenly felt dazed, like she had been hit by a charging bison.

"Tolian sent a messenger to Selissa, then he told me to find something productive to do. I *know* you don't want to split firewood, so I thought we could do some fishing. Asenna, you want to join us?"

"That sounds lovely." Leaving Fen with Juniper and Elyana, the three of them got fishing poles and hooks, then packed food into a basket and walked north through the village. When they reached the best fishing spot, they dug for worms and set the poles into a stump on the riverbank so they wouldn't have to hold them. A large blueberry bush nearby yielded a good harvest, and they laid out blankets under the cottonwoods, making a game of trying to toss the berries into each other's mouths.

"This doesn't feel very productive," Carro sighed as Tira got up to get more berries. He began to roll up his pants and sleeves and Asenna saw a tattoo on his left arm that she hadn't noticed before.

"What's that?" Carro smiled and moved over next to her so she could see the image of a snake wrapping itself around his wrist and hand. Asenna ran her fingers lightly over the black ink forming a jagged pattern of scales on his skin. When she turned his hand over to see the head of the snake, which reached nearly to his knuckles, he curled his fingers up around hers and Asenna felt a shiver go through her body.

"A reminder of what you said to me back in the forest," Carro murmured, "about starting over."

"Did he tell you he cried when he got it done?" Tira asked, coming back with a handful of berries. Carro let go of Asenna's hand and sat up.

"I did not *cry,*" he said firmly, "I don't see you jumping to get one."

"Why would I subject myself to being stabbed with a needle for hours when I could just spend time with you and Gaelin? It's practically the same thing," Tira retorted, throwing a blueberry at his face.

"That's probably fair," Carro laughed and laid back on the blanket so he could feel the sun. Asenna couldn't remember ever seeing him actually be relaxed. He was so relaxed, in fact, that he fell asleep while Asenna laid nearby weaving little flower crowns and Tira lazily tossed blueberries into the river to attract fish.

"He's so different," Asenna remarked after Carro had been asleep for a while.

"Yeah," Tira agreed, rolling her eyes, "he's way more obnoxious now. But it was good for him, I think. Just to be free, not have to answer to anyone. Experience what a normal life is like."

"I'm glad he found that," Asenna said, "but, I'll be honest, I wish you had come back under different circumstances."

"Asenna, we didn't *just* come back to get help from the Kashaitis," said Tira quietly, "if you knew how much he missed you…"

Asenna felt her face burn. "I don't think it's quite what you're imagining."

"Oh, ok," Tira snorted, "then I guess I was hallucinating when I found the two of you behind the house earlier."

"That's not…" Asenna trailed off, unsure of how to even address the accusation, because she herself wasn't quite sure what had happened.

"Look," Tira propped herself up on her elbow, "it took me *years*, and I mean *four whole years*, before I really knew how I felt about Aija. We were both Riders and they paired us together for patrols a lot. I thought we were just close friends, that we depended on each other for safety and we trusted each other and that's why it felt so…different, but in hindsight there was always something else there. I just couldn't admit it to myself until she got sick once and I thought I might lose her. I had to tell her how I felt, even if I didn't really understand it myself, and even if she didn't feel the same way, because I couldn't just…carry it around with me for the rest of my life."

"What did you say to her?"

Tira heaved a deep sigh and Asenna thought she saw a few tears gather at the corners of her eyes. "I told her I couldn't ever imagine my life without her, but beyond that I couldn't ever imagine being with anyone else. Whenever I thought about my future, it was always with her, as a family."

"The way you talk about her is beautiful," Asenna murmured.

"I'm not trying to tell you what to do," Tira said, sitting up abruptly, "I'm just telling you what I see and if there is *anything* there, you can't let it go unsaid. Especially not now that we might be going back and fighting another damn war." Asenna nodded, but did not respond. Tira threw a few more berries into her mouth and then smiled mischievously and motioned to where Carro was still sleeping with his arm over his face.

"Watch this," she whispered, taking a worm out of the cup where they had been keeping them and crawling up beside him on her stomach. Just as she was about to drop the creature into his slightly open mouth, Carro grabbed her wrist, then seized her by one shoulder and flipped her over his body, throwing her directly into the river.

"You *bastard!*" Tira gasped as she came back up, spluttering and laughing at the same time.

"You never learn!" crowed Carro, "you *cannot* sneak up on me!" Tira hissed at him as she hauled herself up out of the water. Asenna was cackling and rolled backwards onto the blanket, but then Tira walked over and grabbed her legs, dragging her toward the water.

"Tira, no!" Asenna screamed, still laughing, but it was too late because Carro grabbed her shoulders and they tossed her into the water. Asenna let herself float there for a moment in that space where everything was still and quiet. Despite the news that there could be another war ahead of them, she found herself feeling happier than ever.

TWELVE: ULVVORI

Tolian's messenger returned from Sciala four days later to tell them that Queen Selissa planned to visit personally to hear their petition. The rumors of a possible return to Esmadia had also spread quickly through the village and there was an excited, anxious buzz in the air. The news had also placed Carro back under the public eye and he could not help but feel a little tense every time he left the cottage. However, since he and Tira had returned, he had only received a few dirty looks and one or two hushed whispers behind his back, and he classified this as progress.

The only real problem that had cropped up for him was Asenna. They had been getting along wonderfully, maybe even too well, but whenever someone mentioned the Esmadian resistance or Selissa's visit, she became cold and silent. In the ten days since his return, Carro had not dared to ask her if she would give her support, but as the meeting drew closer, he knew they needed an answer. Picking the right moment was difficult, since they were almost always busy and rarely alone, but Carro finally found an opening one day while Fen was with Juniper and they were grooming Pan together behind the cottage.

"Have you given it any more thought?" Carro asked as gently as he could while Asenna brushed tangles out of Pan's mane.

"Yes," she said curtly, "but it still worries me."

"What is it that's worrying you?" he asked, coming around to Pan's nose so he could see her face properly. "What can I do to help you feel better about it? If anything…" Asenna thought for a moment while she worked out a tangle, then she sighed and looked at him.

"If we're being honest, Carro," she said, "it's not about Fen...or the throne...or a war. I know my family can take care of themselves. It's...it's about you."

"Me?"

"I need you to answer a question honestly for me, so that I know you're doing this for the right reasons," said Asenna, "why do you want this so badly? Why volunteer yourself? Is it revenge on Azimar? Guilt about the Ulvvori? Do you think I want Fen on the throne and you're trying to do this for me? What is it that's pushing you to fight so hard for this?"

"That was more than just one question," Carro teased, trying to get her to smile, but her face remained serious and he could tell she was searching him for a reaction. He cleared his throat. "I don't know exactly. Maybe I feel like this is the only way for me to...really absolve myself."

"Carro, you've done that already, a million times over. You've made all the right choices. Why do you still feel like this?"

"I absolved myself to you...and the twins, but not everyone else. I helped put Azimar on the throne. I fought for him, all those years, to make him King. I feel like I'm responsible for what's happening now and I need to set it right. Please don't think I'm on a revenge mission, Asenna. I want Azimar held to account for what he's done, but I won't be the one to end his life, I promise," Carro looked over and saw that her face was still stony as she leaned it up against Pan's cheek.

"What happened to not making promises you can't keep?" she said.

"Asenna...that's not fair," Carro muttered, "I'm not that person anymore." Before she could reply, Tira rode up to them on her quick black racing pony, Fitz. She had been going out with the Wolf Rider patrols again since Selissa's message had arrived and now she looked winded and excited.

"She's almost here!" Tira said, jumping down and starting to pull Fitz's bridle off. Carro glanced at Asenna, whose face was still unreadable.

"What should we do?" he asked, "where is she staying?"

"She and her entourage are taking over the council house for at least one night," Tira told them, "come on, Tolian probably wants you two there to greet her." Asenna shrugged and slipped the bridle off Pan too, letting him loose in the field with Fitz.

"Stay away from my garden, you monsters!" she called as they trotted away. She went to go and grab Fen from where he was playing near the house, then they made their way through the village to the main plaza. People had already started to gather as word spread that they were expecting a royal visitor, and Tolian was standing outside the council house with Elyana, Haryk, and Ivarr.

"What's the plan?" Carro asked as they came up.

"Grovel?" Ivarr suggested lightly.

"No one is groveling," Tolian smiled, "Carro, I want you and Tira to simply tell the Queen what you told all of us. Asenna, have you come to a decision yet?"

"I want to speak with Selissa privately first."

"A very wise plan." A trumpet blast sounded from the far end of the village and the gathered crowd parted slightly so that Carro could see a dozen Kashaiti royal guards on white horses coming down the road. As they approached, Carro realized that they were all women, wearing the golden dolphin and sunburst on their uniforms and carrying long pikes. They rode into the plaza and dismounted and Carro noted that they were all at least as tall as him, some taller, and extremely muscular.

"I wouldn't want to go up against them," he murmured, mostly to himself, but Tira heard him and winked.

"I would," she whispered.

"You've been spending too much time with Gaelin," chuckled Carro, craning his neck to see the white carriage where Selissa was riding. It stopped just outside the plaza and her valet opened the door. Selissa stepped out, looking exactly how Carro remembered her: dignified and graceful, dressed in white with the golden crown on her head. She walked toward the council house and some of the Ulvvori began to throw flowers at her feet and call out blessings. Selissa smiled and thanked them and when she reached Tolian, she kissed him on the cheek in greeting. Then she turned to Echo, who was sitting behind them, and put her hand on the giant wolf's nose.

"Please, come inside," Tolian said to Selissa, "you have traveled a long way to speak with us and we are very grateful." Selissa and her valet went into the council house and the rest of them filed in behind her. Selissa settled herself on a stool at the large round table where the Ulvvori's Elder Council had already gathered, greeting each one of them by name as she did. When she had finished, she folded her hands neatly in front of her.

"Thank you all for your hospitality," she said, "I promise that we will not trouble you for long, but I had hoped to see the village during my visit as well. Now, Tolian, your message was rather vague and I would like a full explanation of your request before we go any further."

"Carro and Tira are the ones who brought this to our attention," Tolian replied, waving them over to the table, "so I will let them speak." Carro cleared his throat and stepped forward with Tira beside him. He saw a tiny smile on Selissa's lips as she looked him over.

"I hardly recognized you," she said softly.

"Your Majesty, Tira and I have spent the last year traveling and working in Esmadia," he began, "and we are gravely concerned about the situation with Azimar. He has become a viscous tyrant, even before Asenna escaped he was unstable, but now it has become far worse. I'm sure you have been made aware of this by your own ministers and traders as it has disrupted supply lines between our two countries. It is even worse in Esmadia. Entire fields of crops have been burned and innocent citizens slaughtered on Azimar's orders. There is a great deal of fear and pain."

"I am aware of the situation, yes," Selissa sighed, "and the trade issues have impacted us, you are right. Our merchants no longer feel safe putting in at Ossesh or Anburgh because of the Black Sabers that Azimar has stationed there to search their ships. The loss of innocent lives is considerably more devastating. What can Kashait do?"

"Well," Tira glanced nervously at Carro and he gave her a small nod of encouragement, "during our travels, we met members of a small resistance movement who hope to gain enough support that they might be able to…remove Azimar from the throne."

Selissa nodded slowly. "I am aware of this movement. I believe it was created after the expulsion of the Ulvvori, but it has remained small for quite some time. Now you want our support? Our army, I assume?"

"Yes, Your Majesty," Carro nodded and swallowed hard, feeling his nerves on fire, "we feel it would benefit Kashait to have a stable ruler in Esmadia."

"A stable ruler?" Selissa raised an eyebrow and looked directly at Asenna, who was holding Fen on her hip, "and who might that be? Surely, you do not mean to put a child on the throne. I am not sure how much history you know, Carro, but that sort of thing rarely ends well."

"Yes, Fen would sit on the throne, but Asenna would act as Regent until he comes of age." Selissa was quiet for a moment while she considered his words.

"Asenna?" she said, "what do you have to say about all of this? And what of the promise you made me?"

Asenna stepped forward and hoisted Fen up a little. "I would never break the promise I made to you, Your Majesty. Carro and Tira have assured me that I would not need to return to Esmadia with Fen until after all this is over. However…"

"However?"

"I have…concerns, Your Majesty," Asenna dropped her head a little, "about my own ability to bring any kind of sustainable change to Esmadia. I hoped I might meet with you privately to discuss this." Carro found himself desperately wanting to go and stand beside her, but he held back, knowing she wanted to do this alone.

"I would welcome the chance to speak with you once we are finished here, certainly."

"Thank you, Your Majesty," Asenna gave a small bow. Selissa

considered all their faces for a few moments and Carro could tell everyone in the room was holding their breath.

"As you all know," she said at last, "my decisions and recommendations have no binding power on the Kashaiti Assembly. I am a Queen in name only, I am not an autocrat. Any recommendations I make may fall on deaf ears. Kashait has not mobilized an army since our two countries went to war against one another over two centuries ago."

"We understand, Your Majesty," said Tolian.

"However," Selissa stood up and brushed her skirt off, "I *will* recommend that an army be raised. I cannot sit by while innocent people are killed by those who are supposed to protect them. Asenna, I believe you could bring a desperately needed measure of stability to Esmadia, and it would warm my heart to see the Ulvvori return to their land." Carro grinned involuntarily and Tira punched his shoulder.

"We are very grateful for your support," Carro gave another bow. Selissa came around the table and stood beside Asenna.

"Now, allow me a few minutes alone with the young lady and then I should very much like a tour of your lovely village, Tolian." Asenna passed Fen over to Elyana and then they all filed outside. In the plaza, Elyana set Fen down to play with Sage and then she and Tolian retreated to the side of the building, speaking in heated tones. Haryk and Ivarr slapped Carro on the back.

"If Tolian goes, the Riders will go too," Ivarr assured him.

"Nikke wants to go as well," Haryk said, looking a little sheepish, "she would never forgive me if I didn't come, so I guess I'm in."

"No one is going anywhere if Asenna doesn't agree to the plan," Carro said quietly, "Key told us they won't move forward without her and Fen. There has to be someone left at the end who can take the throne and Fen is the only one with a legitimate claim. Anyone else and it would just throw everything into chaos again." The excitement died down.

"Surely she sees that she can save thousands of lives without risking Fen's?" said Tira.

"I certainly hope so," he replied. Carro started to pace back and forth, chewing on his fingernails and watching Fen roll in a patch of dirt with Sage. Tolian came over to where they were waiting and sat down on the ground beside Echo, who was still guarding the doors.

"You seem a bit anxious," he said to Carro.

"I just…wish we could have an immediate answer about the army."

"Alas," Tolian smiled, "the pitfalls of democracy. Here, come and sit next to Echo." Carro stopped pacing and eyed the huge wolf warily.

"Sit? Next to her?" he asked. He looked over at Tira, who shrugged. Tolian nodded and Carro gingerly lowered himself onto the ground beside

Echo. She turned her head and examined his face with her big golden eyes, then licked him gently on the chin, and Carro felt a wave of composure and calmness fall over him. He leaned back against her and closed his eyes.

"How is that happening?" he asked, "I thought you could only feel them if you had the Wolfsight?"

"The dire wolves can share certain gifts with all of us when they wish to," Tolian said, "Echo says that you remind her of her own son, Storm, and she wants to help."

"What happened to Storm?"

"Sadly, he lost his Rider during the war and now lives with a wild pack in the mountains."

"Asenna told me about them," Carro murmured, "I didn't know the wolves could just…leave."

"They aren't beholden to us. They do make a choice to stay, and when a Rider dies their wolf will usually choose to go into the mountains. Asenna's father, Larke, died when she was very young and his wolf, Briar, still lives. Storm left as well, with others who survived their Riders after the war and the attack on The Den. By all rights, Fennel and Hazel should be there too, since they have no child to bond with." Carro ran his fingers along Echo's neck.

"Do you think they would help us?" he asked, sitting up suddenly, "the wild packs? If we got a message to them, do you think they would come and fight?" Everyone standing around looked at Carro with a mixture of surprise and skepticism. Tolian studied his face carefully.

"I cannot speak for them," he answered at last, "but I do not think sending a message would be out of the question. We can discuss it more once we know whether we have Kashait's support…and Asenna's." Carro nodded and added another piece to the puzzle he was trying to solve in his mind. Finally, Selissa and Asenna appeared at the door and Carro jumped to his feet.

"I can't thank you enough for your kind words and your gift, Your Majesty," Asenna was saying, and when Fen ran up to her, Carro noticed that she was holding a small green book.

"You have quite a remarkable young woman here," Selissa said to Tolian, but her eyes also lingered on Carro for a moment.

"I am aware of it, Your Majesty," Tolian said, smiling, "Asenna?"

Asenna took a deep breath and looked directly at Carro. "You have my support and my permission to go ahead," she said. Ivarr gave a loud whoop and Tira jumped forward to hug her tightly.

"Tolian," Selissa said, "would you humor me with that tour now? I believe these young people would like to celebrate alone."

"It would be my honor," Tolian said, "and I hope you will join me and my family for supper this evening at our home." He took Selissa's hand

and Elyana followed them across the courtyard. Tira, Haryk, and Ivarr started leading the way home, singing a loud marching song, but Carro held back, sensing that she was not in the mood for frivolity. He walked slowly beside her and took Fen's other hand so they could swing the boy up between them as they went. He screamed and giggled, which seemed to improve Asenna's mood slightly.

"What's the book?" Carro asked as Fen dropped their hands and ran ahead to climb on Haryk's back.

"'*The Mandate of the Queens of Kashait.*' It explains their role and how they are supposed to go about making decisions and things like that. Selissa said that they all contribute a little to it at the end of their term, so there's centuries of wisdom in here for me."

"What else did she say?"

"She thinks that I'll do well, but I'm still...uncertain about all of it," Asenna admitted in a soft voice, "what if I let everyone down and then everything just...falls apart again?"

"I think you'll be much better at it than you believe," Carro told her firmly, "you always seem to know what the right thing is and you stick by it no matter what, even when everyone is saying you're wrong or naive. It's one of the things I admire most about you." Asenna's face turned red.

"Oh, there are multiple things?" she laughed.

"You know there are," Carro replied, holding her gaze until she looked away.

"Maybe I'm just too stubborn to admit that I might be wrong," she muttered, "that's not a good quality for a queen to have."

"But you're usually *not* wrong. You're like Selissa. You can just see what's right without anyone having to tell you or convince you."

"Well...thank you for believing in me."

"You believed in me. I'm just glad I can finally return the favor," Carro took her hand and they walked for a few minutes that way until Tira turned around and let out a loud whistle. When they reached the cottages, Fen ran to play with Sage and her brothers. Nikke, who had just returned from a patrol, was getting a fire started, and Juniper, Ash, and Echo were lounging nearby and periodically growling when the pups or Fen tried to climb on them.

"How did it go?" Nikke called to Haryk, who walked over and kissed her on the cheek.

"Selissa is on our side," he told her, breaking into a smile, "she's going to recommend that the Kashaiti Assembly raise an army for us."

"That's amazing!" Nikke said, kissing him back, then she pointed to the table where a basket of vegetables from Asenna's garden was sitting, "Ivarr, you've been volunteered to make supper tonight. Better get going."

Ivarr groaned, but he and Haryk dutifully picked up the knives beside the basket and began to chop carrots while Nikke went to change her clothes. Carro grabbed a knife and began to help with the vegetables, but just as he had finished his fourth squash, Tolian and Elyana returned from showing Selissa around the village.

"Thank you all for getting the food ready," Tolian said, "I'm sure Selissa will be very impressed."

"If Ivarr could impress anybody with his cooking skills, he'd have found someone by now," Haryk teased.

Ivarr pointed the knife at his brother across the table. "You managed to find a bride with absolutely no skills, so I think I'll be alright."

"If both of you worked as efficiently as you talked, supper would be ready by now," Elyana said, giving them a rare smile and kissing Ivarr on the cheek.

"Could I have a word?" Tolian asked Carro. Feeling apprehensive, Carro wiped his hands off and followed Tolian into his cottage, sitting on one of the reed mats that covered the floor.

"When I gave you my judgment concerning your presence here, back in the camp, do you remember what I offered?" Tolian asked.

Carro felt his chest tighten up. "Reinitiation into the Ulvvori…"

"Is that still something you want?"

"I…Of course," Carro breathed.

"You seem hesitant. Do you think I would offer this to you if you had not earned it?"

"No, of course not. I just…I didn't think…"

"You believe you have not earned it yet…" Tolian said gently.

"No, sir. I haven't done--" Carro fell silent as Tolian held up his hand.

"You think I cannot see the hope that has returned to my family's eyes? That is a gift in itself, and one you did not have to give. After what happened to us at The Den, I feared that we would break and scatter, that the wolves would leave us, that even though we still *lived*, the Ulvvori would die out. We were able to stay together and persevere and make a safe haven here in Kashait, but I never imagined we might have a chance to go back and become whole again. You and Tira risked your own lives to bring us this gift, and this is my thanks to you." Carro ran his hands over his face, trying to remain composed.

"If you think I'm ready, then I accept," he said, feeling a wide smile creep across his face.

"Excellent. I will let you know when it is time," Carro stood up and Tolian pulled him into a quick embrace, then they both went back outside. Asenna saw them and cocked her head at Carro as if to ask what had happened, but he kept it to himself while they prepared dinner, not wanting to pull the focus away from Selissa's visit even though he was bursting to tell everyone.

When the Queen arrived, she brought several casks of Kashaiti honey mead as a gift, which they opened and sampled politely. But after Selissa and Tolian had retired for the evening, and Elyana had taken Fen to bed, Tira pulled out some bottles of Esmadian wine she had brought back and Carro told the rest of them his news. The table exploded into cheers and whoops and, in celebration, Tira and Ivarr instigated a raucous drinking game that involved spinning a knife on the tabletop. There was also a great deal of yelling for reasons that Carro could not fully understand because everyone was speaking Ulvvori too quickly and slurring their words. Asenna tried to translate for him as they played, but soon they were all so far gone that she gave up and just laughed at him as he managed to lose round after round. Eventually, Haryk and Nikke went to bed as well and it was only Carro, Asenna, Tira, and Ivarr remaining around the table. However, as they were draining the last of the honey mead, Elyana emerged from her cottage carrying Fen, who was crying softly.

"Bad dream," she said, slipping the boy into Asenna's arms and then retreating to her own bed. Carro, feeling quite blissful, leaned over and squeezed Fen's hand.

"What was it?" he asked, "monsters or bad guys?"

"Monsters," Fen whimpered.

"Oh. Did you fight them off?"

Fen covered his face. "No, too scary." Sage was sitting at Carro's feet and she let out a whine.

"Did you tell them to go away?" Carro asked, "sometimes that works." Fen paused and his brow furrowed as if he had not considered the possibility.

"Go away monsters!" he shouted, clenching his little fists.

"Very good!" Asenna laughed, "I'd better get him settled back down. Just give me a minute." She stood up and walked back to the cottage with Fen in her arms and Carro didn't even realize that he was staring until Tira threw a leftover bread crust at him and he whipped his head around.

"Carro, are you an idiot?"

"Excuse me?" he laughed.

"Am I wrong? Am *I* the idiot?" Tira slurred, looking at Ivarr.

"No, it's definitely Carro," said Ivarr as he drained his cup.

"What?!" Carro almost yelled at them. Tira stumbled over to sit on the stool beside him, putting her hands firmly on his shoulders, but staring at a spot just beyond his head.

"You need to tell her how you feel before you run out of chances. Do you understand me?" Tira shook him a little and Carro dropped his eyes to the ground, feeling his entire body burn with embarrassment.

"I...I don't...that's not..."

"You can't lie to me, Carro," said Tira a little more gently. "I don't think you can lie to anyone, actually, but especially not to me and especially not about this. Everyone can see it. *Do something about it.*" Carro kept his eyes fixed firmly on the table, the soft buzz of the mead quickly vanishing from his head.

"There's no way that she feels--"

"Don't give me that horseshit!" Tira smacked him lightly on the head.

"He can take a couple arrows on purpose but he's afraid of my baby sister," Ivarr snickered, swaying as he stood up. Tira found his words extremely funny and nearly toppled off her stool laughing, but Carro caught her and dragged her onto her feet.

"Come on, you can't sleep out here," he said, wrapping Tira's arm around his shoulder and practically dragging her toward the house.

"Promise me?" Tira murmured as they went through the door, "just talk...to her...please..."

"You won't remember this tomorrow," whispered Carro.

"Yes, I will!" Tira insisted and Carro tried to cover her mouth, but now they were both laughing and Carro realized how unsteady he felt.

"Ok, I promise, but will you shut up? You're going to wake Fen."

"No, *you* shut up," Tira giggled as she dropped onto her bedroll and Carro tossed a blanket over her. Once he was sure she wouldn't get up, he crept over to Fen's room and pulled the curtain back just a hair. Fen was fast asleep again and Asenna was sitting on the floor beside his bed with a hand on his back. She had not had as much to drink as the rest of them, but Carro could tell she was still drowsy. He walked over and touched her shoulder.

"Asenna, come on. You need to get in bed."

"I'm going to sleep in here," she replied, "in case he wakes up again."

"Let me move the blankets then," Carro said, turning around to pick up his own bedroll. Asenna stood up and came over to help him, but she stumbled and leaned against the wall and Carro put a hand on her elbow.

"You alright there?" he chuckled.

"I'm sorry for how I've been acting about all of this," Asenna said softly, "I just...we've been here for over a year and all I've done is garden...and tend chickens...and take care of Fen. And now all of a sudden there might be another war and I might have to be...a real queen. It's just...so overwhelming, but I've been unfair to you and I'm sorry. Can you be patient with me?" She moved toward him and Carro dropped the blankets to put his arms around her.

"I can be whatever you need me to be," he murmured. Asenna leaned into him, resting her head on his chest. The few minutes they stayed together seemed to stretch out as Carro felt her heartbeat and smelled the rosemary oil she used in her hair. He closed his eyes and tried to soak in the feeling of closeness and familiarity before she finally pulled away and looked up.

"Thank you," she whispered, then picked up the blankets and laid them out next to Fen's bed. Carro went into the other room where Tira was snoring softly, but he couldn't sleep. He paced in front of the window for hours, chewing on his fingernails and running his hands through his hair as he tried to piece together the invasion they were planning, while determinedly ignoring the urge to relive the moment with Asenna over and over in his head. Finally, in the middle of the night, he had to walk down to the river and submerge himself in the rushing current in order to get any kind of stillness in his mind.

The next morning Carro was awakened by a loud groan from Tira, who rolled over and spent several minutes trying to extricate herself from her blankets before sitting up. She looked over at him with bleary eyes and seemed confused.

"You're not Asenna."

"A keen observation."

"You look like shit," Tira said, reaching for her water flask.

"*You* look like shit," Carro retorted, rolling over and pulling himself out of the bed, "on your feet. We need food." He pulled Tira up and she walked slowly outside while Carro ducked into Fen's room and found him sitting on the floor beside the bed, playing with some of his little wooden animals. Asenna and Sage were still asleep, so Carro picked him up.

"Come on, little one. Your Mama needs to sleep. You hungry?"

"Horse!" Fen held up one of his toys in Carro's face, "neigh!"

"You are so right," Carro smiled and squinted as they stepped outside. Haryk, Nikke, and Elyana had woken up early and started cooking porridge for everyone. Tira was sitting at the table with a bowl already, holding her head in her hands. As Carro walked out, Elyana came up and tried to take Fen out of his arms, but he turned away from her.

"I've got him, Elyana," he said steadily, feeling like he was staring down an angry cave bear for a moment before she simply scoffed and walked away. Carro sat Fen down on top the table and then got them both a bowl of porridge and a spoon. They ate in silence for a few minutes while Fen made a mess attempting to feed himself.

"So…" Tira finally looked up, "did you talk to Asenna?"

"Damnit," he smiled ruefully, "I didn't think you'd remember that."

"Damnit!" Fen repeated. Tira snorted and covered her mouth, trying not to spit her food out.

"Well, I'm certainly not telling her anything now," Carro groaned, throwing his hands up.

"Telling who what?" asked Asenna, coming up behind him. Carro's eyes widened in horror and he looked over at Tira, who had a fiendish smile on her face.

"That he taught your son to say 'damnit.'"

"Damnit!" Fen giggled.

"Of course he did," Asenna rolled her eyes and reached around Carro to wipe porridge off Fen's face with a rag, "no more babysitting for you two."

"I did nothing!" Tira called as Asenna walked away to get food.

"So, what do you think about the idea of sending a message to the wild dire wolf packs?" Carro asked Tira.

Tira didn't look at him and took a long time chewing before she answered. "Tolian would know better than me."

"You don't think it's worth a shot?"

"I think those wolves left the pack for a reason," Tira snapped, her good mood suddenly gone, "I can't blame them. I left too after I lost Aija and Frost." Carro was surprised at the venom in her voice. She stood up suddenly and left her half-finished bowl on the table.

"What did you do?" Asenna asked as she sat down.

"Nothing!" Carro protested, "I just…I asked her about the idea Tolian and I had to recruit the wild dire wolves to fight with us."

Asenna sighed. "You don't think seeing Aija's wolf again could be painful for her?"

"Oh…no, I didn't realize…I'd better go apologize," he made to stand up, but Asenna put a hand on his arm.

"Let her cool off a bit."

Carro sat back down, but his appetite was gone. "Tolian said your father's wolf is still up there too. Would it be hard for you to see her?"

"No," Asenna said slowly, stirring some blueberries into her porridge, "it was so long ago when he died. I would love to see Briar again. It might be hard for Mama though." Tolian, Ivarr, Haryk, and Nikke came to sit at the table and Carro floated the idea to them as well.

"Who's going to take the message?" Ivarr asked, "we can't send Riders back into Esmadia alone right now." Juniper, who was laying behind Haryk, nudged him with her nose and whined. Haryk looked down at her and tilted his head as he listened.

"She says Fennel and Hazel can go," he said quietly, "they have no Riders. They can carry the message for us." A tense silence settled over them.

"Juniper, we can't ask that of you," Asenna told the she-wolf.

"She says it would be their honor," Haryk told them, "and that, at the very least, if the wild packs won't fight, then her sons will be home."

"There are several other young wolves who were born after we left and could not be bonded to a child," Tolian said, "if they all traveled together it could be safer."

"It's decided," Haryk cleared his throat and stood up, "come on, June." Carro watched them walk away and suddenly felt a little guilty.

"We need to go," Tolian said, standing up, "Selissa will be leaving soon and we must be there to see her off." They all walked down to the council house together with Fen and Sage running ahead, then said their goodbyes to her one by one.

"Thank you again for your hospitality, Tolian," said Selissa, "I hope to see the Ulvvori restored to their lands soon, and many, *many* more children with golden eyes born to you. I will send word as soon as the Assembly votes on your proposal."

"We cannot thank you enough, Your Majesty," Tolian replied, kissing her hand and helping her up into the carriage.

"What do you think they'll decide?" Carro asked Tolian quietly as they all turned to walk home.

"I wish I could say. But whatever happens now, Carro, you have done well and I am proud."

~~~

The messenger arrived two weeks after Selissa had gone, on one of the hottest days of the summer. It was so sweltering that the chickens would not even lay eggs and the dire wolves were spending nearly all their time in the river. The man arrived in the mid-afternoon on horseback, carrying only a small piece of parchment bearing Selissa's seal, which informed them that they had been granted the use of ten thousand infantry soldiers and a small corps of engineers for their mission. Selissa wrote that they should expect Kashaiti military liaisons to arrive within a week so they could begin planning, and with that the entire village was thrown into a frenzy. Planning their invasion left Carro less time to spend with Asenna and Fen, which he regretted since they would be staying behind. However, it also gave him space to try and work through his feelings, because Tira had not forgotten their conversation. She pestered him constantly and he fed her excuse after excuse about it not being the right time. In reality, he had plenty of opportunities to talk to Asenna, but they had fallen into an easy routine together, which mostly consisted of doing chores and looking after Fen, but it felt so natural that Carro was loath to change anything at all.

Nearly two months after the Kashaiti liaisons had arrived, he had still not found the courage to talk to Asenna, and was starting to wonder if he should tell her anything at all, considering the chance that he might not come back from the invasion.

"What purpose would it even serve?" he griped at Tira during one of their spats.

"What purpose does it serve just keeping it all bottled up?" Tira shot back, "you're distracted and useless like this anyway and we're trying to plan a fucking coup. I swear if you don't talk to her, I'll do it for you." Carro was bent over a pile of kindling that he had collected on the ground, but he straightened up and used one of the sticks to whip Tira on her leg.

"You'd better fucking not."

"Watch me," Tira grinned, "besides, I promise you she already knows and she's just waiting for you to figure it out. How do you think that would leave her if you didn't come back? She'd always be stuck, feeling like she can't move on. Trust me."

"I know, I know," Carro sighed, picking up another stick and adding it to his pile, "maybe I really am just a coward."

"That's my working theory, yes," Tira agreed. She glanced up at the sun. "Come on, we'd better get back. Zaki and Kir will be expecting us." The two of them picked up the bundles of kindling that they had been gathering along the riverbank and started back toward the village.

Zaki and Kir, the two Kashaiti advisors sent by the Assembly were serious fellows who detested lateness or any kind of foolishness. They frowned upon the more casual way the Ulvvori did things, but luckily they couldn't deny that the invasion plan Carro and Tira had hatched was workable. They were all feeling especially optimistic since receiving reports from Key that Azimar's army was in chaos due to mass desertions and infighting. It couldn't have been better timing if they had planned it that way.

"Late," Zaki grumbled as Carro and Tira came into the council house. Carro dumped his bundle of kindling by the door and turned to face the older man, who sported a bristling gray mustache and wild eyebrows.

"We have people to care for here," he snapped, "perhaps next time *you* can help with the chores and then we'd be done earlier." Zaki's mustache twitched, but he did not respond. His younger colleague, Kir, was standing at the table, which was spread with papers and maps and markers made from painted rocks. He was a bit more mild-mannered, but still preferred for everything to go exactly as planned.

"We've had news from Sciala just this morning," Kir told them, "our last two companies are on their way to the border. It will take them a week to arrive and then our force will be complete. You and your people need to leave in just a few days in order to meet them and prepare with the Generals. Is that feasible?"

"Yes, we can be ready whenever we need to be," Tira told him.

"And what of the other wolves you had mentioned?"

"No word yet," Carro replied, not meeting his eyes. It had been two and a half months since Fennel and Hazel had left the village and Carro had all but given up on them returning with the wild dire wolves.

"Very well then," Zaki began shuffling some of the pieces of parchment that sat on the table, "then we will depart immediately for the border and bring these plans to our Generals."

"Wait, you're leaving?"

"Tolian has asked us to go before tonight," Kir explained, "some Ulvvori festival or some such going on, isn't there?" Carro glanced at Tira, who quickly looked away from him.

"Not that I'm aware of," he said slowly. Zaki and Kir both shrugged.

"Well, that's what we were told. We shall see you at the border," Zaki reached his hand out and shook Carro's. The two men finished packing up their maps and parchments and then headed to get their horses from the field.

Carro rounded on Tira. "What's going on tonight?"

"Damnit!" Tira smiled, "well, those idiots ruined it, but Tolian was planning your ceremony thing for tonight. We wanted it to be a surprise."

Carro suddenly felt like his entire body was on fire. "Tonight?"

"Well, yeah. He told you they'd do it before we leave and tonight's a full moon." Carro looked down and brushed some bark off the front of his shirt, then looked out the window at the sun, which was barely kissing the horizon.

"What do I need to do to get ready?"

"I mean…you could use a bath," Tira jokingly held her nose, "but other than that, nothing. Don't worry about it." They went over and picked up their kindling and then began walking home. Carro did not like going into new situations completely blind and his mind was spinning with questions.

"Have you seen one of the ceremonies before? What happens?"

"A few times," Tira told him, "it's very basic, don't worry so much. You just have to repeat what Tolian says and get paint on you or something. I don't remember."

"So what happens after?"

"After? There's a big party and then *you* get to stop being so uptight."

"Very funny." They reached the cottages and saw Asenna with Tolian and Elyana standing around the table. Fen was riding in a sling on Asenna's back and he started to squirm when he saw them.

"Pretend like you don't know about tonight!" Tira hissed, digging an elbow into his ribs. Fen squealed, reaching his arms out for Carro, and Asenna reached around to pull him out of the sling and set him on the ground. He came sprinting across the courtyard on his wobbly legs and Carro dropped his stick bundle, scooped Fen up, and whirled him around in the air, spinning until they were both dizzy. When Carro put him down, Fen fell over on the ground giggling as Sage pounced on him.

"Are you busy right now?" Asenna asked. Carro tried not to smile at her inability to be subtle and pretended to think about his non-existent evening plans.

"Uhh...I was going to go get cleaned up...before supper," he said carefully, glancing at Tira, who nodded at him behind Asenna's back.

"Oh, alright," Asenna seemed pleased, "I was going to ask you to go check on the horses, but that's fine. How long will you be?"

"Well...it was hot today and I have clothes to wash, so maybe an hour?" He could tell she was bursting to say something and the infectious smile on her face was making him feel a little giddy too.

"How about I come get you when supper is almost ready?"

"That sounds fine," Carro said, turning to go get his dirty clothes from the cottage before he accidentally let something slip. Tira was leaning on the table, trying not to laugh, and Tolian was glancing suspiciously between the two of them.

Feeling a bit lighter now that he didn't have Zaki and Kir breathing down his neck, Carro walked to his usual swimming hole and tossed his clothes in. Leaving a clean set out on the grass, he stripped down and dove into the water, letting himself sink to the bottom. It was quiet and still under the surface and sitting there for as long as he could always helped him process whatever was going on. Tonight, however, there was so much running through his mind that even the peace of the river didn't help.

The thought of being perceived by everyone in the village sent his heart racing. He pictured Elyana's judgmental yellow eyes, always watching him, and imagined a whole crowd of Elyanas heckling and booing. Shaking the image from his mind, Carro emerged from under the water and started scrubbing his clothes. The sun was starting to disappear and the cool autumn evenings were setting in, so before long he began to shiver and decided to get out. Trying to take his time, he pulled on his clean trousers, then braided his hair back along his head, then started hanging his wet clothes on the tree branches like he always did, all the while listening for Asenna's footsteps. When he finished hanging the clothes, he turned around to put on a clean shirt and saw her standing by the road. She was wearing a long, colorful skirt that looked like a patchwork quilt and a separate top covered in swirling patterns of beads. Tassels of beads hung over her exposed stomach and she had a simple blue shawl around her otherwise bare shoulders. She was also wearing the necklace he had given her and the effect of the fading light made her look like some kind of otherworldly being that had appeared out of thin air to bring him a message. Carro felt his heartbeat quicken as she walked over and held out her hand.

"Tira told me they ruined the surprise for you," she said, "come on. You won't need the shirt." More than a little confused, Carro dropped his shirt on the ground and took her hand, but then pulled her back a little, feeling a tiny spark of bravery come to life behind his pounding heart.

"Asenna, can we talk for a minute?"

"Everyone's waiting," she said, grinning and bouncing on the balls of her feet, "can we talk later?" The spark flickered out and was replaced by apprehension.

"Of course, let's go." She led him through the village to the main plaza. As they approached, Carro could see the crowd gathered and heard drums hammering out a beat that nearly matched his heart rate. Torches burned around the plaza, illuminating the people gathered, who were all staring directly at him now as they walked up the road. There was a narrow path through the crowd and Carro saw as they got closer that there were at least two dozen men standing along it, also bare-chested.

"Asenna, what--" he started to ask, but she put a finger to her lips and pulled him forward. As they walked in between the men, most of whom were middle-aged or older, Carro felt more and more confused until he noticed the torchlight glinting off the jagged, U-shaped brands on all their right shoulders. He released his breath and began to look at their faces. They were all smiling at him and some reached out their hands and patted him on the back or shoulder as he passed. Behind them, the crowd watched and Carro felt their eyes, but he tried not to look at their faces for fear of what he might see. He kept his gaze fixed on the back of Asenna's head as she led him to where Tolian stood in front of the council house. The drums kept beating, imitating his heartbeat and reaching a fever pitch as Carro faced Tolian. Asenna dropped his hand and stood behind her uncle, giving him an encouraging smile. Carro looked out at the crowd and spotted Tira standing with Haryk, Ivarr, and Nikke. Elyana was there too, holding Fen, but she looked like she might be attending under duress. Tolian held up his hands and the drums stopped suddenly, leaving a deafening silence in their wake.

"Carro," said Tolian, throwing his voice so the crowd could hear him, "you come here tonight seeking that which we give our lost sons who have returned to us. We give it to you freely, as your birthright. Tonight, we return to you the family that was taken, the protection of this pack, and the love of Izlani that surrounds and carries all of us. In return, will you renounce all names and titles that have been granted to you by the outside world?"

"I will," Carro responded, feeling his body start to tremble. He tensed all of his muscles, willing it to stop.

"And will you protect and honor your people and your family above all others, for as long as you live?"

"I will."

"Then we welcome you back and mark you as one of our own, erasing all the marks that the world saw fit to give you," Tolian stepped back and Asenna moved forward, holding a small bowl which Carro saw was full of white paint. She dipped her fingers into it and then gently brushed it over the brand on his shoulder. The paint and the air were both cold and he shivered a little, but tried to focus only on her face, letting everything else fade away. Speaking in Ulvvori under her breath, she dipped her fingers into the bowl again and reached up to paint a line down the center of his face from his forehead to his chin, then made two lines under each of his eyes. Carro wanted to know what she was saying, but found that he had lost the capacity to translate or even to think about anything else when she was looking at him. When she finished and stepped back, Carro felt like she took her warmth with her and he was left shivering.

"*E'shayus virra*, Carro, welcome home," said Tolian, holding out his hand. Carro grabbed his wrist and a cheer went up from the crowd. He allowed himself to breathe again just as he was suddenly surrounded by people patting him on the back and congratulating him. Tira fought her way through the crowd and hugged him tight, beaming.

"Welcome home!" she said, her voice trembling a little. The sentiment was repeated by dozens of Ulvvori, including some of the other returned conscripts, who introduced themselves and shook his hand. Carro felt overwhelmed with it all and his limbs still felt a little shaky. Everyone in the village had brought out food and wine, and somewhere nearby a fiddle began to play along with the drums. When Carro turned to look for Asenna, imagining that she might want to dance, she was nowhere to be found. After a few minutes of trying to search the crowd for her, Carro felt a hand on his shoulder.

"You may go if you want to," Tolian whispered, handing him a shirt, "and you might try looking by the fishing hole first." Carro waited until no one was speaking directly to him and then ducked out and went around the back of the council house, pulling the shirt on as he went. Guided only by the light of the brightest full moon he had ever seen, Carro along the riverbank until he reached the spot under the cottonwood trees. Asenna was sitting at the base of one of the trees on a blanket, knitting tiny blue flowers into a crown. Carro's heart, which had slowed down after the end of the ceremony, began to thump wildly again.

"Asenna," he said softly, trying not to startle her, but she smiled when she saw him. "You didn't want to humiliate me with a dance?"

"I thought I'd spare you tonight. You've endured enough," she laughed and her nose scrunched up, making Carro's heart race even faster as he sat beside her.

"What're you doing?" he asked.

"Making this," Asenna held up the flower crown. "And talking to Izlani…and thinking. I…I want to go with you…to Esmadia." Carro leaned away from her, trying to see if she was still teasing him.

"I can't let you do that, Asenna. This will be more dangerous than you can possibly imagine and I...*we* can't afford to lose you."

"I don't want to fight, but...I feel responsible," Asenna replied with a tiny edge in her voice, "Azimar is doing this because of me, because I left. If anyone is going to accept me or Fen on the throne, then I need to show them I'm willing to be there in whatever way I can, even if it's just as a witness. Surely you understand that?"

"You know I do, but I'm just--"

"Then you won't try to stop me from going," she said lightly, as if they had just decided what to eat for supper.

Carro sighed. "I know it's pointless to argue with you either way, you stubborn thing." Asenna leaned over and put the flower crown on his head, letting her fingers rest on his cheek.

"I don't think you can really claim that was a surprise to you," she laughed softly. Carro reached up and covered her hand with his own, then turned his face to kiss her palm. He felt surprisingly calm as their breath mixed together in the chill air.

"No, I love it," he murmured, "I love *you*, actually..." Asenna's face split into a smile and she slipped her hand around the back of his neck.

"I love you too," she said, pulling him in and pressing her lips to his. Carro felt like he was floating in the water again as every sound and sensation was muted except the softness of her mouth and the firmness of her grip, telling him how sure she was. He raised his hands to hold her face and she leaned over, pressing her body against him and making it harder and harder for him to breathe.

"I'm so sorry it took me this long," Carro told her when they finally broke apart, "I just...I didn't understand it, and I didn't think you could possibly feel the same way..."

"Well, you've made quite a habit of being wrong," Asenna teased, kissing him again. Carro leaned over her as she laid back on the blanket and wrapped one arm around her waist. Feeling a burning hunger flare to life in his belly, he moved down to kiss her neck and collarbone, but Asenna let out a small gasp and he pulled back.

"I'm sorry. Do you want me to stop?"

"Don't apologize," she breathed, "and don't stop." Carro obeyed, moving his mouth along her body while his fingers fumbled with the tiny hooks at the back of her beaded top. When it was undone, he threw it aside and wrapped his arm around her again, lifting her off the blanket and pushing her skirt up around her stomach as her chest heaved and her hands clutched at the blanket. Carro traced the inside of her thigh with his lips until he found what he was looking for and her back arched up. With every minute he spent,

Carro could hear her breathing growing more ragged, until finally she reached down and grabbed his shoulder.

"I need you," she murmured, "now." Carro pulled his clothes off and then moved up so they were face-to-face again, groaning as Asenna's fingernails dug into his back.

"I'm yours," he whispered, burying his face in her neck, "every piece of me is yours." As their bodies began to move together, Carro found himself desperate to be even closer to her, to become a drop of blood in her veins and spend every minute of the rest of his existence making her heart pump, or bringing color to her cheeks when she laughed. He couldn't stand the thought of ever being farther away from her than he was at that moment. When Asenna cried out his name, it felt strange and unfamiliar, as if being with her had erased all memories of who he was before. Reaching behind her head, Carro grabbed onto a tree root, using it to brace himself as they both approached the precipice and then plunged off of it. They held onto one another as tightly as they could, drinking in the other's shallow, gasping breaths with their foreheads pressed together, until the waves subsided and they collapsed.

When he dropped his head onto Asenna's chest, Carro realized he was trembling, but he couldn't be sure if it was the crisp autumn air or the strange new feeling flooding his body. He wanted to say it was something like contentment or devotion, or both, but never having felt either, he couldn't be sure. Asenna must have felt him shaking too, because she reached over and pulled the blanket up around both of them, then laced her fingers through his hair and kissed the top of his head.

"Thank you, *lai'zhia,*" she said softly.

"For what…exactly?" Carro asked, tilting his face up and grinning.

"Well, for *that*, yes," Asenna gave a small, breathless giggle, "but also just for being who you are…and for loving me the way I am."

"As if it's difficult to love you," Carro whispered, kissing the place on her chest where he could still feel her heart drumming away.

"I could certainly make it *more* difficult, if you'd like a challenge," Asenna laughed. Carro rolled over onto his elbow and pulled her under his arm, then traced his fingers along her lips and cheeks.

"How about…" he said slowly, "you keep being exactly what you are, and I promise to love you no matter what that looks like…*lai'rani.*"

"*Lai'rani*…like in that song?"

"Yes…because you burned so bright that whatever darkness there was in me didn't stand a chance."

THIRTEEN: THE INVASION

When Asenna woke up, the sun was peeking over the cliffs already. She felt the comforting weight and warmth of Carro's body pressed up against her back and, after reliving the previous night in her head a few times, she rolled over and buried her face in his chest. Breathing in the way he smelled, vaguely like sweat and woodsmoke, Asenna ran her fingers over the spot on his shoulder where the smeared white paint was still half covering the Ulvvori brand. The paint she had put on his face was mostly gone too and she smiled as she traced the lines again, trying to soak up how peaceful he looked when he was asleep. She couldn't remember a time when someone had made her feel so safe or loved, and she was still half afraid she would wake up and realize it had been a dream.

"It's morning, *lai'zhia*," she murmured as Carro began to stir and stretch. It took him a few seconds to get his bearings, then he let out a nervous laugh, draping his arm over her and rubbing his nose against hers.

"I was hoping I didn't just hallucinate all of that," he said, "should we get back?"

"Absolutely not," Asenna put her hand on his cheek and kissed him, "they can wait." She rolled over so she was straddling his legs and felt the same scorching heat in her stomach as the night before, shooting up into her chest and down through her hips to her toes. Carro put his hands on her thighs and pushed her skirt up, but then Asenna paused and tilted her head, swearing she could hear some strange noise in the distance.

"Wait, hang on," she whispered.

"What's wrong?" Carro asked, but she put her fingers over his mouth.

"Shhh, listen." They both heard the howls of the dire wolves start up along the tops of the cliffs at the same time. It was a strange howl that Asenna had never heard before, long and wavering and almost eerie, and it was picked up one at a time by each scout in turn. Asenna looked up at the cliffs, where they saw the silhouettes of Riders racing along at breakneck speed. She stumbled as she stood up, shading her eyes for a better view of the ridge.

"Look!" she cried out, pointing. There were dozens of wolves spilling onto the narrow track from above and running down toward the village, but these had no Riders on their backs, nor any humans with them at all.

"It's the wild dire wolves," Carro breathed, "they're here!"

Once they were both dressed again, Asenna found herself racing Carro down the road as they both sprinted to meet the wolves coming down from the cliffs. They were being led by an enormous white wolf with a missing ear, who let out a loud yip as she ran. Asenna returned the call, tears stinging her eyes, and when they got closer, she slowed down and put her arms out. The white wolf stopped and pressed her huge head into Asenna's chest, nearly knocking her to the ground.

"Briar! Oh, I missed you!" Asenna whispered in a choked voice. The other wolves surrounded them, all yipping and whining and wagging their tails furiously. Asenna could almost feel the elation and excitement of the animals, but also a deep and complex longing that overtook her when she pulled back and looked into Briar's golden eyes. She knew it was the she-wolf's sorrow over losing Larke, which nearly matched Asenna's own, and she kissed Briar on her snout. Looking around, Asenna saw Carro standing behind them, looking intensely uncomfortable as the wild wolves sniffed and inspected him. She reached back and grabbed his hand, pulling him forward.

"Carro, this is Briar," she said, placing his hand on the wolf's muzzle, "she was my father's companion before he died, and she's also Echo's sister."

Carro gave an awkward bow. "It's an honor," he said in a shaky voice. Briar pressed her huge nose, the size of a buckler shield, into Carro's chest, drinking in his scent. He glanced at Asenna with wide eyes and she laughed.

"I think she likes you."

"I certainly hope so."

"Come on," Asenna said to Briar, "let's go find everyone." The two of them led the wild packs back toward the village, where people had started to gather along the road to greet the new arrivals. Some of the Ulvvori wolves, with their Riders, were already racing out to greet their cousins and friends. It was complete chaos and Asenna and Carro barely pulled themselves out of the melee with Briar before they could make their way back to their own home. When they were nearly back, Asenna saw her family standing on the main road. Fen pulled his hand away from Elyana and ran toward her.

"Woofs! Woofs!" he called out, giving a long, shrill howl of his own. Asenna caught him and held him up to Briar, who licked his face gently. When she turned around, Asenna saw her mother standing nearby, tears running down her cheeks. Elyana stepped forward and buried her face into Briar's fur.

"River's gone," Asenna heard her mother sob, "and so many others." Briar growled softly, closing her eyes, and Asenna could tell that she was sharing in Elyana's grief. Haryk and Ivarr came up and put their arms around Briar too, just as Tira ran up to the group, her face wild and strained.

"Rowan!" she called out, desperately searching the shifting sea of wolves. A shaggy red wolf appeared between the others and bowled Tira completely over in his eagerness, licking her face and knocking her sword out of its scabbard. Tira wrapped her arms around his neck and Asenna could tell that her tears were from both grief and joy. She turned to look at Tolian.

"They've come to help us," she said, putting her hand on Briar's neck.

"Thank you, my friend," Tolian said quietly, pressing his forehead to Brair's. They took Briar and Rowan back to their little compound, where the cottages were nearly demolished as Echo, Nettle, Juniper, and Ash came out pouncing and swinging their tails as they reunited with Briar. Sage was a little more cautious meeting her great-aunt, but soon they were all jumping and running around the fire pit, nearly upturning the big table. Tolian suggested to Echo that they take their family reunion to the field behind the houses and the wolves all raced away, yipping and barking. Once they had replaced all the toppled stools and picked up the firewood that had been scattered, Asenna's family gathered around the table to try and finish their breakfast that had been interrupted by the wolves' arrival. Asenna put Fen on a stool beside her and glanced over at Elyana, trying to figure out if her mother would have anything to say about her absence the night before. However, Elyana's eyes were slightly glazed over as she watched the wolves frolicking in the field. Asenna reached over and squeezed her mother's hand and Elyana returned a sad smile, then tried to focus her attention on the food in front of her.

"Can we leave for the border now?" Tira asked, "what else are we waiting for?"

"Yes, I believe it is time to make our preparations and leave as soon as possible," Tolian said. "Carro, we will need to integrate the new dire wolves into our plans. What did you and Tira have in mind?" Carro had been absentmindedly holding Asenna's hand under the table and running his fingers along her wrist, and when Tolian spoke to him he sat bolt upright and cleared his throat, but didn't let go of her. Asenna squeezed his fingers.

"They'll need to stay wherever the Riders are at all times in order for us to communicate with them," he said, "I think I counted about a hundred and fifty or so wild wolves, so we need to divide them up into small groups, maybe ten to fifteen, and assign them to a pair of Riders. Azimar is terrified of the dire wolves, so we may not need them to fight at all. I hope their presence alone will be enough to get him to stand down." Tolian and the others nodded.

"Echo and Briar and I will rally the Riders and begin making assignments," Tolian said slowly, "Ivarr, Haryk, Nikke, I need you three and Tira to go and start spreading the word to the others."

"Yes, sir." They all stood up and went out to the field to extricate their wolves from the play-fight they were engaged in. The rest of them finished eating and after they had cleared the dishes from the table, Asenna picked Fen up and slowly approached her mother, whose face was still tear-stained.

"Are you alright, Mama?" she asked gently. Elyana ran her sleeve over her cheeks and then reached her arms out for Fen. Asenna passed him over, knowing that her mother needed the distraction and comfort.

"I just never thought I would see her again," Elyana said, pressing her face into Fen's mass of black curls, "being able to feel her, even if I can't hear her voice. It's just…it's difficult. She and your father were so alike. It's almost like being near him again." Asenna pulled her mother into a hug with Fen squished between them. Their relationship had improved over the last year, but Asenna knew that it was about to become more strained when she told Elyana about her plans to go with the invasion force, and about Carro. She closed her eyes and tried to savor the brief moment of connection.

"Let's go inside," Asenna suggested, knowing that it would be easier to talk to her mother alone. Once they were back in the house, Asenna tried to surreptitiously change her clothes while Elyana watched Fen play.

"You think I don't know where you were last night?" Elyana said with a tiny smile after Asenna had changed her clothes and sat down.

Asenna squirmed, feeling intensely uncomfortable. "No, I just…I didn't want to upset you by…making it obvious."

"You know," Elyana said, leaning her head back against the wall, "Tolian used to *hate* your father."

Asenna looked up in surprise. "Really? But…they were so close."

"Our parents were already gone when I started bringing your father around, and Tolian couldn't stand how loud and brash he was. He tried to forbid me from seeing Larke. *Tried.* But I was young and in love and I was going to be damned if I had anyone else's babies." Elyana picked at her fingernails as she spoke. "I'm only telling you because…I want you to know…that I don't hate him. Carro, I mean."

"You don't?"

"Oh, I did at first. We all did, save maybe Tolian. I know I haven't been kind to him since he returned, but I could never hate someone who so clearly loves you, and Fen. I just…don't want you to end up like me," Elyana's voice became strangled with emotion, "Senna, I *loved* your father so much. He was my entire world, my best friend. When we lost him...I don't know how I survived. I don't want that for you. Carro's life has been forfeit since the moment he left the Black Sabers. He is about to walk straight back into the monster's teeth and you know Azimar won't just let that kind of betrayal go."

Asenna felt tears slip out of her eyes. "Mama...have some faith in him, and in the rest of them. It's a good plan, and we have so much support."

"I have no doubt the campaign will succeed now that we have the Kashaitis and the wolves, but Carro has already shown that he will put himself in harm's way to protect the people he cares about. You think he won't do that again? For Tira, or Talla, or even Gaelin? He is severely lacking any sense of self-preservation and I think you know that." Asenna nodded slowly and watched Fen balance some of his wooden animals on the deck of the toy ship.

"I'm going with them," she said, knowing that it was better to get it over with.

"What?" Elyana asked in barely more than a whisper.

"I made up my mind weeks ago, Mama," Asenna replied, trying to stay calm, "I'm going with them. How can I expect people to fight for me or follow me, or Fen, if I can't even show my face when there's danger?"

"Asenna...I love you, but you are no warrior," Elyana was keeping her voice even for Fen's sake, but Asenna could see the corners of her mouth trembling, "you expect me to send my only brother, and all three of my children, and Nikke, off to war? After everything I've already lost?"

"Mama..." Asenna felt herself beginning to cry, "I don't expect you to understand, but I *need* to do this! I'm going to be sitting on a throne, Mama, with *everything* on my shoulders, including freedom for our people. Last time, I didn't get to take that burden on my own terms. This time I do, and I'm not going to waste the opportunity to show people what kind of leader I can be, and what kind of leader I'm going to teach Fen to be."

"I see it, *sheyta zhia*, and I know you won't listen to me anyway," Elyana laughed while still crying, "I understand why you need to go, but it will break my heart."

"I love you, Mama," Asenna hugged her mother and kissed her on the cheek, "I should probably go tell Tolian that I'm coming with them."

"I'm proud of you, Asenna," Elyana replied, "I can't deny that you're your father's daughter, and I know he would be proud of you too." Asenna hugged her mother again, then went outside and found Tolian talking with Carro by the firepit. She cleared her throat as she approached them and Carro somehow understood what she was doing, moving to stand behind her.

"I've been thinking about it for a long time," Asenna said to Tolian, "and I've decided that I want to come with you to Esmadia." Her uncle did not react, but quietly considered her words as he always did. Finally, he sighed.

"I suppose that does make sense," he said, "for you to be there, to show the country that you are willing to fight for them. We need to gain their trust if this is going to work. Carro, you have no objections to this?"

"I've already tried, sir," Carro smiled, "it's no use. Anyway, I figure we'd all better get used to taking orders from her, right?"

"A wise man," Tolian said, winking, "very well, Asenna, but I will ask Briar to stay with you at all times for your own safety. I cannot imagine many, even the Black Sabers, will want to tangle with her. Now, if you'll excuse me, I can see some of my Riders coming to pepper me with questions." He walked out into the field behind the houses where Asenna could, indeed, see a dozen or so Riders gathered near the wild dire wolves. She turned to Carro and leaned up against him, letting out the taut breath she had been holding.

"My mother isn't happy, but she's not as angry as I thought she'd be."

"She trusts your judgment," Carro said, "we all do." He put his arms around her and rested his chin on the top of her head.

"She also confessed to me that she *doesn't* hate you," Asenna chuckled, "but she *does* know where we were last night."

"Ah," Carro gave a nervous laugh, "that is somehow both relieving and terrifying." Asenna heard voices coming up the path and turned to see Tira, Ivarr, Haryk, and Nikke, returning from summoning the other Riders with their wolves. All four of them began to smirk and snicker when they saw Asenna and Carro standing together.

"Well, well, well," said Tira, sidling up to them, "I wondered where the two of you were last night and now I think I've got my answer."

"Leave them alone, Tira," said Ivarr, poking Asenna in the ribs from the other side, "I'm sure they're *exhausted*." Asenna took a swipe at her brother, but he dodged.

"Took you long enough," Haryk muttered to Carro.

"We get it, alright!" Carro laughed, "shouldn't you all go and start packing now?"

Haryk cleared his throat and put on a stern expression. "Yes, Tolian said we're leaving in the morning. We have a lot to do before then."

"I'm going too," Asenna told them, "not to fight, just to be there."

"Yes!" Tira cried, punching the air, "I was hoping!"

"Are you sure?" Haryk raised an eyebrow at her.

"Briar will be with me the entire time," Asenna assured him. Haryk looked skeptical, but Asenna could tell that he was too focused on the mission to argue with her. They all went to begin preparations to leave, but as they approached the cottage, Elyana came out carrying Fen in her arms, a stony expression on her face.

"You come back with my daughter or you don't come back at all," she said to Carro, yellow eyes narrowing.

"You have my word, Elyana," he replied quietly. Once Elyana had taken Fen to her own cottage where it was quieter, they all set about packing their things. Asenna carefully took the short sword down from where it hung on the wall of her room and turned it around in her hands while Carro sat on the bed, watching her.

"You aren't afraid?" he asked.

"Of course, I am. But I know there's no safer place for me than with you, and my family," Asenna answered, "are you?"

"Not of the fighting," Carro said, running his hands through his hair, "...maybe...of seeing him again." Asenna put the sword down and sat beside him, gently turning his face so she could see his eyes.

"Why does that scare you, *lai'zhia?*"

"I don't know. I want to face him, to confront him about everything he put me through, but I still feel so...angry and bitter when I think about it. Key wants him arrested so he can stand trial, but...what if I can't stop myself from hurting him? What if I just turn right back into the same person I was? The person *he* wanted me to be?"

"Carro, you are a better man than he could ever dream of being. You can face him knowing that you're finally free of everything he did to you," Asenna pulled him closer, "but, if you decide that it's too much, I promise I'll still love you. So will Fen, and Tira, and everyone here. You're worth more to us than that, and I *know* you'll make the right choice, no matter what."

"Thank you, *lai'rani,*" Carro murmured, pulling her in tighter and pressing his face into her neck.

Their last evening in the village was spent around the fire in the courtyard, with significantly less drinking than before and slightly more nervous, excited energy, knowing what was ahead of them. Asenna cradled Fen in her arms, even after he had fallen asleep, and kissed his little head as often as she could while Carro held Sage like a toddler on his own lap. Her heart was breaking at the thought of leaving him behind, but she also knew that staying was not an option she could stomach. When they all decided it was time to sleep, Asenna slept in Fen's bed with him, while Carro and Sage laid on the floor beside them.

When Asenna woke up the next morning, however, Fen was not with her and she had a moment of panic before she looked down and saw him curled up under Carro's arm, both still sleeping soundly. Their breathing was in sync and Asenna watched them for a few minutes, allowing herself to feel all the sadness and apprehension and love at once so that it caused a few tears to fall from her eyes. Fen suddenly stretched his little body out, punching Carro on the chin as he did.

"Good morning to you too," Carro chuckled, pushing Fen's fists away from his face.

"I was hoping you would keep sleeping," Asenna told him, reaching down and running her fingers along his shoulder, "I wanted to stop everything just like that for a while…before we have to go."

"Me too," Carro said, "it's going to be very different when this is over." Asenna nodded and they let the heavy silence fall over them. After a little while, Carro carefully slipped his other arm out from underneath Fen and got up.

Asenna watched him as he changed his clothes and the sight of the scars on his shoulder and hip caused her to relive the moment he had saved her out on the plains. She remembered hearing his voice screaming Roper's name, trying to draw the attention of the Black Sabers away from her. She remembered looking back over her shoulder to see Talla driving her hatchet into Gade's back, and then the arrow that was meant for her suddenly turning and flying the opposite direction. She remembered watching it bury itself into Carro's body, then watching as the second arrow struck and he had fallen from the horse. She had stopped running then, terrified and frozen as she watched Roper nock another arrow and point the bow back at her. That was the moment the Riders had come, and Asenna shook her head slightly to try and rid herself of the memory of what the wolves had done to Roper. Even then, after she had watched Carro sacrifice himself and his friends to save her and Fen, Asenna could never have imagined waking up in his arms. Still, any vague doubts about her feelings for him had vanished in that moment on the riverbank when he had accepted her decision to go along with the invasion force, and said that he loved her all the more for it.

"Everything alright?" Carro asked as he slipped on his boots.

"Yes, I was just drifting off," Asenna said, pushing the thoughts from her mind and trying to focus on what was ahead of them. Carro kissed her and then went into the other room while Asenna got up and began to change into the clothes Tira had loaned her, then finally knelt down to wake Fen. He stirred and whimpered a little and Sage gave a grumpy little howl, but they both opened their luminous golden eyes and peered up at her at the same time. Once they were awake, Asenna went to her kitchen to get Fen some food and found that Carro had already made a small plate for him and a separate one for Sage before going outside, so she brought them their breakfast in bed. As she watched them eat, Asenna felt like her body was sagging and close to breaking under the weight of wondering when she might see him again.

"You're going to be staying with your Gamma for a while, Fen," she told him, "Mama has to go on a trip." Fen looked up at her and cocked his head slightly.

"I go?" he pointed to himself.

"No, *sheyta zhia*, you stay here with Gamma," Asenna said. Fen seemed unfazed and finished his food, then started chasing Sage around the bedroom. Asenna heard the door open and leaned over to see Elyana holding a large bundle under her arm.

"Carro said you're leaving soon," she said in a far gentler voice than Asenna had heard her use in recent memory, "I wanted to give you this before things got too chaotic." Asenna stood up and took the bundle, unrolling it to find a long dagger in a faded leather sheath. The bundle itself seemed to be a thick, hooded cloak. "These were your father's. I thought you'd get more use out of them than I do."

"Thank you, Mama," Asenna put the cloak and knife on the table and hugged her tightly. Elyana returned the hug and then broke away, trying to disguise her tears.

"Come on, little Fen! Sage!" she said in a bright voice as they ran over to her. Elyana took the two of them outside and Asenna tied the dagger and her sword onto her belt, then threw the cloak over her shoulders. It was slightly big on her but somehow, more than sixteen years after his death, it still smelled like her father. She took a deep breath before doing one last check of her home and then picking up her pack. Briar was waiting just outside the door, her fur slightly damp from the morning dew. She nuzzled Asenna's cloak, breathing in the scent, and her single ear drooped a little.

"I miss him too," Asenna whispered, leaning her face against Briar's cheek. The wolf gave her a tiny lick on the arm as they stood and watched the activity buzzing in the courtyard. Haryk, Ivarr, Nikke, Tolian, and Tira were making final preparations to leave, their faces and arms streaked with red and yellow warpaint. Asenna realized how out of place she felt amongst them, but Briar stuck by her side, making her feel more confident.

"You look like you're ready to lead an army," Tira said with a grin.

"I feel a bit ridiculous, to be honest," Asenna confessed, "I'm just...not a fighter."

Tira took her by the shoulders "That's fine, Asenna! You don't need to be a fighter. There's enough bloodthirsty maniacs in this family, I think, and we're with you no matter what." Asenna laughed and went to lean her head on Tira's shoulder, but Tira pulled back and looked at her with one of those smiles that told Asenna she was about to be interrogated. "Also, you *have* to tell me about the other night, because I'm far too nosy to mind my own business and I--" Tira was interrupted by Carro, who walked up to them leading a pair of horses that Selissa had sent as a gift, and holding two small ceramic jars of paint in his other hand.

"Come here," he said, dropping the reins into Tira's hand and pulling Asenna toward him in a way that made her blush. He dipped his finger into one of the jars and held it up covered in red. "My turn to paint *you.*" Asenna pushed her hair back from her face and tilted it back for him. Carefully and slowly, Carro drew lines across her cheeks and down the center of her face, standing a bit closer than Asenna thought might be appropriate for the occasion. She shivered when his fingers brushed over her lips, recalling the night they had spent on the riverbank. When he was done, Carro stepped back and Tira ventured over to check his handiwork.

"Well?" Asenna asked her.

"You look very intimidating, but I'm not sure I should have watched that," Tira chuckled. Before Carro could offer a retort, Tolian clapped his hands and they all turned to face him.

"Say your goodbyes," he said. Asenna looked over to where Elyana was standing with Fen. Sage was next to her, nuzzled up to Juniper and Ash while Elyana spoke to Haryk, Nikke, and Ivarr. Asenna walked over to them and took her brothers' hands.

"I am so proud of all of you," Elyana was saying, "my boys, Asenna. Your father's heart would burst if he could see you now. Promise me you'll look after one another."

"We will, Mama," they all said almost in unison.

"Nikke," said Elyana, "I know you'll take care of them, and yourself too, fearsome girl." Nikke gave Elyana a firm hug and then turned away, but Asenna saw tears in her eyes too. Haryk and Ivarr gave their mother and Fen one last hug before moving away so that Asenna could take her son in her arms. She pressed her face into his cheek and he giggled when some of the paint came off on him.

"I love you so much, *sheyta zhia,*" Asenna whispered to him, her voice breaking, "I have to go now, but I'll be back soon. You're going to be with Gamma for a while and I need you to be good for her. Promise?"

"Promise," said Fen in his tiny voice.

"I love you, Fen," Asenna repeated it to him over and over until she was on the verge of tears. She felt Carro's hand on her shoulder and then he put his arms around the two of them and held on tight for a few minutes. Fen suddenly reached out for Carro, who took him from Asenna and kissed him on the head.

"See you soon, *lai'rani cyn,*" Carro murmured, "my turn to take care of your mother now."

"Bye-bye, Da," Fen said, wrapping his arms around Carro's neck. Asenna couldn't see Carro's face because it was concealed by Fen's mass of curls, but his hands started to shake as they squeezed Fen tighter, and her own heart flipped over in her chest. She put a hand on Carro's back and he passed Fen back to her, then turned away. Asenna glanced over at her mother, who was suppressing a tiny smile.

"Mama…" Asenna whispered, "did you teach him that?"

"I don't know what you're talking about," said Elyana with a shrug. Asenna shook her head and turned back to give Fen one last hug.

"Bye Mama. Lub you," said Fen, squeezing her neck one more time and then reaching for Elyana. Asenna felt like she was crumbling as she handed Fen back to her mother and knelt down to scratch Sage's ears.

"Please take care of him, Sage." The pup stared back up at her and Asenna felt a wave of loving warmth and reassurance flood her body. When she stood up, she saw Carro waiting next to her horse, a rather jumpy dappled gray mare she had named Scout. She went over and put a hand on his cheek, which was still a little red and damp.

"Are you alright?" she asked with a small smile.

"Yeah," Carro murmured, "just…didn't expect that. Are you ok though? I wouldn't blame you for changing your mind. It's not too late." Asenna blinked her remaining tears away and shook her head.

"No," she replied, "I need to do this." She waved at Fen as everyone around her pulled themselves up onto their dire wolves and Carro mounted the beautiful red roan charger that Selissa had given him, named Caz. Once they were all ready, Tolian waved his hand and they moved toward the main road. Asenna twisted around in the saddle to wave at Fen one more time. He waved back and she was glad to see that he was smiling as Elyana bounced him up and down.

"I love you," Asenna whispered again, blowing a kiss and letting a few final tears slide down her face as they met up with more Riders. Tolian and Echo led the column and they all followed behind him in pairs, with the rest of the Riders falling in as they went, some leading the groups of wild wolves that had been assigned to them. When they reached the edge of the village, Briar threw back her head and let out a long, low howl. The wild wolves joined in, then the Ulvvori wolves. Soon, every dire wolf had added their voice to the chorus and a few of the Riders even howled and whooped along with them. The sound was eerie, but also lifted Asenna's spirits because she knew that she was right where she needed to be as they began to move northwest toward the border.

~~~

Crouching down inside the burned-out shell of the house and stepping over a fallen beam, Asenna picked her way further into the building, holding her shirt over her nose to try and block out the horrific smell. She stopped and peered into one of the rooms at the end of the long hallway, but saw nothing other than more charred beams from the roof, then moved on to the next room. In the cold evening light, Asenna could see the remains of several bed frames and straw mattresses. She took a step further but froze in her tracks when she spotted the figures huddled against the far wall. They were mangled and blackened, nearly unrecognizable as having once been humans, save for the bits of hair and teeth hanging crooked from scorched faces. Asenna covered her mouth and turned to run, feeling the bile scalding her throat. Carro was standing in what was once the kitchen and he caught her as she stumbled out.

"Hey! What's the matter?!" he yelped as she slammed into him.

"I found them," she cried, "the people who lived here." Carro wrapped his arms around her as the sobs overtook her body.

"Damnit! I'm so sorry, Asenna. I shouldn't have let you come in here." Asenna felt the hot tears burning her eyes and she tried to wipe them away, but it was a flood.

"It's my fault," she murmured, keeping her face pressed hard into Carro's shoulder. "I left. I ran away. Azimar wouldn't have done this…" Carro pulled away and lifted her chin.

"Asenna, look at me," he brushed her hair away from her face, "this is *not* your fault. You made a choice to protect Fen, and there is no way you could have known he would do this. Come on, let's get out of here." Carro took her by the shoulders and led her out of the house, back into the street of what had recently been a small farming village. Briar was waiting for them on the road and she nudged Asenna with her nose when they came out of the house, whining softly in concern.

It had been two weeks since they crossed the Kashaiti border back into Esmadia and began moving along the northern edge of the Forever Forest. Thus far, they had encountered only small raiding parties of Black Sabers and there had been several skirmishes between them and the Wolf Riders, but nothing serious. However, everyone knew their movements were being reported back to Azimar, and the atmosphere had been tense as they waited for a larger attack that didn't seem to be coming. The real test, at least for Asenna, had been the devastation and pain they had witnessed. Hundreds of Esmadian refugees were fleeing along the road, trying to reach Kashait, which had set up a camp just across the border. They had also found fields burned and salted so crops would never grow again, villages that had been set alight, and entire pastures of slaughtered livestock rotting in the unforgiving sun. With every encounter, Asenna's feelings of guilt deepened and nothing Carro or Tira or her family said could help her shake it. She had never felt remorseful about fleeing from Azimar, no matter how many Black Sabers had died in their pursuit but now, seeing the sheer destruction her husband had visited on ordinary citizens in his fury, she couldn't help but feel responsible.

When they reached the edge of the village, Asenna was able to pull herself together and put on a brave face for the search party that was gathering back together under a big oak tree. The Kashaiti army and most of the Riders and wild dire wolves were about half a day behind them, but Carro and Tira had formed a small scouting party, which included Asenna, Ivarr, and a few other young Riders. When they had come across the town, they had decided to search the rubble for survivors, but Tira shook her head as they approached.

"Nothing," she said sadly, "nothing but bodies and ash. You?"

"Same," Carro told her, "it's getting late. Let's head to the forest to sleep. We can report back to Tolian in the morning." They all mounted up and began riding back east along the road in silence. Asenna's stomach was still churning with horror at what she had seen, but she tried to put it out of her mind the way everyone else seemed to be able to do. They were nearing the western edge of the Forever Forest and relying on the Kashaitis to engineer a way for the invasion force to cross the Southrun River, near the ruins of the bridge that Talla had blown up. The Kashaiti generals had refused to discuss the issue with the Ulvvori, however, which had caused a great deal more tension than Asenna felt was necessary between allies. Carro had been so agitated about it that he had nearly come to blows with Zaki, and Tira had suggested that they scout ahead in order to get him away.

"Why do you think they haven't attacked us yet?" Tira said to no one in particular as they rode, "they know we're here."

"Azimar will do anything to avoid a pitched battle against the Wolf Riders, especially out here in the open," Carro replied quietly, "I think he's waiting. Once we've crossed the river, we won't be able to escape as easily."

"Then why are we even crossing the river? Aren't we playing into his hands?" Ivarr asked from behind them.

"If we sit here on this side and he sits there on his side, nothing will ever happen, except he'll keep slaughtering everyone on his side of the river," Carro explained, "he won't come out and meet us, so we have to get to him. Besides, the goal was never to destroy his army, the goal is to convince them to come over or at least stand down."

"What about the Black Sabers?" Asenna said, "do you think any of them would leave?"

Carro shook his head. "I doubt it. They know we won't deal as lightly with them, and they're trained to fight to the death. Azimar drilled it into us: *'better off dead than defeated.'* During the war and even after, I carried poison with me on every mission. Don't be surprised if we find some of them have taken it rather than face us." Asenna was horrified at this thought and she pulled Scout a little closer to Caz so she could take Carro's hand. He squeezed her fingers, but his eyes were still focused somewhere off in the distance.

The party fell silent again and didn't speak until they reached a point where they could camp. Riding a little way into the forest so they would be concealed by the trees, they let the horses and wolves go to find their own food. They had no tents to set up and did not think a fire was worth the risk, so they simply spread their blankets out behind a large fallen tree trunk. Asenna volunteered to take the first watch since she had found it difficult to sleep ever since leaving Kashait anyway. She sat with her back up against the fallen log and Carro put his blanket beside her. As he laid down, she pulled his head into her lap and he wrapped an arm around her waist.

"What can I do for you, *lai'rani?*" he asked.

"I just want this to be over," Asenna muttered, then looked down and saw that he already had his eyes closed. "I don't understand how you can all be so calm and sleep so well."

"A lifetime of being trained to repress my emotions at all costs," Carro chuckled, keeping his eyes closed. "Besides, you're forgetting that all of us have already done this once…fought a war. It's your first time, so of course you're worked up." Asenna didn't reply, but sat and ran her finger along the tiny scar above Carro's eyebrow, where she had hit him with the teapot in what felt like a completely different lifetime. The sun was about to disappear and it was throwing the shadows of the trees around them into sharp relief across the ground. Asenna sat and watched them creep, then fade, then vanish as the stars began to come out. Briar returned from the forest and laid down beside her while the scouting party fell asleep one by one until only Asenna was awake, listening and watching the horizon while her thoughts tumbled wildly through her head. All the fear and doubt and anxiety about the confrontation facing them mixed together in her belly and the longer she stayed awake, the harder she found it just to breathe, let alone think straight. She tried to distract herself by watching Carro sleep and thinking about their night on the riverbank, but all that did was make her feel even more desperate and terrified, knowing that she could lose him after they had only just found each other. Elyana's words kept replaying in her mind: *'Carro's life has been forfeit since the moment he left the Black Sabers.'* Asenna knew her mother was right, that if Azimar wanted any of them dead, it was Carro. The feeling of helplessness overwhelmed her, and even when she woke Tira up to take the next shift, she couldn't sleep, tossing and turning under her blanket until dawn.

The following day when they met back up with the Kashaiti army and the Wolf Riders, Asenna's exhaustion did not improve. They were moving slowly along the tree line in the direct sun and the steady rhythm of Scout's gait lulled her into a trance. Although it was mid-autumn, the leaves of the Forever Forest never changed and Asenna found herself hypnotized by the sea of rolling, shifting green that stretched straight out to meet the pale, cloudless sky.

"Asenna. Asenna!" She heard Carro's voice saying her name, but it took a moment to pull herself away and look at him. "You're drifting away from the column." Carro was frowning and Asenna realized that she and Scout were, in fact, moving toward the trees.

"I haven't been sleeping well since we left," she told him.

"I know, and I'm worried about you, *lai'rani*. Come here," Carro said, pulling Caz to a stop and shifting himself out of the saddle so he was sitting on the horse's rump. Asenna swung one leg around and used the stirrups to move over and sit side-saddle in front of him. Carro wrapped Scout's reins around one hand, then put his arms around her so she could lean against him and sleep while he rode.

"Thank you," she whispered as she closed her eyes.

"Just rest. I've got you," Carro kissed her forehead and then pulled her cloak around her shoulders like a blanket. The steady sound of his heartbeat, the *clop-clop* of the horses' hooves, and the dull, thunderous roll of the ten-thousand men marching behind them helped Asenna finally slip into a light sleep.

When Carro gently shook her awake, Asenna opened her eyes to find that it was dusk and they were standing still at the edge of the trees. The Kashaiti army stretched out behind them, but they were no longer on the road that ran along the northern edge of the forest, connecting Kashait to Ossesh. There was some tension in the air and Asenna looked up at Carro to see that his mouth was set in a hard line.

"What's going on?" she asked.

"We're getting close to the river and the wolves smelled something."

"Nettle says it's campfires and a lot of men," Ivarr told her.

"You don't think Azimar sent the army out here, do you?" Asenna said, sitting up rubbing her face, "what about Talla and Andros and Lusie?"

"The wolves can't smell any death," Ivarr relayed quickly, "no fighting, just a lot of men camped nearby."

"We sent some Riders ahead to see what it is," Carro told her. Asenna moved back over to Scout, trying to focus and figure out where they were. It looked like they were coming around the northeastern edge of the Forever Forest and she knew that the plan had been for the Kashaitis to build a new bridge while they waited, then to meet Talla and the other resistance fighters at the farm. However, the looks on the faces of everyone around her told Asenna that the plan would most likely be changing.

"Look!" Tira cried, pointing to the south. Two people on horseback were approaching fast, escorted by four Wolf Riders. Asenna recognized Talla's long, wild ropes of hair flying behind her as she raced toward them, with Andros keeping pace beside her. Talla let out a loud whooping cry and Tira returned it as she rode toward her sister. The two of them almost fell off their horses and seized each other in a fierce embrace, laughing and crying simultaneously. Asenna and the rest followed and suddenly everyone's arms were wrapped around each other as they all dismounted and reunited.

"I was so worried about you," Tira said, holding Talla's face in her hands, "what's going on? The wolves said there's a lot of men nearby."

"We had to leave the farm," Talla said, "too many Black Sabers around. We went up to Ossesh and came back down to lay low in the forest because we knew you'd be coming this way, but…you won't believe me until you see it--"

"*Thousands* of Azimar's men have defected," Andros grinned as he finished her sentence, "our people found them trying to head for Kashait and some of them agreed to join us. And there's Black Sabers, about two dozen of them." Asenna swore she felt her heart stop and then start back up again.

"Are you sure they're Black Sabers?" Carro asked quietly.

"Gaelin confirmed it," Andros told him, "they're all completely unarmed."

"I don't like it," said Carro immediately, "it isn't above Azimar to trick us by sending them out here with legitimate defectors."

"Just come back and see," Talla told him. They began to ride south along the tree line and Asenna heard the Kashaiti officers start barking orders at their men. She pulled Scout up beside Caz and could almost feel Carro's discomfort from several feet away.

"Do you really think it's some kind of trap?" she asked.

"I…I can't say," Carro admitted, "if they're unarmed, that's something, but it just doesn't feel right." After riding for a time, they came upon the outer edges of the deserters' camp, which was stretched out along the river between the edge of the forest and the bluffs. Some of the men had tried to construct crude lean-tos with branches and blankets, but most were sitting on the hard ground around large campfires. Asenna saw several women around as well, one of whom she recognized as a kitchen maid from the palace. As their party approached, Andros gave a loud whistle, pulling all eyes onto Asenna and Briar, who was walking just behind her.

"On your feet for your Queen!" Andros called out. Every man Asenna could see dutifully raised himself off the ground and stood at attention. She watched with some apprehension as Carro drew one of his sabers and moved to ride closer to her, his eyes scanning the crowd.

"Your Majesty!" several of the men called as she rode by. Others called her by name or cried out blessings for Fen. Asenna felt deeply uncomfortable with the displays of devotion that she certainly had not earned, but she gave a polite nod to each group of men as they passed. They all looked dirty, hungry, and defeated. The desperation and grief in the air was almost palpable, as was the tension between the Ulvvori and the deserters.

Carro leaned toward her. "This is exactly the type of thing Azimar would--" he started to whisper, but Asenna cut him off.

"It doesn't seem like a trap to me, Carro. Look at them...they have nothing." She glanced over and could see the struggle behind his eyes. "Please, just trust me?"

"I do..." he said in a strained voice, "I just...I need to keep you safe." They reached what seemed to be the center of the camp, where a large open-sided tent had been erected. Asenna could see a dozen or so people gathered around a makeshift table underneath it. They all turned when the party approached and Asenna spotted Gaelin at the back of the group. Before she could greet anyone, however, Carro leapt down off his horse and put his sword on the neck of a man standing just outside the tent.

"What the fuck are you doing here, Sirota?" he snarled. Asenna quickly slid out of her saddle, exchanging a worried look with the twins. She saw a small group of men standing off to the side that she recognized as Black Sabers, but none of them were carrying weapons and they all looked just as disheartened as the rest of the deserters.

"Captain Morelake. You wouldn't kill an unarmed man," Sirota drawled, putting his hands up and smirking at Carro.

"Care to test that theory?" Carro reached out and grabbed Sirota by the front of his shirt. Some of the other Black Sabers tensed up, ready for a fight. Without thinking, Asenna walked over and put herself in between the two men, placing a firm hand on Carro's chest. She could feel his heart racing and his shallow breaths, but she stared him down.

"Carro, don't," she said sternly, "stop this. Please, *lai'zhia.*" It seemed to take a moment for her words to reach him, but he finally lowered the saber and released his grip. Asenna turned to face Sirota. His gray eyes and pointed goatee were vaguely familiar, but the sight of his black uniform made Asenna's stomach clench with fear and she moved away. Carro put his body between the two of them and Sirota laughed softly.

"I see someone's put you on a new leash, Captain."

"I'd rather be on her leash than Azimar's," replied Carro icily, "I'll ask you again, Lieutenant. What are you doing here?"

"We have left the King's service, just as you did," Sirota replied, raising his chin, "we will not sit by and watch Azimar destroy our country and murder our families."

"How convenient that you choose to leave now, when a foreign army is approaching and your own leadership is in chaos," Carro sneered. Asenna grabbed his arm and squeezed.

"How dare you..." Sirota's smirk twisted into a grimace, but much to Asenna's relief, Talla intervened this time.

"Gentlemen, shall we? We don't have much time before we lose the light. Sirota, cool off," she snapped. Carro snorted and turned away, walking toward the tent. Asenna followed him, looking around and realizing that everyone in the camp had been watching the confrontation. Once people started to look away, she grabbed Carro's wrist and yanked him to the side.

"What the fuck was that?" she hissed.

"Sirota's a snake," Carro said in a hushed whisper, "he's the one who hired Gaelin for me and when he found out Gaelin was Ulvvori, Sirota questioned where his loyalties might be."

"I think that's a pretty fair question where Gaelin is concerned, don't you?" Asenna pointed out, "do you think he might be prejudiced against us?"

"A lot of Black Sabers are, because Azimar told them that the Ulvvori betrayed him after the war. But beyond that, Sirota's always been ambitious and that is *exactly* the type of thing Azimar could weaponize."

"And you don't think it's possible that he has had a genuine change of heart after seeing everything Azimar has done?"

"I'll believe the rank-and-file soldiers defected. They were never treated well anyway. But Sirota said the Black Sabers didn't want to watch their families be killed, but Azimar specifically recruited orphans and unmarried men so that their only loyalties would be to each other, and to him. They're all liars, Asenna!"

"I think you need to try listening to them," Asenna folded her arms.

"I'll believe it when I see them die for this cause. Until then, *you* will stay away from them," Carro spat. He turned and walked away, leaving Asenna shocked by the venom in his voice. She followed him inside the tent, still feeling a little shaky from the confrontation and determinedly avoiding his gaze.

"There he is!" Carro crowed when he saw Gaelin. They embraced and then Gaelin turned toward Asenna and gave a small bow.

"Your Majesty," he said, flashing his pointed teeth and kissing her hand, "welcome home." The smuggler looked completely different than the last time Asenna had seen him, having cut his long hair very short and traded his animal skin clothes for brown and gray cloth to match the other resistance fighters.

"You practically look like a gentleman!" Carro laughed, slapping Gaelin on the back, "Key, you'll have to tell me the secret to getting him to behave." Asenna looked over at the woman Carro had spoken to. She was middle-aged, tall and striking with dark skin and a halo of tight black curls around her face. Asenna felt that there was something familiar about her, but before she could figure it out, Talla clapped her hands and everyone gathered around the table.

"Asenna, this is Key. She's one of the leaders of the resistance here and she'll be in charge of the operation inside the city," said Andros.

"Your Majesty," Key inclined her head, "I cannot thank you enough for agreeing to this. I admit though, I'm a little surprised to see you here."

"I hoped I might be able to offer…something to help, but I'm not sure what that is," Asenna told her. A small smile crossed Key's face.

"I think your presence here is just enough," she said softly, indicating the camp surrounding them. Asenna looked behind her and saw some of the soldiers gathered together, smiling and looking far more optimistic than when they had ridden in.

"We have a plan," Andros said, "we think it'll work, but we want your input while the Kashaitis work on their bridge tomorrow, and it'll need to happen tomorrow night for this to work. For right now, I think everyone needs rest."

"What about Sirota and his men?" Carro asked suddenly, "are they part of this plan?"

"They are," Key told him, "Baine has given us a great deal of valuable intelligence since he arrived."

"He's feeding you false information!" Carro said angrily, bringing his fist down on the table, "it could easily be a trap! Why risk it by letting them be part of this?" Everyone around the table glanced at each other nervously and Asenna dropped her eyes when Carro looked at her.

"Anyone here could have said the same about you not long ago, Carro," said Talla quietly, "don't be so quick to discount others who are following your example." She turned and walked out of the tent with Gaelin, Andros, and Key behind her. Ivarr, Haryk, and Nikke also left, following Tolian back to where some of the other Riders were gathered. Sirota gave Carro a withering look from the other side of the tent and walked back over to his men. Asenna looked over and saw Tira glaring at Carro.

"Talla's right," said Tira, folding her arms, "we don't have any choice but to trust him at this point. You can't pull stunts like this in the middle of a fucking war, Carro! You should know that!"

"I know!" Carro leaned on the table and put his hand over his eyes, "I know! I'm sorry. It's just…I've been in his position. All the doubts and the second thoughts…" His words hit Asenna like a gust of wind, sucking the air out of her lungs.

"You had second thoughts?" she asked softly. Carro seemed to immediately realize what he had said and reached for her hand, but she pulled it away.

"No! Asenna, that's not what I meant! I didn't…I just know he must be questioning himself. It would be too easy for him to decide we aren't worth his trouble as soon as he has more backup." Carro was about to continue trying to explain himself, but Lusie approached the table and Asenna and Tira stood up to hug her.

"I am so sorry you had to leave, Lusie," said Asenna, "where are the children?"

"Oh, I took them to Ossesh to stay with my husband's sister," Lusie's voice was weak and shaky, "it's much safer there, but…I wanted to do my part here. I've made some supper, if you're hungry."

"I promise, Lusie, this will be over soon," Tira said to her, giving Asenna a pointed look as she left the tent, "come on, I need to find Talla and I've missed your cooking." Asenna refused to be the one to speak first, so she sat down in a chair and pretended to look at the map in front of her while Carro stayed frozen in place. Finally, he pulled a chair over so he was sitting in front of her and reached out to take her hands. This time she let him.

"I'm sorry," he murmured, "of course I questioned myself when I left, but I never, *ever* considered going back, Asenna. I swear to you."

"What did you question then?" she asked, feeling her stomach twist as he sighed and looked up at her, his eyes cloudy and pained.

"I wondered if I might just…be better off dead, rather than hurting you and Fen, or having to watch Azimar kill Gade."

Asenna paused for a moment. "Was it any easier to watch Talla kill him instead?" Carro put a hand over his eyes again.

"No, it wasn't. But when I left, I asked Gade to come with me and he said…he would rather take his chances with Azimar. I have to live with the fact that he didn't trust me enough to let me save him."

Asenna put a hand on Carro's cheek and he leaned into her touch. "So maybe," she said, "Sirota and his men have people they want to protect too. You have more in common than not. Gaelin said that to me once, about you, and he was right."

"I know," Carro said, "and I'm so sorry. I was…afraid, and it made me stupid. I'll talk to Sirota tomorrow."

"Thank you, *lai'zhia*."

"What will you do while we're gone? It should be safe here if some of the Riders stay behind with you."

"I'll wait with Lusie," Asenna said, running her fingers along the snake tattoo on his wrist, "and then I'll come once the city is secure. I'd like to talk to a few of the men here about what's been happening."

"I think that's for the best, but just…please be careful," Carro said, "come on, let's go find some food." He stood up and pulled Asenna to her feet, then wrapped her in a tight hug for a few moments before they went to find the others. Once they had eaten the thin soup Lusie had prepared, Asenna helped her clean up while Carro went to get a tent ready. As they were finishing, a light drizzle of cold autumn rain began to fall. Everyone dispersed to their individual tents, or simply laid their blankets out on the ground under the trees, hoping that the thick canopies might block most of the water. Tolian approached Asenna as she was about to go find Carro.

"I wanted to talk to you before tomorrow," her uncle said quietly, "you know how much I trust Carro, but I can only imagine how difficult this will be for him. If he is struggling and we need to pull him out, you must tell us immediately."

"Of course," Asenna murmured. Tolian wrapped his arm around her shoulders and pulled her into a hug.

"Will *you* be alright? I'm sure this is not easy for you either."

"I just…I want it to be over. I hate the waiting."

"We are almost home, little Senna," Tolian said with a tired smile, "almost home." Asenna nodded and then went to find Carro, who had set up their tent far enough back into the trees that the strange, comforting stillness of the forest enveloped them both when he put his arms around her.

"I'm sorry about earlier," he said, leaning down to kiss her neck, "can I make it up to you?" Asenna felt a thrill shoot through her body, but she put her hand on his chest and pushed back a little.

"You think you can get off the hook that easily, do you?" She tried to keep a serious expression, but Carro reached up to hold her face with one hand, while the other one moved down and untied the sword from her belt, and his lips continued to move down her neck. Any trace of anger left in her was burned away by the ravenous ache in Asenna's chest as he ran his hands along her body.

"I think it's worth a shot," he murmured with a sly grin, then bent down and wrapped his arms around her thighs, lifting her off the ground. Asenna squealed softly, folding over his shoulder and laughing as he carried her into the tent. He dropped onto his knees and lowered her onto a blanket on the ground, tossing the sword aside, then leaned in to kiss her and ran his fingers through her hair. Asenna pressed her hips up into his and his hand slipped under her shirt, but before they could go any further, Tira burst into the tent and began heckling them. She threw her blanket out on the ground and started to remove the seemingly infinite supply of weapons she kept tucked around her body. Carro rolled away and let out a loud groan of irritation while Asenna tried to settle herself down by burying her face in the blanket and biting it.

"Don't you have anything, or *anyone*, better to do?" Carro sighed.

"Look," said Tira, throwing herself down on her blanket, "it's raining, so I'm either sharing a tent with you two, or Talla and Andros, and I know you're not as…loud as they are."

"I can be loud if it gets us some privacy," Carro laughed.

"Have at it," Tira winked and laid down, "you underestimate how much I hate sleeping outside in the rain." Grumbling a little, Carro pulled their blanket up and put his arms around Asenna, then slipped his hand under her shirt again, but only to run his fingers up and down her back. Asenna settled into him, still feeling the burning ache for him in her body, but letting it subside as exhaustion washed over her again and she slipped in and out of a strange half-dream.

"*Lai'rani?*" Carro whispered after a while, "are you awake?"

"A little. What is it?"

"What do you think you'd be doing right now…if none of this had ever happened? If we'd both been able to just…live normal lives."

"Hmmm," Asenna thought for a moment, "well, it's autumn, so I'd probably be fishing. Catching a few more salmon before we leave The Den for the winter. And you?"

"That sounds nice. I always liked fishing," Carro murmured, "do you think…we still would have found each other?" Even though there was no longer any light in the tent, Asenna could imagine his expression: a small line between his dark, earnest eyes as they searched her face for reassurance and comfort.

"I think I'd find you anywhere," she whispered, melting into him as he pulled her closer.

FOURTEEN: "TRAITOR"

Carro pulled the black shirt over his head, then slipped on the black gloves and black gauntlets that Key had distributed to everyone early in the morning. It felt strange and wrong to be wearing the color again after having spent so long intentionally avoiding it. Once he was dressed and the sabers felt secure on his back, Carro looked down at Asenna, who was still sleeping. Her arms were thrown up over her head and her black hair was spread out like the feathers of a bird. Trying to savor the moment, he leaned over and ran his fingers over the freckles that dotted her cheekbones and the arc on the bridge of her nose.

"Wake up, *lai'rani*," he whispered, kissing her forehead.

Asenna opened her eyes and groaned. "But it's still dark."

"We're in the forest, remember? The sun's been up for an hour."

"I don't want you to go," she murmured, reaching up and wrapping her hands around his neck, "I just want to stay here in this little tent under the trees forever." Carro slipped his hand around her back, lifting her up as he kissed her.

"Me too. Trust me."

"And I don't like the black," Asenna frowned and picked at the shirt.

"Well, it's just for today," Carro said, "and then you can take it off me." He winked and Asenna playfully pushed him away. Once they were both dressed, they ventured out of the forest and Asenna went to help Lusie sort out how to feed everyone using some of the supplies the Kashaiti army had brought. Meanwhile, on the edge of the bluffs, the Kashaiti engineering corps looked like a colony of ants as they moved around, preparing to start building their bridge. Carro stopped and watched them for a few minutes as they lined up two dozen huge wooden stakes, several coils of rope as thick as his arm, and two lightweight reed boats along the edge of the bluff. As curious as he was about how they were going to go about their task, he heard Tira whistle for him from inside the open-air tent. The twins, Key, Gaelin, Andros, and Sirota were standing around the table with Tolian, Haryk, Ivarr, and Nikke. Several of the Kashaiti generals were there as well, with Zaki and Kir. Looking around at them all, Carro felt more optimistic than he had for a long time about their chances, but Sirota's presence still set him on edge and he tried to push the feeling aside.

"Alright, now that everyone's here, let's go over what's been happening," said Talla, waving her hand at the map of Sinsaya, "after Sirota's men defected a week ago, Azimar closed all the gates. No one is able to get in or out, including the civilians."

"The guards have orders to shoot anyone who approaches on sight, no matter which side of the gate they're on," Key told them, "the people inside the city will start running out of food and water soon. Azimar has barricaded himself inside the palace with the remaining Black Sabers and threatened to set the whole city aflame if the Kashaitis approach."

"What about the smuggling tunnels?" Carro asked, "are any of them still safe?"

"Bastards filled them all in, except this one," Gaelin pointed to the map, "we only finished it a month ago. It's our only way in or out right now and that was part of the plan."

"We have to go in ourselves," said Key, "our plan is to use the tunnel, send in a small force, take out the guards on the gates, then open them."

Carro nodded. "The Riders can come in and secure the city, trapping Azimar and the Black Sabers in the palace complex. We can starve them out if we have to."

"I still say it's a fool's errand," Sirota said, looking directly at Carro, "you can't possibly take out every gate guard simultaneously without alerting the Black Sabers."

"Watch me," Carro hissed. Sirota's mouth twisted into a sneer and Carro had a sudden mental image of slamming his face down onto the table, which he tried to shake away.

"Tolian," said Key in a firm voice, pulling their focus back onto her, "how many Ulvvori do you have that can fight hand-to-hand without the wolves?"

"Any of the Riders can," said Tolian slowly, "although it is not our preference."

"We have fighters too," said Key, "so does Sirota. We'll combine them and make a small force that can get through the tunnel and coordinate their attacks on the city gates." She looked around and no one dared to argue.

"Three groups of ten each," Carro said, "absolutely no more."

"What about the regular army?" Haryk asked, "where are they?"

"They're at the training compound just north of Sinsaya," Sirota explained, pointing to the map, "but it's complete and utter chaos because so many officers defected or deserted. It wouldn't be hard to send your Kashaiti army to hold them there until this is over. I can almost guarantee they'll swear their allegiance to the new King once Azimar is gone."

"Yes," said one of the Kashaiti generals, "this we can do."

"Carro?" said Talla, "what do you think?" Silently, Carro wrestled with his intense distrust of Sirota, but everything the Lieutenant was saying made sense, so he finally nodded.

"You'll need to send scouts to confirm what Sirota's saying before you move in," he said to the general. "And I want all the Riders across the bridge first, with the wild packs, so they can move closer to the city and be ready once we've taken the gates."

"Alright, go choose your teams," Key said to them, "those of you who need weapons will get them once we're inside the tunnels tonight."

As they all dispersed, Carro looked around for Asenna and saw her standing by the big fire pit where Lusie had made breakfast. She was wearing a filthy apron over her clothes and helping Lusie and several others distribute watered-down broth and brown bread to the deserters. A small group of them had gathered around her as they ate and Carro watched her laugh and chat with them. After a few minutes, he realized his entire body was tensed up and his eyes were still scanning the men's faces for any sign of trouble. Asenna smiled and waved when she saw him and Carro anxiously ran a hand through his hair. It was not easy for him to reconcile his fear of losing her with his intense admiration of her boldness and capacity for mercy. Even though he had seen her adorned with a crown and jewels before, she had never looked more like a queen than she did at that moment, and Carro suddenly felt guilty for doubting her instincts. All he had to do was look around at the hopeful faces of the deserters to know that she was right about why they were there. Tira, Sirota, and Key began to return to the tent with their teams and Carro forced himself to turn back to the map on the table instead of watching Asenna.

"Carro, you and Sirota will take eight of his men and go to the east gate," Key told them, "Talla and Andros will go with my people to the west gate. Ivarr and Tira will take the Ulvvori to the north gate. Once you've secured them, Tira will send up the signal and the Riders and the wild packs will come through with Tolian. Clear?" Everyone nodded.

"If this all goes to plan," Andros said, "the Kashaitis won't need to engage at all. They'll just have to hold the army at the compound and deliver the remaining leaders to us. We can sort out loyalties later."

"Asenna will have to be the one to choose new generals, and quickly," said Talla in a softer voice, looking up at Carro, "you think she'll be up to it?"

"She can do it," he said without hesitation.

"Your faith in her is admirable, Captain," Sirota said dryly, "but she's had no experience ruling and will need guidance. Perhaps the Kashaitis--"

"She can do it," Carro said through gritted teeth, "and it's not Captain anymore. Just Carro."

Sirota shrugged. "Then I guess I'm just 'Baine.' Old habits die hard."

"Right," said Tira, glancing between them. "Everyone make sure your teams are briefed on the details and everyone has what they need." Carro moved away from Sirota as quickly as he could, but Tira caught up with him.

"Are you sure Asenna will be alright with all this? Talla told me that a lot of these men think she's some kind of witch and she's going to use her moon powers to call up an army of dire wolves or something like that."

"It doesn't matter what they believe," Carro said, "when they see the truth about her, they'll understand. She listens to people and she actually hears them. It's just...who she is. You think she can do it, right Tira?"

"I think..." Tira replied slowly, "that she's the best of us, and that's enough. Everything else is secondary at this point." Carro nodded and the two of them stood side by side for a moment. Asenna finished what she was doing and then walked over to them.

"How's the bridge coming?"

"Why don't we go see?" Tira suggested.

"Yes!" Asenna bounced on the balls of her feet, "I've been dying to see how they do this." The three of them made their way over to the edge of the river, where the Kashaiti engineers had used grappling hooks and the little reed boats to get four men across the river and stretch the massive ropes between the tops of the bluffs. Each rope was tied to several of the massive stakes, which had been driven into the ground so they were angled away from the edge. As they watched, the Kashaiti soldiers took one of the long wooden planks that were stacked beside the bridge frame and placed it on top of the suspended ropes. Since the eastern bluff was slightly higher than the western one, the men were able to loosely tie the planks to the suspension ropes and then push hard, sending them sliding all the way to the other side. When the planks reached the opposite bank, the men there tightened the knots, securing them to the suspension ropes. They worked their way across the river while hanging at least fifty feet in the air with only their own handiwork between them and the rushing water. It took them only an hour to secure every plank, until the bridge was complete.

"This is amazing," Asenna breathed, "we need this type of work to be done here, by our own people. Can you imagine how much easier things might be if people didn't have to travel all the way upriver to cross?"

"Sounds like something a Queen Regent could do," Carro smiled and she leaned into him. Tolian and Key shook hands with the Kashaiti generals as the engineers set about placing more stakes and running more ropes across the river to create stabilizing handrails along the sides of the bridge. Once it was declared to be finished, the most senior Kashaiti general spoke some sort of blessing over the bridge and then his men gathered around as he prepared to step out onto it.

"But the workers already tested it by running back and forth for the last hour," Tira said under her breath, "why is he acting like he's the first one to cross?"

"Clearly you've never been in the army," Carro smirked.

"Why does the general go first anyway?" asked Asenna, "surely they can't afford to lose him if there's something wrong with it?"

"It's a sign of trust and faith. He's showing that he's willing to stake his own life on the competence of his men. It builds trust and respect." They watched as the general took a confident step onto the bridge, then made his way across, never stopping or faltering in his steps. Once he reached the opposite bank, he held up his hands and a cheer erupted from the Kashaitis and the Ulvvori who had gathered to watch. The realization suddenly hit Carro that it was time for them to cross the river and begin their infiltration of Sinsaya. He felt a pit in his stomach when he looked down at Asenna, dreading having to say goodbye to her. She seemed to be feeling the same way as she accompanied him to get Caz.

"I'll cross with you," she said quietly, "and then say goodbye."

"*Not* goodbye," Carro told her, "just…see you soon." Asenna nodded and they walked back to the bridge, where the small team of Riders were trying to explain to their wolves that they had to stay behind this time. There was a lot of head tilting and whining coming from the animals. Nearby, Key's resistance fighters and the former Black Sabers were staying well clear of each other while making their own preparations. Tira was standing near the bridge with Fitz, her face full of skepticism.

"I don't know," she said to them, "it seems alright, but…"

"You'll be fine," Carro slapped her on the back, "I've seen you swim stronger currents."

Tira rolled her eyes. "It's not the current that worries me. It's the fall."

"Tira, are you afraid of heights?" Asenna laughed out loud, as though she thought it ludicrous that Tira could be afraid of anything.

"No!" Tira protested, then sucked in a sharp breath, "alright…maybe a little. Don't you dare tell anyone!" The three of them moved toward the bridge and Carro felt his stomach lurch as they stepped onto it. Suddenly, he was reliving the moment when the previous bridge had exploded in his face and he felt bile rise up in throat. He reached out for Asenna's hand, but saw that Tira had beat him to it, her eyes clamped shut. Carro grabbed Fitz's reins from her and took a few deep breaths as they slowly walked across the bridge. Once they set foot on solid ground again, Tira uttered a tiny prayer to Izlani and leaned up against Fitz. Everyone else began to cross behind them in small groups and Carro stood back, pretending to check something on Caz's saddle while Asenna said farewell to the twins, Andros, and Ivarr. With his heart feeling heavy and slow, Carro finally made his way over to her. He had never been so afraid to lose anything in his life, but he was determined not to let her see his apprehension.

"My lady," he gave a playful bow, "may I approach?"

"You may, good sir," Asenna smiled and held her hand out for him to kiss, then he put his arms around her and rested his forehead against hers.

"Do you have *any* idea how much I love you?" he asked softly.

"Enough that you won't do anything foolish tonight?" Asenna asked, pulling away so she could look him in the eye. "I can't do this without you, *lai'zhia,* so don't you dare leave me alone."

"I won't. I promise," Carro said, "you don't get to do anything stupid either though."

"I'll try," Asenna half-laughed and half-sobbed. "I love you. Please stay safe."

"I love you too, *lai'rani.*"

"Let's go!" Tira called to him. Feeling like he was being ripped in half, Carro lifted Asenna off the ground and kissed her one more time. She pressed her fingers into the back of his neck and pulled him tighter and closer, then wiped a few of the tears from her eyes as he set her back down. Carro walked backwards so he could see her, trying not to turn around until he reached the others and Tira smacked him hard on the back of the head.

"Focus!" she hissed, snapping her fingers in his face. "Right now we need Captain Morelake, the deadly assassin. Got it?" Carro shook himself as he swung up into the saddle and pulled Caz around to face south.

"Got it," he repeated, "I'm whatever you need me to be now." As much as he hated to do it, Carro took the image of Asenna standing by the bridge and put it into the imaginary box in his mind, then closed it and shoved it away. Tira was right: the person he needed to be now was not apprehensive or impulsive or distracted. Carro tried to go back in his mind to the man he was before, the Black Saber, but he could not reconcile that person with who he was now. Looking around as their party began to move, he saw Sirota walking just ahead and pulled Caz up next to him.

"Baine, I want to apologize for yesterday, and this morning. I know it isn't easy...to leave," Carro said. Sirota looked up and his usual smirk faded.

"All is forgiven...Carro. You know, when I heard that you'd deserted, I didn't believe it. The King's most loyal servant and friend, a traitor, but I knew you were no coward. I knew you must have a good reason, and now I guess...I understand."

"You said Azimar had murdered your families. What did you mean?"

Sirota sighed heavily. "When Jesk and Roper came back without you, Azimar sent a hundred men out with them to track the Queen down. Ten of those men survived the encounter with the dire wolves and came back, including Captain Roeld. They told Azimar you were there, protecting her, and well...you can imagine how he reacted. He ordered them all to be publicly executed, as an example to the rest of us of what failure looks like, and he let their bodies hang up there on the walls for months afterward."

Carro shuddered. "I don't want to believe it, but I do."

"One of those men was my brother, well...half-brother, and the rest were my friends. He threw them away like they were nothing, *after* they had survived the wolves. Roeld was one of his earliest and most loyal supporters against Rogerin," Sirota murmured, "I was able to convince some of my men to leave with me, and I swore I wouldn't allow it to happen to anyone else."

"It won't," Carro assured him.

They traveled south and then west until dusk when they reached the farm, which was intact, but empty. Leaving the horses in a paddock behind the house, they all made their way on foot to a collapsed stone shack that sat just off the main road from Sinsaya. During his year in Esmadia with the twins and Gaelin, Carro had learned that it was actually an entrance to the system of tunnels that had been originally created by smugglers, who were looking to get black market goods into the capital, but were now used by the resistance to move supplies and people. Once they reached the shack, Key reached down and pulled up a trapdoor that was hidden beneath some brush and fallen beams. They had to climb down carefully one at a time until all of them were strung out along the tunnel like a line of ants. Key was at the front, holding a single, weak oil lamp, and once the trapdoor had been closed, they followed her into the sickening and claustrophobic darkness.

Carro blinked as his eyes adjusted to the light in the underground tavern where the tunnel let them out. The tables had all been pushed to the perimeter of the room and there were weapons piled on every available surface, quite unlike the last time he had been there with the twins during their brief foray into the city. After several hours picking their way carefully through the cramped tunnel, Carro's back and neck were on fire and he paused to stretch them out. Gaelin was already walking between the tables, checking the condition of the weapons.

"Those of you that need to arm yourselves, do it now and quickly," said Key, "it's almost time to go up." Sirota's men began rifling through the weapons on the tables, while the Riders and resistance fighters watched them closely. Sirota picked up a large hammer that looked like it came from Ferryn's blacksmith shop and swung it in front of him. Carro looked around at the hodge podge of weaponry and noticed that much of it was old and rusted.

"Nothin' nice enough for you," Gaelin said, sidling up to Carro, "it's all I could get on such short notice. But here, you take mine. I won't be doin' no fightin' today." Gaelin reached into his boot and pulled out a beautifully gilded dagger.

"Gaelin, I can't take this," Carro said, laughing, "I mean…is it even functional? It looks like it's for decoration only."

"Take it or leave it, funny man," Gaelin snapped, pursing his lips to stop a smile. Carro took the dagger and shoved it into his own boot.

"You know, I've never been one for politics," said Gaelin, flashing his pointed teeth, "didn't think I'd enjoy armed insurrection quite this much."

"Would you prefer unarmed insurrection?"

Gaelin barked a laugh, but then his face grew more serious. "I'm also not one for sentiment, boy, but don't you dare do anythin' stupid up there."

"You're the second person to tell me that today," Carro grinned, "it's like you people don't know me at all." Key came back into the tavern and clapped her hands loudly.

"Listen up. It's almost time. Our information says there's twenty-five guards per gate, plus squads of soldiers patrolling the streets. Remember the plan and stick to it. If you don't, everyone else dies and it's on you. There are still Black Sabers in the palace complex and they could have archers, so don't get too close to the walls and stay on your guard. Carro, once the Riders are here, I need you to meet us at the palace gate. If they have archers in there, they could set fires using arrows, so we'll need to get inside quickly." Carro nodded. The twins, Andros, and Ivarr came over to where he and Gaelin were standing and Tira took his and Talla's hands.

"Everyone ready?" Talla asked, reaching down to grab Andros' hand. Carro looked around at his friends, his family, and had the overwhelming urge to laugh and cry simultaneously. Instead, he steeled himself as they turned and moved up the spiral staircase, through the shed, and into the courtyard.

The sky was clear and the moon was bright, which Carro would normally take as a good omen, but tonight he knew it would make them easier to spot as they moved along the streets. Across the courtyard and through Ferryn's shop, Carro tried to push the memory of the old man's death from his mind as they crept out onto Beacon Street. He had never heard the streets of Sinsaya so deathly quiet. Normally there would be a rousing chorus drifting from a tavern somewhere, or dogs baying, but now it sounded like a graveyard and it made him shiver.

Key gave them the signal that the street was clear and the three groups split away from each other, Carro moving up beside Sirota and his men. They made their way north along Beacon Street, keeping as flat against the walls as they could, then turned and headed east toward the gate, encountering no patrols on their way. Once there was a clear view of the east gate, they ducked down and huddled together behind a stack of barrels outside a cooper's shop.

"We have to wait until the others are in position," Sirota whispered, "Carro, see if you can get a head count." Carro nodded and crept around the side of the barrel in front of him. There were six men standing in front of the massive wooden gates, which were barred with a heavy beam, while six more stood on top of the wall above them.

"Twelve that I can see," he told Sirota, "six down below and six up top. I can't see the others anywhere."

"Lazy bastards," Sirota spat on the ground next to him, "probably playing cards in the gatehouse. That makes it easy. Carro, you and I take the ones on the wall. You two, get to the gatehouse and barricade them inside. The rest of you take the six at the gates. I've got an idea to distract them." Sirota mimed pushing the barrels that were stacked beside them and they all signaled their understanding. Just then, a single note split the air, almost like the howl of a wolf, but thinner and higher. Sirota dropped the hammer from his shoulder and tightened his grip on it.

"That's it," Carro said, "let's go." Simultaneously, all ten of them shoved themselves against the stack of barrels, which began to fall and crash against the stone streets. As they had predicted, at least half of the barrels went rolling toward the gate. Carro drew his sabers, running as close as he could to the sides of the buildings as the barrels careened down the street beside him. Sirota had darted across the street and was running parallel to him, while the other men followed.

Carro was the first to reach the stairs that led up the top of the wall and he heard the crash of the barrels hitting the gate and the shouts of the guards as his foot touched the first step. He barely had time to think when he encountered the first two men, who were running down toward the noise. They stumbled backwards when they saw him, but his sabers slashed across their throats before they could react. Carro picked his way around the bodies, flattening himself against the wall, and glanced down to see Sirota's men engaging four of the gate guards, the other two having been struck by barrels. Another guard moved down the stairs above him, face full of confusion and fear. Reaching up, Carro deftly ran his blade across the man's thigh, sending him reeling down the staircase. Although he couldn't see the stairs on the other side of the gate, Carro could hear the ringing of Sirota's hammer as it struck the stone wall, and the sickening crunch as it struck bones. When he reached the top, Sirota was already waiting for him, his face covered in blood splatter.

"The hammer suits you," Carro laughed breathlessly, but before Sirota could respond, he jerked forward and tipped over the battlements, vanishing over the edge with only a strangled cry. When Carro looked up though, it wasn't one of the city guards standing there with a triumphant smile on his face. It was one of Sirota's own men.

"What…" Carro breathed, but the Black Saber raised his sword and lunged and Carro was barely able to block the attack.

"He was a traitorous bastard and so are you!" the man growled. Carro got his bearings and shoved the man back with his sabers.

"You used Sirota as a cover!" he cried, "Azimar *did* send you!"

"You really think he would let you both live after what you did?"

"Both…" Carro stopped fighting, his body suddenly frozen as he remembered the two dozen Black Saber 'defectors' who had stayed behind in the camp, "Asenna…no…" His opponent smiled and then took advantage of Carro's distraction to kick him in the stomach and pin him up against the rim of the wall, forcing him to drop his sabers. Carro tried to raise his arms and push back, but the terror gripping his body at the thought of Asenna being in danger made it impossible for him to break free. The Black Saber brought his sword up, pressing the edge of the blade into Carro's chest and slowly slicing through his skin. Try as he might, Carro felt his strength going out of him and he cried out for Tira and Ivarr as the blade dug deeper into his skin and muscle.

"Oh, I am going to enjoy this," the Black Saber muttered, locking eyes with Carro and sliding the blade further along his chest, "just as much as I'll enjoy watching her dangle from the wall by her pretty neck. After we're done with her, of course."

"No!" Carro roared, rage flooding back into his limbs, blocking out the burning pain from the fresh wound. He managed to get one of his arms free, ducked to the side, then grabbed the back of his opponent's head and smashed it into the stone wall. Before the man could even go completely limp, Carro lifted him up and pitched him over the edge. As the body landed with a crunch beside Sirota's, however, Carro heard more Black Sabers coming up the stairs. He picked up his swords and ran. The panicked pounding of his own heart echoed in his ears as they followed him. He looked north as he ran, trying to see if the Wolf Riders had made it to the city, but having no idea if Tira and Ivarr's team had even taken the main gate. He could hear the men running behind him, shouting and even laughing, and he stumbled on the rough stones. The only thing carrying him forward now was knowing that he had to warn his friends before the Black Sabers reached them.

As he got closer, he spotted Tira and Ivarr standing on top of the wall and then saw the wolves flooding through the gate beneath them. Carro screamed both their names and they turned to look at him with victorious smiles, but when they saw his face they both leapt forward and Tira raised her crossbow. Carro ducked out of the way as she fired, striking one of the Black Sabers in the face. Ivarr engaged another man while Carro slipped between them and then turned around, raising his sabers and trying to catch his breath. Ivarr slashed his opponent across the throat and shoved him from the top of the wall, then put his fingers in his mouth and let out a shrill whistle. In an instant, Nettle bounded up the stairs and put her massive body between them and the remaining Black Sabers. She seized one man in her jaws who couldn't move away fast enough and Carro watched, both fascinated and horrified, as she shook him like a rabbit and then threw the mangled body down into the street. Tira fired again and struck another Black Saber, then the remaining four men suddenly dropped their weapons and put their hands up as several of the resistance fighters came to their aid with more crossbows. Ivarr turned and grabbed Carro by the shoulders, hauling him up from where he was kneeling.

"Aren't those Sirota's men? What the fuck happened?" he cried, but Carro pushed past him and the resistance fighters, sheathed one of his blades, and seized a Black Saber by the throat. The man struggled against Carro's grip, but he only held on tighter.

"I should throw every single fucking one of you to the wolves right now!" Carro shouted at them. "The men you left behind in the camp, were they part of this?" Carro looked around and tightened his grip on the man's neck when his companions didn't answer.

"Carro...what's going on?" Tira came up behind him.

"Azimar sent them," Carro breathed, watching the man he was holding struggle to breathe, "Sirota was the only real defector. The rest were after me...and Asenna." Tira's face fell and she seized another man, bringing her dagger up to his throat and cutting it without hesitation. Her victim fell onto the stones, twitching and bleeding, and Carro shoved his own captive toward her. Tira grabbed him and put the knife to his throat, but then waited for Carro's word.

"Tell me what your orders were!" Carro snarled at the men. "Or so help me, I will let her do that to every single one of you." One of the Black Sabers lost his nerve and fell onto his knees.

"Our orders were to find her and kill her," he whimpered, "but then you were there too and...and..." Carro kicked him in the face and felt a surge of satisfaction when he heard a crack and saw a spurt of blood from the man's nose. The rage boiling up in his chest was threatening to overwhelm him, and he wanted to kill them all, watch the wolves rip their limbs off one by one, but Ivarr put a firm hand on his shoulder.

"We need to find Tolian," he said in his soft voice, which brought Carro back down from his bloodlust only a little, "if she made it out, she might be with the Riders."

"*If* she made it out…" Carro felt his knees go weak again as he turned to look at Ivarr, who had tears gathering in his eyes. The three of them left the Black Sabers with their captors and rushed down the steps with Nettle. Once they were standing in the street, Ivarr jumped onto her back.

"We'll go look for Tolian and Haryk," he said.

"We'll stay here and look for Asenna," Tira told him, then she turned to Carro, "please tell me you're alright, *lai'kheri*."

"No, I'm not!" Carro cried, "I *knew* it was wrong! I told everyone they were lying and you all acted like I was insane! And now…" He felt himself starting to break down as he turned toward the empty road, desperate to hear Asenna's voice or see her face through the darkness. Tira put a hand on his arm, but he jerked it away and walked toward the gate.

"I have to go find her."

"Carro, no, we need you here! We still have to deal with Azimar!"

"I don't fucking care!" Carro rounded on her, "I can't do anything else until I know she's alive, Tira!"

"You think I don't care?" Tira cried back, "you think I'm not fucking scared to lose her? This what we have to do right now! This is what it is to fight a war!" Carro could see tears on her face and he felt the shame spreading through his body, but he turned away. He had only gone a few feet, however, when a great, hulking white shape came into view in the darkness and he started to run before he could even think.

"Carro! Tira!" cried out a strangled voice from up ahead. Carro saw Briar racing along the road, with Asenna keeping pace beside her on Scout, and he felt like he might fall straight through the earth. Somehow, his body felt even weaker knowing that she was safe than when he had imagined her gone. Asenna nearly fell out of the saddle into his arms and Carro caught her, sinking to the ground and pressing his face into her neck as they held each other. He could feel her body heaving with sobs and feel her tears falling onto his shoulder and it nearly broke him to think that she had been just as afraid to lose him.

"I'm so sorry, Carro," she cried, "you were right. I should have listened to you." Carro pulled back and held her face in his hands, soaking in every inch of her as he wiped tears away from her cheeks.

"It doesn't matter now," he whispered, "did they hurt you? Please tell me you're not hurt." She reached up and covered his shaking hands with her own.

"I'm fine. I'm not hurt. I don't know where they got weapons, but they waited until the Riders were gone and most of the Kashaitis were across the river already. The Riders that Tolian left behind and some of the deserters held them off so I could get away with Briar, but...two of the Riders..." Tira knelt down beside them and wrapped her arms around Asenna, who leaned into her chest and began to cry softly.

"You're safe now," Tira murmured into her hair.

"Sirota too," Carro told them, "he wasn't part of their plan. He...he was the only one telling the truth and Azimar used him."

"You're hurt, *lai'zhia*," said Asenna suddenly, sitting up and putting her fingers next to the wound on his chest, which was still oozing blood. Carro wrapped his hand around hers and they pressed their foreheads together.

"You're safe. That's all that matters," he said, standing up and pulling Asenna to her feet, then Tira. "Now we need to get inside the palace and deal with Azimar." The three of them went back through the gate and found Ivarr coming back on Nettle. He jumped down and pulled Asenna into a tight embrace while Carro looked around, trying to take stock of the situation now that he could think clearly. The Riders and the wild dire wolves had made short work of the remaining soldiers in the city, some of whom were being escorted out the gate with their hands behind their backs, and a few civilians were starting to open their doors and look out at what was going on.

"Key and Tolian are up by the palace gate," Ivarr told them as he released Asenna, "they need all of us up there so we can figure out what to do next." He and Tira turned to go, but Asenna grabbed Carro's wrist.

"There's something else," she said, eyes shining, "there was a maid in the camp who worked in the palace kitchens. Before the Black Sabers attacked us, she told me that Ephie is still alive, in the prison block. Carro, I have to go find her. I have to get her out." Carro's heart twisted into a knot, knowing that being away from her again might finish him, but that she was going to go no matter what he had to say about it.

"Asenna, I...I thought I'd lost you. I thought you were gone and it nearly killed me," he touched the wound on his chest, "I want to help Ephie as much as you do, but I can't just let you go again. I need you to stay where it's safe until this is over. Please." Asenna's face fell slightly, but she furrowed her brow and walked toward the palace with Briar on her heels.

"I'll find a way," she said, "and if I can't find one, I'll *make* one." Carro threw Scout's reins over a nearby post and followed her. As they walked, people began to come out of their homes into the moonlight. They looked both fascinated and terrified as they watched Asenna march up the street with Briar towering over her. Carro had to admit that it really did look like she had led an army of wolves into the city, and he suddenly understood the power she held, even without the Wolfsight.

"Bless you, my lady!" some of the people called out to her, "you've saved us! Bless your son, the Prince!"

"Long live the Wolf Queen!" one woman cried, and the call was taken up by others all along the main road. Carro stayed immediately behind her as they walked, his eyes scanning the crowds for any kind of threat. Asenna was as gracious as possible, shaking hands and accepting a half-dead flower from a little girl.

As they arrived at the palace gates, however, she cried out when she saw Tolian sitting up against Echo's flank, an arrow protruding from his upper leg. Nikke and Haryk were kneeling beside him while Ivarr, Key, Andros, and the twins stood nearby with Juniper, Ash, and Nettle, all looking anxious.

"I'm fine, little Senna," said Tolian gently as she ran up to him. "I found out the hard way that they have several archers positioned on the walls." Tira jerked a bolt from her quiver and put it on her crossbow.

"Not for long, they fucking don't," she spat, then moved away toward the wall. Carro and Asenna quickly explained to Key and the others what had happened with the Black Sabers, and Key dropped her face into her hand.

"This has to end now," she said quietly, looking up at the palace. They all heard a loud cry and a *thud* as Tira dispatched one of the archers.

"When we got here," said Andros, "the man on the wall told us that we have two hours to clear the city of our forces and leave or they'll use arrows to burn the city from the other side. They'll also do it if we attempt to break through the gate. What we need now is to get our people into the complex without being seen and try to take out whatever archers Tira can't get from out here, just like we did with the city gates."

"I know a way in," said Asenna softly.

"I'm listening," Key told her.

"When I escaped with Fen, I did it by climbing the wall. There's a spot toward the back where it was destroyed during Azimar's last siege and they rebuilt it in a way that makes it easier to climb over."

Key's eyes widened. "You climbed over that wall…with your one-month-old baby?"

"Yes. It was the only way out."

"Impressive. Alright, Your Majesty, show me." Leaving Tolian and Echo with some of the other Riders, Asenna led the rest of them back through the streets, avoiding the palace walls so that the Black Sabers could not track or shoot them. The street squads had already been put down by the Wolf Riders, and most of the soldiers left in the city had surrendered and were being escorted out, while Key's people moved around offering medical assistance, food, and water to the people coming out of their homes after a week of captivity. When they reached the rough spot on the wall, Key's eyes lit up.

"This might work," she whispered, more to herself than anyone else, "alright. Carro, Tira and Talla, Andros, Haryk, Ivarr. I need the six of you to track down a few of my people who can climb, then get in there, take out the men guarding the gate, and get it open."

"Seven of us," said Asenna, "I'm going too." There were immediate noises of protest from Ivarr and Haryk, and Carro pulled her aside, holding her face in his hands.

"*Lai'rani,* I need you to stay out here with Nikke and the Riders," he whispered, "I can't have you trapped inside with the Black Sabers if something goes wrong with the gate. I felt like I was losing my mind before, when I didn't know if you were alive or dead. I couldn't fight. I could barely even breathe. I need to be able to know for certain that you're safe if I'm going to do this. Please."

Asenna looked at him carefully and Carro could tell she wanted to argue. "Once it's safe, I can go find Ephie?"

"Yes, I promise."

"Alright," Asenna nodded, "I'll stay."

"Thank you," Carro leaned down and kissed her and she moved away to stand with Nikke, Ash, and the other wolves. It took them only a few minutes to find six of Key's fighters who could climb, and Andros began briefing the new recruits while Carro let his mind wander. He had been able to push the thoughts of facing Azimar out of his head until now, but as he looked up at the walls, they were resurfacing with a vengeance. As much as the bitter, vindictive side of him wanted violence, especially after what had happened with Sirota's men, Carro knew he couldn't break his promises to Key or Asenna. He tried to shake the images from his mind, but Tira looked at him and seemed to read his thoughts.

"Are you ready?" she asked, "for Azimar?"

"I've been ready for a long time," Carro replied quietly and Tira put a hand on his arm.

"Once we're inside, I won't leave you until we've found him." Carro put his arm around her shoulders and hugged her.

"We're ready," Talla said, approaching the base of the wall. Tira followed her and the two of them crept up to the top, looking like huge black spiders as they flattened themselves against the stones. Carro climbed beside

~ 233 ~

Ivarr and once all twelve of them were down the other side, they skirted along the base of the wall until they came into view of the gate. There were at least two Black Sabers sitting behind the ramparts and Tira raised her crossbow.

"Wait," Carro told her, thinking quickly. "Alright, Tira, get close enough to shoot those two, and that should draw the rest of them out. Talla, got any fire on you?"

"You know I do," she whispered, reaching for her belt and pulling out a bottle. Carro motioned to Tira, who already had a bolt loaded on her crossbow and was holding a second one in her teeth. She ducked around the side of the wall, scurried closer to the gate, then fired the first bolt, striking one of the men directly in the chest. His companion leapt up and shouted, but the cry was cut short as Tira's second bolt went through his throat and sent him toppling backwards into the street. Carro gritted his teeth when he heard the shouts of more men coming to see what was happening.

"They're inside the wall!" one shouted, "find them!"

"Now it's my turn," Talla murmured, her face breaking into a shameless smile. They all watched with bated breath as she uncorked the bottle and stuffed a cloth into the neck, then handed it to Andros. In one fluid movement, Talla held up her short sword and struck the flint pommel against the steel blade of her hatchet, sparking and igniting the cloth. Andros turned and hurled it toward the Black Sabers gathering near the gate. Carro heard the glass shatter and then saw the flames roar up, silhouetting the men as they cried out and scattered.

"Go!" Tira cried. For a single moment, Carro faltered when the men's familiar faces came into view, illuminated by the flames, but then someone body slammed him to the ground. He looked up to see another Black Saber Captain named Fayel standing above him, curved blades raised and face twisted with anger and fear.

"Traitor!" Fayel screamed as Carro scrambled to his feet and blocked the attack, stumbling backwards, "you abandoned your men! You brought the wolves down on us!"

"Yes, I did!" Carro snarled at him as their blades scraped together, "and you all deserve it for what you've allowed him to do!" As their sabers met again, Carro glanced over and saw Andros and Haryk trying to lift the massive wooden beam that kept the gate locked, while Tira and the others fought all around him.

"Stand down!" Fayel grunted, "you are outnumbered and trapped!"

"I don't have time for this," Carro muttered, ducking down and sweeping Fayel's legs out from under him, sending him crashing to the ground. From the ground, Fayel lunged, but his saber connected with Carro's boot, exactly where he had placed Gaelin's ornate dagger only hours before. Seeing the confusion on Fayel's face, Carro wasted no time, driving a saber into his stomach. Fayel spluttered and choked as Carro jerked the weapon out and then whirled around to help with the gate.

With the twins and resistance fighters covering them, they managed to lift one end of the beam out of the iron brackets that held it and then dropped it to the ground with a crash. The brackets on the other gate ripped free from the wood and the gate swung partially open. Carro was almost bowled over by Nettle and Juniper as they leapt inside. Nikke and Ash, followed by more Riders, poured through the narrow opening like huge, ferocious rats into a pantry. Blood-curdling screams went up from the Black Sabers as the wild wolves tore through the palace grounds and through the front doors. Carro steadied himself for a moment, wiping his blades clean on the grass, then sheathed one of them and searched for Asenna, who came in last with Briar. Carro also spotted the twins standing a little way up the stairs on the wall, looking perhaps a little too gleeful at the unbridled chaos.

"Tira!" he called out, "we need to get inside!"

"Let's go!" she cried, leaping down. Talla followed and they regrouped next to the gate just as Key and her fighters came through with Tolian limping beside them, using Echo for support.

"Good work," Key said, then looked directly at Carro, "now, bring me Azimar. Alive."

"There's probably still Black Sabers inside," Talla warned, "we need a different way in than the front door."

"There's a servant's entrance over here," Asenna pointed and they all followed her to a spot along the wall, but the door was locked. Talla began to hack at it and Asenna turned to Carro, her big, dark eyes burning into him.

"I need to go and find Ephie now," she said, "Carro, I owe her my life. I can't just leave her." Carro tried to think, but the idea of Asenna being away from him inside the palace, so close to Azimar, was making it difficult. Finally, he squeezed his eyes shut and nodded.

"Talla, Andros, Ivarr," he said, "I need you and Nettle to take Asenna to the prison block and help her find Ephie, then get them both to safety. Can you do that?"

"Ephie's alive?" Tira nearly shouted, "Talla!"

"We'll find her," Talla said firmly, "Ivarr, tell Briar that she's too big to fit in the corridors. She'll need to go around and find us inside." Talla had managed to get the door open and Carro realized that they were all waiting for him to give the order to move inside.

"I promised to stay with you no matter what," Tira said to Carro, moving to stand beside him, "Haryk and Juniper, you're with us."

"We'll find Azimar, you find Ephie," Carro said, his voice breaking as he looked around at them. Asenna leaned over and gave him a fierce kiss.

"Don't let him get into your head, *lai'zhia*," she whispered, "just remember how much I love you." She ducked inside the palace with Talla, Andros, Ivarr, and Nettle behind her. Carro and Tira followed them inside with Haryk and Juniper, but they had already vanished down one of the hallways.

Pausing a minute to get his bearings, Carro motioned for them to climb the stairway in front of them. As part of his Black Saber training, he had been set loose in the labyrinthian palace many times with no map, and had to find his way back to the main entrance hall within a certain amount of time. Carro was thankful for it now as he led them through the maze.

"Where is everyone?" Tira whispered as they came out of the corridor into a storeroom filled with barrels and crates. "The servants? Guards?"

"I don't know…" Carro said slowly.

"What about Azimar?"

"We'll check his rooms first. That would be the easiest place for him to barricade. This way," Carro told them as they came into a long, wide corridor lined with arcade windows that looked down into a courtyard. Below, they could see a group of Black Sabers attempting to hold off the Wolf Riders. The nightmarish screams of men being torn apart echoed up through the windows, sending a chill down Carro's spine. As they started down the hall, a group of Black Sabers appeared at the far end.

"Traitor!" one of the men screamed, pointing his saber at Carro.

"Are you getting tired of hearing that word yet today?" Tira laughed.

"So fucking tired," Carro replied with a slight smile. Juniper leapt forward, hackles raised and fangs bared, but this did not seem to deter the men, who charged. They met in the center of the corridor and a spray of blood covered Carro's face as Juniper tore into the nearest man's neck. As she shook the corpse back and forth, her flank hit Carro and threw him into the wall, causing him to drop the saber from his right hand. Forced to block an attack with only his bad left arm, Carro stumbled backwards and his opponent shoved him against the wall hard and dazing him. Before his attacker could do anything else, however, Tira appeared and yanked him away from Carro, running her sword across his throat. Haryk and Juniper had already dispatched the remaining Black Sabers and Tira leaned down to pull Carro to his feet. He felt more than a little unsteady as he stood up, but knew that he had to keep going. They made a few more turns, but encountered no more men until they came to Azimar's rooms.

"Let me go in first," Carro said, opening the door and stepping inside. The room was a disaster, cluttered and filthy and reeking of rotting food. Carro could barely see anything since the heavy curtains were blocking out the pale cast of early dawn that was now illuminating the corridors.

"Azimar?" he called out. There was no answer. Carro turned to leave but then spotted a figure lying on the bed in the gloom. As he approached, he realized with a jolt that it was Ilmira and that she was dead. Carro pulled one of the curtains back just enough to make out the dark bruises around her throat and he felt like he might vomit as he stumbled back out into the hall.

"Just Ilmira," he murmured, "dead. Strangled."

Tira shook her head. "Azimar?"

"I think so," Carro breathed. He straightened up and shook the image from his mind. "We'll check the throne room next." Tira and Haryk followed him with Juniper trailing behind. Walking in silence, they reached a dead-end hall with large ornate doors at the opposite end. The corridor was empty and quiet. *They've all abandoned him,* Carro thought, *he's alone now.*

Slowly, Carro and Haryk pushed one of the doors open just as the first rays of morning sun were peeking through the arched windows and the columns lining the room were throwing long shadows across the floor, making it feel almost like a forest. Sitting across from them in a golden throne on a dais was Azimar. He was visibly and staggeringly drunk, shirtless, with a ceremonial fur robe around his shoulders and a large bottle in his hand. On his head was the ornate wolf's head crown. Carro took several steps forward, but Azimar did not see him standing there for almost a full minute.

"Azimar," said Carro steadily, taking a few more steps.

"Get away!" Azimar screamed, finally noticing them. His eyes seemed to focus only on Juniper, however, and Tira raised her crossbow.

"For fuck's sake, don't shoot him," Carro said, "just stay here." She grunted, but did not lower the weapon. Carro sheathed his own sabers and held his hands up, moving slowly across the room. Azimar squinted at him, then stood and dropped his bottle onto the floor, where it shattered, making Carro feel sick and anxious from the smell.

"Ahh, Carro…" Azimar sighed and then laughed, "I see my Black Sabers have…failed yet *another* mission. An unfortunate trend…as of late."

"Yes, they failed," Carro told him. "And now I need you to come with us, Azimar. It's over."

"Where is she?" Azimar screamed suddenly, lurching forward down the steps of the dais. "Asenna!! Where is my son?!" Carro managed to catch him as he fell, but Azimar shoved him away and sprawled on the floor.

"Asenna's not here and neither is your son. It's just me."

"You…you left me. You promised…you'd never leave me…" Azimar said slowly, meeting Carro's eyes. He looked like he was on death's doorstep. His cheeks and eyes and chest were sunken and Carro could see every rib as he heaved long, ragged breaths. Even his keen blue eyes that would normally see straight through a person looked clouded and heavy. It was clear he had not bathed in a long time and pieces of his curly hair had knotted up into mats. He sat on the floor with his legs splayed beneath him and his words came out in labored gasps.

"I did. I did leave," Carro said, trying to inch closer to him, "you asked me to do something I couldn't do, and now--"

"Oh, you...*fucking hypocrite!*" Azimar screeched with a wretched, choking laugh, "as if you hadn't...killed women on my orders before. She took my son...and you...my brother, you were too much of a coward...after everything I've done for you..." Carro felt a pit open up in his stomach and tried to remember Asenna's words: *Don't let him get into your head.*

"You did *nothing* for me, Azimar," he spat, "nothing that you didn't make me pay for later. Now you need to come with us." Azimar suddenly became far more lucid and pulled the robe tighter around his shoulders, shifting his cold blue eyes over to Carro, who felt his muscles lock with dread.

"They told me you died saving her," Azimar swayed slightly as he spoke, "that you offered yourself up...rather than watch her get hurt. I couldn't understand it...why you would do that for her. Ungrateful bitch."

"*Don't* call her that," Carro said, with more of an edge in his voice than he intended. Azimar's face twisted into a savage grin, exposing several missing and rotted teeth.

"That's exactly what I thought," he cackled, throwing his head back, "oh, I hope you enjoyed her, Carro, even...half as much as I did. She is *so* sweet, isn't she? Especially when she's--"

"Enough!" yelled Carro, squeezing his eyes shut.

"Just wait," Azimar murmured, "until she sees...what you *really* are."

Carro drew one of his sabers and pointed it at Azimar. "She knows exactly what I am," he said quietly, "and she loves me anyway. Something you could never do."

"Of course," Azimar purred, still smirking, "all the times I saved your worthless life...and this is how you've repaid me." The smile fell from his face as he reached down and pulled a ring off one of his skeleton-like fingers, then tossed it across the floor toward Carro, who didn't touch it. "You can give that...to Asenna. A final gift from her *loving* husband. And this...this one is for me." Before Carro could stop him, Azimar had opened the top of a large ring on his hand and dumped the contents of the hidden compartment into his mouth.

"No!" Carro lunged and seized the edge of Azimar's robe, grabbing him by the shoulders and shaking him, but Azimar only laughed.

"Look at me...Carro," he groaned, mouth beginning to foam at the corners. Carro felt a sob escape him as Azimar's body convulsed in his arms, the poison working its way through his blood. "Tell me...you're with me..."

"I'm with you," Carro said the words without thinking, his voice barely a strangled whisper. Azimar gave a final jerk and then went limp, his eyes rolling back as a foul, rattling breath left his lungs. For a full minute, Carro sat frozen, half expecting Azimar to jump up like it was one of the pranks they had played on each other as boys.

When he finally pushed the body away and it fell like a ragdoll onto the tiles, something inside Carro snapped and he let out a savage scream that tore his throat open and nearly caused him to black out. As his vision returned, he could feel his chest heaving so quickly he couldn't catch his breath. He tried to scramble backwards away from Azimar's corpse, but slammed into Tira, who was crouching behind him. She pulled him into a forceful embrace, then dragged him across the floor as far away from the body as she could and let go.

"Haryk, go find Tolian and Key. Tell them it's over," he heard her say, "and then find your sister, quickly!" Carro heard footsteps and Juniper's claws clicking on the stone floors, but every sound seemed like it was coming through water, including Tira's voice. Rage and guilt and grief threatened to swallow him whole as he sat there, unable to feel his own body properly.

"I need air," he murmured, somehow hauling himself up, staggering over to the windows, and shoving one open so he could stick his head out. The breeze hit his face and Carro realized when it stung his skin that he had been crying. He had no idea how long he stood there with his head leaning against the window frame before he heard voices behind him and realized that he could barely hold his body upright. His hip and both shoulders were on fire, the deep wound on his chest was stinging, and he knew he was going to vomit at some point soon from having his head knocked around. Someone put their hand on his shoulder and Carro jerked away, but a pair of arms grabbed him and held him against the window frame.

"Hey!" said a rough, familiar voice. "What happened?"

"Gaelin," said Carro hoarsely, "I didn't do it." Gaelin swung Carro around so his back was up against the wall.

"I don't give a damn who did it," hissed Gaelin, "did he hurt you?"

"No," Carro gasped out a laugh. He felt delirious, as if he had been the one drowning in liquor all night, "tell Key I'm sorry. It's my fault."

"Listen to me right now, boy," Gaelin said in a hushed whisper, grabbing Carro's face and looking him in the eye, "you did everythin' right. That bastard used his dyin' breath to fuck with your head, because he knew that you're a *good man*, somethin' he could never be. He wanted you to blame yourself for his mistakes. Don't let him win that war what's been goin' on in your head since the day I met you. He's gone, and you're here, and now you need to *stay here* for Asenna, and Fen, and the rest of us. You understand me?" The words crept into Carro's head and he was finally able to steady his breathing a little. Gaelin released the grip that was forcing him to stay upright and walked back over to where people were starting to gather around Azimar's body.

"There's a crowd starting to gather outside. We need to show everyone the body," Key was saying.

"I'll take him," Carro said quietly, approaching the group. They all turned and stared at him, but Gaelin gave a satisfied smile and nod.

"Carro, you don't have to…" Tira began to say, but she trailed off as Carro walked over, released the clasp from the robe around Azimar's neck, and removed the golden crown from his head. He dropped them on the floor and then lifted Azimar's limp body in his arms.

"I'll take him," Carro repeated, and no one dared to question him as he followed Key and Tolian through the palace.

FIFTEEN:
THE RESCUE

As Asenna ducked into the palace with Talla, Andros, Ivarr, and Nettle, she realized that she had absolutely no idea how to reach the prison block from their location. All she remembered was that it was on the ground floor, so she picked a hallway at random, holding her sword in front of her and praying she wouldn't have to use it. Talla walked beside her and when they came to another split in the corridor, Asenna looked over.

"I don't suppose Key gave you a map of the palace?"

"Didn't you used to live here?" Talla asked, smiling.

"As if I had a reason to visit the prison."

"We need to find someone," Andros said, "Ivarr, can Nettle hear or smell any people nearby?" Ivarr put his hand on Nettle's cheek for a few seconds, then the wolf gave a small growl and ran down one of the corridors. They followed Nettle's nose, but when they rounded a corner they found themselves face to face with five Black Sabers. Nettle lowered her head and knocked two of them over before they even realized what was happening, while Talla shoved Asenna behind her and threw her hatchet, burying it in another man's skull.

"Keep one alive!" Talla shouted to Andros. A Black Saber rushed at Talla, but Nettle reached over and grabbed one of his legs in her mouth, twisting and pulling him away with a sickening crunch. Finally, there was only one man left standing against the wall with Ivarr's sword on his throat.

"Take us to the prison block," Ivarr hissed as the man struggled.

"Fuck you, filthy inbred cave troll!" the man spat, tilting his head back and flexing his jaw. Suddenly his whole body convulsed and his mouth began to foam. Ivarr grimaced and stepped back.

"Carro warned us that might happen," he said.

"I'll...I'll take you," came a weak voice from behind them. "Just please don't kill me." One of the Black Sabers that Nettle had knocked into a wall was laying on the floor. Andros walked over and dragged him up by his shirt, then ripped the twin sabers from his back and tossed them aside.

"Let's go," he grunted, putting his sword against the back of the man's neck. The Black Saber led them through the maze of rooms and corridors until they came into the kitchen that served the entire palace. There were a dozen large fireplaces built into the walls, plus a cistern, a massive pantry, and several long tables for preparing food.

"That way," their hostage pointed across the kitchen to another corridor, but before they set foot into the room, another squad of Black Sabers entered the kitchen through a pair of double doors and spotted them. They charged between the tables, swords raised, but then a massive white shape smashed through the doors behind them and skidded into the room, placing itself in front of Asenna and the others.

"Briar!" Asenna cried. Using the Black Sabers' distraction to their advantage, Talla and Ivarr raced into the kitchen with Nettle on their heels. Asenna stood just behind Andros, who was still holding their captive by his arm as he watched the fight. Briar was a sight to behold, her sleek white fur stained with blood and her golden eyes flashing as she tore men clean in half with only her teeth. Asenna had never seen her father's companion like this and she felt incredibly thankful and frightened at the same time.

Suddenly, one of the Black Sabers charged Andros and he tried to fend off the attack while still clutching the captive by his arm, but the man was able to pull away and turned on Asenna, who held her sword out in front of her and backed down the corridor.

"Asenna, run!" screamed Andros, but the Black Saber grabbed her and Andros could not break away from his attacker to help. The man's eyes were wide with panic and his hand quickly found Asenna's throat as he shoved her against the wall. Asenna dropped the sword as his hand tightened, cutting off her air and stopping her from crying out for help.

"Ulvvori bitch!" he snarled in her face. As she struggled and her vision started to go dark, Asenna remembered her father's dagger tied on the back of her belt. She spat in the man's face, causing him to close his eyes and let go just long enough for her to reach down, pull the dagger out, and plunge it between his ribs. The Black Saber gasped and immediately dropped his hand, but Asenna withdrew the dagger and stabbed him again in the soft flesh of his belly. Before he dropped to the floor, he let out a wheezing cough, spraying blood across her face. Horrified, Asenna stumbled away toward the kitchen, trying not to look back at her victim gasping on the floor. Talla suddenly grabbed her around the waist from behind and hauled her away from the corridor. The other Black Sabers were laying scattered in pieces around them and Asenna had to avert her eyes from the detached limbs and entrails that decorated the room. Andros was leaning up against an overturned table, holding his legs, where he appeared to have been cut badly along the backs of his knees.

"You did good," Talla panted, waving at Asenna's attacker, who was still twitching and bleeding out on the floor. She let go and went to examine the wounds on Andros' legs.

"I didn't…I didn't mean to…" Asenna felt herself start to shake and she dropped the bloody dagger onto the table, "I wasn't even thinking." Talla pulled two bandages from her belt and quickly wrapped Andros' legs, then picked up the dagger, wiped it on her shirt, and put it back in the sheath.

"You did exactly what you needed to do, Asenna," she said, "now we have to find Ephie." Asenna looked around for Ivarr and saw him across the room, kneeling on the floor. Nettle was laying on her side in front of him and Asenna felt like the floor had fallen out from under her.

"Ivarr, no!" she gasped, rushing over to her brother and grabbing his shoulders. He looked up and Asenna could see that the shining, glimmering light of the Wolfsight had already faded from his golden eyes.

"I…I didn't get to her in time…" Ivarr stammered. His hands and face were covered in the blood pouring from a wound on Nettle's neck. The wolf's eyes were closed and she was not breathing. Behind them, Briar threw her head back and let out a low, heart-rending howl that reverberated around the kitchen like a bell. Asenna looked back at Talla and saw tears on her face.

"Ivarr," said Asenna, kneeling down and taking her brother's face in her hands, "*lai'kheri*, listen to me. We need to go. They'll find us again if we stay here. I swear to you, when this is over we'll take her home and bury her. She won't stay here, but right now, I need you to get up. I can't lose you." Ivarr leaned over and buried his face in the black fur around Nettle's neck, letting out a howling scream like Asenna had never heard from any creature before. He lifted her head off the ground and kissed her muzzle and Asenna heard him whispering in Ulvvori, words that made her feel like she was the one who had been torn open by a blade.

"I love you, my beautiful girl," Ivarr said as he tried to stand. Asenna put her hands under his arms and practically lifted him to his feet, then threw his arm around her shoulder and steered him over to where Briar was standing, sniffing the air in the corridor that the Black Saber had indicated. She gave a low growl and had to crouch down in the small passageway to lead them away from the kitchen. Andros was limping badly and Asenna could see the bloody makeshift bandages that Talla had tied around his legs becoming more saturated as they went. She could also feel Ivarr shaking and his breath becoming more ragged, and she felt panic rise up in her throat. Asenna had never been with anyone when they had lost their dire wolf before and she was terrified of what might happen to him. Finally, they turned and found a large iron gate in front of them.

"That's it!" she cried. The gate was ajar, so they all pushed inside and then Talla used her sword to bar it shut. There was a questionable-looking staircase that led down into what was merely a pit with partial stone walls and a roof. The prison was one long, narrow room where huge iron cages had been placed at intervals, with crude walls built between them using piles of logs. The few windows were small, high, and barred, allowing very little light inside, and the stench was so horrific that Asenna felt sick when she breathed in. Talla grabbed a burnt-out torch from the wall and wrapped it with cloth, then soaked it in lamp oil from her belt and lit it. As she began to examine the cages, she let out a loud string of curses in Ulvvori. Asenna led Ivarr over to a large pile of hay and dropped him onto it. He sat there, completely still except for the shaking, holding his head in his hands, while Andros leaned on the wall. Asenna turned to follow Talla and Briar down the row of cages, holding her shirt over her nose.

"This is beyond the pale," Andros whispered. Half the prisoners were deceased, and it appeared that some of them had been that way for quite some time. There were flies everywhere and rats ran in front of their feet as they searched. Behind her, Asenna heard Ivarr retch and vomit. Many of the prisoners who were still alive could barely move and when they saw the great white wolf standing outside the bars, some began to sob or scream, imagining that they were entering some kind of bizarre afterlife. Asenna heard a voice calling from the end of the row and saw a hand stretched out from one of the cages. When she reached it, she found an older, balding man who seemed to be in far better condition than the others. He looked familiar, but Asenna could not place him with the dim light and the grime covering his face.

"Your Majesty," he breathed when he saw her, "oh, thank goodness you're here. Please, we need help." Asenna knelt in front of the bars and Talla held the torch over her, throwing the prisoner's face into sharp relief. Asenna felt a stab of recognition.

"Bernart…Greenlow? Right? You were one of Azimar's ministers?"

"Yes, Your Majesty, but I was imprisoned here for speaking out against his cruelty," Greenlow cried, "please, you must get help."

"We're here with the Ulvvori to liberate the city," Asenna told him, "you'll all be released soon, I promise, but I'm looking for my maid, Ephie. Is she here?" Greenlow's beady eyes widened and he scrambled to the back of the cage, where another person was laying on the floor under a blanket.

Asenna saw the white hair and let out a loud cry.

"She's here," said Greenlow softly, "she's in very bad condition, Your Majesty, but she is still alive." Asenna shook the bars of the cage.

"Ephie!" she cried, feeling wild and desperate, "hang on! How do we open it?"

"I...I don't know," Talla said. Asenna felt tears on her cheeks as they looked around for keys or any kind of tool they could use to open the big padlock on the cage door. Briar approached and Greenlow shrunk back from her, but Asenna could see that the she-wolf understood what they needed.

"It's alright," she told Greenlow, "she's going to help." Briar examined the lock for a moment, then gingerly hooked it with one of her huge canine teeth and, in one swift motion, jerked her head down and snapped it in half. Asenna yanked the door open and ran to Ephie. She was so thin that Asenna could feel every bone through her threadbare clothes. Her hair was falling out in chunks and her lips were cracked and caked with dry blood. Trying to be gentle, Asenna rolled Ephie onto her back.

"Ephie, I'm here. It's Asenna." The old woman opened her eyes and raised a thin, feeble hand.

"Oh, my *sheyta zhia*," she whispered, "you came back."

"Asenna, we need to get them all out. Now," Talla said from behind her, "I'll take her. Briar can open the rest of the cages and then we can barricade the gate so that no one can get in while we figure out what to do." Asenna wiped the tears from her face and stepped out of the cage while Talla knelt to pick up Ephie's skeletal body.

"Hello, Auntie," Talla whispered, and Asenna realized that, in her desperation, she had forgotten about Ephie's connection to the twins. She suddenly felt a little guilty and selfish for spearheading the campaign to rescue her friend when Talla could have been used elsewhere, but Talla took Ephie over to the haystack and laid her down gently beside Ivarr. Asenna sat between them while Briar opened the rest of the cages. Talla and Andros gathered half a dozen living prisoners near the haystack and then set about double-checking all the cages to make sure they hadn't missed anyone. Greenlow stumbled over to them and sat down beside Ephie. He was trembling and Asenna handed him a thin blanket that was sitting nearby.

"Greenlow," she said, "you have to tell me how this happened."

"I don't know, Your Majesty," he murmured, "the King's condition has...deteriorated rapidly the last few months. He took near full control of the government, trade, everything, using the Black Sabers to carry out his orders. Myself and other ministers on his council were kept in the dark. Some were put under house arrest, some were exiled, some were even murdered, with their families. I managed to stay with him the longest and I tried to prevent the things I could. When the Kashaitis crossed the border two weeks ago, he told me about his plan to bar the city gates and burn it if the army approached. I protested, and he put me down here. I didn't know about the conditions in the prison and I..." Greenlow dropped his head into his hands and began to cry softly.

"What about Ephie? How is she still alive after all this time?" Asenna asked.

"There were a few kitchen maids who would bring her food and water in between the jailer's shifts," Greenlow said, his breath steadying, "they told me they'd been doing it the entire time she's been here, taking care of her, because she was like a mother to them. But when Azimar barred the gates a week ago, he sent all the servants and maids and even the jailer out of the palace, so none of us have eaten or had any water since then." Asenna looked down at Ephie and bit her lip.

"When can we leave?" she asked Talla quietly.

"Carro and Tira know this is where we were headed. They'll send someone to find us. For now, we're safe so we just have to wait."

"And Ivarr?" Asenna looked over at her brother, still as a statue.

"Losing the Wolfsight..." Talla murmured, "it's like a fever. It has to burn and burn and it will get worse before it gets better. He'll survive, even if he doesn't feel like it. And then he'll have to mourn her. That takes...considerably longer..." Asenna watched as Talla's pale yellow eyes filled with tears again.

"What can I do for him?"

"I won't lie to you, Asenna. There were times after I lost Flint that...I nearly killed myself. Tira felt the same way, worse since she lost Aija too. Our friends, Andros, and our father, they had to convince us to keep living. You and your family might have to live for him, keep him going, until he can...stand on his own two feet again." Talla turned away to check on Andros and the other prisoners, clearly not wanting to discuss the topic any further. On Asenna's other side, Greenlow cleared his throat.

"Your Majesty, you must know that the King imprisoned me because he could not afford to kill me," he said, "I am more knowledgeable about the laws of Esmadia than any other person living, and if you are amenable to it, I would gladly serve you. And Prince Elijas too."

"His name is Fenrinn," said Asenna sharply, then she sighed and softened her tone, "I'm sorry. You couldn't have known that. Yes, my son and I would be grateful for your loyalty and your help, Greenlow. Thank you."

"Then, Your Majesty, if I might--" Greenlow was cut off by a loud banging on the gate.

"Asenna! Ivarr!" cried a voice from above them that she immediately recognized as Haryk's. Talla ran up the stairs and unbarred the gate for him and Juniper to come in.

"Haryk!" Asenna hugged him tightly, "what is it? Where's Carro?"

"It's over. Azimar is dead and the Black Sabers are defeated."

"Dead?" Asenna felt unsteady and Talla had to hold her by the arm as she took a step backwards, "what do you mean? He was supposed to be arrested. Carro didn't…"

"No, it wasn't Carro," Haryk reassured her, "Azimar poisoned himself. Tira sent me to find you. There's a crowd starting to gather outside and they'll expect to see you soon."

"Asenna, you go," Talla said gently, "Andros and I will stay with Ephie and Ivarr. Haryk, tell them we're down here and we'll need help to carry these people out, and immediate medical attention."

"What happened to Ivarr?" Haryk asked, going to kneel in front of his brother.

"Nettle's gone," came Ivarr's cracked voice. He raised his head and Asenna saw that the golden color in his eyes was already beginning to fade to yellow. Haryk cursed and pulled him into a bone-crushing hug.

"It's over now," he murmured, "and they'll pay for it. You stay here and I'll send someone for her body. We'll take her home."

"Haryk, do…do I have to go up now?" Asenna murmured, "I just…I thought I'd have more time before…"

"Key needs you, and Carro does too. He's…not doing well."

"Is he hurt?" Asenna asked, her heart twisting in her chest.

"No," Haryk said, "come on, I'll tell you upstairs."

"Please, Your Majesty," said Greenlow, coming up behind them, "if you would allow me to accompany you. I have information about the laws and procedures that must be followed to ensure that the succession is legitimate."

"Yes, of course. Thank you, Talla, Andros. I'll come and find you later. Please take care of Ephie and my brother, and yourselves." Talla put her arms around Asenna.

"You can do this. You were meant to do this," she said in a firm voice as Andros stood behind her, nodding.

"Thank you," Asenna said softly, feeling like somehow Talla's encouragement was more meaningful because it was so rarely given. Asenna followed Haryk and Juniper out into the corridor with Greenlow trailing after them and Briar at her side, helping steady her when she stumbled or went a little off course. It felt like she was walking upriver through a current as they passed through corridor after corridor and room after room that all looked exactly the same. The moment had been coming for months and yet, now that it was actually here, it felt strange, as if it had been sprung on her without warning.

Finally, they stopped outside a door and Asenna recognized the small meeting room adjacent to the balcony where she had been brought the day of Fen's naming ceremony. She looked past the curtains out the windows and realized that the low buzzing noise she could hear was a crowd gathered on the palace grounds.

"Tell me what happened with Azimar," she said as Haryk steered her over to a chair and sat her down.

"We found him in the throne room. He was drunk and he said some...awful things," Haryk said quietly, "then Azimar took poison and Carro had to just sort of...hold onto him while he died..." Asenna let out a breath and allowed the anger to wash over her.

"Of course, he couldn't even kill himself without making sure he hurt someone in the process," she murmured, rubbing her forehead, which was beginning to ache.

"Your Majesty," said Greenlow, coming to stand beside Asenna, "there is something that you should know before you present yourself—"

"Give her a damn minute!" Haryk barked at him.

"No, Haryk, I'm alright. What is it, Greenlow?"

"I assume that you plan to place your son on the throne and then act as his Regent, but I would like to offer you an alternative, if I may. There is a relatively obscure law, which was intentionally kept obscure by your husband and his predecessors, which allows a *widowed* Queen to assume the throne in her own right, as long as she has a legitimate male heir who is still a child. She can rule by her own power until the boy turns twenty years old, at which time she must formally abdicate in his favor."

"I don't understand," said Haryk, "what's the difference?"

"It grants the Queen more autonomy to make decisions," Greenlow explained, "rather than being beholden to a Regent's council made up of lords and ministers who may or may not truly be loyal to you and your son. Additionally, it would allow the young prince more freedom. You see, when there is a Regency in place, the King may not leave the capital."

Asenna looked over at his drawn, wrinkled face, her heart sinking. "You mean...Fen wouldn't be allowed to leave Sinsaya *at all* until he turns twenty? If I were Regent?"

"That is correct, Your Majesty. As I'm sure you're aware, our history books are full of stories about the pitfalls of placing young children on the throne. It would be for his own safety, of course, but I believe in your...particular circumstances, it would be quite difficult," Greenlow glanced at Briar and Juniper, who were sitting in the corridor outside.

"Yes, it would be," Asenna said slowly, "what's the catch? Surely they would never just...allow a woman to take the throne by herself?"

"Naturally, there are conditions. The Prince must still spend a certain amount of time here, learning about his duties. *You* must also sign a binding document naming him and only him as your heir, agreeing to abdicate on his twentieth birthday, and agreeing not to remarry until he assumes the throne in your place."

Haryk made a noise. "She can't remarry? Fen isn't even two yet. That's eighteen years. What if she wants to have more children?"

Asenna let out a loud, involuntary laugh. "Haryk! Our parents had three children without being married. If Fen's freedom is contingent on me remaining, legally, a widow then that's what I'll do. I want to do this by following the laws, however…archaic they might be. They can be changed later, the right way. I won't start off as an autocrat."

"I can draw up the document immediately, if Your Majesty wishes," Greenlow said, "but you will need to decide very soon."

"I've decided already, Greenlow," Asenna said, "do it."

"What about Carro?" asked Haryk quietly.

"He'll understand that it's for Fen." As she said it, there were voices in the hall and Key came sweeping into the room, accompanied by Tira, Gaelin, a Kashaiti general, and Tolian, who had been given a crutch to help him walk. Asenna stood up just as Carro came in behind them, carrying a half-starved and limp body in his arms, which he laid out on the long meeting table in the center of the room. Greenlow began to sputter in protest as Asenna walked slowly over to the body, feeling like she was in a horrible dream.

Her husband's face was wretched-looking, thin and gaunt and lined, like he had aged ten years since she had last seen him. Asenna reached out and gingerly pushed the matted black curls off his forehead. His skin was impossibly pale and already felt cold. She half expected him to start breathing again as she put her fingers lightly on his hand. The tears sprung into her eyes and Asenna took a deep, ragged breath, trying to hold them back. She could not cry in front of all these people, not when she was about to be presented as their Queen, and especially not for the man who had caused her and her family so much pain, but the tears came anyway and she leaned on the table to steady herself. A warm, familiar hand grasped her arm and she turned to look at Carro. She could feel him trembling as they embraced and the pain in his eyes as he touched the dried blood on her face was almost palpable.

"Are you hurt?" he asked.

"No, I just…had to defend myself."

"*Lai'rani*…I'm so sorry. I should never have let you go."

"It's over now," Asenna sighed, glancing around and realizing that everyone was watching them, "I need to talk to you. Alone." She took his hand and led him out into the corridor.

"What do you need?" Carro asked, leaning against the wall.

"You remember Greenlow, right? We found him in the prison block with Ephie and he told me something," Asenna tried to explain quickly, "if Fen is named King now and I'm Regent, he wouldn't be allowed to leave the capital until he's twenty, when he can take the throne. I don't want that life for him, Carro. I want him to be able to grow up like I did, to be with my family and the wolves in the mountains. There's a law that would allow me to be Queen, in my own right, until Fen comes of age, and then I would abdicate in his favor."

"That's wonderful!" Carro said, giving her a genuine smile, "you can do so much more that way…you look worried though. What's the problem?"

"There's a condition: I have to maintain my status…as a widow. I can't remarry until Fen takes the throne," Asenna twisted her fingers through his and looked up at him, "I love you, Carro, and I don't want to lose you, but if marriage is something you need…I can't give you that…"

Carro shook his head and laughed. "Asenna, I don't care about any of that. All I want is *you*, for as long as you'll have me, and however you'll have me. You do what's best for Fen, and yourself, and I'll be here no matter what." Asenna leaned up and kissed him and he lifted her off the ground.

"Are you two done now?" said Tira, coming out into the corridor, "they're all getting a little restless." Asenna and Carro went back into the meeting room, where Greenlow appeared to be explaining to Key what he had explained to her.

"Is this what you want?" Key turned to ask Asenna, "to take the throne yourself?"

"Yes, it is."

"Good enough for me. Now, we need to show them," she motioned to Azimar's body, still lying on the table. Carro stepped forward, sliding his hands under Azimar's shoulders and knees. Asenna wanted to say something to him, but she could tell he was set on this, just as she had been set on rescuing Ephie, so she stood back. Key and Greenlow went ahead of Carro to the balcony, where Key held up her hands to the massive crowd that had gathered below. Asenna's heart began to hammer when she saw how many people there were, spread out on the palace grounds, covering every available space between the balcony and the wall, with even more standing along the tops of the walls. Tira came up behind Asenna and turned her around to wipe off the dried blood.

"What happened?" she asked.

"I…had to put your lessons to good use," Asenna replied, feeling her hands start to shake, "Tira, I killed someone…and I don't…" Tira pulled her into a fierce hug.

"You did *exactly* what you had to do, and I am so proud of you, Asenna. You'll get through this, I promise. We're all here with you." Asenna didn't reply because her voice was stuck in her throat and she tried to listen as Key began speaking outside.

"Esmadia!" she called out, her voice reverberating around the palace grounds, "your ordeal is now over! The coward Azimar chose to take his own life, rather than submit himself to justice. This kind of instability and evil can never be allowed to throw your nation into chaos again." The crowd sent up a deafening roar and Key motioned for Carro to come forward. He laid Azimar's pale, fragile body on the wide railing of the balcony and then stepped back. Asenna could see the people in the crowd craning their necks to look and she felt like she wanted to vomit. When Key seemed to be satisfied, Carro lifted Azimar up and brought him back inside to the table. One of the resistance fighters removed her cloak and tossed it unceremoniously over the body. Outside, Key continued her speech and Carro came to stand with Tira and Asenna, putting his arms around both their shoulders as they listened.

"I now present to you Queen Asenna, returned from her exile, who will assume the throne and rule in fairness and justice until her son, your Prince Fenrinn, comes of age," Key continued, "will you accept her as your sovereign?" Another cheer went up from the crowd and Asenna stepped out onto the balcony, her legs wobbling. As she stood there, waving and listening to the roar of the crowd, she felt like she wanted to laugh hysterically.

"Your Majesty, do you wish to speak?" asked Greenlow. Asenna shook her head.

"Let's get you away, then," said Key quietly, taking her arm above the elbow and addressing the crowd again, "please, return to your homes. The city is secure and you are safe, but your Queen has much work to do on your behalf!" The crowd heeded her words and began to pour out of the palace gates as Key took Asenna back inside.

"Maybe *you* should be queen," Asenna gasped, leaning on a chair and trying to control her shaking legs, "you're much better at that than I am."

"My own mother taught me well," Key replied, folding her arms, "and it looks like she was also right about you, Asenna. I know you'll do well." Asenna searched Key's face and suddenly realized why the resistance leader had seemed so familiar to her since they met.

"You're Selissa's daughter," she said, and immediately heard small gasps and whispers behind her. Asenna wondered if she had made a mistake by saying it, but Key smiled gently.

"Yes, and not many are aware of it, but I thought that perhaps you all should know now. There are many in Esmadia who would not take kindly to the offspring of a foreign monarch interfering in their affairs, but I am not here to serve Kashait. I am here as a private citizen who believes strongly in this cause, and in you, Your Majesty."

"Selissa told me that she had agents in Esmadia. She meant you?"

"That's how she already knew about the resistance when we told her," Tolian smiled, "Selissa is always one step ahead of everyone else." Key merely nodded, obviously keen to put the subject behind them.

"I only mention my mother, Your Majesty, to explain why I cannot be the one to advise you for much longer," Key said, then turned to Greenlow, "you, what needs to happen next?"

"First, I suggest that we…either remove this corpse from the table or select another meeting place, then I would be happy to walk Her Majesty through the next steps." Key snapped her fingers and several of her fighters stepped forward.

"Move the body somewhere secure and guard it until we decide what's to be done," she said, "get Ilmira's body and bring it there as well."

"Ilmira's dead?" Asenna asked.

"We found her in Azimar's chambers," Carro said quietly, "strangled to death."

Asenna's stomach lurched. "His own mother…" she whispered, "I can't say that she'll be missed. But still…"

Key and Greenlow escorted Asenna out of the chamber with Carro and Tira and everyone else falling in behind, trailed by the wolves. As they walked, Asenna explained to Key about Talla and the people in the prison block, and Key sent some of her people to assist them. Once a suitable meeting room had been located, they settled around the large table and Asenna felt all eyes shift to her. She was glad when Carro came to stand behind her with his hand on her shoulder. Even though he didn't speak, having him there made it easier to wade through the quagmire of decisions that needed to be made and issues that needed to be discussed.

The next hours were a blur as Asenna began to try and rebuild everything Azimar had destroyed, with gentle guidance from Tolian, Key, and Greenlow. At least two dozen messengers were sent off in all directions to recall ministers who had been placed under house arrest and the refugees who had fled Azimar's reign of terror, and to reestablish contact with officials in Ossesh and other cities. Asenna made sure that there was also a message for her mother to bring Fen to the capital as quickly as possible, and to tell the Ulvvori that they were free to return to the mountains. Then, there was the army and the remaining Black Sabers to deal with, a job which Asenna did not relish because she knew that it might eventually involve signing orders of execution.

By late afternoon, Asenna was beginning to fade and realized that she had not eaten at all since the previous night. She looked around the room and saw Carro sitting in a chair in the corner, his head balanced on one hand as he slept. Haryk was also beginning to nod off at the other end of the table and Tira looked like she might collapse at any moment. Even Key was hiding a few yawns as she tried to listen attentively.

"Mr. Greenlow," said Asenna quietly, "I'm sorry to interrupt, and I know how important this all is, but I think everyone here needs to rest and eat. What can we do about finding beds and food?"

Greenlow looked a little embarrassed. "Your Majesty, I am so sorry. I believe there are temporary accommodations being set up in the entrance hall of the palace, but if you would like a more private room, I will have to send someone to check."

"Thank you," Asenna said, standing up, "my old rooms will be fine, if they are still intact. If not, I can go to the hall with everyone else." Asenna went over to Carro and knelt down, running her hand along his arm.

"Come on, *lai'zhia*," she said, "you need rest. We all do." Carro startled awake and they shuffled through the corridors in silence, making their way up the stairs to where Asenna's old rooms were, but she stopped just outside the door.

"Suddenly, I don't know if I want to go in," she said.

"Are you afraid he destroyed it?"

"No, but it feels like…stepping back into the way things were before." In spite of her doubts, Asenna turned the doorknob and entered the room, which looked exactly the same as the night she had left, except for the thick coating of dust over everything. She walked to the bed and ran her fingers over the tiny basket where Fen had slept that first month. On her vanity, the comb and jars of makeup Ephie had used the day of the naming ceremony were still sitting open and slightly askew, as if she had just put them down. The big copper bathtub still sat in the antechamber, now full of dead spiders and mice. Asenna turned back to Carro, who was standing in the doorway turning something over in his hands.

"The teapot," he smiled ruefully, "that you threw at my head." He held up the chunk of floral ceramic and tapped the tiny scar on his eyebrow. Asenna couldn't help but smile too, even though the memory was a painful one. She walked over and took the piece from him.

"I think you probably deserved that one."

"No, I *definitely* deserved that one."

"You know…" Asenna leaned her back against his chest, "it's a little ironic, isn't it? I never wanted to get married, but I did it anyway when I wasn't even in love. And now that I've found someone I actually love and want to make a life with…I can't get married."

"Well," Carro said softly, "I, for one, don't need Greenlow breathing down my neck to sign a piece of paper telling me what I already know."

"And what is it that you already know?"

"That you are the most beautiful and incredible person I've ever known," Carro said, leaning down to kiss her neck, "that I never want to belong to anyone else. And that I plan to spend every single minute of the rest of my life making sure you know how much I adore you." Asenna felt the warmth of his words spread down her body to her fingertips and she turned around.

"That sounds like a lot of work," she said with a wide smile.

"You are well worth it, *lai'rani*."

"I'm not afraid of a little hard work either," Asenna said, wrapping her hands around the back of his neck, "so, I promise that you will never go a single day without knowing how much I love you, and how thankful I am that I found you, and how proud I am that you're mine." Their lips met and Asenna allowed the sensation to burn through her body and overwhelm her, blocking out the horrors of the day for a few precious moments.

"Those didn't count as marriage vows, did they?" she laughed when they broke apart.

"I won't tell if you won't," Carro replied, rubbing his nose against hers and grinning, "come on, there's nothing for us here." Asenna tossed the piece of the teapot onto the floor and they walked back down the corridor.

When they reached the entrance hall, Asenna was stunned to see that dozens of citizens had come into the palace from the city and the countryside beyond, bringing cots and bedrolls, blankets, medicine, bandages, food, water, and even flowers for the resistance fighters and the Ulvvori. Through the windows, Asenna saw that several of them had even built fires out on the palace grounds and were already cooking large batches of food, while others were tending injuries. A few of the resistance fighters were sleeping already, and many of the Ulvvori were resting with their wolves up against the walls. Asenna saw Briar curled up with Echo, Juniper, and Ash in a corner. They were all quiet and could not even manage to prick up their ears when she came over. Asenna could feel the sadness and pain from Nettle's death as she leaned against Briar's shoulder.

"Ivarr lost Nettle," she told Carro when he came over with a blanket for her, "and Andros was injured badly. I have to find them, and Ephie and Talla."

"You need to sleep," Carro said, "you have more work to do than anyone here. I'll go find Ivarr and the others."

"But you should rest too. And you need to get this looked at," she brushed her fingers over his chest next to the wound. It was no longer bleeding, but she could see Carro wince every few minutes and she knew it was hurting him.

"I'll find someone to check it, but I got a bit of a nap during your meeting. I certainly don't envy you having to listen to Greenlow drone on like that." Asenna shook her head and laid down on Briar's paw, letting Carro cover her with the blanket.

"Don't let me sleep too long," she murmured.

"You'll sleep as long as you need to, and if Greenlow comes anywhere near you with his inane horseshit, I will cut him. I know he remembers me, as much as he wants to pretend he doesn't."

"No cutting anyone, *lai'zhia*," Asenna said sleepily. Almost immediately, she felt Briar's emotions shift from sadness to calm, and the feeling enabled her to slip into a dreamless sleep.

When Asenna woke, it was dark outside. The hall was still and quiet, but every cot and bedroll was occupied, and the walls were lined with sleeping wolves and their Riders. Carro was beside her, resting his head on Briar's other paw, while Tira was curled up against Rowan nearby. She could also just make out Juniper, Haryk, Ash, Nikke, Echo, and Tolian lying further down the wall, but saw no sign of Ivarr. Asenna got up and wrapped the blanket around her shoulders, then picked her way around the sleeping bodies that littered the floor and slipped out the main palace doors, which had been left slightly ajar. The moon hung over the rooftops and the walls of the palace, lighting her way as she searched for her brother. The palace grounds were full of wild dire wolves, sleeping peacefully in piles on the grass, but Asenna could also see dozens of bodies, human and wolf, lined up along the base of the wall, wrapped in white linen and covered with flags or bits of colored cloth. Toward the back of the complex, she finally spotted a lone figure with a familiar silhouette sitting on one of the battlements. Asenna climbed the steps and pulled herself up beside Ivarr, who was hunched over with his head thrown back, staring up at the moon. He turned to look at her and Asenna felt her skin crawl at the sight of his pale eyes. With his dark hair and sunken cheeks, he looked like a spirit.

"I can't live without her, Senna," he said hoarsely, "I can't do it. I don't want to."

"You have to!" Asenna reached over and grabbed his hand, "I know this isn't easy, but you *can* live. Look at the twins and Mama. If you can't keep going for yourself, do it for us. I need you, *lai'kheri*, please, now more than ever. How can I do this without you?"

"It's so quiet…"Ivarr murmured, "it's so quiet in my head. Is this what it's like for you? All the time?"

"Yes," Asenna let out a small laugh, "it's very quiet most of the time."

"I hate it," Ivarr put his head down and a few tears fell onto his legs, "I hate it, Senna. I just want to hear her voice again. I can't stand this. I miss her so much." His shoulders began to shake and Asenna reached over and pulled him into a tight hug. She let him cry, let him sob and scream and curse, for as long as he needed to, and when he became quiet again, Asenna leaned over and looked him in the eye.

"No matter what happens now, I'm here," she said gently, "so is Haryk, and Tira, and everyone else. Whatever you need from me, just say it."

"Can I stay here with you?" Ivarr whispered, "I want to bury her in the mountains, but then...I don't think I can stay. It would hurt too much."

"Of course you can stay with me." There was a long silence as they both looked up at the moon.

"I'm proud of you, Senna. I don't know how you've made it through this without breaking down," Ivarr said, leaning his head on her shoulder.

"Ah, well," Asenna smiled, "I'm sure I'll have to carefully schedule my breakdowns with Mr. Greenlow from now on. Come on, let's get you inside. It's cold tonight."

"For what it's worth," Ivarr swung his legs around and stood up, "I think this is what you were born to do." They walked back to the entrance hall together and Asenna held onto Ivarr's arm to steady him. Tira was awake and offered for Ivarr to come sit beside her and Rowan so they could talk, so Asenna went back to where Briar and Carro were sleeping. Briar opened her big golden eyes when Asenna sat down and leaned against her head.

"I *can* do this, can't I, Briar?" Asenna asked quietly. Briar pulled her lips back in a soft growl and nudged Asenna gently with her muzzle as if to say: *"Of course you can, silly girl."*

CARRO'S EPILOGUE

The southern sun beat down mercilessly as Carro pulled Pan to a stop and jumped down onto the hard packed red dirt, shielding his eyes to look up at the big red house. All the months he had spent there in his youth with Azimar seemed like a dream now, like something he had read about in a book. Carro wished he could forget all of it, but knew that was unrealistic. His memories of their time spent down on the beach hunting for sand sharks and buried treasure might fade with time, but the memory he could not escape from was the one of Azimar's ragged final breath and the way death felt in his arms. In the back of his mind, Carro knew that Azimar would have died anyway. He would have been executed for the safety of the kingdom, but at least that would have come with a warning, time to prepare, and the option of witnessing it. Carro had not been given a choice and still could not shake the guilt and grief that were tucked away in the corners of his mind, jumping out when he least expected them. Once he had ensured that Asenna would be safe in the capital, he had asked for permission to do the one thing he needed in order to rid himself of those feelings. It had taken all his powers of persuasion to convince Key to let him take Azimar and Ilmira's bodies. She and the others had hoped to burn them publicly so that any surviving Black Sabers who were harboring loyalties for Azimar, despite their new oaths to Asenna, might be taught a lesson. In the end, however, Key had relented and Gaelin had helped him load the bodies onto the cart and bring them to the coast.

"So, this is it?" Gaelin asked, jumping out of the cart beside him, "looks like a *qehogar*."

Carro gave a weak laugh. "Yeah, I'm sure it's awful compared to the cave where you grew up, you troll." Gaelin snorted and they turned around to pull the bodies, which had been wrapped tightly in black linen, off the cart and carry them one by one up the stairs and into the atrium. The pool had long since dried up and the wilted husks of the water lilies and vines that had once decorated the room now littered the blue tiles at the bottom of the pool. They placed the bodies along the far wall and then began hauling the bundles of firewood from the cart and tossing them unceremoniously into the empty pool, working in silence. Carro gathered up all the dried vines and other plants and threw them in too.

"Ready?" Gaelin asked, holding up a bottle of brown liquor they had purchased from a tinker along the road. Carro walked over as Gaelin opened it and took the first drink, then gagged. "What the fuck *is* that?"

"Well," Carro said, taking a drink and nearly choking on the foul liquid, "it's not as if we came for a good time anyway. Wait here. I'll be back." He took the bottle, then picked up a jug of lamp oil and wandered into the grand entry hall.

Carro walked slowly between rooms, letting the lamp oil trickle out onto the floor and furniture as he went. The villa had not been lived in for years. Azimar had effectively abandoned it when he had become King, and much of it still looked the way Carro remembered, just with a thick layer of grime, bird droppings, and sea salt. He walked through the portrait gallery in the library, trying to avoid the gaze of generations of Sinsayed generals and lords. On the large desk beside the window, Carro paused and shuffled through some of the letters and maps. In one of the drawers, he found a leather-bound sketchbook with Azimar's name stamped on the front in gold. He sat in the creaky chair and continued to drink from the liquor bottle as he flipped through the sketches.

Before the need for control and power had fully consumed him, Azimar had a talent for drawing. Whenever they had come to stay at the villa, he had spent hours on the beach sketching whatever strange sea creatures Carro could spear from the water. When he found the drawing of a bizarre-looking blobfish they had found once, which Azimar had embellished with a mustache and a monocle so it resembled his old tutor, Carro actually found himself smiling a little. At the back of the book, however, were two sketches that immediately opened back up the bitter wound in his stomach. The first was a rough self-portrait of himself and Azimar as young teenagers. He remembered how they had posed themselves in front of a mirror for hours, their arms growing tired, while Azimar worked to get it right. In the picture, Carro was grinning, with his arm thrown around Azimar's shoulder, while Azimar's eyes looked more serious and focused on the image in the mirror. Carro stuffed the paper into his belt and then picked up the second drawing, which was of Asenna. It had to have been one of the last sketches Azimar did before the war had truly pulled him away. In it, Asenna was leaning on the railing of her balcony, looking wistfully out over the cliffs. At the bottom of the page, Azimar had scribbled *'my love.'*

Carro crumpled the sketch up and let it fall to the floor, then put the sketchbook under his arm, kicked the desk over on its side, and covered it with lamp oil. He took another swig from the liquor bottle and left the library as quickly as he could. Once he had doused the entire house in oil and nearly drained the bottle of drink, Carro went back to the atrium, where Gaelin was waiting, drinking from his own flask.

"What's that?" Gaelin asked, motioning to the sketchbook.

"Something for Fen," Carro murmured, "when he's ready. Come on, let's get this over with." Carro grabbed another jug of oil and started to soak the pile of firewood in the empty pool, then they carefully placed Azimar and Ilmira's bodies on top of the pyre. Carro took the sketch of himself and Azimar out of his belt and Gaelin looked over his shoulder as he began to fold it lengthwise.

"Not bad. He should've stuck to drawin'," muttered Gaelin as Carro handed him the paper. Using a flint and the blade of his dagger, Carro lit the sketch on fire and tossed it in between the logs, igniting the oil. The flames began to rush around the edges of the pool, licking and biting, until they finally reached up and began to consume the bodies too. When the flames finally caught the trail of oil leading into the rest of the house, Carro and Gaelin quickly walked outside and down the stairs. They moved the cart away to a safe distance, then sat back to watch the smoke pouring out of the windows and twisting across the clear blue sky, until it disappeared into the ether.

"Now it's done," Carro said quietly, "let's go home."

SIXTEEN:
THE MIDWINTER CROWN

~ One Month Later ~

As Asenna and her party neared the farm, her heart nearly burst with joy to see Lusie's children spilling out of the house. They ran out to greet them, dodging between Pan's legs and hugging his nose and trying to race Tira and Fitz down the dirt track. She didn't dare go too fast though, since she was riding with Fen sitting in front of her on the saddle, so the children got a good head start and beat her into the yard.

"Talla!" she cried as she slid off Fitz's back with Fen in her arms, "Andros! Lusie!" Asenna rode into the yard, and behind her, the mismatched royal guard made up of Wolf Riders and resistance fighters dismounted too. Lusie and Talla came out of the house and Asenna was momentarily taken aback by how different Talla looked in her plain clothes, with her hair cut to her shoulders and not a single weapon on her body. After the invasion, she had decided to put aside her hatchet and her little bottles of sunfire and move to the farm to help Andros and Ephie recover. Now, she looked far more relaxed and happier than Asenna had ever seen her.

"They've turned you into a farmer!" Tira laughed.

"A little," Talla said, "but they'll never get me into a dress." Asenna came over and hugged Talla and Lusie.

"Give me that little one!" Lusie exclaimed, holding her arms out for Fen. Tira handed him over and Lusie went into the house while her children followed, making faces to try and get Fen to laugh.

"How is everything?" Tira asked her sister, "Andros? Ephie?"

"Everything is wonderful. Come inside," Talla said, leading them into the kitchen, where Andros was sitting at the table. The wounds on the backs of his legs had proven slow to heal, and Asenna knew he had a great deal of trouble walking now, so she went over and hugged him.

"Where's Carro and Gaelin?" he asked.

"A few more Ulvvori arrived from Kashait yesterday," Asenna told him, "so they're managing everything at the palace with Ivarr, but I was finally able to get away, so we had to come and see you. Is Ephie awake?"

"Here," said Talla. She led Asenna down the hall to one of the bedrooms. "Auntie? Look who's here to see you." Ephie was laying in one of the narrow beds along the wall, looking a thousand times better than the day Asenna had found her in the prison block, but she was still impossibly thin and had a nasty, lingering cough. Asenna sat on the edge of the bed and hugged her for a long time.

"I brought Fen too," she said softly, "but he's with the children right now." Ephie raised a bony hand and pushed Asenna's hair back.

"You have grown so much," the old woman said, smiling, "a real queen now. Magnificent. I am so proud. Tell me everything you've been doing, *sheyta zhia*."

"Well…" Asenna wasn't sure where to begin, so much had happened in only a month, but she knew there was one particular bit of news that Ephie would want to hear. "Some of the Ulvvori have started coming back from Kashait already. I've asked them to stop in the city before they go home because there's something Tira and Ivarr have been helping me with. I came today because I wanted to tell you first. We're creating a sort of registry…to try and reunite Ulvvori families with their sons."

Ephie's eyes immediately filled with tears. "My boys?" she whispered.

"Yours was the first name in the book," Asenna told her, trying to hold back her own tears, "I've given orders for every Ulvvori soldier to come to the palace and register themselves too, and then we can try and match people based on whatever information they can give. Tira said she won't rest until she finds your boys, and Issi too, so don't worry." Ephie took Asenna's hand and squeezed it with all her meager strength.

"Oh, thank you, sweet girl. I knew there was a reason Izlani kept me alive in that cage. What else? How is your family?"

"My family is…well enough. Ivarr lost his dire wolf in the invasion and it's been difficult for him. Managing the registry and helping resettle the Esmadian refugees is keeping him busy, and Tira keeps him distracted with her terrible jokes." Ephie tried to laugh, but it turned into a hacking cough and Asenna grabbed a cup of water from the windowsill for her.

"Poor girl inherited Ferryn's sense of humor," Ephie said after drinking, "what else?"

"Haryk and his wife Nikke are still in the city, but I know they plan to go back to the mountains after the coronation. Briar and the other wild wolves went home too. I hope Tolian will stay to look for his son though, and my mother would never part with Fen, so she's going to stay too," Asenna continued, "but I couldn't stand for us to live in the palace. Too many bad memories. We've moved to an old estate house in the city for now while they use the palace as a shelter, and to sort out all the soldiers."

"And…what else?" Ephie asked, a small smile playing on her lips. "You know, Talla already told me about you and Carro. I'd like to hear *that* story one day, when I'm not so tired."

"I wasn't sure if you would be upset," Asenna mumbled, looking down and picking at the blanket, "considering…"

"Considering that he was the one who arrested me? Or considering that he was the one who made sure I survived down there?"

Asenna jerked her head up. "What do you mean?"

"He didn't tell you? The day after you escaped, one of those young Black Saber recruits came to see me," Ephie explained, "I think his name was…Gade. He said that Carro ordered him to make sure I was looked after, and I told him to talk to the girls in the kitchen. If it weren't for Carro, no one would have known I was there and I would have starved to death long ago." Asenna felt a tear slide down her face and pushed it away.

"He never told me that," she said quietly.

Ephie patted her leg. "Some people are knotted up inside and it just takes time for them to undo all of it," she told Asenna, "I'm glad you found one another. You deserve to be loved, sweet girl, just as much as you love others." Asenna watched as Ephie's eyelids drooped and she rested her forehead against the old woman's shoulder for a moment.

"I'll let you rest, Ephie," she whispered, "and I'll bring Fen to see you before we leave."

"Thank you," Ephie closed her eyes and slid down in the bed. Asenna went back to the kitchen, still feeling emotional, and drank her tea quietly while Tira and Talla exchanged stories about Issi and their cousins. Asenna shared their hopefulness that the registry might prove effective in reuniting families, but it broke her heart to think that the success might not extend to the people she loved the most. She spent the rest of the afternoon itching to get back to the city to see if any progress had been made.

When they arrived back on the palace grounds early that evening, Asenna quickly found Elyana and asked if she would take Fen back to the estate for dinner.

"Of course, but I think Tolian wants to speak to you," Elyana said, taking the boy from Asenna's arms. "He's in the hall with Ivarr and Haryk."

Asenna gave Fen a kiss and then she and Tira went inside. It was bustling with soldiers and refugees and some of Key's people who had stayed to help things run smoothly, even though Key herself had returned to Kashait. Asenna spotted Tolian sitting on the staircase at the back of the room, talking to her brothers. The wound on his leg had also been slow to heal, and the sight of him limping everywhere pained Asenna, who had always seen her uncle the same way she saw the mountains: still and silent, but also constant and indestructible.

"How was your visit with Ephie?" Tolian asked as she walked up.

"It was wonderful. She's beginning to seem more like her old self again," Asenna said, "what's been happening here?"

"Nothing new today, but I wanted to tell you that I've decided to go back with Haryk and Nikke," Tolian said in his calm, even voice, "we plan to leave the morning after the coronation."

"But...I thought you wanted to look for Kirann?"

"I've held onto the hope that he is still alive for far too long," Tolian said sadly, "but there were so many young men lost in the war between Azimar and Rogerin. It helps me to think that maybe he died fighting alongside the Riders, or that maybe I shook his hand in passing and never realized it was him. That has to be enough for me, and I'm needed at home now."

"I'll keep checking the registry," Asenna told him, "I promise."

"I've made peace with it, Senna. I know you want to fix everything that was ever broken in this country, but some things, and some people, cannot be healed. You must focus all your boundless energy and love on the things and the people you *can* help, because there are many," Tolian said, putting his hand on her arm.

"I know," Asenna replied, glancing over to where Tira and Ivarr were flipping through the newest pages of the registry book, "but if I don't try, I'd never forgive myself. You, the twins, Ephie, Carro...you all deserve answers."

"Has he checked it yet?" Tolian asked quietly.

Asenna twisted her fingers together. "No. He says it's pointless. Tira's been checking it, but even if there was something, I'm not sure he'd want to know. It's so painful for him."

"Well," Tolian wrapped an arm around her shoulders, "I know you will be there for all of them when they do find something. Are you sure you can't persuade Ivarr to come home?"

"I've tried," Asenna told her uncle, "at least here, he'll have the twins and Mama. They understand what he's going through."

"I know it's for the best, but it will be difficult for Haryk, with only me and Nikke to order him around," Tolian winked.

"I'll still see you at the coronation, yes?"

"Of course, little Senna," he smiled and gave a small bow, then Asenna went over to where her brothers were standing with Tira near the table with all the registry books.

"Where's Carro? And Gaelin? Weren't they supposed to be here helping?" she asked.

"They said they had to go back to the estate for some reason, but that was hours ago," said Ivarr, "I didn't even realize they'd been gone that long." Asenna glanced over at Tira, who shrugged and laughed.

"Whatever it is, with those two it can't be good. We'd better go."

"We'll be there later," Haryk said, "still a few things to be done here. Save us some food though, alright?" Asenna nodded and she and Tira went back out to the paddocks where the horses were kept. As they rode through the city with two Wolf Rider guards behind them, Asenna found herself more at ease with the attention she received. In fact, now that the pressing crowds had died down, she enjoyed being able to stop and talk to people on the street, to hear what was happening in the city, and to better understand what she could do with her newfound power. When they finally arrived back at the estate, which was a large manor house surrounded by gardens and a tall wrought-iron fence, the guards escorted them onto the grounds and they were greeted by Sage, who was completely covered in dirt.

"That's what happens when you leave her home alone all day," Tira laughed, trying to brush her off before Sage followed them inside, "don't worry, we can toss her in the horse trough after dinner. I'm starving." Elyana and Fen were already almost done eating when Asenna and Tira sat down, and Elyana quickly excused herself to get a bath ready for Fen. As she left, Gaelin came into the dining room, followed by Carro, who immediately scooped Fen out of his chair and flipped him upside down.

"Argh!" Carro cried, "I've captured the Princeling and his little wolf! They'll make a fine addition to my pirate crew!" Fen cackled as the food in his hands fell to the floor, where Sage gobbled it up.

"Carro! He's eating!" Asenna laughed and he stopped a few feet away from her.

"Oh, where are our manners, Fen?" said Carro in a stuffy, formal voice, "*Our Most Gracious and Exalted Queen!*" He gave a deep bow, dangling Fen just above the floor where Sage began to lick his face. Fen squealed with delight and Carro flipped him back over and set him down. Asenna tried to hold back a smile as Carro walked over and pulled her chair away from the table, putting his hands on the arms and leaning in close to her.

"I missed you," he whispered, and Asenna felt herself melt as his lips barely grazed hers.

"I was only gone for one day," she breathed, "but I missed you too." Carro kissed her and Asenna heard exaggerated gagging noises behind them.

"Can I finish my dinner before you do that, please?" Tira grumbled.

"My thoughts exactly," Gaelin said, eyes twinkling as he sat down.

"Absolutely not," Carro taunted them, trying to lean in for another kiss, but Asenna playfully pushed him back.

"I *will* shoot you," Tira pointed her fork at him, "I keep the crossbow downstairs just in case you or Gaelin get out of line."

"Hey, I'm a reformed man now," Gaelin said as he pulled a platter of food toward him, foregoing the use of any utensil and eating with his hands.

"Yes, I can see that."

"Are you done eating?" Carro asked Asenna softly, "I have a surprise for you." She stood up and let him lead her out into the hallway, where he pulled a piece of cloth out of his pocket and stood behind her to tie it like a blindfold.

"Is this the surprise?" Asenna said breathlessly.

"Well, it wasn't supposed to be, but now I'm rethinking my plan," Carro replied, running his hands along her back and sending shockwaves through her body as he kissed the top of her shoulder. He took her hand and pulled her forward through the house, then out a door and down some steps. Asenna could tell they were outside in the garden, but she had no idea what to expect as he removed the blindfold. The previous owner of the house had planted orange trees along the ivy-covered back wall, and Asenna gasped when she saw that each tree had been hung with a dozen tiny oil lamps, like the ones that had illuminated their family courtyard back in Kashait. Someone had also dug up all the garden beds around the base of the trees and planted bunches of tiny blue flowers.

"Carro…this is beautiful. Did you and Gaelin do all this today?"

"Most of it. Sage helped with the digging of course. You told me how much you missed the lanterns in the trees back in Kashait, so I wanted to make sure you still had that here."

Asenna knelt and looked at the flowers. "Forget-me-nots. This is wonderful. Thank you, *lai'zhia*."

"I know things are going to be harder for you now," Carro said, "but if you need to be alone, you can come out here. Just tell me and I'll light the lanterns for you." Asenna leaned against him, closing her eyes, and they swayed on the spot together almost like they were dancing.

"Ephie told me something today," said Asenna after a while, tilting her head back to see his face, "she said the day I escaped, you sent Gade to make sure she was taken care of in the prison. Is that true?"

Carro's eyes shifted to the ground. "Yes…I did ask him to do that."

"Ephie said the only reason the maids knew she was down there is because of you. Carro, you saved her life. Why didn't you tell me?"

"I wasn't even sure Gade had done it until you found her," he replied, "and then it didn't seem to matter anymore because at least she survived." Asenna put her hand up to his cheek and Carro closed his eyes, leaning his face into her palm. She knew he was thinking about Gade.

"I know you don't want to talk about it, but thank you."

"Are you ready for the coronation?" Carro asked, and she could tell he was trying to change the subject.

"Definitely not. All those people just staring at me? And I have to say words? In public? I wish I didn't have to do it," Asenna sighed.

"What can I do?" Carro rested his forehead against hers and laced their fingers together, "please give me something to do."

"You can stay by my side the entire day and make up excuses for me to leave if it gets to be too much," Asenna told him as she breathed in the comforting scent of the beeswax he had started putting in his hair again, "and then...you can take me somewhere they won't find us, and keep me there as long as you want."

"Hmmm," Carro murmured, "I'm not sure I'm qualified for that. Maybe we should do a test run? Just to make sure?"

Asenna threw her head back and laughed. "A very practical idea," she said, taking his hand and pulling him back into the house. They went upstairs to their room and Carro sat on the edge of the bed to take his boots off. Asenna turned around and stood in front of him, indicating the laces at the back of her dress.

"Can you...?" she asked. Carro began to untie them but when he reached up to pull the dress down over her shoulders, Asenna took a step away and began to pull it off herself, revealing the silk shift underneath that she knew clung to her body like a glove.

"Asenna..." said Carro softly, "don't do that..."

"Do what?"

"You know exactly what," Carro reached out and pulled her backwards, then pressed his face into the curve of her lower back. He wrapped one arm around her waist and then pulled the shift up and slipped his other hand between her legs, gripping her tightly while she braced herself against his shoulders. After a few minutes, Asenna felt her knees start to shake and she let out a loud groan. Carro grabbed her by the hips and spun her around.

"How am I doing so far?" he whispered with a grin on his face. Asenna pulled his shirt off and leaned down to kiss his neck, just above the bandages that were still covering the jagged new wound he had earned.

"I haven't decided yet," she said quietly, "I may need to see a little more." Carro reached up and laced his fingers through her hair.

"Oh, I can do more..." he said, tightening his grip just enough to make her gasp.

The coronation was a simple affair, but the tension in Asenna's chest didn't come from the pomp or the pressure to impress the very few Esmadian Lords who deigned to attend. It was strictly related to the sea of eyes that burned into her no matter where she went. When she woke up, she found that a small crowd had gathered outside the iron fence of the estate, tossing flowers through the bars and calling out to the family's dire wolves. When she went outside with Fen, Carro, Tira, and her mother to climb into the small carriage that would take them to the palace, there were people lining the streets, calling out their names. When they rode through the palace gates, there was already a steady stream of people moving through to watch the ceremony.

"How long is this going to take?" Asenna asked Greenlow when they arrived at the palace and met him in the room behind the balcony.

"Your Majesty," the little man mumbled, "I will try to make it as fast as I can, but there are protocols to be followed and--"

"I would be *very* grateful if you could keep the protocols to a bare minimum," Asenna said pointedly. Greenlow bowed and looked like he was about to speak again, but then Key appeared in the doorway and approached Asenna. She was wearing a long white gown and her halo of thick curls was held back with a golden cloth band that made her look like a sun goddess. She was carrying a carved wooden chest in her arms, which she set on the table and wrapped an arm around Asenna's shoulders.

"Welcome back," Asenna told her.

"My mother sends her regrets that she couldn't be here today," said Key, "but she wanted you to have this. A gift from the people of Kashait." She lifted the lid of the chest and Asenna gasped as she pulled out a beautiful, deep blue cloak. Asenna pulled her hair aside, allowing Key to wrap it around her shoulders and fasten it at the neck. It was flowing and soft, with luxurious white fur around the collar and golden trim that matched Key's headband. Asenna felt safer wearing it, like it was a shield between her and the spectators.

"May I also receive the gift of knowing your real name, my friend?" Asenna asked Key, who tossed her head and laughed.

"I'm not sure I can legally refuse now, Your Majesty, but I will make you a deal. You come visit me in Kashait, and I'll tell you then."

"I think I can do that," Asenna smiled.

"What about a crown?" Carro said to Greenlow, "isn't that part of it?" Asenna knew he was thinking about Azimar's horrible golden wolf's head crown, but she had ordered it to be melted down immediately after the invasion.

"I believe I have what you need," said Tolian, pushing through the small crowd of family and friends who had gathered around Asenna. He was holding an object wrapped in deerskins and Asenna took it from him, pulling the coverings back. In her hands, she held a simple, delicate, white crown carved from what appeared to be a single piece of mammoth tusk. The tines twisted and crisscrossed each other and then met in points at the top, reminding Asenna of her father's old fishing nets. She turned it in her hands and saw that there were Ulvvori blessings and symbols carved on the inside.

"Where did it come from?" she asked Tolian.

"It is called the Midwinter Crown. As you know, for two thousand years the Ulvvori were ruled by their own sovereigns, independent from the rest of Esmadia," Tolian explained, "we gave up that way of life, but this crown has been kept by the Wolf Riders as a symbol of our people's survival and longevity. The legend says that all the wisdom of the Ulvvori leaders who came before you, the Midwinter Kings and Queens, is contained in it, and they will speak to you when you wear it."

Asenna's eyes burned with tears. "Thank you, Tolian."

"Now, Your Majesty," said Greenlow anxiously, "you will step onto the balcony with me and I will present you, you will need to simply affirm your oath, and then the crown will be placed by someone of your choosing." Asenna looked around the room and her eyes fell on Elyana, who was bouncing Fen on her hip toward the back of the room.

"Mama?" said Asenna, "I'd like you to do it."

Her mother looked up in surprise. "Me?" she asked, "surely…Tolian…or Key…" Asenna shook her head and Carro went over to take Fen. Asenna firmly placed the Midwinter Crown in her mother's hands, then nodded to Greenlow, who led them out onto the balcony. Carro followed and stood behind Asenna, holding Fen up on his shoulders so that the crowd could see him as well. Fen waved enthusiastically, delighted at the loud cheers he received, but Asenna felt her heart hammering in her chest at the sight of all the curious eyes burning into her.

"Esmadia!" Greenlow called out in a surprisingly strong, clear voice, "we come here today to crown a new Queen, one who will lead us into an era of justice and prosperity such as this country has never seen before."

"No pressure," Asenna murmured under her breath, making Elyana chuckle.

"I call on each citizen here today to bear witness as Queen Asenna makes her oath to you," Greenlow turned so that he was halfway facing Asenna and halfway facing the crowd, "do you, Asenna, daughter of Elyana of the Ulvvori, swear this day that you will honor and protect the throne of Esmadia; that you will act always as the loyal servant of your people; that you will maintain their best interests even above your own; and that you will faithfully execute the duties to which you are obligated under the laws of this nation?"

"I do so swear," Asenna said, trying to throw her voice.

"And do you also swear to abide by the conditions set forth by those laws: that you will act as Queen under your own power until such time as your eldest son and heir, Prince Fenrinn, comes of age; that you will foster him to succeed you in your duties; that you will maintain your status as a widow; and that you will abdicate the throne in his favor upon his reaching the age of twenty years?" Greenlow continued.

"I do so swear," Asenna repeated, feeling her knees start to buckle until Carro placed his hand on the middle of her back, steadying her.

"Then I do hereby name you Asenna, Queen of Esmadia!" Greenlow finished and stepped aside so Elyana could place the crown on Asenna's bowed head. Once it was secure and Asenna had straightened up, Elyana took her hand and squeezed it, then they both turned to face the crowd, who were still deathly silent, as if they were waiting to be given a signal.

"The Midwinter Queen!" Elyana cried out, raising Asenna's hand in the air. The crowd broke and suddenly Asenna was overwhelmed with the cheering, whistling, screaming, and the flowers being tossed onto the balcony. She tried to smile and wave as long as she could, but after several minutes she threw a pained look at Greenlow and he nodded. Once they were back inside, Asenna collapsed into a chair and Carro slipped Fen into her lap. The boy rested his head on her shoulder, exhausted from all the excitement, and Asenna ran her fingers over his back, humming softly. The room was buzzing with excited chatter around her, but it all seemed to fade away as Asenna closed her eyes and tried to listen for the ancient voices that Tolian said would speak to her through the crown. She heard no words, but the new weight on her head felt comforting and liberating, rather than burdensome, and Asenna knew that somehow, she had always been meant to wear it.

ASENNA'S EPILOGUE

The mountain air was chillier than Asenna remembered and she pulled the big fur cloak tighter around her shoulders. Early snow was already capping some of the Midwinter peaks, but the bite in the air told her that the harshest months were yet to come. She looked back at where Ivarr sat beside the fire with Fen, teaching him how to safely roast little chunks of meat on a pointed stick and then feeding them to Sage. Her son was nearly three now and all the pain and heartache that Asenna had felt since his birth was still being washed away slowly, but her first year on the throne had been difficult.

It had been difficult to watch Ephie slowly decline and then pass away only a few months after being liberated, but Asenna was thankful that at least it had happened in a warm bed with herself and the twins there. It had been even more difficult to repair the deep wounds that Azimar had left on the country, and on the people Asenna loved. Andros had extreme difficulty walking now and was in almost constant pain, leaving Talla and Lusie responsible for the farm. This kept Talla so busy that she was rarely seen at the palace. It had taken Ivarr months before he was willing to visit the Ulvvori again after burying Nettle, but he refused to stay, and Asenna had given him a job in the palace library to keep him busy. Tira had enthusiastically taken over command of Asenna's new Queen's Guard, but she hated to sleep alone. Many nights, Asenna would wake up to find her curled up on the couch in their bedroom, calling our for Aija or Frost or Ferryn in her sleep. Carro still woke up drenched in cold sweat when Azimar's voice and face visited him in his dreams as well, and it was all Asenna could do to comfort either of them during those moments. Just like the scars they all bore from being cut, shot, or branded, the invisible damage would never quite leave. The mountains carried their share of scars as well, and it had taken months for the Ulvvori to locate and deal with the mines Azimar had dug, which had tainted parts of their water supply.

Suddenly, a gut-wrenching cry shattered the night air around them and Asenna saw Carro's entire body flinch. Tira grinned and hit him on the knee.

"You know that's normal, right?"

"It's awful," Carro said, "it sounds like she's dying." Another cry rent the night and Asenna went over to stand behind him.

"She might as well be. It's been hours now. Tolian, when do we get help?" Another cry came from the tent behind them, this one ending on a piercing note that hurt even Asenna's ears.

"They're getting closer together. I think it's almost over," Tolian said quietly, "Nikke's strong. She'll make it." Carro turned around and pressed his cheek against Asenna's belly, which was round and heavy with their own child, a little brother or sister for Fen.

"I don't know if I can watch you go through this," he murmured.

Asenna ran a hand through his hair. "You are *not* letting me do this alone," she laughed, "I'm still your Queen, if not your wife."

"You know I would never," Carro kissed her stomach and then her hand, "but I might have to close my eyes a few times." Asenna scoffed and gently pushed his face away from her, still smiling. Another scream came from the tent and Asenna could hear Elyana, Haryk, and Nikke's sister, Cylia, calling out their encouragement. Finally, the screams stopped and were replaced by the sound of a newborn baby's first wavering cry. Everyone around the fire stood up and watched the tent and Asenna could sense their overwhelming anxiety. Haryk and Nikke's child would be the first born since the Ulvvori's return home, after three years of exile which had seen dozens of children born without the Wolfsight. A few tense minutes later, Haryk emerged, his face exhausted, but shining with joy.

"Come on!" he said, waving them all inside and Asenna took Fen's hand and led him in first. Elyana and Cylia were sitting beside Nikke on the far side of the tent, while Ash and Juniper had stationed themselves on either side of the reed mattress like great statues at an ancient temple. Nikke was holding a small bundle wrapped in blue cloth and beaming widely.

"It's a girl," she whispered, "her name is Hasti." Asenna looked at Haryk and she could tell he understood her question.

"And she has the Wolfsight," he said. Asenna let out the breath she had been holding as she peered down and saw a pair of tiny golden eyes blinking back up at her.

"We did it," Tolian breathed, "it came back." He grabbed Ivarr by the shoulders and Asenna saw a rare smile spread across her brother's face.

"She look like me, Mama," Fen whispered, tugging on Asenna's cloak.

"Yes, she does," Asenna murmured, feeling her own voice catch in her throat, "and you two will be the best of friends." Nikke began explaining to them that a litter of pups had just been born the previous week, but Asenna suddenly felt suffocated in the tent, with the candles and people and wolves. She stood up with some effort to excuse herself, but Elyana put a hand on her arm.

"I'm fine, Mama. I just need some air." Elyana pulled Fen into her lap as Carro walked Asenna out of the tent and they stood together, letting the clean breeze wash over them. After a few minutes, Asenna found herself crying and Carro pulled her chin around to look at him.

"What's wrong, *lai'rani?*"

"It's really over now," Asenna said, "we did all of this for them, for our children, and now they can live the way we were meant to." Carro wiped a tear off her cheek and kissed her on the forehead.

"*You* did this, Asenna," he told her firmly, "if you hadn't been brave enough to leave then none of this would have happened. *You* saved them. You saved all of us, actually." Asenna leaned her head back on his shoulder as she looked out over the moon-drenched mountains. She knew they couldn't be her home again for a long time, and she knew there was still so much work she needed to do, but the prospect of it no longer frightened her. She relished the challenge, and even though it ached, every minute spent away from her people was worth it for them to be back where they belonged, finally free and safe and whole again.

ULVVORI LANGUAGE GUIDE

- *cyn* (little/small)
- *dria skana* (giant mountain deer)
- *e'shayus virra* (we welcome you home)
- *ialas* (yellow; a Rider who has lost their dire wolf)
- *Izlani* (the Moon, or the spirit of the Moon)
- *Kharia* (the earth, the body of Izlani)
- *Kusa* (the Sun; Izlani's lover)
- *lai'kheri* (my brother)
- *lai'rani/lai'rani cyn* (my light/my little light)
- *lai'zhia* (my heart/my love, in a romantic sense)
- *no'shela skana* ('star-deer')
- *qehogar* (shithole)
- *rani no'shela* or *no'shela* ('light before people'; the stars)
- *shela* (humans/people, other than the Ulvvori)
- *sheyta zhia* (sweetheart, nickname for a child from a parent)
- *ulvvi* (dire wolf); *ulvvia* (dire wolves)
- *vikmiri* (an diseased animal; or a social pariah)
- *zai hana eilli* ("you [zai] look [hana] beautiful [eilli]")

ACKNOWLEDGMENTS

I would be remiss if I didn't thank my incredible husband first. He has been far more patient with me during this process than he should have been, considering that I wouldn't let him read a single word until it was ready to be published. I also can't leave out my family, especially my amazing mom (who encouraged me to read and write probably a *little* too much), and my fabulous beta readers: Wren, Bridget, Tessy, and Ashlee. Y'all were the first ones to fall in love with this story and these characters (especially Gaelin) and your feedback was absolutely invaluable. A very special thanks to my sweet friend Chelsea, who hyped me up every day *and* drew the beautiful artwork for the chapter headings, and to everyone out there in the weird little corners of the internet who encouraged me along the way. Stay strange and wonderful, my darlings.

Finally, I want to thank a few people that I've never met, nor will ever meet, but who have had such an impact on my life that I'll never be able to adequately put it into words: David Clement-Davies, Tamora Pierce, Suzanne Collins, Christopher Paolini, Scott Westerfield, Lois Lowry, Cornelia Funke, Philip Pullman, Brian Jacques, Robert C. O'Brien, Hayao Miyazaki, C.S. Lewis, Louisa May Alcott, Richard Adams, Jean Craighead George, Scott O'Dell, Michael Dante DiMartino, Bryan Konietzko, and too many others. Thank you for giving me so many worlds to get lost in and friends to get lost with.

ABOUT THE AUTHOR

R. H. Linehan is never gonna give you up, never gonna let you down, never gonna run around and desert you. Never gonna make you cry, never gonna say goodbye, never gonna tell a lie and hurt you.

Gotchya ;)

While you're here, don't forget to follow me on **Instagram (r.h.linehan.author), Facebook, and Goodreads** for updates, giveaways, general silliness, or to send me fan art and memes.

Contact Email (also good for fan art & memes): rhlinehan.author@gmail.com

Made in United States
Orlando, FL
21 April 2024